Felicity Hayes-McCoy

The MONTH *of* BORROWED DREAMS

HACHETTE
BOOKS
IRELAND

First published in Ireland in 2018 by HACHETTE BOOKS IRELAND

First published in paperback in 2019 by HACHETTE BOOKS IRELAND

1

Cataloguing in Publication Data is available from the British Library

ISBN 9781473663671

Typeset in Bembo Book Std by Bookends Publishing Services

Printed and bound in Great Britain by Clays Ltd, Elcograf S.p.A.

Hachette Books Ireland policy is to use papers that are natural, renewable and recyclable
products and made from wood grown in sustainable forests. The logging and manufacturing
processes are expected to conform to the environmental regulations of the country of origin.

Hachette Books Ireland
8 Castlecourt Centre
Castleknock
Dublin 15, Ireland

A division of Hachette UK Ltd
Carmelite House, 50 Victoria Embankment, EC4Y 0DZ

www.hachettebooksireland.ie

For Mary in Kilmaley

and

Martine in Tralee

Visitors to the west coast of Ireland won't find Finfarran. The peninsula and its inhabitants exist only in the author's imagination.

Prologue

From her seat to one side Hanna could see in two directions. To her right, the front row of faces was tilted upwards, visible in a spill of steel grey light. To her left, the boy walked into silver water. The sound of it moving against his legs could be heard above the music, which pulled and tugged like the sluggish waves that rolled onto the beach. A camera on a tripod stood on the sand, and out to sea a distant ship was waiting, half lost in a shimmering heat haze.

The sun burned in the sky. The boy was as slender as a sally rod or as gaunt as a famine victim. When the waves reached the tops of his thighs he turned and looked back. You couldn't see his face. He was only a figure washed with shining light, looking back from a distance, inviting the watcher to follow him. As the music rose and fell like the sea, the words of a folksong hung in Hanna's mind.

I wish I was on yonder hill
'Tis there I'd sit and cry my fill,
And every tear would turn a mill ...

Her eyes flicked right, towards the audience. Each face had the same rapt expression and wide eyes.

On the screen, the boy bent one arm and put his hand on his hip. Standing in profile, he slowly raised the other arm and held it out, a dark smudge against the haze. Then, curling his fingers, he cupped the burning eye of the distant sun. The classical music swelled, then ebbed like dragging shingle.

I wish, I wish, I wish in vain,
I wish I had my heart again,
And vainly think I'd not complain ...

Back on the beach, the watching man slumped sideways. Tugged by a restless wind, figures from earlier scenes came and went about his lifeless body. Then the yearning music took over and the film came to an end.

The screen went black as a long list of names scrolled upwards. Actors, cameramen and assistants, dressers and makeup artists. People who had told the story from all its different angles: in light and paint and movement; in fabric, music and sound. In the spaces that were filled and those that had been deliberately left empty. In what was spoken and all that remained unsaid.

When Conor flicked a switch and the lights came on, the reading room in the library was totally still. Then someone coughed, and people began to turn in their seats or reach into handbags. You could hear phones being switched on, and murmured conversation. And the inevitable sounds of ripped foil and crumpled paper, as Ann Flood from the pharmacy opened a double Chunky KitKat.

Chapter One

At first Hanna Casey's idea for a monthly film club in Lissbeg Library hadn't worked. She'd decided that the members would see a film at one meeting and discuss the book it was based on at the next, having borrowed it from the library in the weeks between. And, as it turned out, plenty of people were happy to come to the films. The club was a great idea altogether, they told her, the way you could save yourself the cost of something like Netflix. Also, they loved the tea and biscuits.

But, as time went on, there was a lot of muttering about being too busy to read, and suggestions that, compared to a film, a book could be fierce heavy going. After a while a good many people stopped coming.

So Hanna put up a notice. 'Due to popular demand,' it said, a film would now be screened at each meeting, not every second one. Across the bottom, in smaller writing, members were informed that meetings would begin with a brief discussion of the film shown the previous month.

Conor, her library assistant, was scathing. 'God, you'd think they'd manage to read a book when you gave them the full four weeks.'

'Well, some people did and they still will. Others won't, so they'll purposely turn up late and miss the discussion. But they'll come through a library door, and that's the point, Conor. So don't go looking at them sideways.'

She knew he wouldn't, though. Conor might be in his early twenties but he was absolutely reliable. He just liked things to be organised and expected plans to be followed.

In hindsight Hanna realised it had been daft to expect much interest in the nuance of adaptation, particularly when there was a great stretch in the evenings and the whole Finfarran peninsula was gearing up for summer. Easter had come early, and March and April had been chilly enough for her to light a fire each evening when she got in from work. But while May had begun as a blustery month it was now as mild as milk.

This was the time of year Hanna loved best. Having left Finfarran at nineteen and spent most of her adult life in London, she was intensely aware of new life springing up in the fields. Driving to work between ditches smothered in tangled weeds and flowers, she could feel a sense of potential and promise she'd lost in those long city years. Perhaps it was because she'd moved on at last from a difficult divorce, or because a new relationship, begun in shyness and uncertainty, was now flowering as happily as the primroses up on the ditch.

And she wasn't just projecting her own feelings onto the world around her. It truly was a glorious time of year. According to Conor, whose family farm was a few miles beyond the town of Lissbeg, there was grand bite in the grass at last and the lambing was going great guns.

This month the film club was going to watch the film of *Brooklyn*, Colm Tóibín's best-selling novel about love, emigration and choices, set in 1950s Ireland and New York. Hanna locked the library door at five thirty as usual, and went back to her desk. There were always bits and pieces of admin to be dealt with towards the end of a week, and she was glad of the time to catch up with them before the club met at seven. Conor, who had shot off early on his Vespa, would be back soon with very clean hands and damp hair, having helped his older brother Joe with the milking and taken a hasty shower.

After tidying her desk and shutting down her computer, Hanna went to the kitchenette to make a coffee. Often, on film club nights, she'd nip over to the Garden Café for a wrap or a salad, to save herself the trouble of making a meal later on. Tonight her daughter Jazz was coming to *Brooklyn* so they'd planned to eat together after the film. Like many others who'd joined with initial enthusiasm, Jazz had become an erratic club member, more likely to miss a meeting than to turn up, but today she'd sent a text saying she'd be working late in the office and might as well come to the film when she was done.

As Hanna waited for the kettle to boil, she calculated the number of chairs she'd need. *Brooklyn* would pull a crowd. With a rural Irish setting, three 2016 Oscar nominations and a BAFTA Best British Film award, it should appeal to a wider audience than a classic like *Death in Venice*, which she'd chosen the previous month.

There'd probably be greater interest in borrowing the book as well. Even though they'd loved the film, more than a few film club members had picked up Mann's *Death in Venice*, seen it was a translation from the German, and put it back on the shelf. But Colm Tóibín was a writer everyone had heard of, and the fact that he had a pronounceable name would give him a head start. She'd learned that, if nothing else, from her screening of Dostoyevsky's *The Brothers Karamazov*.

By a process of osmosis the town had agreed that a brief discussion starting at seven meant the film would begin at seven thirty, though a hard core always came early to get first go at the biscuits. Tonight, long before Conor had set out the chairs, Ann Flood from the pharmacy was hovering near the tea urn, where the plates of digestives and rich teas were augmented by chocolate fingers.

Among the early arrivals was a knot of readers eager to discuss *Death in Venice*, and one was determined to make it tête-à-tête. Fixing Hanna with a beady eye, she bore down on her inexorably in a whirl of scent and beads. Avoiding the claw-like clutch at her arm, Hanna smiled brightly. 'Conor's about to bring in the cups. Do help yourself as usual.'

She moved away to greet the next influx, which included a group of pensioners, Conor's fiancée, Aideen, and a couple of guys who worked in the council offices over the way. As she smiled and shook hands with the newcomers, Hanna could hear the disgruntled enthusiast behind her announcing that cheap tea always turned her stomach.

The council offices were housed in a block that had once been Lissbeg's convent school, where the library was accommodated in the former assembly hall. When she'd left her English husband

and returned to Ireland, the fact that she herself had been a pupil here had added to Hanna's sense of disorientation. Working in the dark-panelled room where she'd giggled and whispered as a schoolgirl had somehow brought back a teenage sense of inadequacy, making her prickly and aggressive at a time when she'd badly needed friends. And at first she'd actively disliked her job, not only because of its setting. She had left school with the dream of a career as an art librarian in London, so ending up in Lissbeg local library had felt like failure. But now both the library and her attitude towards it had changed.

Previously enclosed by a grim, grey wall that encompassed the school and the convent, the buildings had been developed to provide offices, low-rent workshops and studios for start-up businesses, and a public space with a café in the former nuns' garden. In the process, the library had been extended to include a state-of-the-art exhibition space as well as the airy, modern reading room that Hanna used for the film club.

Those changes had vastly improved her workplace. The dark-panelled hall had been linked to the new spaces by glass partitions, so the library, which used to rely on ugly strip lighting, was now lit by daylight from two sides. And because the exhibition space displayed a medieval psalter, which had proved a magnet for tourists, the library's amenities had been improved as well. Along with the digital screens installed in the exhibition space, Hanna's reading room had been equipped with blackout blinds and a projector, and a screen that still gave her a secret thrill whenever she hit the button to lower it from the ceiling.

Admittedly, the kitchenette where she and Conor made tea

and hung their coats was still the size of a shoebox, but that was nothing compared to all the rest.

Now she moved to the front of the room. There were plenty of vacant seats at the back; a few couples had gathered in the centre; and a phalanx of pencils and notebooks was twitching in the front row. Dead centre was Mr Maguire, a retired local schoolteacher. And on a chair that had somehow migrated to the right, Ann Flood, with a teacup at her feet, was unwrapping a chocolate finger.

Hanna was about to kick off the discussion when Mr Maguire sprang to his feet and swivelled to face the audience. In his well-manicured hand a copy of *Death in Venice* bristled with brightly coloured sticky notes. It was a Knopf hardback edition, Hanna noticed, so he definitely hadn't borrowed it from the library. She could see the guys from the council offices, who'd known him in their schooldays, looking resigned.

'The *first* question is why the director perversely chose to make the hero a *composer* when the author made him a *writer*. Any meaningful comparative discussion must begin from that starting point. So let's take it from there.' With the air of a man who had set out his stall, Mr Maguire sat down again.

Hanna looked at the faces around her, whose expressions ranged from bafflement to boredom. From his position at the back of the room, Conor flashed her a grin.

A woman with a gauzy scarf over her dark hair leaned forward, and Hanna heard herself responding rather louder than she'd intended. 'Yes! Saira! Did you want to say something?'

There was a gleam of amusement in Saira Khan's eyes. She was a quiet woman in her forties with a daughter who'd recently gone off to college, leaving her with spare time on her hands. 'Actually, I thought the film threw new light on the book.' She turned to Mr Maguire. 'And it's good to have one's assumptions about a work of art challenged. Don't you think?'

Mr Maguire was squaring his shoulders when Aideen, Conor's fiancée, raised her hand. She was sitting in the centre row beside her cousin Bríd. 'I dunno if I should say this because I haven't read the book.'

Several people who clearly hadn't read it either looked encouraging. Aideen hooked a curl behind her ear. 'If they hadn't changed the hero from an author to a composer, would the music in the film have made sense? Because the music was the best bit, I thought. And the costumes. And the light on the water. I mean, I've been to Italy – not Venice, Florence. Me and Conor went there. The light's amazing. And, in the film, the way the music and the pictures work together is fantastic.'

In a pained voice, Mr Maguire asked Hanna if they weren't straying from the point. 'I believe we're here to discuss a classic work of modern literature.'

Aideen turned scarlet and Conor immediately spoke from the back of the room. 'Well, I *have* read the book and it seems to me that Aideen's bang to rights. Spot on.'

Hanna was torn between sympathy and annoyance. Conor hadn't read *Death in Venice* – he'd told her so that morning when he'd returned the copy he'd borrowed. He'd had a couple of goes at reading it, he'd said, but he'd been up with the sheep all hours for weeks and kept falling asleep.

Now his eyes met Hanna's over the heads of the audience. With his damp spiky hair and sunburned face, he was an unlikely picture of chivalry, but his blazing stare dared her to undermine his stance. She could think of no other circumstance in which he was likely to challenge her, but where Aideen was concerned he was Galahad and Lancelot rolled into one. So, feeling she had no option, she said his point was well made.

With the arrogance of a man who'd spent forty years in undisputed authority, Mr Maguire ignored the interruption and told Saira Khan that, unlike literature, films weren't Art. 'And books are made to be read, not fiddled about with.'

Hanna mentally counted to ten and refrained from asking why, in that case, he'd bothered to join the club.

Saira Khan's eyes gleamed again, but before anyone else could speak, the door opened to a stream of new arrivals. It was five to eight and Lissbeg had arrived in force to see *Brooklyn* – a brilliant film, as someone declared loudly, though how come the tea was all gone?

Chapter Two

There was still light in the evening sky when Hanna and Jazz left the library. Hanna paused for a moment to check that she'd set the alarm properly, then ran down the steps to the flagged courtyard. Linking arms, she and Jazz went through the arched gateway into Broad Street.

This gate had been the entrance to the school, though the nuns themselves had never been known to use it. They had moved through private doorways linking the school to the convent, which in those days had been an inviolate sanctum. The idea that Jazz now had an office there was extraordinary to Hanna, but Jazz saw nothing strange in it. Neither, of course, thought Hanna, did any of that generation: the changes that had come to Finfarran in only a few decades were immense.

Edge of the World Essentials, the organic cosmetics company Jazz worked for, had been one of the first start-ups to rent in The Old Convent Centre. Jewellers and other craft workers, artisan chocolatiers, artists and picture-framers had followed, filling what had once been classrooms, the nuns' parlour and their dormitories. Since then the domestic-science rooms had been refitted for a residential cookery course, and the upper storeys of the two buildings were still being redeveloped.

Hanna asked what Jazz had thought of the film.

'I liked it. D'you reckon she was right to get on the boat and go back to the guy she'd married over in Brooklyn? Or should she have stayed in Ireland and built a new life?'

'Well, that's the eternal dilemma, isn't it?'

'Knowing the right thing to do?'

'Well, yes, but not just that. Actually having the courage to choose.'

Jazz linked her arm through Hanna's. 'So, what are we going to eat?'

'Smoked salmon.'

'Yum. With potato salad?'

'No, but I did make brown bread.'

'And, while I think of it,' Jazz turned back the flap of her bag to reveal a cardboard box, 'I got cheesecake from the deli. A slice of salt caramel and one of Morello cherry. We can arm-wrestle for them, if you like, or chop them into trendy tasting-portions.'

'Or, in my case, put some away for tomorrow.'

'Don't be such a wuss! I bet you haven't eaten since lunchtime.'

Looking at her daughter's slender wrists and the bony shoulders under her expensive T-shirt, Hanna wondered when Jazz herself had last had a proper meal. Sustenance, she suspected, had become a matter of sandwiches wolfed at meetings, and far too much coffee. But, at twenty-three, Jazz could still revert from competent executive to stroppy adolescent so, wary of saying the wrong thing, Hanna laughed.

They drove in convoy through the streets of Lissbeg where the first of the season's tourists were out seeking pub music. Then they made their way along country roads to the clifftop field where Hanna's house was. It was coming up to ten o'clock in the evening and the edge of every fluttering leaf was still clear against the sky.

The low stone house with its little rear extension stood at the top of the field, its back to the road and its front door facing the ocean. The narrow plot sloped steeply down to a boundary wall beyond which a grassy path followed the curve of the cliff: the path was only a few feet wide and the sheer drop to the waves below was breathtaking. Rounding the gable end of the house, Jazz called over her shoulder, 'It's still a lovely evening. Shall we eat outside?'

'A bit chilly now the sun's set. Let's take some wine down to the bench first, though.'

In the distance gulls were coasting on the wind and the faint trace of the lost sun glimmered on the horizon. As Hanna fetched wine from the kitchen, Jazz wandered down the field and climbed the stile to the wooden bench at the far side of the wall. Following with the bottle and glasses in her hands, Hanna watched her daughter settle on the bench and tip back her sleek head. With her hair streaming sideways, tugged by the wind from the ocean, Jazz's thin shoulders visibly relaxed as she raised her face to the sky.

Later, having sauntered back up the field, they sliced salmon and brown bread, piled salad onto plates and sat down to eat. In addition to the small, built-on bathroom and utility area, Hanna's house consisted of just two rooms: her tiny bedroom and this open-plan living space with its kitchen at one end, fireplace at the other, and a table under the window looking out at the huge sky.

Squeezing lemon juice onto a sliver of salmon, she looked across at Jazz. 'How's Louisa doing in London?'

'Fine. I spoke to her this morning. She's been networking with investors. In a nice Home Counties way, of course, and interspersed with visits to John Lewis's.' Jazz buttered a slice of bread. 'Gosh, this is gorgeous. I'd no idea I was so hungry.' Taking a large bite, she spoke with her mouth full. 'She doesn't seem to be seeing much of Dad.'

'But isn't she staying with him while she's over there?'

'Mm. But she's always out doing things. Bank manager. Chatting up contacts. All good stuff. And brilliant from Dad's point of view because he doesn't have to be bothered with her.'

'Oh, come on! She's his mum and he adores her.'

Jazz made a cynical noise and speared a slice of salmon. 'So long as she needs no attention when he's otherwise engaged.'

Hanna gave up. Jazz was right. Malcolm did love his mother, just as he loved his daughter, but essentially he was selfish through and through. Yet despite all the revelations and recriminations they'd been through and dealt with as a family, she still felt Jazz should be spared that unvarnished truth.

Jazz shrugged. 'Look, Dad's a demanding little boy disguised as a high-profile barrister. I know that. Granny Lou knows it. We all do, Mum. It's cool.'

Recognising a warning to back off, Hanna said it was great that Louisa was lining up investors. Jazz added a squeeze of lemon to her salmon. 'Who knew that she'd turn out to be such a sharp businesswoman? At her age! And how lucky am I that she decided to set up Edge of the World Essentials. I mean Granny Lou! Twinset and pearls and croquet on the lawn!'

The company had been set up by Malcolm's widowed mother who'd decided her English country home was too big to live in alone. The decision had astonished Jazz, to whom Louisa had just been a granny. But Hanna hadn't been surprised. She'd known there was far more to her ex-mother-in-law than her genteel appearance might suggest.

It was Louisa who'd laid the social foundations for Malcolm's stellar career as a London barrister by inviting the right people to the charming manor house in Kent, and creating a necessary network of obligation and support. It was a subtle process, requiring shrewdness, tact and hard work. No one knew that better than Hanna, on whom the role had devolved as soon as she'd married. Giving up her cherished dream of being an art librarian, she'd spent most of her time supporting and advancing her husband's career – until she'd found Malcolm sleeping with a woman she'd always believed was her friend.

There was no doubt that Louisa was enjoying her new role in business, but Hanna knew that her taking it on hadn't been entirely a matter of choice. Louisa could easily have retired in comfort on the proceeds of the sale of the manor, but instead she'd set herself the task of establishing yet another career. It was a duty as well as a pleasure, she'd told Hanna confidentially, crossing her elegant ankles and folding her hands in her lap: Malcolm's disgusting behaviour had left Jazz rootless, and his late father would have wanted that put right.

Jazz transferred a cherry tomato straight from the bowl to her mouth. 'Oh, Mum, I never said. Dad's put the London house on the market.'

'What?'

'I know. Weird. He must be having a mid-life crisis. Louisa says he wants a flat in a glass box near the Tate Modern.'

'But – he's selling the house? How do you feel about that?'

'Me? Fine. Why should I care?'

Dozens of answers jostled in Hanna's mind. *Because it's your home. The house you grew up in. Because you still have a room there – okay, a room where you probably keep three jackets and a hairbrush. But it's your room. I painted the walls for you. I sang you to sleep there at night.*

It was she who'd found the tall Georgian house in the first place, and tirelessly worked to turn it into a home. She'd installed the oil-fired range in the basement kitchen and planted espaliered pear trees in the brick-walled garden, envisaging tea and sponge cake by the range on winter evenings, ice-cream and lemonade on a sunny bench in summer.

That work had been an act of faith in the first year of her marriage, after she'd miscarried a baby she and Malcolm had longed to have. She'd needed to believe she'd get pregnant again, and that next time things would be perfect. For months she'd scoured salvage yards, finding cast-iron baths and fire grates, a deep butler's sink and cut-glass doorknobs. The reception rooms were hung with hand-printed paper, and the curving mahogany banister was sanded till it felt like silk, then polished with beeswax. It had taken nearly a year for the house to be ready, and by the time they moved in, Hanna had been in love with it.

On their first evening there, she and Malcolm had wandered hand in hand till they came to the master bedroom, where Hanna had chosen soft grey fabrics to go with the sage-green walls. When Malcolm opened the door she'd seen a bottle of champagne in a silver wine cooler standing on the bedside table. He'd laughed at her astonishment.

'Doesn't it fit? It's supposed to be Georgian.'

It was, and it was perfect. As he'd poured the champagne, he'd told her how much he loved her, and the following morning he'd cancelled a meeting and they'd stayed in bed till noon.

They'd been in their early twenties then, and it had taken eleven years and many tests and interventions before Hanna conceived again. Yet she hadn't become obsessive or disheartened. Instead she'd devoted herself to supporting Malcolm – caring for the house, where she threw networking dinner parties, and finding a cottage in Norfolk where his colleagues could come and spend relaxing weekends. In all that time she'd never questioned his love, or doubted that one day they'd have a child.

She'd been sitting in the moonlit garden one night when Malcolm came home with a bouquet of white jasmine from Louisa. Hanna had breathed in the scent, and shown him the blurry scan she'd been given that day at the clinic. And together they'd decided to name their daughter Jasmine.

Long afterwards, putting two and two together, Hanna had realised Malcolm's affair had begun in the weeks when she herself had been choosing paints and fabrics for the London house. She'd found them there in bed together when Jazz was sixteen.

'Mum?'

'What?'

'You're worrying about me, aren't you?'

For a moment the vivid, accusing face looked exactly like Malcolm's.

'How many times do I have to say that you did the right thing? You found out Dad was a lying cheat so you grabbed me and whipped me off to Ireland. Okay, maybe it was a bit sudden, like The Bolter in a Nancy Mitford novel.'

'Hang on, I was nothing like The Bolter. She was married about seven times!'

Jazz giggled. 'Whatever. It's ages since I read the books.'

'Where did you find them anyway? We didn't have them at home.'

'I dunno. I expect Granny Lou had them in Kent. Anyway, the point is that you made the right choice and it didn't blight my life. And if I fussed a bit at the time, Mum, I got over it. So I wish you would.'

Hanna hardly knew whether she felt like laughing or crying. Leaving Malcolm hadn't been part of a conscious, responsible plan. She'd simply found him in her bed with Tessa Carmichael, one of his colleagues, and left for Ireland that evening with no plan at all. It was later that she'd discovered how long Malcolm had been cheating on her with Tessa, and realised there was no way back.

But, whatever the provocation, plucking a teenager out of her home and school had been reckless. To make matters worse, she'd tried to conceal Malcolm's betrayal from Jazz for far too long. Whatever Jazz might say now, the whole mess had been traumatic. And, no matter how much she'd wanted to, Hanna hadn't been able to fix it: it had taken Louisa's intervention, and the establishment of the business, to give Jazz her present sense of being rooted here in Finfarran.

So, yes, she did worry, and often she felt guilty. But neither worry nor guilt had flooded her mind just now. Instead she'd seen sage-green painted walls, smelt beeswax and remembered moonlight. The thought of her perfect bedroom and of blossom shining on the pear trees had, for a moment, blotted out all sense of the years in between.

Chapter Three

There was a movement by a clump of thistles in the ditch, and Jazz saw a pointed face blink in the spill from her car's headlights. Pulling in at a farm gate, she switched off the lights and lowered the window to watch a badger cross the road a few yards up ahead. His powerful legs seemed too short for his heavy grey body, and his black and white face gleamed in the moonlight, like a mask. She knew he was aware of her because he'd turned his ponderous head as she'd stopped at the gateway. But he seemed untroubled by her presence. Instead of freezing or retreating, he continued his steady progress and, ducking his long snout into a mass of briars and nettles, disappeared into the further ditch.

It was a quarter to twelve and the night was so still that Jazz could hear the sound of cattle pulling grass in the field beside her. She was about to start the car again when a second stripy face appeared, framed by thistles, and with the same plodding concentration a smaller badger crossed the road at the same angle as the first.

Jazz had read somewhere that successive generations of badgers would follow well-worn paths for centuries, steadily walking established routes despite obstacles and change. As far as she could remember, the underground systems they lived in were inherited as well. Hundreds of years of instinctive excavation must have gone into the tunnels that lay here beneath tarmac and turf. And this road probably hadn't existed when forebears of the creatures she'd just seen had first stumped across what, by now, had become their ancestral territory.

Pleasantly tired after her meal with Hanna, Jazz continued on her way home, still thinking about the private midnight world she'd glimpsed on the road. She wondered if new tunnels were dug when populations got bigger, or if badgers threw out extensions for the hell of it, like humans building conservatories and sheds. One thing she knew was that badgers' tunnels and chambers could extend for half a mile and even more. They lived in clans and mated for life, though, so you could see why they'd like some elbow room in the home.

Ten minutes later, when she got to the flat, she found Sam sprawled on the bed watching telly. He lowered the volume slightly as she came in. 'Good dinner?'

'Lovely.' She walked round the silver mesh partition to put the box of cheesecake into the fridge. 'God, I can hardly move in here, what's all this?'

Sam rolled off the bed and came to look. 'That's what we call washing-up.'

'But couldn't you have done it? And put it away, maybe?'

'Sorry. It was just a tin of tomato soup. And stuff.'

He tried to kiss her but she slipped past him, catching her elbow on the handle of a pan and splashing the front of her T-shirt. 'Dammit!'

This was the second time in a week that Sam had left a pan soaking on the hob, and plates and dishes piled up in the sink.

'Oh, no! Really, Jazz, I'm sorry.' He dabbed at her T-shirt ineffectually.

'It's okay. It's fine. It'll wash.' With a determined smile, she went and sat on the bed, which was supposed to be folded away as soon as you got up. Kicking her shoes off, she glared round crossly. The studio flat had seemed rather sweet when she'd rented it, but now, with Sam here as well, it was just cramped.

Most days they were both out working and didn't get home till fairly late at night. But two days a week, when Sam worked from home, the place became chaotic. While Jazz generally cleaned as she went along, he let things accumulate. So, by the end of his days alone in the flat, there were papers and mugs everywhere, and half-eaten plates of food on the rumpled bed. But, to be fair, Sam was big and so was his laptop, far too bulky for a console table exactly the width of her own, carefully chosen, MacBook. The bed was really the only space where he could work.

They'd met in Carrick, Finfarran's county town, which was about twenty miles from Lissbeg. While the centre of Lissbeg had once been a muddy cattle market, Carrick had grown up at the feet of an Anglo-Norman castle, which, as time went by, had made it the focus of far more genteel commerce. It retained a sizeable medieval cathedral, and an imposing courthouse, now the county museum. But unlike Lissbeg, which so far had no chain stores, its Victorian shopping streets had disappeared behind the plastic fascias of coffee shops and computer outlets. And its slightly dilapidated Georgian squares and terraces were jostled on all sides by ribbon development.

Yet, from Lissbeg's point of view at least, Carrick still had notions. Its tourist office had grandly styled it the 'Gateway to Finfarran's Glory', and its chamber of commerce doggedly attended international trade fairs at which companies considering relocation were wooed by promised local-government tax breaks. Jazz found the Lissbeg–Carrick rivalry pathetic, but she recognised there were nuances in the relationship, which, as someone born and raised in London, she'd never understand.

On the day she'd met Sam, she and her friend Eileen had been having coffee in Castle Street, and he'd been sitting alone at the next table, checking his emails. Eileen's dad owned Dawson's AgriProvision, the biggest business of its kind in the west of Ireland, and, with his fortune made, he was about to splash out on a lavish wedding for his daughter. Jazz had been chosen as chief bridesmaid and they'd met in Starbucks to discuss the latest twist in Eileen's plans.

'So, hang on, let me get this right. You're making it a double wedding?'

'That's the plan. Me and Joe, Conor and Aideen.'

'But when was this decided? And why?'

'Well, you know Joe and Conor have been running their family farm, right? And their dad's been off work for ever because he tripped over a cow?'

'Not quite the story as I heard it, but yeah.'

'Well, my dad has offered Joe a job in the Dawson's office in Cork. Management, obviously.'

'Obviously.'

Oblivious to the amusement in Jazz's voice, Eileen had nodded. 'Which would leave Conor struggling to cope on the farm.'

'Especially as he's also my mum's assistant at the library.'

'I know, and he's been faffing about for ages, trying to decide whether to stick with farming or go off and become a librarian.' Eileen, who'd caught sight of her own eyebrows reflected in the window, frowned at them sharply before deciding that they'd do. '*Any*way, the thing is that the farm can't just be left to die the death. I mean, that's what Joe says and I do see his point. So he's going to cover the cost of a labourer's wages. And Conor's going to chuck the library thing and choose life on the farm.'

'And when you say Joe's going to cover the cost of a labourer, you mean your dad is.'

'Of course.'

'What does Conor think?'

'He's over the moon. Because this settles things. Plus they've been saving up for about a year to get married, so Joe said why not have a double wedding and do the thing in style?'

'And you're up for that?'

'Oh, come on! Why wouldn't I be? I'm not a total egomaniac.'

'Well, I admit that "the bigger the better" has always been your motto.'

'Aideen and Conor are dotes and they could never afford a big do.' At that point Eileen had slammed back her chair and gone to fetch more coffee, and the violent impact on Sam's table had caused him to look up.

Catching his eye, Jazz had smiled apologetically. 'Sorry. My friend tends to do things at speed.'

He'd smiled back and said it didn't matter, and there'd been an awkward pause in which they'd both felt that if Eileen weren't in the offing they might have begun to chat.

Now, sitting on the edge of the bed, Jazz pulled her T-shirt over her head. 'Imagine if we hadn't met again after that first day in Starbucks.'

'Why? Would you rather we hadn't?'

'No, idiot, of course not! But it was just chance, wasn't it? And, look at you. Here you are.' She looked at him, marvelling at how great it was.

Sam shrugged. 'Isn't that a definition of life? You walk through one door, one thing happens. Choose another and it's something else instead.'

'Definitely chance, not Fate, then?' Seeing his bewildered expression, she laughed. It had been a daft question anyway. Sam was an inveterate pragmatist and the idea that Fate might intervene in his life would never enter his head.

Yawning, Jazz rolled off the bed and went into the tiny bathroom. When she came back, Sam had shuffled his work into an untidy pile on the floor and was under the duvet with the light off.

Snuggling in beside him, Jazz mentally ran through a checklist of all she had to do tomorrow. At least, she thought, it only took five minutes to get to the office. Rental property round Broad Street was as scarce as hen's teeth but, having found the perfect office space, she'd been determined to avoid having to drive to work. So coming upon an ad that offered 'a dream studio apartment' had been a triumph.

Stretching out under the duvet, she found Sam's foot and tickled it with her toes. It was wonderful to have someone she loved so much to come home to. Though sometimes she wished they could tunnel through her flimsy walls, like a couple of stripy badgers, and turn her studio apartment into something less like a cell.

Chapter Four

Conor reckoned that the best part of his library job was the couple of days a week he spent on the road. He'd taken over the mobile-library run from Miss Casey last winter, when she'd suggested that the hours involved would give him more time on the farm in the mornings. Then, when it turned out to be the perfect arrangement, she'd told him to carry on.

To give Miss Casey her due, she was good that way. You wouldn't find her sticking her nose into your business but she was always one to come up with suggestions that helped. When Conor had started at the library, people had called her a dragon. She'd been stand-offish and po-faced back then, running the place like clockwork with hardly a civil word. But you couldn't blame her. Finfarran was a great place for gossip and, having been posh Mrs Turner in England, it must have been hard to come back to Lissbeg with a kid and a broken marriage.

Sticking his elbow out the open window, Conor continued to ruminate as he bowled towards Ballyfin. According to his mam, Miss Casey had had every reason to fear gossip. By all accounts, the ex-husband had been loaded, but she must have made a pig's ear of the alimony because she'd hardly been home when she'd had to apply for a job. She'd changed back to her maiden name too, which suggested a nasty divorce.

But she'd relaxed a lot in the last few years, especially since she'd got together with your man Brian Morton, the County Architect, who was kind of reserved in his own way but decent enough. Most people liked her now and just called her 'Hanna'. He'd never got the hang of that himself, though. She was the boss, so Miss Casey seemed more the thing.

Today his route took him through the northern foothills of Knockinver, the mountain range at the end of the peninsula. Ballyfin, at its most westerly point, was his final stop. He had several other halting places before it, scattered villages where he pulled into a church car park, or by a little post office, where villagers and people from outlying farms stood in groups by the roadside, or sat chatting on walls while they waited for him arrive. The queues for the van were great places for gossip, and he knew that much of it now was about himself. A double wedding was big news in Finfarran. He didn't mind, though. The questions he had to keep answering made it all seem properly real.

He still couldn't quite take in the idea that next year they'd be married. He and Aideen had been saving for so long with no real timeframe, and whenever they'd sat down to talk about it the future had seemed less clear. It wasn't just the money. It was the fact that the whole thing had turned into a class of a Gordian knot.

Before getting together with Aideen he'd had plans to be a librarian, though he hadn't really been certain because he loved farming as well. Anyway, how could he go off to college? Who'd give him a student loan and how would he pay it back? Besides, he was needed at home. With his dad, Paddy, unable for heavy work after an accident, he and his brother Joe were hard pushed to keep things going. And with the farm not yielding a decent income for the lot of them, his library-assistant work made a real difference to the family budget.

People kept telling Conor they should sell the farm and get shot of it and, okay, selling would release cash. But what would happen then to his mum and dad? That land had been farmed by McCarthys for six generations. Paddy lived with chronic pain and suffered from bouts of depression. What would losing his home do to his health? And being engaged to Aideen had added more complications. How could they afford to get married if he was a student? Where might they have to move to when it came to finding a job?

And then, out of the blue, Joe had announced his engagement to Eileen Dawson, and with one swipe the Gordian knot had been cut. Admittedly, the solution had scuppered Conor's notion of being a librarian. But it had saved the farm and kept him on the land. And, best of all, he and Aideen had been able to set a date.

The idea of the double wedding had come out of the blue as well, and Conor hadn't known what Aideen would think. It was Joe's notion but Eileen had leapt on board with all guns blazing, full of plans for cakes and cards and where to hire cars. Aideen seemed fine, though. While she might be quiet, underneath she knew her own mind. That was part of what Conor loved about her. Look at the way she'd decided not to change her name when they got married, which, as far as he was concerned, was game ball. He wouldn't be up for changing his name, so why should she?

Eileen, of course, was all set to be Mrs Joseph McCarthy. But that was par for the course. Anyway, the bottom line was that Aideen seemed happy with everything, and so long as she was happy so was Conor.

The road snaked through a pass that, according to Paddy, had once been a drovers' way. For hundreds of years it had been used to bring cattle to market, until a new one was built leading directly from Carrick to Ballyfin. People called that 'the motorway', though it was really just a dual carriageway. It ran down the centre of the peninsula and round to Ballyfin from the south, where the side of the mountain had been blasted away with a grant from the EU. Some people said it was great because it halved your journey time to Carrick. But God help you if you needed to cross it in a tractor with a trailer full of beasts.

As his steady climb began to yield glimpses of the ocean, Conor told himself potholes put fierce wear on your tyres. He loved driving the back roads, though. You could take your time and daydream, and from the library van you could look across fields as if you were up in a tractor. Nothing like being in the car or on his Vespa, when you sometimes felt you were whizzing along through tunnels of green leaves. There were no trees at this height, just towering masses of black rock and miles of rough grass and purple heather. People from the farms below grazed sheep here, trusting to dogs to round them up when it came time to go to the mart.

Lissbeg, to the south of the motorway, was the only sizeable town west of Carrick. There was still a mart there but most years brought rumours of plans to close it, and letters to the *Inquirer* from people like his dad. According to Paddy, the powers-that-be had no interest in agriculture. They'd kill farming with neglect if they could, just like they'd sat back and done nothing while the fishing industry died. But, as Joe said, that was just Paddy grousing. And how could you blame him when he was stuck inside with online forms and paperwork, and dying to be out working in the fields?

There was a bit of truth in Paddy's grousing, though. Farming was a precarious way to make a living. But, as he breasted the top of the pass, Conor knew that he'd made the right choice.

Cruising down the drovers' way he could see Ballyfin below him. Dazzling light reflected from the ocean around it, and local fishing boats and expensive yachts were bobbing on the waves. The boats were tied up to a stone pier in the old harbour, and the yachts were moored by landing stages jutting out from the marina, where shops sold deck shoes and sunglasses and mugs saying 'Captain's Mate' and 'Ship's Cat'.

He parked in his official spot by the green above the harbour and, seeing that no one was waiting, took out his phone. There was a text saying 'Done & Dusted!!' from Aideen, with a photo of two boxes of sandwiches wrapped up in cellophane with 'HabberDashery' printed on the labels. She must be having a busy day at the deli.

HabberDashery, which Aideen and her cousin Bríd had set up in partnership, was just beginning to show a return for all their hard work. It did corporate deliveries as well as takeaway, and made sandwiches for the Garden Café as well. Conor took a thumbs-up selfie and pinged it back to Aideen. This time next year, he told himself happily, they'd be an old married couple, working together. Already she had plans for sourcing ingredients for the deli from the farm. She had notions of the place going organic too, though he wasn't sure how that would go down with Joe and Paddy or his mam.

Everything in life seemed to be changing, the way the peaks of Knockinver turned from white to black and green in spring. It was all good. You had to get your head round it, though. Like when old Dawson offered to upgrade the farm machinery, airily calling it a wedding present. Neither Conor nor Paddy had liked that, but it was kindly meant and the gear was badly needed so, in the end, they'd accepted the offer as a loan. Eileen had laughed and said they were pure daft. The thought that you might not like to be beholden wouldn't occur to the likes of Eileen, who'd never had a day's worry about money in her life.

Conor had been a bit shocked when Joe had backed her up, saying the gift would work as a tax write-off for old Dawson. No doubt it would but that wasn't the point. Taking a labourer's wage from Joe made sense because he was family and, in the end, when Paddy was gone, he'd come in for his share of the farm. But taking gifts from Dawson was something different.

There was a knock on the side of the library van and Chris Ford from the bank stuck his head through the window. 'How's it goin', Conor?'

'Sound out, Chris. How's life?'

'Tipping along, you know yourself. Waiting for the bulk of the tourists.'

Ballyfin advertised itself as 'Ireland's best kept secret', which was a laugh. Its smart hotels and miles of beaches brought hordes of tourists each summer, including celebrities pretending to be incognito who always ended up on the front of *Hello!* and *OK!* magazines.

'How're the wedding plans going?'

Conor shrugged. 'I just sit back and leave the women at it.'

That, in fact, was a massive, whopping lie. Still, Chris would probably die laughing if he heard Aideen was basing her dress on a picture they'd seen in a gallery, so it seemed best to come out with the standard line. Especially since the design of the dress had been Conor's own idea. They'd found Botticelli's *Primavera* on a weekend they'd spent in Florence and, while you mightn't want your bridesmaids going round in see-through outfits, one girl in the painting, in a proper, flowery dress, was the spit and image of Aideen. Right down to her gorgeous eyes and wavy hair. Aideen had shaken her head when Conor had pointed out the resemblance, but she was well up for the notion of recreating the dress.

Chris thumped the van again and said he'd better get going: he was due for a drink down in the Marina Hotel. 'Now, there's a great place for a wedding. Though you'd want to get your women moving because it gets booked up months ahead. Give me a shout, though, if you're pushed, because I'm good mates with the manager.'

With a strong memory of Aideen saying she'd rather be dead

in a ditch than have a reception at the Marina, Conor said he'd be sure to give him a call. Actually, he agreed with Aideen a hundred per cent. The Marina was full of plastic lobsters and seahorses and, for all the fancy cocktails they served, they couldn't pull a decent pint. Fortunately a kid turned up at that moment, carrying a pile of returns, and as Conor jumped out to help her, Chris strode away.

The next hour passed in a flash, what with loans and returns, and the inevitable tourists who took the van for an information point, and a woman who insisted on presenting Conor with a box containing two kittens. They were a present for his mam, who Conor knew wouldn't want them. Still, he hadn't the heart to turn them down so he said they were great altogether.

The woman was dying to hear what the girls would be wearing at the wedding. 'I'd say it's a secret, though, is it? Sure, whatever they wear, don't you know they'll both look lovely?'

Conor smiled back at her. 'They will of course, aren't the two of them only gorgeous?'

That was a fat lie, though. Deep in his mind he was certain that nothing worn by Eileen could match the beauty of Aideen in a dress embroidered with flowers, with bare feet and a wreath of carnations and daisies in her hair.

Chapter Five

'Have you just sold the last chocolate brownie?' Aideen lifted the Perspex cover and called across to Bríd, who was lowering the blind on the door.

'Yep, to Mary Casey.'

Bríd came back to the counter, struggling with a difficult knot in her apron strings. She took it off and hung it on the storeroom door. 'What's the problem?'

'Nothing. Just that Eileen's a great one for brownies.'

'Well, she'll have to whistle for them, won't she? Give her a huge slice of Death by Chocolate. That might shut her up.'

Bríd went round to brew fresh coffee as Aideen took off her own dark green apron, with 'HabberDashery' embroidered across the bib. The logo was part of their newly designed branding, a signal to the world – or at least to Lissbeg – that their business had taken off. She glanced at Bríd, who was looking a bit ratty. They had a full evening ahead of them, checking orders and paying invoices, so Eileen's impending arrival wasn't convenient. The trouble was, she'd rung up and kind of invited herself.

Rattling three mugs onto a table, Bríd shrugged. 'I suppose it's better to cope with her now than invite her to the house.'

'Well, yeah. I thought so. I mean, she just wants to take a photo to stick up on Instagram. I couldn't say no.'

'Is that what she's into now? Instagram?'

'Yeah, she's set up a new account. I think it's specifically for wedding stuff.'

'Holy God, she's starting a bit early.'

'Well, you know Eileen.'

'I do.'

'So, what kind of a photo?'

'I dunno. "Here's me with Aideen and her bridesmaid." Smiley face, smiley face, huge big heart.'

'Well, she'll bore people rigid if she gives them months of that.'

'Yeah, but next month it's sure to be something else. She gets notions, and the easiest thing is just to play along.'

'This is your wedding too, though, remember? Don't let Eileen tell you what to do.'

There was a pause in which Aideen grinned at her and Bríd looked sheepish. Then she gave Aideen a slap. 'Okay, I know what you're thinking. But I'm different. And you know I'm right.'

Aideen laughed and went to cut the cake. Bríd, one of a large family of cheerful, competent siblings, had always behaved to her more like a sister than a cousin. Aideen, whose unmarried mother had died giving birth to her, was an only child brought up by their gran and their elderly Aunt Bridge. Gran had passed away after years of being bedridden, and Aunt Bridge had died when Aideen was just finishing school.

Her dad's people didn't come into the picture. He'd been a married man with a wife and kids who'd wanted nothing to do with her and, except for Bríd's family, the relations on her mum's side took much the same view. Though it hadn't happened often, Aideen had had enough schoolyard questions about her parents to make her sensitive, and Bríd's continuing bossiness arose from an instinct to protect her.

When Aunt Bridge died, Aideen had moved in with Bríd's family for a while. It had all felt a bit noisy and strange after what she'd been used to, but Aunt Carol and Uncle Justin were kind, though Aideen had wished Bríd herself had been there to help her cope with the weirdness. Bríd had been off doing a culinary-science course by then, and when she came back to Lissbeg six months later, they'd joined forces and opened the deli. By then the formal stuff to do with Aunt Bridge's will had all been completed, and Aideen had found she'd been left the house she'd grown up in. The decision to live there with Bríd had been a no-brainer. They got on well and could share the household expenses, and the idea now was that, after the wedding, Bríd would stay and they'd put a lodger in Aideen's old room.

There was a tap on the door and Eileen arrived in a wave of expensive perfume. Having kissed Aideen and hugged Bríd, she accepted a coffee and took her phone out of her bag. 'Okay, here's the thing. I've got this app for shooting black-and-white photos. Really edgy, you know, like film noir? And I thought I'd do a series on Instagram as a big wedding build-up.'

Bríd sat down at the table. 'But isn't film noir about pessimism and menace?'

'Well, yeah, okay, not film noir exactly, but that's not the point. The *point* is that the app can pick out certain features in colour.' Eileen rounded her wide eyes and pointed at them. 'Look at me. Brown eyes. Right?' She held out her phone triumphantly. 'And look at *this*!'

The image on the screen was a black-and-white selfie in which Eileen's eyes were a startling sapphire blue.

'How cool is that? There are so many options! What d'you think?'

Without waiting for the others' response, she swiped to the phone's camera. 'So what I thought was, let's do a shot of the three of us and give us bright red lips!'

Her hair was expertly tousled and her makeup looked freshly applied. Evidently she'd prepared for this with an afternoon at a salon.

Out of the corner of her eye, Aideen saw Bríd looking bolshie. A long day behind the deli counter had left them both feeling knackered, and no app was going to make them look half as good as Eileen. Then, to Aideen's relief, Bríd summoned a smile and nodded. 'Okay, let's do it but, for God's sake, get a move on.'

Eileen bit her lip. 'Oh, I'm sorry! Am I being awful? I didn't mean to turn up at a bad time.'

Aideen felt dreadful. 'Of course not. You haven't. Anyway, I told you to come. Look, have a piece of cake first and we'll do the photo in a minute.'

'Not at all, I won't. We'll do it now. I'm in your way.' She shuffled her chair, held out the phone, and the others leaned in on either side of her. 'Okay, all together, big cheesy smiles!'

Having fired off a burst of shots, Eileen swiped through them on the screen. Each photo showed her looking even more fabulous, while Aideen and Bríd's expressions ranged from fatuous to mad.

Catching Bríd's eye, Aideen fought to keep from giggling. The addition of bright red lips was going to make the three of them look like a freak show, but Eileen seemed to think they were perfectly fine. Shrugging on her jacket and putting her phone in her bag, she enveloped Bríd in another hug and blew Aideen a kiss. 'You're both stars, and I'm so glad, and I'd love to stay but you're up to your eyes and, besides, I have to fly because I've got another appointment. Check out the pic when I put it up. See you soonest!'

As the door slammed, Aideen halved the slice of chocolate cake, pushing a fork across the table to Bríd. They ate several bites in silence before Aideen spoke. 'I am going to contain this, I promise.'

'Don't be daft, you're the bride. I'm the one who's supposed to deal with the crap stuff.'

'But you can't deal with Eileen. All you can do is play along, and I don't want you to have to.'

'What you mean is you know that if I took over, sparks would fly.'

'All right, yes. And I don't want them to. Eileen's mad as a box of frogs, but she's Joe's fiancée, and Joe is Conor's brother.'

'So?'

'I don't want Conor upset.'

'Oh, Aideen!'

'What?'

'There's months of this ahead of you. You haven't even set the actual date yet. If Eileen's pushing you around over a stupid photo on Instagram, what's she going to be like when you get to the real stuff? And, incidentally, when's that going to happen? You can't book a venue till you've settled on a date.'

'I know. And I have asked her. But she's awfully hard to pin down.'

Bríd abandoned the chocolate cake and started to clatter the plates onto a tray. Feeling a lump rise in her throat, Aideen put her head down and said nothing. Suddenly Bríd sat down again, her hands still gripping the tray. 'We're not at school now, you know.'

They'd all known each other at school, when Eileen had been a prefect while Aideen was a lowly junior. And when Bríd had been in fifth form Eileen had already left. Aideen sighed. Of course the obsolete pecking order should be irrelevant now, but maybe it wasn't. Or maybe it was.

'Ade, if you don't want a double wedding, you've got to come out and say so.'

'I do want one.'

'Why? So Eileen's dad will put money in the farm?'

'Stop bullying me. It's complicated. It's not just about the money. And it's not just about me. This is Conor's wedding too, and Joe's his brother. And Eileen's going to be my sister-in-law. I want us to get along. It's about family, Bríd. My new family.'

Looking up, Aideen saw Bríd's face. 'Oh, *don't*. I'm not saying you're not family. I'm not. Of course you are. That's why you're my bridesmaid. And I'm not saying you're not right about stuff because most of the time you are. But, honestly, Bríd, I've got to think about Conor. That's what marriage is about.'

Chapter Six

The place known as the Hag's Glen was called Móinéar na Méine in Irish, which was why the site Brian Morton had bought there appeared on the map as 'Moneymenny'. When you typed the Irish name into an online translator it came up as 'the meadow of desire', followed by stipulations that it could equally well be 'the rough grassland of yearning' or 'the poor place of need'. But having spent years working in a council planning office, Brian was well used to anomalies thrown up by translations of Irish place names.

The origins of the Hag's Glen name were a mystery, though Fury O'Shea insisted it was barely two hundred years old. The houses there had been abandoned, he said, back in the time of the Famine, but one old crone who'd refused to leave with her family had lived on alone.

'And, what, people called her a witch or something?'

'Not at all, man, she was a perfectly respectable woman. She just didn't fancy taking the American boat. You couldn't blame her at her age – they say she was pushing ninety. Anyway, she stayed on and lived till she died and they called it "the Hag's Glen".'

The trouble was that you couldn't believe a word Fury said.

He had a firm belief that architects, like dogs, had to be taught their place in a pack and, in this instance, it was well below the youngest labourer's: Brian wasn't just an architect but a blow-in to boot.

Well into his seventies, Fury O'Shea was a byword for eccentricity. Despite this, and Fury's mendacious claim that he couldn't do forms or estimates because he'd never learned to read, Brian always championed him as the best builder in Finfarran. And despite Brian's refusal to be bamboozled by his posturing, Fury held that, for a blow-in from Wicklow, Brian was game ball.

Brian hadn't argued about the name of the land he'd bought. There had been plenty of other things to argue about – including whether it was a proper place to build a house at all. And there were lots of people whose initial response was to tell him he was mad. Chiefly his colleagues in the planning office, who were rigorous in their capacity as professionals and bewildered when they talked to him as friends. Why would anyone make a planning application with so many inherent difficulties? And was he out of his mind entirely deciding to build in the back of beyond?

With boxes to be ticked, letters to be written, and endless justifications to be made in the course of the planning process, Brian could have fallen out with people he needed to have onside. But, by doggedly sticking to facts and containing his feelings, he'd jumped through all the required hoops and got his permission in the end. And now, long months later, the house in the Hag's Glen was almost complete.

He'd discovered the upland river valley last summer, on a sparkling day when every blade of grass seemed tipped with light.

Turning off the motorway halfway down the peninsula, he'd taken a road that ran between cliffs and forest, and struck inland along a farm track, planning a mountain hike. Having left his car near the farmyard, where a sheepdog had growled warningly, he'd set off across little fields that soon gave way to commonage studded with heather and furze. Then, following sheep paths, he'd zigzagged towards Knockinver's northern shoulder.

The rising ground was treacherous in places, where old turf cuttings half filled with water were overgrown. Brian was absent-mindedly wishing he'd brought a stick when a steep scramble took him to the rock from which he'd first seen the valley.

It was stunning. Broad-based and with curving sides, it tapered to a rocky cleft at its head, where the peat-brown river fell as a slender waterfall, before widening into a broad stream. Grouped on the riverbank were the ruined walls of half a dozen dwellings. From his vantage point Brian could see that a spur from the track he'd taken as far as the farmhouse ran on round the base of the hill to the entrance of the valley. There couldn't be more than five hundred yards between the fallen walls below him and the point where the spur petered out. Yet no farm or road would be visible from the valley and, except for the sound of the waterfall, there was no sound at all.

His hike forgotten, he'd climbed down, taking photos all the way. The soil in the valley was stony and the ruined buildings small, and he'd understood why it might have been called 'the poor place of need'. But, for him, from that first moment, it was the meadow of desire. He'd known at once that he wanted to build a house there.

His flat in Carrick had never been more than a staging post, though somehow he'd found himself stuck there for years. Privacy was important to him and the impersonal low-rise apartment block provided plenty of that. In one sense the valley offered more of the same, but it was the wild beauty of the place that enchanted him, and the chance to design a space that was wholly his own. When he'd first brought Hanna up to the site, she'd understood exactly what he meant.

'It feels like a haven. Or, no, since it's you, maybe I mean an artist's palette.'

Someone else might have bustled in and started telling him how he ought to design it. Hanna had sat beside him in silence as they drank in the view.

Fury had been scathing from the outset. 'Name of God, do you know the cost of dragging the makings of a house all the way up there?'

'I do.'

'And you're going to put in an access road, I suppose, and sink a well and generate your own power.'

'That's the plan.'

'And you've noticed there isn't a pint of milk to be had within miles.'

'I have, yes.'

Fury, a scarecrow figure standing on the empty site in a torn waxed jacket, had thrown up his beaky nose with a sniff of disgust. 'Well, you're a fool, man. And I'm telling you that from the start, so don't blame me later.'

'You're up for the job, though?'

'Oh, I'll take it, I suppose, if the money's right. Anyone planning to build up here will want to have deep pockets, so be warned.'

They'd agreed on a notional price there and then, and shaken hands on it, something that Brian had no intention of letting anyone know. His colleagues would think that he'd lost what wits he had left to him, but he knew Fury of old. Arrogant and bolshie though the old man might be, he was honest to a fault, and nobody took a greater pride in his work.

Having spat on his palm and shaken hands, Fury had turned and tramped down the valley to where he'd parked his van next to Brian's car. His little Jack Russell terrier, known as The Divil, flung itself barking against the windscreen as soon as it saw them approach. Ignoring him, Fury had leaned against the van and extracted a roll-up cigarette from behind his left ear. 'Will we have a drink to seal the bargain?'

'I suppose we should.'

'Trust me, by the time this job's over, you won't have the price of this fag, let alone a drink.'

In a little pub over a couple of pints, with The Divil eating Tayto at their feet, Fury had cocked a shaggy eyebrow at Brian. 'I wouldn't have had you pegged as a man for romance.'

'And now you have?'

'Well, can you blame me? Jesus, you must have been reared on the Lakeland poets. Or Walter Scott.'

'And there was I believing the story that you've never read a book.'

Fury shot him a sly grin. 'You learned poetry by rote in my

day. The master bawled out each line and the lads all gave them back.'

'And Walter Scott?'

'God, I loved that film *Kidnapped*. All them gloomy castles in dark, mysterious glens.'

'Robert Louis Stevenson. Not Scott.'

'Really?' Fury scratched The Divil with his boot. 'Well, that's me. Illiterate. Still, I well remember the poems. "Childe Roland to the Dark Tower Came ..."'

'Browning. Not one of the Lakeland poets.'

'Are you sure?'

Brian finished his pint and put his glass on the table. 'When can you start?'

'The job? Soon as you like.'

'Because now that I'm good to go I want to get on.'

Leaning back in his chair, Fury had smiled knowingly. 'You see, that's what I mean. Romantic. You're building a house for Hanna Casey, aren't you?'

'What?'

'Well, it's no secret the two of you are an item.'

'God, Fury, you're a hell of an old gossip. No, I'm not building a house for Hanna Casey. She's got a house of her own.'

'Oh, right so. Well, maybe I'm the romantic.'

Pointedly refusing to rise to the bait, Brian had nodded at The Divil. 'Will we have another round?'

'My shout. You'll probably go getting smoky bacon and he's a salt and vinegar man.'

Over the second drink, they'd roughed out a broad schedule,

starting with access and the generator, then working through the phases of the build. By the time The Divil had fallen asleep with his nose in his crisps packet, Fury had lost his customary air of languor and Brian himself had been itching to begin.

That had been more than a year ago, and in the following months he'd been consumed by the complexities of the task. Now, however, with the house only weeks from completion, he found himself focusing more and more on something he had to tell Hanna.

Chapter Seven

Jazz glanced down at the nuns' garden. One of the nicest things about her office was having this desk by the window. It overlooked a fountain where water gushed from stone flowers round the feet of a statue of St Francis. The shallow basin with its broad rim was the centre point of the garden, in which the carefully tended herb beds were separated by box hedging and narrow gravelled paths.

Although an old wall had been taken down to make an entrance from Broad Street, the nuns' garden still retained a sense of cloistered tranquillity: the visual rhythms of its formal layout were soothing, and the trees were full of birdsong. Each morning one of the volunteers who worked there waded through the water to pour birdseed into the weathered saint's extended hands.

This ritual, begun by the nuns, must by now have become part of the birds' communal memory. As Jazz watched, a flight of goldcrests swooped from an alder to the fountain, pecking and snatching at the food and whirling back to the trees. The flurry of gold and olive plumage echoed the colours of the stained-glass roundel in the window at her elbow. It would be hard to think of a better place to work.

The door opened and Saira Khan stuck her head in, asking if Jazz was free.

'Sure, come on in. I'm due to have lunch in the café with Eileen but I'm not moving till I see the whites of her eyes. She's twenty minutes late already.'

Saira murmured that Eileen must be very busy. 'Weddings take a lot of work.'

'Oh, she thrives on wedding stuff. She just doesn't know the meaning of turning up on time. Did you want to say something?'

'It won't take a minute.' Saira sat down. 'Don and I have been running through the list of our growers.'

Jazz nodded. Saira's family in Pakistan had made herbal cosmetics and cures for generations. She'd been a volunteer in the nuns' garden before she was offered a research-and-development job at Edge of the World Essentials, and was proving an invaluable liaison point between Don, who managed production, and his suppliers.

'Well, I've tracked down more local people who garden organically and either grow herbs already or are willing to begin. Right now we are fine, of course, with what we buy from the garden here and our other current suppliers. So this is looking ahead.' Saira glanced at a notebook she'd opened on her knee. 'But I've noticed that we're building a really diverse list. At one end of the spectrum I have young people who've gone organic because of concerns about the environment, and at the other I have pensioners who've never thought of gardening any other way. So I thought this might be a story for a magazine. Or one you could use on the website? A kind of "Meet Our Growers" feature.'

Jazz was already three steps ahead of her. 'Could we get

attractive photos? Things we could blow up and use on marketing material. Shop displays, say?'

'Well, yes. So long as you're not expecting people who look like fashion models. Johnny Hennessy must be eighty and he doesn't have many teeth!'

'He has a wonderful face, though. And a gorgeous garden. I can see how this would work.'

'I'm glad.'

As Saira got up to go to the door she turned back, looking thoughtful. 'Some of the younger growers have kids, who'd be very sweet in photos.'

Jazz laughed. 'I'm supposed to be the sales and marketing person, remember? But you're absolutely right. Images that span generations would be great. Leave it with me and let's talk about it again.'

Saira agreed and left the room, her sandalled feet moving as softly as those of the nuns in the past.

Jazz was still at her desk by the window when she saw Eileen bounce through the entrance from Broad Street. She reached the café just as Eileen bustled back out.

Eileen waved. 'There you are! I'm sorry I'm late. I've ordered wraps and coffees. Let's find a table by the fountain.'

The Garden Café didn't do table service, but that wouldn't bother Eileen. Unerringly, she'd have spotted a member of staff willing to break the rule and bring out a tray. Somehow she always got her way, yet no one could fail to like her.

As Jazz sat down at the sunny table she remembered the first day they'd met. It was halfway through the spring term at St

Enda's in Lissbeg – a rotten time to turn up as a new girl – and, standing with her back against the school wall, she still hadn't taken in what was happening in her life. All she'd known was that, when they'd turned up the previous week on her nan's doorstep, Mary Casey hadn't been expecting them.

Finfarran hadn't been strange to her: she'd holidayed at Mary's bungalow every summer since she was a baby. But the thought of living there permanently had been a shock. Her mum and her nan had never got on brilliantly, and Jazz herself had always been a daddy's girl. Besides, divorce was something that happened in other people's families. Up to then she'd seen her parents' marriage as rock steady. In the end it was Mary who'd made a pot of tea, sat down and tried to explain things. But Jazz could tell she was floundering through a mass of half-truths and lies.

It was Eileen who'd made St Enda's bearable. Her assured air when she'd sauntered up and introduced herself had made Jazz assume she'd been sent officially to mentor the new girl. It hadn't seemed likely that she was just being kind. Later on Jazz had discovered that assurance and kindness were Eileen's defining characteristics. Shyer, quieter personalities found her overwhelming, but Jazz had her own streak of assertiveness fostered by an equally privileged background. So, in time, they'd found a balance.

Eileen had been the perfect friend for someone screwed up and stroppy. Being cheerfully involved in her own affairs, she asked no intrusive questions, and a total lack of imagination meant that her instinct for kindness was never subverted by fear of saying or doing the wrong thing. And, unlike many of their schoolmates, she lacked the sense of tribalism that, at the start, Jazz had frequently fallen foul of. Instead of taking umbrage when the new girl dismissed camogie as a weird game for savages, Eileen had cornered her after school and asked if she played tennis. She had a court at home, she'd said, and a spare racquet. And if Jazz wanted to borrow some kit she had masses of T-shirts and shorts.

The Dawsons' home five miles out in the country had become an unlooked-for oasis in a desert of confusion. While Mary Casey's bungalow was full of hidden tears and suppressed fury, Eileen's house, with its shady lawns and tennis court, reminded Jazz of her grandparents' home in Kent. JohnJo Dawson and his fat, chatty wife were nothing like Granny Lou or Grandpa George, but they were cheerful and hospitable, happy to let their daughter's friend come and go as she pleased.

Actually, her arrival had been a godsend for the Dawsons. The tennis lessons Eileen had from a coach each Wednesday were part of an attempt to live up to the house JohnJo had bought as an emblem of his success. So were the drinks parties on the Dawsons' boat in Ballyfin marina, and the afternoon teas served by a Polish au pair. But few kids at St Enda's played tennis, and biking five miles for a dainty sandwich wasn't really their style. Back then, Eileen had needed a friend as much as Jazz did and, despite the differences in their personalities, her uncomplicated companionship had made them friends for life.

As soon as the coffees and wraps arrived, Jazz put her elbows on the table. 'Look, have you actually got your head around the practicalities of this wedding? Because it strikes me that by now I should be liaising on things with Aideen's bridesmaid.'

'Why?'

'Because otherwise, Eileen, it's you and me doing the organising and Aideen having no say.'

'We're not organising. Not at this stage. We're brainstorming.'

'You texted to say we're off to a wedding fair!'

'Yes, but it's just a fair. You know, champagne and canapés and lots of little goodie bags. It's fun, that's all. What's the point of being engaged if you can't have fun?'

'But shouldn't Aideen be having fun too?'

'Well, of course, if she wants.'

Eileen reached for her phone but Jazz stopped her.

'Wouldn't it be better to ditch the fair, and sit down instead with Aideen and discuss things?'

There was a pause in which Eileen fiddled with her iPhone. Then she thrust it back into her bag. 'Actually, I did ask Joe if he thought she'd want to come. He said she's not the wedding fair type.'

'If that's the case, a fair isn't the best point to start from.'

'But who doesn't like wedding fairs? She'd love it.'

Jazz took a deep breath. 'Well, if she would, shouldn't you have asked her to come along?'

'I thought you said I should cancel it.'

'Oh, Eileen! What I'm saying is that double weddings are complicated.'

'I know. I'm not stupid. Which is why I've decided we're going to have a wedding planner.'

Jazz blinked. 'And that "we" would be you and Aideen, would it? You've asked her?'

'Why are you being difficult?'

'Because you're not getting the point. You can't just go round making decisions because you're the one with the credit card. Can't you imagine how Aideen might feel?'

Eileen pulled a face. 'According to you, I've got no imagination.'

'In this instance you don't need it. You just need to sit down and talk to her.'

'Okay, you're right, I will. The thing is, I don't really know her. Look, the double-wedding idea was Joe's, not mine. But I'm totally cool with it. And I know she's going to love this wedding planner. He costs a fortune but apparently he's brilliant.'

'You've booked him already, haven't you?'

Eileen made wide, guilty eyes at her. 'He gets booked up, like, *centuries* in advance, Jazz, I promise you. He's got a regular slot on morning TV.'

Chapter Eight

The sun pouring in through her bedroom window filled Hanna's wakening consciousness with dust motes dancing in light. The room was just big enough to take her double bed, a chest of drawers, a chair and a built-in cupboard. As she wriggled upright against her pillows, she could see a pile of Brian's clothes folded neatly on the chair.

The sound of a boiling kettle made Hanna stretch luxuriously. It was Sunday, the weather was gorgeous, and there was a whole day of idleness ahead.

Brian appeared round the door carrying two mugs. 'Tea here or shall we go outside?'

Faced with a choice between two equally pleasant prospects, Hanna hesitated so long that he put her mug on the windowsill and climbed back into bed.

'Oi, I was making my mind up!'

'Yes, and in the meantime this was getting cold.'

She took her mug and settled herself back against the pillows. The tea was made exactly as she liked it. Brian's, she knew, would be brewed black and have several sugars in it, a legacy, he claimed, of a lifetime of tea drunk on building sites.

At forty-eight, he was four years younger than Hanna, a

disparity that had bothered her at first. Having been the focus of gossip as 'Miss Casey with the broken marriage', she hadn't fancied the role of a divorcée who chased younger men. Though, in fact, it was Brian who'd done the chasing. Famously solitary and uncommunicative, he'd pursued her doggedly despite all her qualms. But, unlike Malcolm, he'd never been manipulative. Instead he'd waited with what Hanna now felt had been superhuman patience while she'd offered a million excuses before admitting that she was just scared. To find love again after all she'd been through had seemed incredible, and to believe that this was someone she could trust had required a leap of faith.

And here they were a few years later, propped against pillows in the sunlight, established as far as Finfarran was concerned as an actual, official couple. Yet, even here, she clung to a sense of emotional and physical privacy, fiercely cherishing her reclaimed independence. Although she and Brian never discussed it, they meticulously avoided leaving personal belongings in each other's territory. Whereas Malcolm would have felt challenged by this, Brian understood. His long years of solitude had become a habit, and autonomy was as important to him as to her.

There were so many things they were happy to share, though. As she finished her tea Hanna asked if he fancied a day in the garden. 'I was thinking of digging a new ridge for the spuds.'

Brian placed his mug on the floor and crossed his arms behind his head. 'Truthfully? I'd hate it. I've been dreaming of a boot-free, trench-free day all week.'

'Okay. Dumb suggestion. How about a picnic on the beach?'

'Now you're talking.' He pushed back the duvet and swung

his feet to the floor. 'Maybe I'll skip a shower and settle for a swim.'

Hanna got up and reached for her kimono. 'Have a shower while I chuck together a picnic. You can't go out unwashed on a Sunday. What if we met a priest?'

He pulled her close, loosening the belt she'd just tied and drawing back the coloured silk to plant a kiss on her shoulder. 'We're past praying for by this time. Imagine what your great-aunt Maggie would say if she saw what was going on under her roof.'

Hanna laughed. 'For all you know, Maggie Casey could have been a right goer. She certainly didn't have much time for the priests.'

His arms tightened, and Hanna briefly touched her forehead to his collar bone. Then she pulled away, retying her belt, and told him to have his shower. 'If we go back to bed now we'll miss the best of the day.'

'That's a value judgement. I'm not sure I share it.'

'Well, be that as it may, bugger off to the bathroom. I'm going to root in the fridge.'

As she cut sandwiches and packed fruit in the kitchen she could hear him whistling cheerfully in the shower. It was strange, she thought, how she relished the contrasts her new life had brought. The emptiness of this house when she was alone gave her almost as much joy as the warmth of Brian's presence. Maybe because, when she'd first moved in, the house had been her fortress, a place where she could hide and lick her wounds.

She'd made the move as soon as Jazz had finished school and left home. The years spent in Mary's bungalow had been fraught with unspoken tensions, and the longing to get away had increased as time went by. The little house on the cliff had been derelict then, and the field was a wilderness, but at least they were her own. As a child she had dug potatoes and run errands for her great-aunt with no idea that the old lady would leave her the place in her will. As far as Mary Casey was concerned, the bequest had been more of an insult than a gift, but for Hanna, who'd almost forgotten she'd been left it, the house was a refuge, and the months of restoration on a minuscule budget had done much to restore the confidence she'd lost since her divorce.

The drive to the beach took less than ten minutes. They left the car and sauntered along a sandy path between marram grass and thistles till they reached a place where folds in the rocks made a kind of ladder. It was a bit of a scramble down to the beach, but it wasn't high and, provided you kept up your pace, it was safe enough.

This side of the peninsula was less rugged than the other, where the stony inlets that fringed the base of the sheer cliffs were mostly inaccessible. Here the horseshoe bay enclosed a sloping stretch of golden sand with a flat spit of rock reaching into the turquoise waves. Towing Brian, who was carrying the picnic in a backpack, Hanna waded upwards through sand that streamed behind her, the shifting surface revealing a darker, colder layer beneath. When they reached the point where the cliff met the spit they sat down against a boulder. Drawing her knees up to her chin, Hanna brushed away the shining flecks that clung to her bare feet. 'I never know why I bother to do this. They only get covered in sand again, as soon as one moves.'

Brian pushed a folded sweater behind his head. 'Did you really dance on the spit with seals when you were a kid?'

'Well, we jumped up and down and waved our arms to spook them. I told you. We wanted to hear the splashes when they lumbered into the sea.'

'And there was me seeing a selkie dancing on fairy foam.'

When Hanna snorted he turned his head and looked at her. 'Why not? Look at you. Huge grey eyes. Dark hair. Alabaster skin.'

'Don't be ridiculous. Anyway, selkies are Scottish, not Irish.' As soon as she'd spoken, she felt rueful. Compliments always unnerved her, but why be so ungracious when he was being nice?

Brian reached out and touched her cheek with his finger. 'It's true, though.'

'Fairly middle-aged selkie.'

'Selkies are ageless. Anyway, your beauty is in the bone.'

'Not the alabaster skin?'

'Not just that. And if you don't stick some factor thirty on it you'll probably end up freckled as a hen's egg.'

He raised his own face to the sun and closed his eyes with a small contented grunt. Hanna looked down at his lean body and smiled. Lazy days on the beach like this were one of the pleasures of having returned to Finfarran. There was never any pressure. A picnic with Brian meant lounging, swimming, and wandering about peering into rock pools, exactly as it had meant when she was a child. The sandwiches might get sandy, or a sudden shower might result in a scramble for shelter, but Brian, with his long limbs and sun-bleached hair, was very different from Malcolm, whose dark hair, sleek as a seal's back, never got wind-tossed. When she'd been married and her weekends were spent in Norfolk, they'd often take friends out on a yacht from Great Yarmouth. But, back then, the proper male attire had been polo shirts, guernseys and peaked caps worn at a rakish angle, and the picnics had come in a hamper, carried aboard by the skipper. Malcolm had liked his pleasures well organised.

Plaiting her hair at the nape of her neck, Hanna wriggled out of her jeans and shirt and began applying the sunblock. As she adjusted the straps of the swimsuit she'd worn under her clothes, she asked Brian if he'd ever read *Brooklyn*.

'Nope. I saw the film when it came out, though. Why?'

'I've just remembered the bit about struggling to get into togs under a towel in 1950s Ireland.'

Brian laughed. 'Before my time.'

'Mine too, as it happens.' As she made a face at him she realised with a rush of pleasure that the difference in their ages had become a cause for laughter, not concern. 'So, what, you just threw caution to the wind and didn't care?'

'As far as I can remember we went in for a lot of skinny-dipping. That was when I was pre-pubescent, though, so perhaps it didn't count.'

Hanna knew very little about his childhood. She'd gathered that, unlike Mary Casey, his mother had been self-effacing, a typical company wife who'd followed her husband around a series of jobs in oil companies abroad. The family home in Wicklow had been sold when his father was offered a placement in Dubai.

Brian and his sister had been sent to English boarding schools at the company's expense. According to Brian, who'd only been twelve, school was an endless round of midnight feasts and cricket matches, and he'd spent the holidays with a couple of aunts in England whom he'd adored.

'But didn't you miss your parents?'

'Well, we flew out and saw them too. But, no. It was a great school – a sort of grown-up version of *Jennings and Darbishire* – and I'd never really seen much of my dad at all.'

'Gosh! I can't imagine childhood without my dad there as a touchstone. At home he always played second fiddle to Mary, but he and I used to sneak off together and have fun. We were friends.'

'I had a master at school who served that function. We still keep in touch.'

Following her train of thought, Hanna had frowned. 'You know what I can't imagine either? A father not wanting to be there while his son grew up.'

At that point Brian had turned his head and, fearing she'd touched a nerve, she'd said no more.

It had often struck her that Brian's fierce sense of personal privacy must be rooted in his self-sufficient childhood. That and what had happened in his late twenties, when his wife of only a few years had tragically died of cancer. It was a blow so sudden and brutal that he hadn't been able to cope. Irrationally, he'd gone to ground, locking his door and refusing to answer his phone. As a result, his fledgling architectural practice had lost a big contract. And, stricken by guilt, he'd sold his home, pushed the proceeds in an envelope through his business partner's letterbox, and disappeared without leaving a forwarding address.

Three or four years ago, when Hanna had first met him, he'd still been working in a council job he'd drifted into in Carrick, over-qualified, truculent, and as lost and confused as she had been herself. They'd both come a long way since then, though, and one sign was the extent to which he enjoyed his new job as Finfarran's County Architect. Now, looking at the relaxed, sun-tanned figure sprawled on the beach beside her, Hanna remembered his former tension and the constantly wary look in his hooded eyes. If ever she doubted his love for her she had only to think of the day on which he'd told her the story of his past. She'd known as soon as he'd opened up how much it had cost him to share it, and that he'd consciously let down his guard that day so she could lower her own.

Chapter Nine

The piece of paper said 'Mrs Khan. Tea Room. 3.30'. The woman at the desk read it out loudly, as if Rasher was thick.

Rasher took it politely. When he'd heard about the halfway house he'd been warned that places here were like gold dust and you needed to spend your whole time saying thanks. Probably this woman with the frizzy hair and the flowery shirt didn't have the authority to kick him out. She was only a volunteer, like Mrs Khan who was coming to 'have a chat' with him. Still, he smiled and thanked her. You got used to hot showers and a warm bed and not being pissed on, so he didn't fancy ending up back on the street.

One of the rules was that you couldn't wear a hoodie with the hood up indoors. Another was that you had to be bang on time when they fixed you an appointment. There were a lot of appointments, and most of the time they'd do your head in. Rasher had had an assessment the other day from a woman who wouldn't believe he wasn't a minor. When he'd shown her his passport, taking care to be cheerful, she'd gone off with it, saying she'd need to check his status. But he knew that was fine. He'd had his eighteenth birthday a couple of weeks earlier, so no one could try sending him back to his mum.

You had a choice of whether you had your chat in the tea

room or a cubicle. It was a no-brainer in his case. Being cooped up in a little curtained space with Mrs Khan, whom he'd never met, would have been weird. Anyway, the cubicles reminded him of hospitals. All those afternoons spent hanging round on plastic chairs doing his homework while he waited for Mum or Dad to finish a shift. And later on, when Dad was dead and homework no longer seemed to matter, all those nights in A & E waiting for someone to patch Mum up before taking her home to get smacked about by her new boyfriend.

This place had all the hallmarks of a hospital, from the inmates' air of mingled gratitude and resentment, to the bossy kindness of the overworked staff. From the moment Rasher had crossed the threshold he'd hated the smell and feel of it. But whenever he'd been tempted to walk out again he'd remembered the time he'd opened his eyes one morning under the viaduct and seen an old guy who'd never wake up being carted off on a stretcher. Rasher had grabbed his own stuff and the old fella's – which had turned out to be useless – and dodged away while the paramedics were putting the stretcher in the ambulance. Then he'd faced the fact that if he didn't do something, he too could be out on the streets for life.

Mrs Khan was probably about his mum's age. When Rasher arrived in the tea room she was sitting at a table with a notebook. She had a long floaty scarf over her hair and thrown back across her shoulders. He sat down warily, suspecting that the notebook was full of stuff about himself. But she put it away, saying she'd been catching up on some work while she'd been waiting. Rasher stiffened. 'Sorry, I didn't think I was late.'

'You're not. I was early. I came on the bus from Lissbeg.'

There was a bit of a silence. Then he asked if Lissbeg was where she lived.

'Yes. For nearly twenty years now. My husband manages an IT support centre. But, of course, we're not Irish, as you can see.'

Rasher didn't say anything.

She held out her hand. 'My name is Saira. It's nice to meet you, Adam.'

'I'm called Rasher.'

He'd found out ages ago that being Rasher rather than Adam Rashid could sometimes save him a kicking. Not that anyone stopped to ask your name when you were sitting on a corner begging. If you had dark skin and black hair, you were a feckin' foreign scrounger and that was that.

'Would you like some tea?'

He wasn't particularly thirsty but he never refused a freebie. When she came back with the mugs, she folded her hands on the table and asked if there was anything in particular he'd like to talk about. 'I expect you already know why you've had me assigned to you. Basically, I'm here to answer questions. I can give you practical information, and maybe offer advice.'

He noticed she'd been assigned to him and not the other way round, which seemed to fit in with the way this place did things. Very eager to be client-friendly, probably so's to tick some funding box. Martin the warden was a big slab of a priest in his mid-forties, who looked like he knew how to handle himself. He'd interviewed Rasher the first day and rattled off a list of rules at him but, according to what you'd hear on the street, he was an okay bloke. Rasher wished to hell he hadn't dumped this oul one on him, though.

There was another awkward pause before she spoke again. 'You're not from Finfarran yourself?'

Rasher said he wasn't. 'I was born in Dublin.'

'Well, if we're going to get to know each other, perhaps I should tell you how I came to work here. I'm a volunteer, which you already know, I'm sure. I have two daughters, one about your age and one who is younger. And, as I said, I live in Lissbeg.'

'So why get on a bus to Carrick and come here?'

The question sounded ruder than he'd intended but she didn't seem upset.

'Partly because of my girls, I suppose. Ameena, who's your age, is very bright. She's gone to university. I like to help people like you who maybe haven't had the chance to make choices as she has.'

Rasher shrugged. 'Yeah? Well, I didn't even get my Junior Cert.'

'Paper qualifications are not all that count in life.'

Rasher didn't argue, but this was clearly a waste of time. He was here *because* of paper stuff, for God's sake. That was what he needed. A PPS number, so he could work. An address, so he could have a PPS number. Some kind of letter or certificate or diploma that would get him through a door.

Suddenly hopelessness descended on him. When Martin had shaken his hand the other day he'd said, 'Don't panic. We'll get you there. I've never had a case through these doors that I couldn't crack. You'll be back on your feet in no time.' That night, in an actual bed in a room with a lock on the door, Rasher had almost believed him, and he'd woken up determined to give it a go. But what kind of help was he going to get from a woman whose kids went to uni and whose husband could afford to let her go off and play at being Mother Teresa?

He swept a sideways look at her and found that she'd caught his glance. Her hands were still folded on the table and she laughed and spread them out. 'You're checking out my filthy fingernails!'

'No. I wasn't.' Though now that he came to look at them they did look kind of rough.

She leaned forward. 'Let me tell you something about myself, Adam. I've always had a home, so I've been lucky. I've always felt safe and protected. But sometimes that can cut you off from life, and that isn't good. And one thing I've learned from coming here is that living on the street can chew up your self-confidence. You eat and sleep and walk among throngs of people, but you feel completely alone. It's as if you're living behind a wall of glass. Well, that's exactly how I used to feel in my own home. I know it sounds strange, but it's true. My spoken English wasn't great when I came to Ireland so I made no friends. My husband worked hard and I stayed at home and looked after the children. And, as time went by, I hardly ever went out. My whole life was about being a housewife and taking care of my kids.'

She stopped talking. Rasher wondered if she thought he hadn't been listening so, to be polite, he nodded, trying to look involved. She didn't seem very convinced, but she smiled and went on.

'Here is the point. I had no qualifications. Nothing that would allow me to take a job. Then my daughter took me to a public garden in Lissbeg. It's part of The Old Convent Centre – do you know it?'

He shook his head. He hadn't been to Lissbeg, which, he knew, was way smaller than Carrick. You never got much hanging round in a place that had no fast-food shops, and no supermarkets where people would spend a fortune and then feel guilty and chuck you a handful of change.

'Well, it used to be the nuns' herb garden. And now it's run by volunteers.' Mrs Khan held up her hands. 'And growing herbs is something I do know about.' She laughed and looked at her nails. 'It takes a serious moisturiser to cope with the wear and tear.'

Rasher wondered if she imagined that rough sleepers sat around cheerful camp fires exchanging tips on cosmetics. He knocked back his tea in one slug so she wouldn't see scorn in his eyes.

'So I took the first step. And it was terrifying.'

Looking up, Rasher saw that she'd pressed her fingers to her lips.

'I'm sorry. It still makes me emotional. Because it was a hard thing to do. But I did it. I volunteered to work in the garden.'

'For free?'

'Yes. I volunteered.'

'So it wasn't a job, then?'

'No. And a job is what you want, I know that.'

'It takes money to pay rent.'

'I know. And I was lucky. How to pay rent was not one of my problems. But finding friends was. Discovering that I could talk to people. Realising that I had something to offer. I'd always thought I had nothing. Maybe I thought that everybody knew all about herbs.'

'You went to work in a garden for free and made friends.'

'I did. And I found I was good at something that other people valued. And eventually someone offered me a job.'

'Paid?'

'Yes. And, at the moment, part time. But it's a proper job, with a proper title. I'm a research and development officer for a cosmetics company in Lissbeg.'

Rasher frowned. 'So why are you still doing volunteer stuff?' He couldn't work out what she thought she was going to get by hanging round a halfway house.

'It's not a matter of one thing or the other, or of doing something just to get something back. Or not for me. Of course, not everyone views things the same way. People make choices. But you have to get to a point at which there are choices for you to make.' She stood up and asked if he'd like another tea. As she walked away to the counter Rasher watched her thoughtfully. He wasn't a fool and he kind of saw what she meant.

Chapter Ten

Five of the six copies of *Brooklyn* Hanna had ordered through the central system had been borrowed. The sixth, and two of the three on her own shelves, awaited collection. This was a pretty impressive number of loans, amounting to nearly half the film club audience, and as members often arrived to borrow the book at the last moment, more applications were likely. Mr Maguire, of course, probably had his own first edition.

It was pensioners' computer-class day in the library and Pat Fitz, who taught it, was chatting to Hanna. Pat, who was Mary Casey's best friend, was a pensioner herself. As she rested her oilcloth bag on the desk, her brow was furrowed. 'Do you know what it is, Hanna? I'm halfway through *Brooklyn* and one thing keeps leaping off the pages.'

Two of Pat's sons had made their homes in Canada so when Hanna had chosen Tóibín's novel for the film club she'd imagined Pat would relate to its central themes of loss and emigration. Now she hoped her choice hadn't stirred up painful memories. People so often projected their own dilemmas and dreams onto books they borrowed from the library that sometimes she felt librarians ought to have specialist training in counselling.

Pat's forehead creased again and she looked earnestly at

Hanna. 'Did you ever wonder if writers know that repeated words have a real effect on a reader? Well, what am I saying? Of course they do. Isn't that a writer's trade? I don't know how they do it, though I've been reading all my life.' She paused and cocked her head, like a robin ready to pounce on a worm. 'No, but the thing is that in a novel – say, like *Brooklyn* – you'd get drawn in by particular words that would conjure up the experience of a whole generation.'

Hanna nodded sympathetically. Pat's sons had been out of touch for years, and the family had only grown close again in the few months before her husband had died. Now the wasted decades must be preying on Pat's mind.

'Like cardigans.'

'I'm sorry?'

'Cardigans. The word "cardigan". Did you notice the way it's repeated a lot in *Brooklyn*?'

'No, I don't think I did.'

'Well, now, that's because you and I are different generations. My poor mother set great store by a cardigan. She'd have a new one for Christmas or for a wedding, say, and a black one with jet buttons for funerals. The good coat would be enough for most funerals in those days, but with close friends or relations, my mother was one who liked to mourn to the skin.' Pat nodded emphatically. 'And, do you know what it is, the cardigan thing went through to the 1960s. Myself and your mam, now, were always buying knitting patterns. When the angora wool came in, sure you couldn't hold us back. There was a shop in Carrick used to get it in lovely pastel colours. It cost the earth, so maybe you'd do your cardi in merino, and use the angora just for your collar and your cuffs.'

Hanna said that the film's costumes had certainly featured cardigans.

'I know. Weren't they lovely? I think it's a great book.' With a decisive nod, Pat went off to prepare for her session and, as Hanna returned to her search for a missing email, the members of the computer class began to trickle in. The Old Convent Centre included a day-care facility to which pensioners from outlying villages came on a subsidised minibus. For some, it was just a chance to have a cup of tea in pleasant company but others were eager to brush up on their skills.

Among them was Mary Casey, rigid with disapproval at the thought of being classed as a pensioner but determined not to miss the chance of a free lift into town. Unwilling to spend her afternoons with what she called 'a crowd of old bores eating Bakewells' she'd signed up for the computer class, but as she seldom listened she hadn't learned much.

Scrolling rapidly through her inbox, Hanna gave her mother a wave. Mary immediately adjusted her course and sailed majestically towards her. With a sigh, Hanna asked if something was wrong.

'You may be sure it is! Did you not get the text I sent you?'

'You know I don't keep my phone on here in the library. And I hope you've turned yours off, now you're here.'

'I have not, and I'll tell you why. Because it's my lifeline. A poor widow living alone with no one to keep an eye on her! What if I fell and nobody knew?'

Hanna closed her eyes and prayed for strength. At Mary's own suggestion, her home had been remodelled to include a flat for Louisa, who'd wanted a pied-à-terre close to Lissbeg. It was the perfect arrangement for two elderly widows, but Mary's clutch on martyrdom was tenacious.

'You don't live alone, you live with Louisa.'

'Louisa skites off to London whenever the mood takes her.'

'And when she's away Johnny Hennessy always looks in on you.'

'What if I took a queer turn on a bus?'

'Well, unless you've taken to driving one, you wouldn't be on it alone.'

Mary snorted. 'Ay, it's easy seen *you*'ve got your health and your strength.'

'I'm sorry I missed your text. Was it important?' Feeling guilty, she opened her phone and saw the text at once. Mary only used capital letters and never stooped to punctuation.

AM COMING TO PATS YOKE THOUG% GOD ALONE KNOWS IF THE BUS WILL TURN UP ON TIME

There was a pause in which Hanna raised her eyebrows and Mary placed her hands on her ample hips. 'I could have been in extremis!'

'Well, you're perfectly safe for the next hour, Mam, so please turn off your phone.'

As Pat gathered her flock to lead them away, Mary opened her mouth, determined to have the final word. Pat took her firmly by the elbow. 'Ah, Mary girl, would you give it a rest and not be tormenting Hanna? Let's go through and see if you can follow a few instructions on a screen. Though, since you can't find Shift on a keyboard, I wouldn't hold out much hope.'

Amid winks and nudges from the rest of the class, who never failed to be entertained by Mary, Pat and her pensioners disappeared into the reading room. Torn between amusement and mild resentment, Hanna tried and failed to refocus her mind on her work. Dealing with Mary was taking increasing amounts of time and energy. And, of course, Hanna reminded herself, there was nothing unique in that. The world was full of people trying to juggle lives and jobs with the need to cater to the growing demands of elderly parents.

Though she'd never admit it, Mary had secretly been in her element when Hanna and Jazz had arrived unannounced on her doorstep. The need to cosset her troubled granddaughter, and to castigate Hanna, had given her what had amounted to a new lease of life. After those unexpected years of renewed purpose, Mary had been unsettled by Jazz's departure and Hanna's move to Maggie's place so, when Louisa had decided to set up her business and share the remodelled bungalow, Hanna had hoped that the company, and the new source of interest, would fill a void. To a degree, it had, and even Mary wouldn't deny it. But the bottom line was that she lacked the inner resources to cope well with moving on in life.

Hanna always tried hard not to make comparisons, but they were evident. Louisa had faced the loss of Malcolm's dad with quiet courage; and Pat, Mary's best friend, always turned every obstacle into a challenge. Even Pat's computer literacy came from a determination not to lose touch with her emigrant children, and the class now gave focus to a life that had grown even lonelier since her husband, Ger's, death. But, besides being infuriating, Mary's acerbic martyrdom impeded every attempt Hanna made to help her. Still, Hanna knew there was no changing her now. You had to take her as you found her; and, however annoying she might be, she was a shrewd judge of character, and a rock of strength in times of crisis, ready to take on all comers in defence of her family or a friend.

With the pensioners gathered in the reading room and no one else in the library, Hanna completed the work at her desk and went over to Children's Corner. There had been a group of toddlers there earlier and, despite their mothers' efforts to tidy up after them, picture books were buried under beanbags and the toy basket on the bottom shelf was looking suspiciously empty. As Hanna gathered up the books and pursued pieces of Lego, she remembered visits to her local library in London when Jazz was small.

They'd always walked there, usually chatting so intently that it seemed to take no time. Then, on their return with their arms full of books, they'd stop to feed birds in the park. At home there was an armchair in the conservatory, next to the window, where they'd sit together and read. Even when Jazz had graduated from picture books to classics like *Alice* and Noel Streatfeild's *Ballet Shoes*, they'd sometimes squash into the chair together and read aloud to each other. It was a ritual that became the bedrock of the underlying sense of togetherness that had sustained them through the troubled years ahead.

Picking up a copy of *The Story of Babar*, Hanna made a mental note to order a new one. The damage was evidence of fervour, not destructiveness – it was remarkable how much fervour the average kids' book could take. A tattered copy of *Goldilocks*, which she'd loved for its illustrations, had survived her own parents' move from her childhood home to the bungalow, and become a part of the holidays that she'd spent there when Jazz was little. And Jazz had had a copy of *Where's Spot?*, which she'd loved to disintegration. Unbidden memories like that one could still bring a lump to Hanna's throat. Though *Where's Spot?* had probably gone to a jumble sale long beforehand, she often feared it might have been lost in the turmoil of the divorce. She'd never returned to the London house since she'd found Malcolm with Tessa, but she knew that all the familiar clutter of Jazz's childhood was gone.

Now, rounding the end of a bank of shelving, she discovered an intimate reading party on the floor. Propped up against alphabet blocks, the library's collection of stuffed toys was sitting in a circle round an open copy of *When We Were Very Young*. A large, floppy dinosaur dominated the group, in which Piglet and Eeyore sat cheek by jowl with Paddington and Moomintroll. Peter Rabbit was perched on the end of a shelf above them, and bitten-off bits of jelly bean had been placed by each toy's paw.

In the context of what she'd just been thinking, it looked almost like a set-up. Grinning, Hanna told herself that, even for a distracted, guilt-prone mother, sniffling over A.A. Milne was a step too far. Anyway, it was high time to give up on the guilt. Jazz was fine. Mary might be a trial but she'd settled down with

Louisa. Brian was happy building his house, and she herself was more than happy in the home Maggie had left her. So, from her family to her love life to her choice of *Brooklyn* for the film club, everything right now was pretty much perfect.

Chapter Eleven

May was foxglove time of year. Clusters of purple flowers on tall green spires lined the ditches as Aideen sped along, and, though the droning of bees was lost in the sound of her Vespa's engine, she was aware of their fuzzy gold and black bodies and sunlight flashing on bright transparent wings. It was astonishing how clearly, in spite of her speed and her helmet, she could envisage what was happening all around her. Leaning into the curve as she turned a corner, she wondered how intensely memories of the past affected how you saw the present. Once you'd peered into its tubular flowers and felt its fleshy stem, could you ever see a foxglove, even from a distance, without an awareness of how it appeared close to?

That was how it had been when she'd seen the painting in the gallery in Florence. It was on the first holiday she and Conor had taken together, when they'd grabbed a budget deal and flown off, not knowing what to expect but certain it would be great. Neither of them had been to Italy before, though Conor was always talking about it. When he'd started working in the library, Miss Casey had shown him a book of Italian Renaissance paintings, and afterwards he'd typed 'Images + Italy' into a search engine and been blown away by the old paintings and cool photos, including guys on Vespas whizzing round squares. That was what had made him get himself a Vespa of his own.

In a way Aideen was sorry that she now had one too. Travelling on the back of Conor's bike had been really close and romantic, even though the Irish weather made it a bit damp at times. The first night they'd slept together, in a backpackers' hostel in Florence, Conor had told her that Italy was the land of lovers because it was the most romantic place on earth.

On that trip they'd gone off into the countryside where olive trees really did grow in straight lines on terraces; and the buildings had crinkly tiles on the roofs; and the churches had dim, peeling paintings on plastered walls. They'd wandered round Florence, drinking coffee from little booths in backstreets and avoiding expensive cafés in the tourist spots. Then, having hoarded their money, they went to the Uffizi Gallery, where they found Botticelli's *Primavera* and Conor was blown away.

Aideen had been thinking about paintings ever since. The thing was that you had to stand back if you wanted to look at them properly. But then you had to get in close, to see what was actually there. Half the women in the *Primavera* were basically wearing chiffon and looking as if they could do with some time at the gym. The one who was meant to be the goddess of love had a kind of a sulky face on her. But another one, off to the side, had a truly amazing dress.

It was covered in flowery embroidery and her arms were full of roses, not like the roses you'd buy in a shop but flatter, like the pink ones that grew on the ditches back home. When you moved in to get a closer view, you could see that the flowers looked real. Or, rather, they were flowers embroidered by someone who knew what real flowers looked like. And they'd been painted by someone who knew he was painting embroidery but had real flowers there in his mind as well. You could see what he'd been aiming at. Because, according to the leaflet, this was the goddess Flora, who was the spirit of flowers and fertility imagined as a girl.

Anyway, the dress was a dream, and when Conor had had his brainwave Aideen saw what he meant. You couldn't do a recreation that was exactly like the painting. The sleeves were some kind of a scaly fabric she wasn't sure of at all, and there was a big wreath round the neck that'd scratch your ears. You couldn't see the back of the dress either, so you'd have to reinvent it in three dimensions. But you could use it as the basis of a really amazing design.

Ever since, Aideen's mind had been playing on perception. The important thing about a wedding dress was that it had to work as effectively at a distance as close to. You were making a personal, private promise on a big public occasion, and the way you looked needed to be an image of both things at once. If it hadn't been for that painting she'd never have thought of it that way but, as soon as she'd worked it out, she'd known that that was the crux of the matter. And now, whizzing down the road to the farm, it all fell into place. Her embroidery would be as detailed as her memory of bees and flowers, and to the congregation she'd look like a foxglove growing high on a ditch.

Turning into the farm driveway, she saw Conor and Joe up in the yard in heavy boots and overalls, doing something energetic with shovels, so she took the bike round to the kitchen door. Una, Conor's mum, waved her in.

'Come and give me a hand.'

Aideen loved this kitchen. It was a square room with a flagged floor and two windows. One looked out on the little paved yard outside the back door, and the other overlooked a garden with apple trees and a washing line and steep hills beyond it, where sheep grazed in stone-walled fields. There were masses of worktops and an oven and things on the left-hand side of the kitchen, where the sink stood under a window, and a range and a couple of easy chairs on the right. At the moment the big table in the middle of the room was spread with sheets of newspaper and Una was shelling peas into a bowl.

Aideen took off her helmet and shook out her hair. 'It's a gorgeous day.'

'Isn't it? These peas are from the polytunnel but I've already got a crop doing well in the garden. I'd say we'll have a good summer.'

Una pushed half the pile of pods across the table and Aideen sat down to help her. There were squares of light on the flagstones, made by sunshine pouring through the window above the sink. As Aideen ran her thumb down the inside of a pod, one pea missed the bowl, bounced on the table and, before she could catch it, rolled onto the floor. Immediately, two ginger kittens leapt from one of the easy chairs and chased it under the range.

Una raised her eyes to Heaven. 'I'll swing for those blessed kittens! You can't keep them out of anything.'

Having abandoned their attempts to locate the pea, the kittens now appeared to be playing hopscotch on the flagstones, chasing each other's tails across the grid of shadows and light.

'Where did they come from?'

'Ballyfin. Brought by Conor. One of his old library biddies sent them to me as a present. Wouldn't you think he'd have more sense than to be taken in by a line like that?'

'But they're dotes!' Aideen was on her knees, teasing the kittens with a string from one of the pods. 'Oh, my God, they've got green eyes!'

Una laughed. 'I know. They're cute, aren't they? As like as two peas. But I don't need them. And poor old Marmite's gone on strike and stalked off to the barn.'

'Doesn't he get on with them?'

'Well, that's his chair they've colonised, and at his age he can do without babies trying to play with his whiskers.' Una began to roll her empty pea pods up in the newspaper. 'People are always trying to get rid of kittens and Conor knew fine well that I wouldn't want them. He just hadn't the heart to turn them down. Isn't that him all over? I don't know where he gets it. It surely wasn't from me.'

Hiding a smile, Aideen picked up the wriggling kittens and settled them back on the chair. Everyone knew that Conor got his sweet nature from Una who, even though she didn't want the Ballyfin woman's surplus kittens, clearly wasn't going to send them back. He even looked like her – slim and wiry, not huge and heavy like Joe, who took after their dad. Seeing Conor and Joe together you'd hardly think they were brothers, though they shared Paddy's steady, thoughtful manner. Una and Paddy were both essentially gentle. Aideen, who'd been terribly shy about meeting them, had been greeted with warmth since the first day she'd visited the farm.

Everything about this tight-knit, rooted family was different from her own. On the one hand, they joked and laughed together, almost as if they belonged to the same generation. But sometimes Conor and Joe behaved as if Una and Paddy were the ones who needed looking after. This was remarkable to Aideen: in her family grown-ups had been grown-ups, and the thought that they could be inadequate or mistaken was inconceivable. Most of all, the McCarthys shared an unquestioned sense of belonging, both to each other and to the family farm. Even Joe. It was clearly understood that, while he'd be off to live in Cork as soon as he married, he'd retain a share in the business and a site to build a house on if he came home.

It didn't bother Aideen that, except for Bríd's lot, she'd no long list of family to ask to the wedding. She'd already told Aunt Carol that, since the rest of her mum's relations had stayed away till now, they wouldn't be welcome. And she knew that her dad's crowd wouldn't dream of coming.

Conor and Joe, on the other hand, had a rake of cousins and family connections up and down the peninsula, and Eileen had five hefty brothers, three of whom were rearing kids of their own. Sometimes the thought of the lot of them turning up on her wedding day daunted Aideen, but whenever she thought of her future here in the farmhouse she couldn't stop smiling.

Now, gathering up her own discarded pea pods, she caught Una's eye.

'You're looking happy.'

'I was just thinking how much I love the farm.'

'Well, that's nice to know. We're looking forward to having you here.'

Bríd's response when she'd heard what was planned had been different. 'Live with your in-laws? Are you stone mad?'

'I knew you'd say that.'

'It's a recipe for disaster.'

'The trouble with you is you're way too conventional.'

'For God's sake, Aideen, there's a reason for all those proverbs about the hideous danger of brides sharing a home with their husband's mum.'

'What proverbs?'

'Oh, I can't remember, but there's loads of them.'

They'd backed away from the subject then, knowing it would get heated, but later on Bríd had tried again. 'Honestly, Ade, I only want you to be happy.'

'I know.'

'I don't even think you understand what the farmer's-wife thing means. It's not all roses round the door and pet lambs by the Aga.'

'Ah, for God's sake, I'm not thick.'

'How are you going to cope with the broken nights when Conor's up with a farrowing sow or something?'

'He doesn't keep pigs. We might, though. If we went organic the deli could use the bacon. And that's what I mean. We've talked about it. It's not just all in my head, Bríd. Conor and I have rational discussions.'

'Okay, I'm sorry. I know you do. Actually, producing for the deli's a good idea. We should all discuss it. But there's a difference between that and dealing with all the family stuff. What about his dad's condition? Depression's not easy to live with.'

'I know. We've talked about that too. But Paddy's lovely. And Una says I really cheer him up.'

It had ended with Bríd wrinkling her nose and saying unconvincingly that no doubt Aideen knew best.

Afterwards, Aideen had lain in bed feeling doubtful. Paddy's clinical depression wasn't the same as just being moody. And most brides didn't fancy moving in with their in-laws. She'd realised that she'd always lived with people who organised her. Aunt Bridge, who'd been brisk and business-like, and Bríd, who was definitely bossy. Was that why living in the farmhouse seemed such an attractive prospect?

Now, scattering pea pods on the compost heap, she tried to banish the memory of those troublesome midnight doubts. But, whatever Bríd might think of her, she wasn't completely naive. The fact was that the kitchen, with kittens by the range and the smell of home baking, wasn't your typical setting for a young married couple. It was the picture-perfect image of a cosy family home. If she weren't so deeply in love with Conor, she might be wondering if she wanted to marry his parents instead of him.

Chapter Twelve

Brian had known from the outset where his builder had got his nickname. From his first day on the Hag's Glen site, Fury had gone about the job like a whirlwind, coordinating deliveries, berating and cajoling workmen, and overcoming obstacles with a mixture of bloody-mindedness and inspired lateral thinking.

On several occasions the lateral thinking had caused spats with Brian, who'd turned up to find undiscussed changes to his design. Dealing with a beaky-nosed whirlwind as temperamental as a diva had required all the tact he could muster. Ultimately, however, they'd always emerged with honour intact on both sides.

Now, with the last of the scaffolding down and the heavy machinery banished, the valley was recovering from the ravages of the work. Where earth had been churned up and re-levelled, grass and furze were beginning to reassert themselves; and the house itself, positioned by the river with its back to the rearing mountain, seemed hardly more present than the low, ruined dwellings that stood around it.

Driving up to view the site one evening after a long day in the office, Brian was greeted by The Divil. The little dog appeared on the doorstep and barked at him shrilly, then retreated inside. It was an evening of pearly skies tinged pink after mist and rain.

The waterfall at the head of the valley was a single thread of light and, overhead, swifts wheeled through the air catching insects. Fury's red van was parked nearby, but it was evident that the other workers had downed tools at their usual time and gone home.

Brian looked at the house with a surge of satisfaction. His design and choice of materials had arisen from an impulse to refer to the past by blending in with what was already here. It was a two-storey structure built of stone laboriously carried from a local quarry and chosen to match the field stones that had been used in the old dwellings. Solid and square, with a flat roof, which Brian intended to turf, the building consisted of an open-plan space with a loo and a bathroom on each floor, and a glass veranda running across the front at ground level. Once the green roof was established, and planting inside and out had softened the lines of the veranda, it would be easy, at first glance, to mistake the new building for part of the ruined village. This was exactly the effect that Brian had wanted, and Fury had been scathing at every turn.

The roof had produced the first spasm of outrage. 'Holy God Almighty, man, could you not use decent slates like anyone else? And don't give me any old guff about capturing airborne pollutants. You're halfway up a bloody mountain, not surrounded by dark, satanic mills!'

They'd been sitting in the cab of Fury's van, with The Divil between them and the specification spread out against the dashboard.

'Did no one ever teach you that flat roofs are disastrous?'

'They're not if they're properly built.'

'Do you tell me that? Well, let me tell you I was building sound roofs when you were in nappies. And have you any idea what the wind up here will do to this fancy membrane?'

'I took that into account. By the way, planting typically extends the life of the membrane by a factor of three.'

'You believe that, do you?'

'I do. And, after all, I'm the eejit who'll have to live with the result.'

Slightly mollified, Fury had folded the papers. 'You said it, not me. But I'm telling you this. The men who built here in the past didn't have sod roofs so's to feel at one with the landscape. They'd have grabbed at slate if they hadda had the money to afford it. They weren't putting up houses as bloody design statements. They were thinking about keeping the heat in and the wind and the weather out.'

It hadn't been the right moment to mention water run-off mitigation, so Brian had remarked that green roofs were known for keeping heat in. In the end Fury had gone away and mastered the specification so well that he'd subsequently given Brian a series of lectures on the subject, all of which Brian had endured with good grace.

They'd had similar tussles over the generator; where to sink the well; and whether the house should have double or triple glazing. But, no matter who won the battle – and usually it was Brian – Fury had brought meticulous standards to everything that was done.

Leaving his car parked next to the van, Brian followed The Divil into the house. Inside, Fury was hanging the ground-floor bathroom door.

'For heaven's sake, what are you doing? You should have gone home hours ago.'

Fury sniffed and, getting up from his knees, opened and closed the door. Brian stood back and admired it. 'It's looking good, but installation was part of the deal when we ordered them.'

'Ay, well, if you think I'm going to let them lads hang a door in a house of mine you've another think coming. The men that crowd sends out are no more than bloody van drivers. Delivery boys!'

Kneeling down again, Fury inspected a hinge. The Divil observed him intently for a moment, then pattered off with an air of great decision. With his head against the door jamb, Fury reached out and groped on the floor for a screwdriver. Brian was about to hand it to him when The Divil reappeared round a corner, dragging a claw hammer. Arriving at Fury's side, he dropped the hammer and sat down triumphantly, his head cocked and his pink tongue lolling between his teeth.

Fury looked round and raised his eyes to Heaven. Then, taking the hammer, he patted The Divil on the head. 'Good man. You're a great dog altogether. Go on now. Go out and wait by the van.'

As the little dog trotted away obediently, Fury scowled at Brian. 'There's no call to go looking sideways at me, I know I'm a right fool.'

Setting down the hammer, he picked up the screwdriver and turned back to the door. Then, without looking at Brian, he began to explain. 'He did it one time when he was a pup and, as it happened, a hammer was what I was reaching for. So, of course, I made a big fuss of him and told him he was great. Then, the next time it happened, I was reaching for a chisel. So all the lads made a joke of him when he went off and got me a hammer, and you should have seen the look on the poor dog's face. He was scalded with embarrassment.'

Swinging round, he faced Brian truculently. 'So, I told him he was great again, and that was the rock I perished on. He's been doing the same damn thing ever since.'

'Bringing you a hammer.'

'No matter what I'm reaching for. And I've been letting him think he's a great man.'

Contriving to keep a straight face, Brian enquired how long this had been going on.

'Ten years. No, all right, twelve. Maybe eleven.' Fury glowered at him. 'It's my fault, not his.'

'No, I see that. Yeah. Absolutely.'

'I'd normally keep him shut in the van if there's other lads around.'

'Yes, well, probably best.' Brian indicated the door. 'It's looking good, that.'

'Well, it is now it's properly hung. I might let those wasters that drove it here stick a window into a wall, maybe. But there's an art to hanging a door.'

'The whole place is looking pretty damn good, actually.'

Fury glanced around the room grudgingly. 'When are you bringing herself up for a look?'

'Hanna? She's seen it.'

'Ah, would you cop onto yourself, man, you're fooling no one.

Doesn't the whole world know she's the one you're building it for?'

Brian's jaw clenched. 'Who says so?'

'Not me, anyway, so you can stop glaring like a basilisk. I keep my beak shut till I've good reason to open it. Most people round here don't, though, and that's a fact.' Having regained the advantage, he pointed the screwdriver at Brian. 'I'm telling you this too, though you won't thank me for it. I've never known a woman take to a house she wasn't consulted on. Mark that.'

'But this is total nonsense. We've no plans for Hanna to move in with me.'

With a disdainful snort, Fury thrust the screwdriver into his pocket. 'Well, if you say so, I suppose I have to believe you. But if that's the case, you're a bigger fool than I thought.'

Brian turned away, then swung back again. 'Christ, man, did you never hear of timing?'

'I did. And I heard of fellas that went and missed their chance.'

Chapter Thirteen

Jazz felt the water stream over her head and told the disembodied voice that the temperature was perfect. Last night she'd been struck again by how much she had to be grateful for. A job handed to her on a plate when other people were struggling with unemployment. A place to live that perfectly met her requirements, even if it was tiny. And Sam, whom she'd met by chance and was now so essential to her happiness.

It was gratitude that made her work so hard, determined that Louisa's investment should result in a successful business. But yesterday, coming home late to find Sam slumped in front of the telly, she'd worried that he might be feeling neglected. They hadn't gone out on the town or even had a proper night in together for ages. So today she'd got up at the crack of dawn, done a full day's work before lunchtime, and booked an afternoon appointment at a beauty salon in Carrick.

If Sam was right, finding love was just a crazy lottery, so what could be more dreadful than to lose what she had found? And, considering the amount of time she spent in the office, you couldn't blame him if he felt he came second to her job. He hadn't said so, or even hinted at it, but Mum had spent twenty years or something failing to see what was going on in her marriage so, as soon as the thought had crossed Jazz's mind, she'd felt that she must act on it.

The disembodied voice asked if she'd like conditioner. 'We have coconut or almond blossom.'

'Er, you don't have rosemary, do you?'

As soon as she'd spoken, Jazz realised she'd clicked back into work mode. Edge of the World Essentials was developing a range of organic herbal hair products and, according to the latest focus group analysis, rosemary was coming out way ahead of the rest. But today she was supposed to be a domestic goddess, not a marketing geek. 'No, look, it doesn't matter. Almond blossom is fine.'

She lay back, breathing in the sweet scent and enjoying the sweeping touch of the brush on her scalp. Later, wrapped in a gown with a towel round her shoulders, she smiled into the mirror at the stylist standing behind her.

The girl smiled back. 'I'm Mandy. Just a trim and blow-dry today, is that right?'

Jazz nodded. 'Thank you.'

She left the salon two hours later with perfectly blow-dried hair swinging just above her shoulders, waxed legs, and subtle nude polish on her nails. Having decided to go the whole hog, she'd had a pedicure as well as a manicure, and a shoulder massage while she'd waited for the nail varnish to dry.

It was a balmy day and Carrick was looking its best. The lamp posts along Main Street were hung with baskets of blue and white lobelia, and people were sitting outside cafés chatting in the sun. Jazz's plan was to spend the next couple of hours buying food for a special meal, and to be back to Lissbeg in time to spend the evening cooking and eating it with Sam. She knew he'd be there when she came swooping in to surprise him. He was a freelance HR consultant and today was one of the two days a week when he set up jobs and did admin stuff from home.

Inevitably, the flat would be chaotic when she got in. But that wouldn't matter. It was so small that tidying up really didn't take all that long. The bed would have been left down but that wouldn't matter either. She'd plan a meal that could happily be eaten side by side, propped up against the pillows. She and Sam were basically ready-meal people but, so long as she went for something suitably special or exotic, ready-made would be fine. Scallops in a gorgeous creamy sauce, say. Or an artisan beef and ale pie, which Sam would probably prefer.

One of Carrick's department stores had a small upmarket food hall and, wandering round, Jazz found a pie made with beer from a local brewery, and dauphinoise potatoes for two that came in an ovenproof dish. The guy behind the counter recommended a selection of what he called rainbow salads.

'Lots of colour on the plate, see? Beetroot. Lovely green kale leaves. Edible flowers – look, borage and marigolds. Colourful seeds and toasted nuts. All this dreamy golden fennel, and strips of gorgeous crunchy rainbow chard.' He was ladling salads into separate bowls as he spoke and, assembling them on an oval plate, he spread his hands dramatically. 'See what I mean? So inviting!'

What Jazz saw was that the whole lot was going to cost a fortune. But it did look delicious, and in her mind's eye she could see the plate on the floor beside the bed, like a shot in a lifestyle magazine. She nodded, and he swathed the assemblage in cling film, then eased it into a cardboard sleeve with 'Recyclable Packaging' stencilled on the side.

With the pie, potatoes and salads packed in one of the store's lifetime shopping bags, she selected two pots of chocolate mousse and a bunch of grapes with bloom so dark that they almost looked black. Then, having bought a bottle of wine, she threw caution to the winds and took the lift up to the lingerie department. If tonight was going to be a turning point in how she and Sam saw their relationship, something in oyster satin and lace seemed the right thing to wear.

Even before she'd become a workaholic Jazz hadn't had much luck finding boyfriends. Looking back, she could see that the move to Finfarran hadn't helped. In her Lissbeg schooldays, most of the time that she hadn't been over at Eileen's she had spent locked in her bedroom, feeling grim. If Nan had had her way she would have been hoicked out of there, but Mum, whose parenting at that stage had amounted to walking on eggshells, had always announced that she needed time to adjust.

The result, Jazz supposed, was that she'd ended up being a late developer. She'd already left school and was working before she'd fallen in love. Her job, as a cabin crew member with a budget airline, had brought her the freedom to travel, but the hours had been unsocial and, inevitably, that first love affair had failed. Afterwards she'd moved on to a series of short-term relationships, many of which had hardly been more than extended one-night stands. At the time it had seemed like a buzzy, exciting lifestyle but, ultimately, it had left her feeling even more rootless than before.

Actually, working as what he'd described as a 'trolley dolly' had largely been a way of annoying Dad. Even though he'd doted on her, she'd always resented his arrogance and, besides, she'd still been screwed-up by the divorce. As far as Dad was concerned, his precious daughter had been destined for university, so choosing to thwart him had given her a pleasing sense of control.

Anyway, it hadn't lasted long. Exactly as she'd been whipped off to Ireland with no prior warning, her job with the airline had come to a sudden end. One moment she'd been driving her car without a care in the world, and the next thing she'd known she'd woken up in hospital with people saying she'd been lucky to survive a head-on collision with a wall. It had literally been a life-changing experience, and in the weeks of convalescence that had followed the crash, she'd realised it was time to put down some roots. Changing career course and coming back to work in Finfarran had seemed counter-intuitive at first. But London no longer felt as if it belonged to her and, having no ties anywhere else, she'd embraced Louisa's project with a huge sense of relief.

Now, as she hovered between satin and silk, she told herself Sam was wrong. Life actually wasn't a crazy lottery. Everything was ruled by Fate, not chance. What if she'd married her first love and that had been the end of things? What if she'd kept on travelling the world and never returned to Finfarran? Either of those things might well have happened but they hadn't. Because the universe had been driving her inexorably towards Sam.

She drove home to Lissbeg with a bubbling feeling of

excitement, music playing at full volume and the windows wide open. Her perfectly polished nails on the wheel and her hair blowing in the wind made her feel like a film star. And that was just what this evening was going to be like. That bit at the end of *Brooklyn* when Saoirse Ronan is standing on the ship's deck, having chosen to follow her heart.

Jazz could see it all again as the car sped towards Lissbeg. The director had done this amazing close-up on the actress's huge eyes, and you could see the character's certainty and serenity as she stood there with the wind in her hair. There'd been this little insecure girl standing behind her, scared and not knowing what might lie ahead. But Saoirse, who played Eilis the heroine, turns round and tells her she's going to be fine. She mustn't be afraid because she has her whole life ahead of her, and you can move on and leave behind the confusion of your past.

And, later, at the big ending, Eilis is standing on a street in Brooklyn waiting for Tony, the American guy she's in love with, to finish work. There's this great shot of her leaning against a wall, knowing he's there across the road and willing him to come out. And then he does, and the music goes crazy, and their eyes meet and, next thing, they're in each other's arms.

This evening was going to be just like that, except that she'd be bursting into the flat and Sam would look up and see her. She'd be in jeans and a shirt, not one of those 1950s full skirts like Saoirse's. And Sam – who was no film star – would probably be watching telly in his pants. The chances were that the place would be like a bombsite but it wouldn't faze her because none of that day-to-day stuff would even matter.

Pulling into her parking space, she lifted her Bag for Life off the back seat as if it were lighter than air. She'd bought a bouquet of lilies that they'd put on the console table or, if there wasn't space there, in a corner on the floor. As she climbed the stairs to the flat, she realised the scent of the lilies might be a bit overpowering, so maybe they'd need to sleep with the window open or stick the vase out on the landing as a last resort.

Giggling at the thought of what the neighbours would make of lilies on the landing, she struggled with her latchkey, and pushed open the door. The flat was spotless. No papers on the floor, no dishes in the sink, no rumpled bed. The console table was bare except for her MacBook. The bed was folded away and every surface and corner was clean.

For a moment, thinking Sam must have had the same impulse that she'd had, she looked around as if there were some place from which he might appear. But, of course, there wasn't. Maybe he'd cleaned up like mad and gone out to buy wine and flowers and something for dinner. Everything looked lovely anyway so, crossing the room, she dumped her bags and the bunch of lilies on the table. Then she turned and saw the note that was taped to the wardrobe door.

Chapter Fourteen

Driving back to work from a meeting at the County Library, Hanna noticed the increasing number of coaches using the motorway. By the start of the second week in May, the tourist season in Finfarran was always well established, and from now on Lissbeg would see an influx of visitors drawn by the medieval psalter. Fortunately, the exhibition had its own entrance and was manned by volunteers, so the crowds beyond the glass wall behind Hanna's desk made no difference to her workload. They added to the dynamic of the library, though, and increased her sense that summer was on its way.

For the last week she'd been wondering about her next choice for the film club. *Brooklyn* had been a winner. Far more people than usual had emerged from the film wanting to read the novel, and several readers who hadn't been to the screening had turned up the following week requesting the book. Hanna had noticed that the majority were women, possibly drawn by the cover image of Saoirse Ronan and the handsome American actor who'd played the hero in the film. Sometimes she thought that, while people like Mr Maguire arrived seeking a pulpit from which to pontificate, others came to her library simply wanting to borrow dreams.

Mr Maguire's latest contention was that the film club's programme should be decided by secret ballot, but when this had been mentioned in Hanna's hearing she'd turned a deaf ear. She knew from experience that a vote system inevitably provoked lobbying followed by fierce recrimination; and that, as a result, the film club would simply peter out. By making the decisions herself at comparatively short notice, she could preserve anticipation, and absorb the blame afterwards if anyone hated her choice. This time she'd decided to go for a contrast, so the posters for the June film club meeting advertised a screening of *The Revenant*, starring Leonardo DiCaprio and based on the novel by the American author Michael Punke.

Conor had frowned and said he'd never read it. 'I didn't see the movie either, but the poster was kind of striking. Wasn't DiCaprio covered in ice and eaten by a bear?'

'That's the one. But he isn't eaten by a bear, he's mauled by one when he and his son are guiding a group of trappers somewhere up in the frozen north. Most of them abandon him, and one chap, who's been paid to stay, tries to kill him but, in the kerfuffle, stabs the boy instead. Then, against all the odds, DiCaprio survives and tracks down the murderer. The book's subtitled *A Novel of Revenge*.'

'Not exactly a date movie, then?'

'No.'

Conor considered for a moment, then chuckled. 'Kind of depends, though, doesn't it? Different strokes for different folks.'

He was holding the fort now, having had his lunch break earlier, and Hanna had eaten a sandwich before leaving Carrick so she planned to spend half an hour or so out in the nuns' garden. It was a sunny day with a hint of a breeze, and goldcrests were nesting in the conifers by the old convent wall.

As she walked through the archway from the courtyard to the garden she stopped short, just avoiding someone hurrying by, head down and shoulders hunched. About to apologise, she realised who it was. 'Jazz! Hello ...'

Opening her arms for a hug, Hanna paused and stepped backwards. Jazz had clearly been crying and, equally clearly, she wanted to hurry away.

Fearful of doing or saying something wrong, Hanna dithered. Then, as Jazz gave a forced smile and tried to keep moving, Louisa approached from the other side of the garden.

For a moment, Jazz reacted like a cornered rabbit. But as Louisa came close enough to realise what was happening, the hunched shoulders dropped and Jazz raised her chin, daring them to comment on her puffy face and red-rimmed eyes. It was obvious that she'd tried to conceal the evidence with makeup, but anyone could see that she must have been in tears all night.

'Sweetheart ...'

'Look, I'm sorry, I should have been in the office this morning.' Ignoring her mother, Jazz spoke to Louisa who, Hanna could see, was taking care not to look shocked. 'I had a bad night but I'm fine, and I have a meeting with Saira. I ought to get on.'

'Darling ...'

'I have a cold. It's ghastly, but I don't think I'm infectious. So I'd better get to that meeting.' Jazz made to walk on. Then she turned back and looked directly at Hanna. 'Sam and I have broken up. He's moved out, actually. So he won't be coming to lunch at the weekend.' Her face flushed, and she controlled her voice with an effort. 'I'm so sorry but I'll have to cancel as well. There'll be all sorts backed up on my desk since this morning. Sorry, Mum.'

Hanna and Louisa watched her stride off towards the entrance to the convent centre. Then, with one accord, they made their way across the garden, skirting the fountain and finding a secluded bench. Hanna folded her arms across her chest. 'I don't think she had any idea this was going to happen.'

'Oh dear!' Louisa sighed. 'Men can be dreadfully callous.'

There was an awkward pause in which the spectre of Malcolm's perfidy hung in the air between them. Then Hanna broke the silence. 'I suppose it could just be a tiff.'

'Well, if he's moved out, it does sound serious. Poor child! I doubt if we'll hear many details. She's not going to confide in her grandmother.'

'And she certainly won't tell me.' Hanna pulled a face. 'These things happen, but I so wish it hadn't. I hate to see her upset.'

'Of course you do, dear. But she's young. Youth is resilient. It's when we get older we're less able to cope. I hope she won't make this a reason to throw herself into more work. She does too much already, and she won't be told.'

Hanna laughed. 'Well, she comes from stubborn stock! Look at my mother.'

'Yes. Perhaps. But she gets it from both sides, you know.' Louisa plucked a sprig of mint from the herb bed beside them. 'Over in London I was so annoyed by Malcolm. He refuses to believe I know what I'm doing with the business. And he won't accept that it's none of his concern.' Crushing the mint in her hand, Louisa breathed in the sharp scent and dropped the bruised leaves into the herb bed. 'The fact is that he hasn't considered what he intends to do next. There's only so much consultancy that's going to be required of him – particularly at the fee he charges – and so many after-dinner speeches he'll be invited to give. You've heard of his plans to sell the house?'

Hanna nodded. Louisa shot her a glance and looked away.

'It was always yours more than his, wasn't it? In terms of involvement?'

'Yes, but a long time ago. Water under the bridge.'

'Is that really how you feel? I mean about the sale?'

Hanna wondered if Louisa might be thinking about money. When she and Malcolm had broken up she'd rejected his offer of alimony and, though in hindsight she'd recognised how daft that was, she didn't regret her decision. Telling him where he could stick his wealth had given her a degree of confidence at a time when she'd badly needed it.

Mary Casey, of course, had been outraged. In her view, a cheating husband ought to be taken for every cent he had. But, for Hanna, all that had mattered then was that Jazz should be looked after and, to be fair to Malcolm, he had never failed to do that.

She looked at Louisa. 'Jazz seems to be fine about him selling and, at this stage, it has nothing to do with me. How about you? After all, it's been your London pied-à-terre.'

'Yes, but no more than that. I shall be quite happy in a hotel or staying with friends when I go over. Now that my own house is sold, and the business is up and running, I really feel that Ireland is my home. Having you and Jazz living so close to me is wonderful, and the flat in the bungalow suits me down to the ground.'

Remarkably, Louisa really did seem contented at Mary Casey's. She was a great people-watcher, and nothing that Mary said or did seemed to faze her. Hanna's own childhood relationship with Mary had been difficult, and forced proximity as an adult had done nothing to improve it. She'd emerged from a lifetime of hectoring determined to avoid inflicting the same thing on Jazz. Yet at times she harboured a sense of fellow-feeling for her mother. It was hard not to wade in with solutions when you saw your child in trouble.

Now, as if she'd read Hanna's mind, Louisa gave her a smile. 'It's not just mothers and daughters who have their moments. I mean, Malcolm's in his fifties, and here am I fretting as if he were going off to school. He's never been any good socially when thrown on his own resources. And, while he's in his element in a court room, I'm not sure he knows how to buy himself a dish mop or set up a broadband account. So heaven alone knows how he'll cope with this move.'

Remembering her marriage, Hanna thought Louisa was probably right. When Tessa had finally left him a few years ago, Malcolm had installed a series of youthful girlfriends, who'd presumably acted as social secretary and housekeeper as well as mistress. Hanna hadn't kept count of them. Given his charm and his money, she'd assumed that Malcolm would continue to attract companionship. But, apparently, he was now living alone.

Louisa shook herself briskly. 'I refuse to make it my problem and it certainly isn't yours. You should know, though, that I think he may be planning to make us a visit.'

'Is he? Why?'

'Well, to see Jazz, of course. Though, if the truth be told, I suspect he's also feeling rather bored.' Glancing at her watch, Louisa picked up her handbag. 'I ought to go into the office. I said I'd go over some figures with Jazz and Don.'

Though the idea of Malcolm planning a visit was startling, Hanna's mind was still focused on Jazz. 'Give me a ring later, will you, and tell me how she seems?' As soon as she'd made the request she retracted it. 'No, look, that's daft. Forget it. You don't need to. She'll be fine, I'm sure.'

Of course Jazz would be fine, she told herself, as they strolled down the gravel path. She was well settled now in Finfarran, with a flat and a job and a loving family around her. This was only a hiccup and she'd sort herself out in time. Then, as she turned to kiss Louisa goodbye, a new thought struck her.

'Oh, poor child! Isn't she going to be Eileen Dawson's bridesmaid? That's not a job you want to do when your love life's just crashed and burned.'

Chapter Fifteen

Rasher no longer needed to sit on street corners. He had three meals a day now, so he wasn't hungry and, anyway, if he tried to scrounge a few euros, the guards would be sure to spot him and pass the word back to Martin. Most of the police in Carrick were decent enough, but everyone knew they were hand in glove with the crowd at the halfway house and, having got himself in here, Rasher wasn't about to take the risk of being thrown out.

Mind you, there was one guard you'd want to be sure to avoid. A big sergeant, who looked easy-going but was known for every dirty trick in the book, from deliberately waking you up whenever you'd found a corner to sleep in to 'accidentally' spilling his coffee on you as he walked by.

You'd think Dublin would be a bad place to be out on the streets living rough. You'd be right too, as Rasher knew well. That was why he'd got out of it. He'd been shit scared of the junkies who'd kick your head in for a quid, and terrified that, if things got bad, he might end up on drugs himself. So, the first chance he'd got after he'd left home a year ago, he'd headed down to the country, vaguely thinking that things would be safer there. For a few months he'd lived in a squat in Nenagh, but then a dealer had moved into the house and things had got heavy. Knowing that going back made no sense, Rasher had travelled on. Someone he'd met in a caff on the road had turned out to come from Finfarran and, for the want of anywhere else to go, he'd headed for Carrick.

It wasn't as scary as Dublin but it was no bed of roses. Almost as soon as he'd hitched into town, he'd been targeted by the sergeant. Being an outsider made you easy to spot. Though your man, whose name was Nugent, wasn't above going for locals too. Even old fellas like Tommy Banjo, who was cracked and had lived on the streets of Carrick for ages and was always going round shaking your hand and thanking you when you hadn't done anything for him.

No one in the halfway house would kick you, and that was brilliant. Still, it was boring playing snooker all day in a place that stank of disinfectant, and having to toe the line when they called your name. This time, when they gave him a shout, the guy at the desk handed back his passport, trying not to look surprised that somebody called Adam Rashid could be Irish. Rasher said thanks and went to stick it in his locker, giving the door a shake when he'd closed it and shoving the key down his sock.

After that he decided he couldn't face going back to the snooker. Outside, it was a windy day with no clouds in the sky. Walking into the centre of town, he found a park bench near a bandstand. He was wearing jeans and a sweatshirt that he'd washed himself in the laundry room, and a pair of new trainers. Some shop had donated a boxful to Martin, probably because no one would buy yokes so startlingly unfashionable and white. In fairness, though, they were comfortable enough. So were the bright white socks he'd been given with them. He'd managed to tone the trainers down by scraping them on the grass, and his jeans were a bit long, because he'd lost weight recently, so they covered the socks, even sitting down.

Spring had been wet and cold this year and, though he'd told himself he'd get the weight back on with a few feeds of McDonald's, he never had. He was aware of the hard slats of the bench underneath him and wished he had a bit of cardboard to shove under his arse. The weight loss was because of a dose of flu he'd had a while back, which, along with the shock of the old guy who'd died under the arches, had made him see that he'd got to find a way back to ordinary life. The crowd he'd been dossing with at the time had taken him to A & E with the flu, and after that he'd spent a week or so in an emergency shelter. He'd got out of that as soon as he could though, and probably far too soon.

Sitting on a park bench was a step up from being hunkered down on a pavement, when people around you were reduced to a forest of legs passing by. Rasher had heard it said that people like him were treated as if they were faceless but, the truth was, it worked both ways. They stopped seeing you as people, and you just thought of them as legs. Every so often, though, he'd been sure that he'd seen his mum walking towards him. He knew it was mad because, at this stage, she wouldn't be wearing the same clothes she'd worn when he was a kid. But he'd see her between the passing legs, crossing the street or hurrying round a corner, her red coat flapping open and her hair looking messy, not up in a neat knot like she'd worn it when he was small. The figure would always turn out to be someone who actually looked nothing like her – an older woman or a schoolgirl who happened to be wearing red and have blonde hair. Whoever it was would pass by, ignoring him, and the tension that had built up inside him would slowly drain away.

A bunch of schoolkids was crowding onto the bandstand, carrying instruments. Under instructions from a harassed teacher, they opened stools, set up music stands, and started to play tunes from some musical Rasher couldn't name. Something ancient like *Oklahoma!* maybe, or *Cats*. Back before his dad died, his mum had been in the chorus of the R&R. Dad used to call it the Rathmines and Rathgar *Mew*sical Society, and tease her by saying they sounded like shrieking cats. They'd been pretty good, really, and she was never bothered by Dad, who was only messing. Not like Fergal the bastard boyfriend, who'd picked away at the last shreds of her confidence and sneered at her when she'd try to boost it with drink.

According to Martin, the plan was to find Rasher a job and a place of his own to move into. He'd leaned across the desk and said they'd have to be pragmatic. 'Jobs don't grow on trees, you know, and affordable accommodation is scarce enough in Carrick. What sort of work would you fancy if you had your choice? Which you probably won't have, so don't get your hopes up.'

Rasher had said he didn't know.

'What did your da do, say?'

'He was a pharmacist. Worked in a hospital.'

'Right. And your mam?'

'She was a nurse.'

'And you've no aspirations in that direction yourself?'

'No.'

'Ah, well, let's think about getting you a wage to start with anyway. It might be a case of a live-in job that would come with a room.'

Rasher had said nothing because there didn't seem much to say. He couldn't imagine what kind of job might be out there for someone like him. Chances were that, whatever it was, it would turn out to be crappy. The thought of a room was good, though, so long as he didn't end up as some kind of slave in somebody's house. He'd met a guy on the road, up in the midlands, who'd told him farmers put immigrants in sheds and paid them nothing for their labour, saying the work was the price of the roof they'd been given over their heads. Rasher had been green enough then to protest that he wasn't an immigrant. He wouldn't bother now if he met the same fellow again. It wasn't worth the energy it took you to answer back.

Martin was so full of energy that he'd almost knock you over. He'd grabbed Rasher round the shoulders as they'd walked to the door of the office, and you could feel the strength of his fingers and the muscles in his arm. He had a thick culchie accent on him, and the story was he'd gone into the priests off a pig farm. Other people said he'd been a navvy over in London, working for British Gas. Rasher reckoned it wouldn't be wise to ask.

'I know it's fierce confusing now but, take it from me, Rasher, we'll get you settled. Just stay out of trouble in the meantime. Have you got that?'

The crowd on the bandstand moved on from musicals to marches. The girls wore awful tartan kilts halfway down to their heels, and green jumpers. The boys had the same jumpers, grey trousers and school ties. They were probably sixth years doing some kind of cultural project. Actually, there was a board by the bandstand with a poster on it, but Rasher couldn't be bothered going over for a look. There were a few people sitting round listening to the music, parents maybe, or teachers from the school. Next year, this crowd crucifying 'The Minstrel Boy' would be off at uni, like the Khan woman's daughter. If things hadn't gone wrong after Dad died, he might be in college himself, with God knew what career ahead of him. Before his dad died he'd had a notion he might be a chef. That wasn't something he'd mentioned to Martin. It seemed as pathetic now as saying that, as a kid, he'd thought he'd grow up to be an engine driver. Or fly to the moon.

Looking beyond the bandstand, he tensed up, seeing a familiar figure. Nugent was walking across the park in his direction. Rasher measured the distance between them with his eye, deciding it was safer to stay where he was than to scarper. Better to be in the open than to retreat under the trees where your man could easily corner him. 'The Minstrel Boy' finally fell and the band immediately started 'The Battle of Aughrim'. Getting to his feet, Rasher drifted towards the noticeboard. Nugent had stopped and was leaning against a lamp post, apparently a benign uniformed figure watching a community event. Rasher could feel the cold eyes boring into him. Since he couldn't stand looking at the poster for ever, he moved to sit on another bench by a woman with two small kids.

'Do you mind? It's nice to be near to the music.'

She looked a bit nervous but smiled and nodded. Secure in the knowledge that he didn't smell and was wearing clean clothes and new trainers, he relaxed and smiled back at her, hitching his jeans up at the knees to reassure her with the bright white socks. Over by the lamp post, Nugent's mouth twisted into a sneer.

Chapter Sixteen

A cloud rolled away along the shoulder of the mountain carrying rain eastwards from the peak of Knockinver. Far below it, where sunlight was bright on a wheeling hawk's wings, Hanna reached up for Brian's hand. He pulled her up to join him on a massive boulder that projected from the hillside, and together they looked down at the Hag's Glen.

Seen from this height Brian's house, by the river below, seemed part of the landscape. 'It's wonderful.'

An expression she didn't understand crossed his face. Then he smiled. 'Thank you. I think it works. The planting on the roof makes a big difference, and it'll be even more effective once it begins to mature.'

'Are you going to have a garden?'

'At ground level? No, I don't think so. Not formally.'

'But you'll have to set a few spuds. Look, you can see where there used to be ridges.'

When Brian had first shown her around the site the shallow ditches and hummocks had been lost in ground cover, but from here you could see that there'd once been cultivated plots between the ruined buildings. He nodded. 'I know. And there were larger fields running back from the village. Most of the evidence got scraped away by the build.'

The hawk above them began to spiral downwards at an angle and suddenly swooped on some creature in the heather. Hanna looked up and saw it rise with its prey held in its talons, then sheer off towards the rolling clouds. Beneath her feet she could feel the curve of the boulder's pitted surface, and off to her right, other grey rocks marked the point where the river poured into the valley. 'How come it's a valley, but they call it a glen?'

Brian shrugged. 'Technically they're much of a muchness, except that "valley" usually assumes that there's water running through it. The word "glen" comes from the Irish. I guess that's what people who lived here in the hag's time would have spoken.'

'If you believe she existed.' He had told her Fury's story about the name, and Hanna, who also knew Fury of old, had been sceptical.

'Yes, but you don't have to believe in the hag to know that the village actually was abandoned during the Famine. And most of the peninsula would have been Irish-speaking in the mid-nineteenth century.'

He had hunkered down and was sliding cautiously over the edge of the boulder. Hanna followed, and the conversation lapsed. Each of them had done enough walking on the foothills of Knockinver to be wary of the treacherous roots and ruts beneath the thick vegetation. They were safe on a sheep path that snaked towards the head of the waterfall before Hanna pointed west to where the sun was a flaming ball. 'You won't get the sunsets.'

'Nope. But I face south, so I do get the sun for most of the day.

Masses of light, and trees swaying down below in the distance. And from the roof I can look out across the forest and catch a glimpse of the ocean.'

'I bet you're glad you're no closer to the salt spray. In winter my windows are practically opaque.'

'Whereas I shall be sitting in my glass veranda admiring a gorgeous view.'

'Not a sea view, though.'

'True. Not from the veranda. But I have my own river. And this.'

They had reached the granite lip from which the narrow torrent spilled over into the valley. Fearful of slipping, Hanna knelt gingerly and reached down to dip her fingers in the amber-coloured water. Brian sat on a rock and smiled at her. 'Beautiful, isn't it?'

'I can see why you'd want to live here.'

'Can you? Why?'

'Well, it's not just beautiful. There's an austerity about it. No, I don't mean that. Something that's essentially remote.'

'And you associate that with me? Personally?'

'I'm not complaining.'

Brian frowned. 'Am I remote? It's not intentional.'

'Actually, it's rather attractive.'

He burst out laughing and Hanna made a face at him. 'Oh, shut up! Maybe I should have said reticence. I admire it as a quality, that's all.'

'Even after what you went through with Malcolm?'

'Malcolm wasn't reticent, he was a liar.' Hanna reached up and touched his cheek. 'You have no idea what it means to have found someone I can trust. I never dreamed I would. And then there was you.'

Brian grasped her hand so tightly she almost yelped in protest. He opened his mouth for a moment, as if about to speak. Then he relaxed his grip and looked down at the valley. 'It's not particularly remote physically. Well, I suppose that depends on where you measure from. I don't view Carrick as the centre of my universe. People lived and thrived here for hundreds of years before the poor hag and the Famine. Maybe even thousands.'

'How do you know?'

'We found a sluice box. It emerged when Fury was digging my foundations.'

'But what is it?'

'Basically a box that lets water through. It's filled with material to catch gold deposits washed down from the mountain. Gold is dense, so you can trap it when lighter stuff flushes through.'

She scrambled up beside him on the rock. 'Seriously? Actual gold?'

'Sure. There was lots of gold prospecting in ancient Ireland. They found a huge sluice box, thousands of years old, in Woodenbridge, up in Wicklow. There was a kind of gold rush there in the eighteenth century. I remember getting all fired up when I heard the story as a kid. I went scouring riverbanks for nuggets.'

'But the box you found here, is that ancient?'

'It's not always easy to be sure. The designs hardly change, so you need to carbon date them if they're early. But, no, I should think this one was made in the nineteenth century. Maybe the hag stayed behind because of the gold.'

Hanna rested her chin on her knees, envisaging the valley filled with noise and bustle, and the sweet smell of turf smoke. When you realised that a million people had died, and a million more emigrated, during the potato famine, it was easy to understand why emigration had become such a towering image in the Irish imagination. Even now, the poignant emigrant themes of aspiration, loss and yearning tapped into something visceral for those left behind.

Brian, who had been ruminating too, leaned back on his elbows. 'Actually, if there *was* a memory of gold being washed down in the river, the poor bastards faced with famine might have made a desperate attempt to catch some. There probably wasn't much to be had by that stage. Well-known sources often got worked out.' He looked up at Hanna. 'You know the story of Jason and the Golden Fleece?'

'What about it?'

'Well, Jason sets out to find the fleece of this mythical golden ram.' He sat up and put his arm round her. 'It hangs in a sacred grove, defended by bulls with brass hoofs.'

'And a fearsome dragon.'

'Exactly. So our hero yokes the bulls, defeats the dragon, and ends up with the fabulous golden fleece.'

'Is there a reason you're telling me this? Because I did do tales from Greece at school.'

'Yes, there is a reason, so shut up and wait for it. That story may have been inspired by the practice of trapping gold by stuffing sheepskins into sluice boxes.' Keeping his arm round her waist, Brian gesticulated at the valley. 'Imagine an ancient community down there on my doorstep, lifting glittering fleece out of a river running with gold.'

Hanna drew in her breath. 'That's extraordinary. This really is a pretty magical place.'

'Do you think so? Because ...'

'Gosh, you know what? I nearly forgot to tell you ...'

They'd started to speak simultaneously. Hanna laughed. 'Sorry, go on.'

Brian, who had taken a deep breath, let it out. 'No, you first.'

'Okay, but it's irrelevant, it's just about Malcolm.'

'What about him?'

'It's nothing. Well, actually it is, it's something Louisa said the other day. She thinks he's planning to come over, and I bet she's right. Apparently, he's all alone again. The latest girlfriend is gone.'

Brian took his arm from her waist and, bending down, plucked a sprig of heather. 'It's amazing to think what poor soil some things run riot on.' Stripping the tough, wiry stem, he allowed the purple bells to drop from his hand. 'When does he arrive?'

'Oh, Heaven alone knows. That's Malcolm. He's a law unto himself.'

Hanna was still looking down at the quiet glen beneath them. Fury's van was parked by a fallen outhouse and the steady clink of a hammer on stone was the only sound to be heard. She reached out without looking at Brian and laid a hand on his knee. 'Awful to think of those famished emigrants setting off for America.

How could they be sure that leaving home was the right choice to make? Still, even if they feared they'd made the wrong one, I guess there was no going back.'

Brian nodded. 'I wonder how many bought into the dream that streets could be paved with gold.'

Chapter Seventeen

Without anyone being conscious of the exact moment of change, The Royal Victoria in Carrick had gone from a place where you took your granny for tea to a cool, happening hangout.

It was an imposing hotel, faced in granite, set in a Victorian terrace off Main Street. A broad flight of curved steps led to mahogany double doors with brass fittings and etched-glass panels. Everything in The Royal Vic was well polished, from the massive, carved furniture in the reception area to the gleaming rows of glasses hanging above the bar in the lounge. It had a ladies' coffee room with writing tables, embossed notepaper and brass inkstands; loos with real towels; and a grill room much frequented by accountants and bank officials. The front-of-house female staff wore dark suits with crisp cotton shirts and gilt name-badges. And PJ, the head barman, wore a spotless white jacket and a tartan bow tie.

Eileen had fixed to meet Jazz in the lounge bar at three thirty. Jazz had taken the call on a crackling phone line. 'Sorry, Eileen, my reception's crap and I'm on my way to a meeting. Did you say tomorrow?'

'Well, The Royal Vic's heaving on a Sunday, these days. All those brunches in the bar they do now, and the cream tea deal.

Saturday's nearly as bad, but PJ's promised to keep us a quiet table.'

'It's a bit short notice ...'

'Stop being a bore. You're just trying to avoid me.'

'No, I'm not.'

'Yes, you are. I want to hear what's happened. The word is that Sam's gone.'

Jazz groaned. 'Okay, yes, he has. And I'm busy, Eileen. I'm not sure I can make it tomorrow.'

'Well, that's tough, because the table's booked and I've told Aideen. And I've messaged Owen that we'll all be there at four.'

'Who will?'

'For God's sake, Jazz, keep up! You, me and Aideen. So Owen can get a sense of where we're at. But you and me to begin with. To get me up to speed on you and Sam.'

'Hang on, is this Owen the wedding planner?'

'Yes. Of course. I told you I'd been in touch with him.'

'You also said you'd back off till Aideen was on board.'

'How do you know she's not?'

'Because I know you. Did you talk to her before you fixed this meeting?'

'It's not a meeting. Just a get-together.'

'That's a no, then. You haven't talked to her. Not properly. Does she even know you've invited Owen along?'

'Look, this is a foul connection and I'm in a rush. See you tomorrow, and don't be late. We'll have a quiet drink before the others descend on us. I'm your best mate and I need to know what's happening in your life.'

She had rung off before Jazz could protest any further and, feeling there was no help for it, Jazz had come along. For once, Eileen had arrived early. She was sitting on a cushioned banquette at a window table and PJ was standing beside her with a polished tray in his hand. Jazz approached, feeling confident that, though she looked tired, she wasn't the red-eyed, swollen-faced wretch she'd been a few days before.

As she joined Eileen at the table, PJ bowed from the waist, revealing an age-spotted scalp under a brilliantly greased comb-over. He was as much an institution in Carrick as The Royal Vic itself and, with its new lease of life as a happening venue, had even appeared in a magazine feature, posed behind the bar with a cocktail shaker and a Noël Coward air.

Eileen announced that she'd ordered a gin and tonic. 'PJ's special. He'll do one for you as well. And bring us some olives and snacky things, PJ, will you? They're gorgeous! All made right here in the kitchen, according to *Irish Country Living*.' She leaned over and kissed Jazz, who told PJ she'd like a glass of tonic water.

'Ice and lemon? Or would you prefer lime?'

'Lemon's fine. Thank you.'

PJ moved away across the crimson carpet, his shoes creaking slightly.

'So, what's the story?'

'You're going to drag it out of me, aren't you?'

'Crap. You're dying to talk. What happened? Did you throw Sam out?'

Jazz suddenly realised that she was indeed dying to talk.

No matter how inappropriate Eileen's advice might be, there'd be no doubt about whose side she'd be on. In her world, mates supported each other and women stood shoulder to shoulder against the iniquities of men. There were times when Jazz, who prided herself on being egalitarian, resisted the idea of life as an unexamined battle between the sexes. But, right now, what she wanted was sympathy.

Eileen raised her glass. 'Here's to the enemies! Tell me all.' She was a skilled interrogator. 'You may as well say what you found him at, or I'll sit here thinking it was worse.'

'I didn't find him *at* anything. It was all my fault.'

'God, Jazz, this is so *you*! I bet it wasn't. Even if he didn't rifle your purse or shag another woman, it's *never* one person's fault when things go wrong.' Eileen crossed her legs and took a decisive sip of gin and tonic. 'How did it end?'

'He just disappeared.'

'What?'

'Well, he left a note.'

'A *note*? He moves in with you. Everything's grand – this is according to you, mind – and then he fecks off without a word, leaving a note! And it's all your fault? Ah, would you cop yourself on, girl, you're well rid of him.' Eileen rapped on the table. 'I suppose you have the note by heart? Go on. Spill.'

She did, in fact, remember every word of it. '*I'm sorry. Really. But this isn't going to work. You're not to blame yourself. We're in different places in our lives, that's all. There's no point in raking stuff over. Love, S.*'

'I burned it.'

'Where? In the large, baronial fireplace in your weeshy studio flat?'

'Okay, I didn't burn it.'

She had crumpled the note in her hand and tried to stuff it into the kitchen bin along with the expensive dinner, then sat on the floor and cried when the bin was too small.

'I chucked it. He just said things weren't working. And if I didn't see that myself, Eileen, then, yes, it was my fault. I've been so buried in my job that I haven't been paying attention.' To her horror, Jazz found her lip trembling. She took a determined pull at her tonic water and managed a crooked smile. 'The crap thing is, though, that I'd actually realised that. Well, not how bad things had got, obviously, because I thought I could fix them. I swept into the flat, all got up like a film star. And I'd spent a fortune on food and flowers. It was going to be the first day of the rest of our lives.'

'Ah, Jaysus!'

'Yeah. And instead it was me in my spotless bijou apartment, drinking an entire bottle of New Zealand red.'

'Did you ring him?'

'I've tried. He won't pick up. He's right too. We'd only be raking over dead coals.'

Eileen nodded at Jazz's glass. 'Would you not have a drop of gin in that?'

'God, no. I still haven't really recovered from the bottle of red. Between throwing up and roaring all night, the next day was gruesome. I may not face another drink for a month.'

'You've got to stop the self-blame, though. If things were

going wrong, then at least you tried to fix them. Definitely beats clearing off without even making an effort.'

'I suppose.'

'I'm telling you! Oh, wait, hang on, there's Aideen.' Eileen stood up and waved vigorously. Jazz shot her a warning look as Aideen walked towards them. She didn't need to, though. Whatever Eileen might say to her face, she'd never let her down in front of someone else.

PJ appeared and, eager to make Aideen comfortable, Jazz said she'd join her in a coffee. Aideen gave a distracted nod and looked at Eileen. 'You said in your text you'd invited someone called Owen?'

'Oh, right. Yes. He should be here soon.'

'But who is he?'

So, Aideen hadn't a clue. Furious, Jazz glared at Eileen across the table. Ignoring her, Eileen stood up again and gesticulated at PJ, who obediently went to welcome a guy who had just appeared at the entrance to the bar. He was stocky and tanned, with an air of relaxed assurance, and when PJ ushered him to the table, Eileen was all gush.

'Now, isn't this great? How good of you to join us! I saw you had a roadshow in Carrick this weekend and, when I realised you were staying at the Vic, I thought I'd just ping you a text.'

She fussed him into a seat, introducing him as Owen, then turned to Aideen with a laugh. 'But what am I saying, who doesn't know Owen Dunphy? Sure, we've all seen him on the television and listened to his advice!'

Jazz suspected that, like herself, Aideen hadn't. Though it

would have been hard not to see Owen's face on the cover of celebrity magazines. He accepted the offer of a coffee and sat back, apparently assessing the situation. Presumably he was used to dealing with people like Eileen, who, having greeted him as a superstar, was now subtly suggesting he was being interviewed for a job.

'There's nearly a year before the wedding date, so Aideen and I are still dipping our toes in the water. But, as I said when I talked to you a while back, I really admire your work.'

Aideen's bafflement had changed to consternation. Reaching under the table, Jazz hacked Eileen on the ankle. Then she turned to Owen, ignoring Eileen's subdued yelp. 'Of course, they're not even sure it's the kind of event that will need a wedding planner. I'm Eileen's bridesmaid and, to be honest, I haven't begun to engage my brain yet. Bríd's going to be your bridesmaid, isn't she, Aideen? I suppose she and I will need to sit down together some time.'

Owen indicated the gleaming mahogany bar. 'This place is amazing. Like a film set. Is it going to be your venue?'

'It's charming, I know, but I'd say we'd do better in Cork. I mean, there's hotels there that are really set up for a proper big wedding.' Eileen looked sharply at Owen. 'But do you think that by next year the Vic could be a go-to venue? If we used it, might your programme show my video?'

Owen smiled, revealing dazzling teeth. 'The TV stuff is down to the people at the station. You'd never know, though. It's not inconceivable. It'd be a matter of separate arrangements, of course. One with me and one with them. And, naturally, neither would depend on the other.'

Obviously he was Eileen's equal when it came to negotiation, and just as accustomed to keeping his options open.

Aideen put down her coffee cup and spoke directly to Eileen. 'Conor will want to be part of any decisions.'

For a moment Eileen looked taken aback. Then she laughed. 'Ah, come on, Aideen, what red-blooded man wants to ponce around making wedding plans?'

There was a shattering silence in which Eileen went scarlet and Jazz watched Owen trying to keep a straight face.

'I didn't mean ... I wasn't suggesting ...'

'Of course you weren't. That's just what comes of starting on the gin too early!'

Leaning across the table, Owen gave Eileen a charming smile and patted her on the arm. It was all that was needed to defuse the situation but, to Jazz's dismay, Eileen continued to burble. 'No, but ... honestly ... I wouldn't dream ...'

'It's fine. Truly. Don't apologise. But, look, I really must get back.'

There was a subtle creak of shoe leather and PJ appeared beside them. Before Eileen could move, Owen reached across the table and signed the tab.

Eileen's colour mounted again. 'No, please, you mustn't! I invited you.'

'It was my pleasure. If you need to get in touch about the wedding, just give my people a call.' Standing up, Owen shook hands with Aideen. Then, as he turned to go, he winked at Jazz. 'You know, that's a hell of a responsibility you've taken on. Saving your bride from herself can be two-thirds of the job.'

Chapter Eighteen

The weather was getting warmer by the day and Hanna had taken to setting her alarm early so she could eat breakfast in the garden. Muesli and coffee were twice as good consumed sitting in sunshine with your face raised to a wide expanse of sky. Her coffee was made from freshly ground beans and, while it brewed, she lifted a bowl from the painted wooden dresser, one of the few pieces of Maggie's furniture that remained in the house. The biscuit-coloured pottery bowl, the size of a large cappuccino cup, had a pattern of yellow flowers glowing beneath its worn glaze. Like the shawl she kept on the back of her fireside chair, it had belonged to her great-grandmother.

According to Mary Casey, who had thrust it at Hanna as a moving-in present, such bowls, once used for drinking tea, were locally known as basins. Though Mary would never admit it, the gift had been an unspoken apology for her aggression during their claustrophobic years together in the bungalow. Hanna had received it in the same spirit, knowing that acceptance would be recognised as a complementary gesture. Back then, words, no matter how well chosen, might easily have sparked another row.

She had seen similar bowls in Brittany and France, wide

enough to require two hands to grasp them and deep enough to allow you to dip a croissant into your coffee. But croissants were weekend fare so, as the coffee filled the kitchen with the rich scent of morning, she pottered about mixing oats with chopped nuts, apple and a handful of seeds. Having added yoghurt to her plate of muesli, and milk to her bowl of coffee, she took them outside to sit on her doorstep.

When she opened the door to the pale sunlight a triumphant voice was singing in a nearby ash tree, and broken yellow snail shells were scattered on the stone step. A thrush had had breakfast there already. Hanna brushed the shells away with a slippered foot and, carrying her coffee, went to inspect her rockery.

Dew-spangled cobwebs trembled on marjoram and marigolds, and lay like gossamer shawls on the bush where she usually spread her tea-towels out to dry. Maggie had called spiders 'night knitters', a term Hanna had never heard used by anyone else. She'd mentioned it once to Mary, who'd tossed her head and declared that Maggie Casey had always had notions. The having of notions was the ultimate put-down in Mary's terms: and, though the old lady had been long dead when they'd talked about the night knitters, it was clear Mary felt that if given an inch she might somehow come back and take an ell.

Hanna was often puzzled by the sense of frustrated entitlement that seemed to possess so many of Mary and Maggie's generations. Yet was it so surprising? Maggie had lived through Ireland's war of independence and been old enough to be aware of the rebels' aspirations for a state founded on the principle of equality. Yet she'd been hounded out of her home by a parish priest who'd seen her in the woods with a man. And her brother had accused her of leaving their mother uncared-for, though he himself had joined the rebels without a backward glance.

Maggie's seducer had faced no retribution, and her brother, who'd ended his life as a drunk, had been a local hero. Yet her own life had been overturned and she'd died an aggressive recluse. Had she asked herself how Ireland's dream of equality had dwindled to a reality in which women lacked both power and respect?

And that was the Ireland Mary had been born into — a smug, impoverished, Church-ridden world, which simultaneously treated women as inferior and equated them with the virgin mother of a patriarchal God. Whenever Hanna felt tempted to strangle her mother, she reminded herself of that toxic inheritance. Could you really blame Mary if impotent rage had made her overbearing? How could you expect her to be aware of what she hardly understood?

With her coffee balanced in one hand, she reached out to pull a weed from the rockery. Then she found herself smiling. Plenty of Irishwomen of those generations had risen above their circumstances, so it had to be nature as well as nurture that produced a Mary Casey. That being so, she told herself she'd be well employed keeping a sharp eye on her own behaviour. When Louisa had talked about Jazz's inherited stubbornness, citing Malcolm and Mary as examples, she might well have pointed out that Hanna had her own share of it too.

*

Having eaten, showered and got ready for work, Hanna was cheerfully putting her bag on the car seat when a buzz announced the arrival of a text.

JOHNNYS DRIVING ME TO SNITCH AND BITCH

Waiting for the next, which she knew would come, Hanna concentrated firmly on the may blossom in the hedgerow. There was another buzz and she looked again at her screen.

STICH NOT SNITCH THESE KEYS ARE 2 SMALL % ULL HAV2 GET ME A NEW ONE

She punched OK CU LATER into the phone, thinking she ought to have it as an automatic reply to all texts from Mary's number. It would certainly save a hell of a lot of time.

As she left her car at the library car park, Conor cruised past on his Vespa. They met in the courtyard, and as soon as Hanna had opened up, he went to set chairs for the morning's Knit and Natter session, always referred to by its members as the Stitch and Bitch.

Like every small town, Lissbeg had its share of serial joiners. Usually they were interested, interesting people with time on their hands, but among them were prima donnas of both sexes seeking a captive audience. Occasionally, Hanna had her work cut out to woo newcomers to the library's groups while making sure that her stalwarts didn't feel threatened by their arrival. The serial joiners could be infuriating but they also tended to be indefatigable volunteer workers, without whom the Stitch and Bitch or the weekly Children's Storytime just wouldn't happen.

As always, the first-comer was Darina Kelly, who'd started the group earlier in the year on the basis of a cross-stitch kit she'd received as a Christmas present. It was a lovely thing to get, she'd informed Hanna, and once it was done she'd have a gorgeous footstool. But there was an awful lot of work in it and you got bored on your own. 'Mind you, I have the kids round my feet, so it's not like I'm lonely! And I do have a vibrant inner life, which I'm constantly tapping into. But I love your creative writing group and I *long* for each film club meeting. So, I said to myself why not Stitch and Bitch? It's so fun and people can bring whatever they're working on. Or we could all get together and make quilt squares for Africa. Or – wait for it – do knitted knockers!'

Hanna had recognised yet another excuse for Darina to leave her undisciplined, noisy kids with the au pair. But she knew of similar groups making items for sales of work, and knitting cotton breast prosthetics for cancer survivors, so she'd happily agreed. Now, months later, Darina was still stabbing doggedly at her cross-stitch, but several other members of the group had combined to knit and sew for charity. Their fortnightly sessions in the library often continued as convivial lunches in the Garden Café and, now and then, there was even some chat about books.

Mary Casey attended only sporadically, and Hanna was continually torn between welcoming the fact that she'd made the effort and finding her presence irritating. She arrived today on Darina's heels, armed with a large knitting bag and demanding to know when Hanna would take her to Carrick to buy a new phone. Luckily, the rest of the group turned up promptly and before long they'd assembled in a circle.

Hanna watched from her desk as they jockeyed to sit near friends and avoid sparring partners, fished crochet cushion covers and babies' bootees out of bags and looked round distractedly for their glasses. Some were getting organised quicker than others. Two young mums with infants beside them in buggies were already hard at work knitting knockers. Pat Fitz was crocheting a blanket. Darina was still struggling to erect the adjustable stand that had come with her cross-stitch kit. Beside her, Carol Garvey, who was Aideen's aunt, was setting a section of fabric into a workmanlike embroidery hoop, with yards more of it carefully folded on a neatly placed sheet at her feet.

As Conor got on with shelving returns, Hanna turned her attention to her computer screen. Scrolling through a series of forms sent by the council's health and safety office, she could hear voices from the circle rising and falling.

Darina's, as ever, was the loudest. She'd been watching an episode of *Downton Abbey* on Netflix the previous night. 'And do you know what occurred to me? That really *Downton* is just Jane Austen with sex and different bonnets.'

One of the knocker knitters looked up in surprise. 'But Jane Austen's massively sexy. I mean Colin Firth's a bit long in the tooth, these days, but he's seriously fit in that thing *Pride and Prejudice*. It was on telly again a while ago and I watched every episode.'

'Yes, but that's the adaptation. Not the book.'

'It's the same character, though, isn't it? Or wasn't Mr Darcy in the book?'

'Well, of course he was, but that's not the point I'm making.

Jane Austen doesn't have him rising out of a lake as if he's in a wet T-shirt contest.'

Carol Garvey drew a silk thread through her fabric. 'You're right, though. Her books are basically family sagas, aren't they? Same as *Downton*. Just without the *Upstairs, Downstairs* bits.'

Several older women in the group agreed that *Upstairs, Downstairs* had been proper television, and a parallel discussion began between them about Mrs Bridges' wig. Carol ignored it. 'The costumes in *Downton* are brilliant. It's a better period to design for.'

'No! How can you say that? Think of Emma Thompson in those chip hats and the lovely Empire line dresses.'

Pat Fitz, who'd been contributing to the discussion on Mrs Bridges' wig, glanced round at Darina. 'That was *Sense and Sensibility*.'

'No, it wasn't.'

'Yes, it was. And it was a film. Actually, it's one that Hanna could do for the film club.'

'Are you sure? I mean, wasn't Emma Thompson Elizabeth Bennet in the film?'

The second young mum said that she thought they'd said *Pride and Prejudice* was on telly.

Pat looked at them mildly over her glasses. 'Yes, it was. And then it was a film, starring Keira Knightley as Elizabeth Bennet, Darina, not Emma Thompson. Though of course there were other films of it before that. I thought Laurence Olivier was a wonderful Mr Darcy.'

Darina frowned and said she must Google it.

'Well, you can if you like, but I know I'm right. Emma Thompson worked on the script of the film of *Pride and Prejudice*. She wasn't in it. Then she wrote the whole of the script for the film of *Sense and Sensibility*. And played Elinor Dashwood.'

Darina stabbed herself with her needle and sucked her finger violently. 'Damn! I'm always doing that. It's just as well I chose to make these roses red.'

Pat spread out her blanket on her knee. 'I wasn't sure what colour I'd do this. I mean, these days no one cares about pink for a girl and blue for a boy, do they? But would you say orange on a cot might be a bit raucous?'

Everyone assured her they wouldn't – except Mary, who snorted loudly – and Pat continued serenely with her crocheting. The Mrs Bridges' wig discussion resumed, with one side of the circle insisting it must have been nylon.

Carol turned to Darina. 'I think you're probably right. Jane Austen's just *Downton* without the sex. And, okay, don't shoot me down, anyone. I mean overt sex. Rolling in the hayloft stuff.'

Pat shook her head decisively. 'Actually, *Sense and Sensibility* is all about money.'

Darina frowned. 'No, it isn't.'

'Yes, it is. Well, marrying for money. Having it. Losing it. Having a moral right to it. Ending up without it.'

Mary Casey snorted again and pointed a worsted weight knitting needle at Pat. 'Now, *there's* a subject we could all write a book about.'

The Mrs Bridges discussion stopped abruptly. Having gained

her audience, Mary placed the needle against her lips. 'That's to say, we could if we were let.'

She shot a significant glance in the direction of Hanna, who cursed her inwardly.

'Oh, yes.' Mary addressed the Aran sweater held low on her lap. 'There's many a fool of a woman who married into money and lost it. Talk about having a moral right and ending up with nothing! But, of course, it's never talked about. Even when the guilty party decides he's going to add insult to injury.'

The eyes of the whole group swivelled towards Hanna. At the far end of the room, Conor, who was lifting a book from the trolley, looked round, as if feeling the tension. It was so precisely like a scene from a film that Hanna couldn't decide whether to laugh or be furious. One thing was certain, though. Either Jazz or Louisa had told Mary that Malcolm was selling the house.

Chapter Nineteen

Jazz was sitting on a high cliff when Mike fell over her. It wasn't an auspicious way to meet but, on the other hand, it hadn't been his fault. She was curled in a patch of sunlight reading *Brooklyn* and he'd rounded a corner, tripped over her feet, and sent the book flying. *Brooklyn* landed safely on its face a few yards away, but he'd fallen heavily on his hands.

He looked up apologetically. 'Oh, God, I'm sorry, did I hurt you?'

'I'm fine, but are you?'

He had rolled over and, though his left palm was bleeding, was anxiously checking a camera that was slung around his neck. Jazz scrambled to her knees. 'That looks expensive. Is it okay?'

He wiped the blood off his hand and stood up. 'It's fine. I'm fine. I should have looked where I was going.'

Jazz went to fetch the book, which had narrowly missed a muddy patch by a rock. As she smoothed the pages he came and joined her. 'It's a library book, isn't it? I'm so sorry.'

She could tell by his accent that he was English. 'It's fine too. Really. How's your hand?'

'I'm not going to say fine again. It's grand. Isn't that the proper Irish response?'

'Yes. But I'd stop there if I were you. I mean, I wouldn't say "top of the morning" or "sure and begorrah". Just in case you had that in mind.'

'I'll make a note.' He held out his right hand and smiled at her. 'My name's Mike.'

'I'm Jazz.' She could see his attention straying back to the camera. 'Are you a photographer?'

'Yeah. Well, a video journalist. But sort of at the start of my *über*-sensational career.'

'Would that be the point before it actually becomes sensational?'

'Got it in one.'

His handshake was firm and he was tall and fair, probably the same age as she was. Far slighter than Sam and with long, floppy hair.

Jazz gestured at the deserted cliff. 'Not much round here for a journalist.'

'Not if you're chasing news, perhaps. But I'm doing a travel series.'

'Like for National Geographic?'

'Oh, God, *everyone* asks me that! No, not National Geographic. I wish, though.' His eyes strayed again, this time to the horizon where an island wreathed in mist appeared to be floating on polished silver.

Jazz could see he was dying to lift the camera. 'Why don't you go ahead and shoot it? You know you want to.'

He laughed and, choosing a springy clump of heather, sat down. 'No, I don't. Anyway, I've got enough for today. If I'm not careful I'll end up with a six-hour series, and the most I'm going to sell is some pathetic two-minute clips.'

'Of Finfarran?'

'I'm travelling along the west coast. Cashing in on The Wild Atlantic Way.' Nodding at *Brooklyn*, he asked if she was a student.

'Nope. I'm in marketing. The book's relaxation.'

'And you're from here?'

'Mm. Well, I live in Lissbeg.' Jazz sat down beside him. 'I was born and raised in London, though. My mum's from here. You're a Londoner, aren't you?'

'Middlesex. I grew up in Petersham.'

'Still counts as London. I mean it's within a spit of a District Line station.'

'That sounds like nostalgia.'

Turning the book over, she straightened its plastic cover. 'I guess I'm a bit like the girl in this novel. Have you read it?'

Mike squinted at the title. 'No. I'm not a reader. More a marathon man. I've seen the movie, though.'

'Yeah, so have I. That's why I'm reading it. My mum's the librarian in Lissbeg. She runs a film club.'

Mike looked at the cover. 'So how does the book compare with the film?'

'Well, I haven't finished it.'

Actually, she'd only read a few chapters.

When Mum and Louisa had heard about Sam's departure, Mum's reaction had been to back off, registering that she didn't want to pry. Louisa's had been different. She'd turned up and cornered Jazz in her office. 'I don't want to see you responding to this break-up by taking on extra work and becoming overstressed and unwell.'

'Of course not.'

'Because marketing a start-up business is a formidable task.'

'I know.'

'And you can't be useful in a creative capacity if you never raise your head from your computer screen.' She must have seen Jazz's expression because she laughed. 'You don't have to be a business mogul to know that, dear. When you're as old as I am you gain a modicum of sense.'

Jazz knew the admonishment had contained as much concern for herself as for Edge of the World Essentials so, feeling chastened, she'd gone to the library that lunchtime and borrowed a copy of *Brooklyn*. She had no inclination to attend the next meeting of the film club, but maybe in a few weeks' time she'd be more disposed to. Anyway, escaping with a book to some private corner had once been her favourite pastime and now, with Sam gone and weekend work forbidden, there was far too much time to be passed. She'd done a lot more daydreaming than reading since borrowing the book, though. Idiotic dreams in which Sam kept coming back.

Mike, who had picked up *Brooklyn*, was inspecting the cover illustration. 'So who do you think you're like? Saoirse Ronan?'

Did he think she was looking for compliments on her appearance? 'No. Well, yes. Her character. Eilis.'

'Why?'

'I suppose because I'm caught between two countries.'

'Not two men?'

For a moment Jazz wondered if this was a come-on. Then she realised there was nothing flirtatious about how he'd asked the question. He simply wanted to know. 'No, nothing like that. It's just that sometimes I wonder if this is where I want to be.'

Sam's disappearance had brought back her old sense of rootlessness. In the days that had followed, a series of memories of London life had engulfed her. Crossing Waterloo Bridge on a bus and seeing the Thames Clippers churning their way down towards Greenwich. Wandering round Tate Modern or Whitechapel Gallery, or choosing from dozens of cinemas when you fancied seeing a film. Crocuses in Kew Gardens and Green Park in springtime, and ice skating at Somerset House under twinkling Christmas lights. More than once when she'd been trying to read *Brooklyn*, she'd found herself dreaming of Hampstead and Marylebone High Street, pop-up boutiques in Smithfield and street food in Hackney. She'd even woken up one night from a dream of Columbia Flower Market and winced at the memory of the scent of lilies the night Sam had left.

'So why not go back to London?'

'Because I've got a job here. And family. And I've been mad enough to agree to be a head bridesmaid at a huge double wedding next year.'

She'd realised recently that the wedding stuff was beginning to do her head in. Still, she couldn't leave poor Eileen in the lurch just because Sam had walked out.

'No family over there?'

'My dad. Who's the reason I ended up here, actually. He and my mum split up.'

'I've got Irish family, though I've never been here before. I can't think why not. It's stunning.' He was lolling comfortably in the heather not showing any inclination to go.

Jazz tucked *Brooklyn* into her bag and relaxed beside him. 'So, what do you mean you're a marathon man?'

'I run them. London. Paris. Los Angeles next year, if I'm lucky.'

'That's cool.'

'It allows me to travel. That's the point of the travel journalism too.'

'I used to work for an airline.'

'Now, that's really cool.'

'Not really. It was a budget airline, and most of my flights were to places like Alicante. I did share a flat in France with a bunch of other trolley dollies, though.'

'A bunch of what?'

'Cabin crew. That's what my dad called us. He's such a snob.' She turned her head and looked at Mike, half surprised at how willing she felt to confide in him. It was almost as if his easy, self-contained air was in some way familiar. 'You know, I keep thinking I've moved on from all that crap and then it ambushes me again. Still, it's behind me now. I'm here in Lissbeg with a different job and a flat that's all my own.'

And no Sam, said her mind, *so what's the point of any of it?*

Suddenly she felt awkward. 'Is this what they taught you in journalism school? How to grill people for the story of their lives?'

'Was I grilling you? Sorry, I don't mean to. Anyway, no, that's not what they taught us. It was mainly software and microphone add-ons, and what kind of filter to use for African sunsets. That sort of thing.' He indicated the ocean. 'Literally, that sort of thing.' The setting sun was producing spectacular effects on the sky behind the island, framing its rocky outline with streaks of crimson light. 'It's amazing. Very Bali Ha'i.'

'As in *South Pacific*? You're on the Wild Atlantic Way here, remember? That's not Bali Ha'i, mate, it's Hy-Brasil.'

'Really? That's what it's called?'

'No, not really. Hy-Brasil is Ireland's mystical, magical island. It appears every seven years, wreathed in mist. Same sort of thing as Bali Ha'i, though. The Land of Heart's Desire. The idea of a dream place on the horizon must be some kind of universal theme.'

'Every seven years, huh? You've got to admire our timing.'

Instinctively they leaned forward, as if drawn by the shimmering island.

'What's its actual name?'

'Big Rock.'

'Seriously?'

'Yup. Carraig Mór. I love how people who invented romantic notions like Hy-Brasil came up with prosaic place names like Big Rock and High Hill.'

'I've never been to a musical, but we saw the film of *South Pacific* at college. It's a kind of watershed moment in movie history. A crossover point between stage lighting and film. Lots of pink, blue and gold filters, and an island out in the distance creating unreal effects.'

'Like that?' Jazz gestured at the ocean where a shivering path of blood-red light stretched from below the cliff where they sat out to Carraig Mór. The sky was now streaked with blue and gold and, as they watched, the clouds round the island shifted and it disappeared in a swirl of amber mist.

Mike burst out laughing. 'Exactly like that.'

Scrambling to her feet, Jazz brushed dusty pieces of heather from her jeans. 'You know, I really ought to go – I've been here ages.'

He stood up too and she wondered if he was planning to walk with her. Instead, he shook her hand again and smiled. Then, as he turned away, he glanced back. 'How come you know *South Pacific*? It's a bit ancient, isn't it?'

'Yes, but it's based on a book of short stories.'

'So?'

'My mum was planning to show it at the library film club, so we watched it together one night. She decided not to show it in the end. I quite liked it, though.'

They'd watched it together in Mum's house one evening last December, snuggled together in a shawl. Now, walking back towards Lissbeg in the warmth of the May evening, Jazz could almost feel the rough wool and smell its oily scent. She'd sat on the floor by the fireside chair with her arm across Mum's knees. The wind was screaming so loudly through the ash trees that, at one point, they'd had to raise the volume to hear the film. Rain hurtled against the windows and occasional drops had spewed down the chimney, spattering the broad hearthstone with black spots. Mum had been burning black turf and salt-crusted driftwood, and spurts of blue and green had leapt through the red-gold flames as the scent of the woollen shawl had mixed with the scent of smoke from the fire.

As Jazz turned inland towards the town, the thought of that night sparked childhood memories of London, where Mum had read aloud to her as they'd sat together in an armchair in the conservatory. It had had velvet-covered feather cushions, and there was a polished table next to it where they used to stack their library books.

Maggie's place was titchy compared to that tall terraced house in London. Jazz loved it, though. Its low ceilings, thick walls and little windows, and the wide stone hearth where firelight made coloured patterns, spoke to her of an adult, not a childish, sense of security and belonging. Finding out what a rat Dad had been had stripped both Mum and herself of a vital sense of assurance. Rediscovering and settling into Maggie's house had been part of Mum's healing process. Now, without Sam in her life, Jazz feared she might never complete her own.

Chapter Twenty

The next time Rasher was due to meet Saira, he was given the message by Martin. 'She'll be here at two.'

'Right.'

'So, make sure you're punctual.'

'Okay.' He was getting a bit pissed off by all this fuss about timing. Living in the halfway house was far too much like being back at school.

Martin produced a letter from the piles on his big, messy desk. He beamed all over his craggy face and waved the page at Rasher. 'What would you say if I told you I'd got you an interview for a job?'

Rasher looked at him cautiously, thinking this might be a joke. Ever since his bout of flu he'd felt mentally knackered, like he hadn't the strength to cope when people messed him about. The trouble with Martin was that he went in for boisterous stuff, so half the time you couldn't be sure he wasn't having you on. Still, the letter looked convincing. It was headed 'The Royal Victoria Hotel, Carrick', in curly writing, and it turned out that Martin wasn't holding it out to be read. It was more of a flourish, a sort of dramatic gesture, like the way he jumped up and came round the desk to give Rasher a thump on the chest. 'There y'are now!

This is the first step on a long road to where you want to be, boy. Make sure you pin back your ears and listen to Saira. She'll give you the low-down on how to make the right impression.'

'So, what's the job?'

'It's a foot on the ladder, that's what it is. And that's how you've got to see it. More to the point, it's live-in, so it gives you a proper address.'

'But what do I have to do?'

'You've to keep your head down and your nose clean and give them no reason to sack you. D'you hear me? I spend half me life trying to place the likes of you, boy. Crawling to the feckers that run this town, telling them God will smile on their sins if they give a poor bastard a job. And, lookut, one eejit with his hand in a till can stymie things for everyone. So, I'm warning you, if you end up in a police cell, that'll be the least of your troubles. Because when they let you out I'll track you down and kill you. Have you got that?'

Rasher didn't know if he meant it. Though he had a feeling he might. The word on the street was that Martin had been what they called a late vocation and the bishop himself wasn't sure what he might do if he was roused. Probably the Church had to take what they could get, these days. You wouldn't find many normal people wanting to be a priest.

'Two o'clock, right? And mind your manners with Mrs Khan. She's a great woman altogether.'

That seemed to be that, so Rasher decided to wait and ask Mrs Khan what the job was. By the sound of things, it was likely to be shite.

Bang on two o'clock he turned up in the tea room and found her at a table reading a book. 'So, what's this job, then?' He hadn't intended to sound abrupt but, having hung around, he'd got more and more nervous since the talk with Martin. The job was going to be awful. Or scary. Something he'd hate or wouldn't be able to do. And even if it turned out to be fantastic, he'd have to go through an interview. He'd never had a job in his life, not even a paper round. His mum and dad had always said he'd be better off doing his homework and, anyway, there'd been plenty of money at home. Nothing crazy, but two decent wages, and he'd been an only kid. So, he hadn't a clue about interviews. Would whoever it was ask him awkward questions? Would they know before he arrived that he'd been living rough on the street?

His mind was so full of questions that he hardly heard the Khan woman asking him to sit down. And – Holy God – that was exactly the sort of thing that would go wrong. He'd turn up at the interview and they'd ask him something – his name, say, or what age he was – and his head would be all over the place and he wouldn't hear the question. Because, look at him now with Mrs Khan smiling at him, and she'd just said something else and he hadn't heard that either, and here he was, still standing up like a fool.

He sat down on the plastic chair and heard it give a loud crack, like he might have broken it. Mrs Khan closed her book and didn't seem to notice he was sweating.

'The Royal Victoria Hotel is looking for a kitchen porter. Martin has spoken to the management and they're happy to speak to you.'

'And that would be the interview?'

'Yes, and it won't be formidable, Adam, I assure you. Just a chance for them to meet you and see if perhaps you might suit.'

Rasher frowned. 'So, what's a kitchen porter?'

She spread out a piece of paper on the table, 'Someone very, very low in the kitchen pecking order. But you won't mind that. See for yourself.'

The page looked like a printout from the internet. It began with shouty red writing saying that being a kitchen porter could be the most important step in your life. Then it went on in smaller black writing to admit that it was what was called 'an entry-level position', requiring discipline, stamina, determination and a pair of rubber gloves.

Underneath that was a list of FAQs. The first was 'What will I actually be doing?' Rasher checked out the answer and looked up at Mrs Khan. She turned the paper round again and read out another shouty red bit about how chefs such as Michel Roux recognised and celebrated the importance of a kitchen porter in helping a commercial kitchen to run smoothly.

'You see? It says there is even an annual Kitchen Porter of the Year awards ceremony, to celebrate the vital role that porters play.'

'Doing the washing-up.'

'Collecting it. Doing it. Checking all the surfaces are clean. Organising the storeroom. It will all matter. And your attitude will be important, Adam. As it says here, no matter how great the chef may be, if there are no clean pans nothing is going to get cooked.'

'Right.'

'It says conditions are tough. You need to be fit. It's hot and crowded. People shout and swear.'

'Yeah? Well, I'll be fine dealing with all the shouting and swearing. Plenty of experience there.'

'Adam?'

'What?'

'It also says the next step up is being a kitchen assistant. That from there you could look to becoming a trainee chef.'

'With no Junior Cert?'

'You could study in your spare time for that. It's not impossible.'

Against his will, Rasher found he was getting a bit excited. 'Yeah, but they're not going to take me, are they? Not if there's other people up for it. They won't want a guy who's been living on the street.'

Mrs Khan pushed back her chair. 'Don't underestimate Martin's powers of persuasion. Or your own abilities. Would you like some tea?'

Feeling he ought to show a bit of politeness, Rasher stood up and said he'd get them in. 'What way do you want it?'

'I won't have any myself, thank you.'

He wondered if she thought he had fleas or something, but she smiled.

'It's Ramadan. I'm a Muslim and during this festival we fast until sunset. But get yourself some. Then we'll talk.'

Rasher went and joined the queue at the counter. He'd gathered that Ramadan worked a bit like Lent. You didn't just give up chocolate, though, or say you'd keep off the fags.

It was cold turkey, nothing at all, not even a cup of tea. He didn't know much more about it, though people often assumed he was Muslim. Which was ironic because Mum and Dad had always been totally down on religion. They'd sent Rasher to Catholic schools because there wasn't any option but, like half the kids, he hadn't paid any attention in RI. At national school the religious stuff was mostly drawing pictures, anyway. That and boasting about how much money you'd got for your First Communion. And in secondary he'd always tuned out and sat at the back with his phone.

All of which made it *really* ironic when Fergal arrived, after Dad died, and began making comments. Rasher had hated the sight of him from the first day that Mum had brought him home from some pub. He was a freckled git with a big belly on him, and a snide way of talking even when he was sober. You could tell he was a user and a loser, but Mum had bought into his macho crap and the smarmy pretend sympathy, and his stupid boxes of chocolates and bunches of flowers. He was nothing like Dad. But because Dad had always teased Mum and kind of made fun of her, she hadn't spotted, like Rasher did, that this guy who'd picked her up was a proper dangerous bully. And because she'd taken to drinking herself, to numb the way she was feeling, she'd been okay with him lying around, knocking back cans of beer.

More often than not, it was when he was pissed that Fergal would start on Rasher. Not much to begin with, mainly corny, heavy-handed stuff that just about passed as a joke. After a few weeks, though, he was calling Rasher a mongrel.

'Rashid! What kind of name is that?'

The answer was 'It's Egyptian, you stupid, thick bastard', though Rasher tried to keep his mouth shut. But if you ignored Fergal, like people said you should with bullies, he kept on needling until finally you'd crack. Mostly Rasher would slam doors and Mum would get all weepy. But one day he'd lost it with Fergal and thrown a six-pack of beer at him, and Fergal had knocked him across the room and given him a fractured wrist.

That was when he'd first called Rasher the son of a bloody ISIS terrorist, and told Mum that she'd want to watch out or the guards would raid the house. Rasher had known damn well what that was really about. He'd gone into Mum's room one day and found the stash of weed Fergal kept under the bed.

Then, because he was staying out a lot, to avoid the stupid bastard, your man went round warning the neighbours that Rasher was radicalised. Which was totally mad, because he'd never been in a mosque and he'd run a mile if a bearded weirdo came near him. But one guy a few doors down had always muttered about foreigners handing out drugs in Irish hospitals, and soon he'd begun throwing Rasher dirty looks. Then, next thing, someone at school had scribbled 'Allahu Akbar' on his desk.

For a while he'd hung in there, because sometimes he'd manage to protect Mum when Fergal got vicious. And when he couldn't get between them, at least he'd be there to take her to A & E. He'd always had to cart her across to St James's on the south side because she wouldn't want them to see her in the hospital where she worked.

After six months or so of this she'd stopped going in to work altogether, and at the time Rasher had been furious because none of her colleagues seemed to care. Which wasn't really fair of him, because what could they do? They'd been nice enough when she'd first started missing shifts after Dad died, and someone from HR had rung more than once, but she'd just cut them off.

His Irish grandparents had always been iffy about Mum's marriage to Dad. If Rasher had turned out looking like Mum, things might have been different. But he hadn't, so they weren't. Anyway, the grandparents lived miles away and Mum never rang them, and after a couple more months she'd pretty much stopped going out at all. Mostly she lay around on the couch, drinking with Fergal, and Rasher could tell from the rows they had that money was getting low. He'd kind of got his hopes up then that, once there was nothing left, Fergal would leave.

But instead, one day when Mum was at the off-licence, Fergal began to swear again about having to raise a dirty little towel-head. And Rasher had gone on a rampage through the house.

He didn't know how long it lasted, but when he'd stopped hitting things he'd looked round and seen the devastation. The telly was smashed and so was the couch, and he'd thrown Mum's laptop at the mirror in the living room. Upstairs, her bedroom looked like a bombsite and downstairs half the stuff in the kitchen was on the floor.

Fergal had made for the door as soon as the furniture started flying, but Rasher had known he wouldn't call the guards. There was no way he could face Mum when she came back, though.

So, he'd taken the roll of twenties Fergal kept upstairs with his stash and, with a vague notion of selling it, robbed the weed as well. Then he'd shoved some clothes and his passport into a backpack and taken off. And on his first night on the Dublin streets he'd given the weed away to a guy who'd threatened him with a knife.

Chapter Twenty-One

Una McCarthy cracked an egg into the sizzling frying pan and, having given it a shake, turned to the sausages under the grill. It was seven a.m., the day promised to be fine, and Conor and Joe would soon be in for their breakfast. She'd propped the back door open as soon as she'd begun her work in the kitchen: there was no fear of field mice running in at this time of year and anyway Marmite was curled on his chair by the range. Having begun life as a barn cat and a famous mouser, he was getting more domesticated in his old age. Nevertheless, he remained lord of the farmyard, and even the rats still kept their distance, as if word of his exploits had become part of their folklore and they knew better than to approach his realm.

Though the ginger kittens had hardly been in the house ten days, they, too, had learned to respect him. When Una crossed the sunlit kitchen, she could see four bright eyes peeping out from under the range. In a week or so they'd be old enough to be banished up to the sheds to hunt for their food; right now, they were anticipating their breakfast, knowing that when Marmite had eaten his they'd get their own share of the scraps she'd place on a tin plate in the yard.

Una smiled, thinking of how pleased Aideen had been to hear

that the kittens were staying. Whether or not they'd let her touch them when they'd gone up to the barn and the sheds, and were practically feral, was another matter. But Marmite, now that he'd taken to his chair, was willing to accept a certain amount of petting, and Aideen was as soft-hearted about old age as she was about the fuzzy babies mewing under the range.

As she moved from the dresser to the table, laying out plates and cutlery, Una glanced at Paddy, who was sitting opposite Marmite, reading the *Farmer's Journal*. He was far too sedentary for a man of his age, but what could he do? Chronic pain and depression made for a miserable combination, and on bad days, which could stretch into weeks, he couldn't even face going out for an evening in the local where, because of his medication, he wasn't allowed his pint.

There was the sound of the tap being turned on in the yard and vigorous splashing as Conor and Joe cleaned their boots. When they came into the kitchen in their stockinged feet Bid, the sheepdog, stuck her nose round the door. To Una's dismay, Paddy scowled at the sight of the enquiring, furry face. Getting to his feet, he snarled, 'Geddout, you,' with such force that the dog, who'd never been known to cross a threshold uninvited, jerked back with a yelp. Aware that the rest of his family was carefully avoiding comment, Paddy went and sat at the table and asked where his breakfast was. Conor watched as Una controlled her face with an effort and turned back to the pan.

They'd all become so used to such moments that their shared responses were both dulled and heightened, the sharp sense of each other's distress routinely smothered by the need to act as if nothing untoward had happened. The fact that Paddy was frequently guilt-stricken didn't help matters either. Now only Bid reacted without constraint: bewildered by this injustice from the master who had trained her, she continued to whimper pathetically outside the door.

As he joined his dad at the table, Conor wondered if it was wise to say what he and Joe had been doing. As sometimes happened, they'd set out that morning with one job in mind and been sidetracked by another. It was a case of taking a decision promptly to avoid wasting time and they'd both known that, if Paddy had been with them, he'd have made the same call. The trouble was that Paddy could flip if he heard you hadn't stuck to what had been agreed. It was just frustration and mostly he said sorry afterwards, but neither Conor nor Joe could bear to see him humiliated by the need to apologise.

Sometimes Paddy was relaxed enough about the role they'd agreed to call farm manager. There was plenty of planning and form-filling to be done, and masses of changing government regulations that someone had to keep tabs on or they'd all be up the creek. Things had been difficult immediately after the accident, because Joe had already transferred the management stuff from paper to digital and Paddy hadn't been handy with the computer. He'd gone on a course, though, and properly got to grips with it. And, while it wouldn't be Paddy's way to say so, Conor reckoned his dad was proud of what he'd managed to achieve.

But the bottom line was that a real farm manager didn't just sit in behind a desk. Not on a farm their size anyway. He'd be operating machinery too, or overseeing maintenance, or standing in a muddy field talking to a vet. Paddy couldn't even get himself up on a tractor without his back going crazy, and even when he was just out walking, on bad days he'd have to use a stick.

Sometimes the kind of irritation he'd shown to the dog was a sign of a bad day to come. But as Mum put the sausages and eggs onto the table you could see him making the effort to give her a smile. Relaxing, Conor told him they'd found a few yards of fence down and got it fixed before getting on with the ear-tagging. It was a mobile-library day, so Joe was going to be finishing up there, then tailing the lambs, while Conor was on the road.

Paddy shrugged. 'You did right, I suppose. Well, you couldn't do otherwise. Did you say Aideen was coming for her tea this evening?'

It was great the way Aideen always seemed to lift Paddy's mood. Often he'd complain that he'd been awake half the night, and stump off to bed in the evening before they'd sit down to their tea. But if Aideen was coming he'd usually make the effort to stay up. There were even times when he'd hardly speak a word all day long and she'd manage to have him chatting before she left. Old Dawson's injection of money was going to make a big difference on the farm, and two full-time workers instead of one and a half would be great. But Conor's mum had told him a while back that the thought of Aideen as part of the household was the thing about the double wedding that pleased Paddy most.

When they'd finished breakfast Conor got a couple more hours in with Joe before setting off for Carrick on his Vespa. He left the bike in a staff placc in the County Library car park and picked up the keys of the van at Reception. Today his route would take him along the southern side of the peninsula. The landscape was gentler there but the roads were just as narrow as those through the foothills of Knockinver to the north. Among the books in the back of the van was a copy of *Brooklyn*, which had been returned by a borrower and was now going out to the classroom assistant of the school in the seaside village that was his first stop.

Kids were playing in the May sunshine as he cruised downhill towards the school. Beyond the yard there was a little pier and a narrow cove where gulls and gannets floated above jade-green waves. As Conor pulled in by the school gate, the children formed a straggling queue, and Marian, the classroom assistant, came to greet him.

It was a two-room national school, exactly like the one that Conor had been to himself, and it had two entrances to the lobby, with 'Girls' carved on the lintel over one and 'Boys' over the other. One of these was now blocked by wheelie bins and clearly hadn't been used for some time. As Conor jumped down to open the van, a stream of kids of both sexes appeared on the steps of the other door and ran into the yard. For the next while he was fully occupied taking returns, handing out loans and listening to enthusiastic critiques of books the kids had just read.

One small girl confided in a throaty whisper that *I Want My Hat Back* by Jon Klassen was the best book in the world. 'Actually, not just the world. The universe. The *galaxy*. Honestly, Conor, you have to read it. It's seriously great.'

'What's it about?'

'A bear. He's lost his hat. And nobody anywhere in the whole world has seen it.'

'So what happens?'

'Well, I can't tell you that, can I? If I did you'd know the end.'

'But sometimes that doesn't matter. People read books over and over. Especially if they like them.'

'Yes, but the first time is the *best* because it keeps you in suspense.'

Marian winked at Conor over the little girl's head. 'We learned that word in reading class yesterday, didn't we, Shauna?'

The child looked conspiratorially at Conor and lowered her voice even further. 'Actually, I knew it already but I didn't want to be rude.'

Having delighted Shauna by offering to bring her Klassen's *This Is Not My Hat* next time, Conor dealt with the rest of the kids and the few adults who'd joined them, and set off in the van for his next stop. Making his way back up the hill from the village, he told himself that he really ought to read *Brooklyn*. Marian now had one of the last copies for loan from a Finfarran library but he could whip in and borrow it when she returned it. It'd be good to have it read before the next film club discussion, especially as Miss Casey had known damn well that he hadn't read *Death in Venice* when he'd stood up last time and dissed Mr Maguire.

What with the farm and the library, it wasn't easy to find time for reading. Maybe if there was an audiobook he could get that and play it as he made his rounds in the van. The thing was that every spare minute he had was spent with Aideen, and when he stayed over at her place they didn't exactly sit around analysing books. The other night, when he'd been there, Bríd had started teasing, saying they'd be totally jaded before they got to the altar. According to her, the fashionable thing now was to take a sexcation before you went off and got married.

'A what?'

'Like a vacation or a staycation.' Bríd had made big eyes at Aideen. 'It's a total break from having sex.'

'That's mad.'

'No, it's not. It makes the wedding more romantic and exciting.'

'So how long is a sexcation supposed to last?'

'Don't ask me. I'm not an expert. You could Google it.'

'Yeah, right. Like you haven't made it up.'

They did Google it later and found that, instead of being a break from sex, it meant the exact opposite. Basically, you went to bed together and didn't get up for weeks. Which Bríd had probably known all along.

Now, driving between hawthorn hedges loaded with white flowers, Conor remembered Aideen lying on her stomach with her laptop on a flower-patterned pillow, and the look she'd given him when she read out the Google definition. There was nothing more romantic or exciting than Aideen's bedroom when she'd lit candles on the dressing table and poured wine into the long-stemmed glasses they'd bought when they were in Florence.

They hadn't done much more talking that night, though the following day Aideen had told him that they'd need to get themselves sorted fairly soon. Apparently Eileen was being a dork about how they'd organise the wedding so, at some stage, they'd have to sit down and thrash the whole thing out with her and Joe. According to Aideen, they'd better get Bríd and Jazz there too, and make a plan before Eileen lost the run of herself entirely.

Wrapped in dreams of Aideen's bed reflected in her flickering dressing-table mirror, Conor happily steered the van towards his next destination. Sooner or later he'd probably get around to reading *Brooklyn*. And it'd be time enough to get wedding stuff fixed when he and Joe had the muck and the fertiliser spread, the cattle off the silage, and the last of the lambs castrated.

Chapter Twenty-Two

Midges were dancing in shafts of sunlight as Hanna drove home from the library. There were swifts nesting in a cattle shed near the corner where she turned off the motorway, and the light on their wings almost dazzled her as they swooped past her windscreen catching insects. This meandering back road, which led to her house and the fields around it, delighted her. At this time of evening, after the thundering rush-hour traffic on the motorway, its tranquillity was almost startling.

On the seaward side, where the fields were narrow and sloped to the cliff-edge, not much thrived without constant care and protection. Hanna could remember Maggie stumping down to her newly made potato ridges, carrying seaweed hauled from the beach by a farmer who'd taken annual pity on his elderly, bad-tempered neighbour. In Maggie's childhood every cliff field here had had its stone cabin; and households, often composed of three generations, were fed with the produce of those salt-scoured strips of land. Now Hanna's was the only remaining house on the cliff side of the road and the little fields around it had long regressed to scrubland.

On the opposite side the land, which was better, was protected by high, earthen ditches. The former patchwork of stone-walled plots had disappeared, and larger fields had been established, wide enough to support bigger herds or be worked by machinery. Hanna could see cows gathering by gates as she passed, ready to be herded back to farmyards for milking.

Up ahead, where there was a pull-in by her own gate, she saw a red van she recognised at once as Fury O'Shea's. As she drew in behind it, The Divil appeared round the gable of the house. His demeanour was proprietorial. Back when Hanna had restored Maggie's place, Fury had been her builder and, as always happened when he worked on a house, he and The Divil continued to treat it as if it belonged to him, rather than to her.

Walking down the path at the side of the house with the little dog behind her, Hanna saw Fury at the end of the field staring up at her roof. She moved down to meet him, the waving fronds of tasselled grass almost touching her elbows. Except for the herb rockery and a couple of flower beds close to the house, this year she'd allowed the field to turn into a meadow. Now it was starred with wildflowers, and full of the quiet drone of bees and insects. Millions of small, noisy lives were being lived out all around her and, though Maggie would certainly have castigated the waste of a good vegetable plot, the sense of busy wildness enchanted Hanna.

'How well you didn't call me out earlier!'

Fury was standing with his back to the ocean glaring up at her roof. A ridge tile had come off in a storm a couple of months ago, and though Brian had offered to borrow ladders and fix it, Hanna had known she'd not be forgiven if he did. It was still Fury's roof and no one else could touch it. She'd also known that phoning

Fury was useless. He never picked up calls or responded to texts on his mobile, so the only way to summon him was to engage in a process he always referred to as 'putting out the word'.

When she'd first encountered him, this had driven her to distraction. Accustomed to employing tradesmen in London, the thought of mentioning a vital repair to the postman or the hairdresser and waiting for Fury to pick it up on the grapevine had seemed absurd. In time, however, she'd discovered it worked and, though they'd fought like a bag of weasels to begin with, he was now someone she thought of as a friend.

Propping herself on the wall beside him, she looked up at her roofline, where the missing ridge tile showed like a broken tooth. 'I told Brian weeks ago to let you know it was off.'

'And I suppose it's smashed to bits too, is it? You never told him to tell me I'd need a replacement.'

'Actually, it's not. I found it next morning.'

Leading him up the field to the shed, she produced the terracotta ridge tile. 'See? Slightly chipped but absolutely fine.'

Fury sniffed dismissively. 'I'll be the judge of that.' He turned the tile in his hands and said he'd be round to fix it tomorrow. 'I've no roof ladder in the van now and I'm not risking me neck without one. So you'll have to wait.'

Hanna, who'd waited patiently for weeks and had just been accused of failing to act promptly, smiled and asked if he fancied a mug of tea.

Fury glanced down at The Divil and shrugged. 'Maybe. If you're making one. You'll have a saucer for himself.'

'Does he still take sugar?'

'No, he had to give it up. The vet said he'd have his teeth ruined. I'd say he'd take a biscuit, though, if you happen to have one to hand.'

Indoors, she put the kettle on and made tea while Fury wandered round inspecting things. The Divil settled down with his nose in the silken ashes of last night's fire. Having fiddled with window locks and frowned at a light switch, Fury considered the dresser by the chimney breast, which filled its alcove, reaching from floor to ceiling, a solid piece of hand-built furniture made of driftwood collected from the beach. With cracked glazed doors and jammed drawers, it had been in a sad, shabby state by the time Hanna inherited it, and she'd thought of pulling it out and installing shelving instead. But Fury had refurbished it without consulting her and sanded back the grubby paint to reveal the original colour underneath. 'And, as it happened I had the makings of it back in my shed so I mixed it for you.'

Faced with the fait accompli, Hanna had blinked. It was a peculiar shade, somewhere between wine and brick red, which clashed violently with the rest of her colour scheme. To begin with she'd said nothing, planning to repaint it in dove grey as soon as the place was finished and Fury was gone. Later, and to her surprise, she'd come to welcome the jarring colour as a continuing token of Maggie's acerbic presence in the house.

Fury had observed her initial reaction with a shrewd glance and no comment, and they'd never spoken of it since. Now he remarked casually that the paint was wearing well. Hanna nodded. In fact, it had darkened with time to a more acceptable muddy brown.

Fury cocked an eyebrow at her. 'I could always slap on another coat, though, if you wanted one.'

Refusing to rise to the bait, Hanna bent down to scratch The Divil's back and asked if all was going well at Brian's.

Fury shot her an appreciative glance. 'Did no one ever tell you builders are like doctors? We never discuss a case.'

Hanna said nothing. Having lived through a project with Fury herself, she wasn't sure whether he or Brian was more deserving of sympathy. Though, since they were both professionals and she'd been a rank amateur, it could be that they enjoyed their apparently endless running battles.

The integrity of the Hag's Glen site seemed to be a constant flashpoint and, looking at it objectively, Hanna could see why. Fury took perverse delight in casting Brian as a woolly-minded romantic and himself as a put-upon pragmatist. The truth lay somewhere in the middle. Each was sensitive both to the beauty of the glen and the ruins among which Brian's house was emerging. But Fury had long ago learned the value of assuming a volatility that gave him the upper hand. In his view, a craftsman's contribution far exceeded that of the mere employer who paid his wages so, for a job to be done properly, the balance of power needed to be redressed.

According to Brian, a major part of an architect's skill was understanding the psychology of his builder. 'Fury was working on sites in London before I was born. You've got to respect that, even if he's slightly behind on the use of contemporary materials.'

'Slightly?'

'Okay, completely.' Brian had grinned. 'But I can't diss a

lifetime of experience. It might have been a good while back but, you know, he worked on buildings that are London icons. And he catches up on things incredibly fast. You can see the wheels going round like mad behind the supercilious face.'

Leaving The Divil to lap his tea, Hanna looked at Fury. 'Did you know there's a book that's a biography of London? It's a huge bestseller.'

'I did not. But I know a daft notion when I hear one. How would you write a biography of a place?'

'Well, that's the point. Ackroyd, the guy who wrote it, perceives London as a city full of shadows of people who built it and lived there in the past. He calls it "echoic".'

'He does, of course.' Fury looked round aggressively. 'Where's the poor Divil's custard cream?'

Custard creams had always been available when he'd been working on Maggie's place, but Hanna knew she had none in the house now. Remembering that her last packet of biscuits had been bought when Jazz was visiting, she asked if The Divil might fancy a Blueberry and Orange Seedy Crunch.

'Why call it a biography if it's really a class of a history?'

Hanna crumbled a biscuit into The Divil's tea. 'Well, because he goes further ...'

'Don't you know he does?'

'... and sees the city itself as having personality. Well, landscapes holding specific memories that, over time, became the characteristics of each place. Actually, no, it's more than that. Because what he suggests is that urban landscapes affect people who live in them. And that people respond to landscape according to associations that have been made with particular places in the past.'

Fury's face assumed precisely the supercilious expression Brian had described.

Hanna pressed on. 'Okay, look, I'm putting this badly. There's another guy, Alan Garner. He started as a children's author. I thought of him when I first saw the Hag's Glen. He went on to write adult books. There's one called *Thursbitch*.'

'Right. Good title.'

'He has this thing about "sentient landscape". That there are places where the land remembers what happened there in the past. And people can feel it.'

'Well, sure, everyone knows that.'

'They do?'

'Isn't that what haunted houses are about? And uncanny places where locals won't go at night? And isn't it the same with sites people call sacred? Say, holy wells. Did you ever notice how Christian churches got built on top of Roman temples?'

'Well, yes, that's what Ackroyd writes about ...'

'There's a church now in London, called St Bride's. I worked on a site near it when I was over there as a lad. That has six earlier churches underneath it, and a Roman temple beneath that again. And the St Bride it's dedicated to is St Bridget. Well, there you are! Aren't half the holy wells you'll find called after St Bridget? And most of them belonged to some pagan goddess long before she came along. But of course you haven't noticed. Nobody does.'

'Well, Garner and Ackroyd ...'

Tipping more tea into his mug, Fury waved his hand at

Maggie's dresser. 'You never noticed the hell I went through and I putting down your blasted slate floor.'

Hanna remembered the standoff they'd had when he was installing her kitchen. Maggie's floor had been of cement laid over the original earth floor of the house. Fury had insisted that Hanna would want timber flooring, because the slate tiles she'd told him she wanted would be far too cold underfoot. In the end, she'd won the battle, and her floor, with its uneven surface and multicoloured patches, was one of the things she now loved most about the house.

Under Fury's accusing eye, she went to look at the section that ran under Maggie's dresser. Kneeling down to inspect it closely, she realised that the tiles had been carefully cut to accommodate the dresser, the top of which touched the ceiling, while the feet still stood on Maggie's cement beneath the stone.

'You try cutting Chinese slate with that kind of precision. I'll have you know I nearly burned out the angle grinder, and I totally buggered me disc.'

'You're right, I never noticed.'

'People never do.'

By way of inadequate compensation, Hanna returned to the table and offered him milk. The Divil immediately raised his head and she hastily took the teapot to his saucer. As she was trying to fill it while avoiding the little dog's quivering whiskers, she frowned and looked up at Fury. 'But how come you didn't take the feet off the dresser? If you had, it wouldn't have been too tall, and you could have just stood it on the slate.'

'Holy God, woman, would you look at the size of it? How

did you expect me to lift it out or, for that matter, get it back? Or deal with the fact that the ceiling would probably come down if I moved it at all?' Having vented his usual outrage, Fury shrugged defensively. 'Anyway, like yer men say, places carry stories. Don't you feel Maggie here yourself sometimes? The same thing will happen when you move on and make way for the next person. And whatever poor bastard comes to change that floor or shift that dresser will be able to tell that, in my time, I was here too.'

Chapter Twenty-Three

The table in Jazz's office was scattered with paperwork, the residue of a long and successful meeting. Don, in charge of production, had given a presentation that had managed to be exciting as well as detailed; Saira had talked about plans for a follow-up to the range of rosemary hair products; and Jazz herself had shared rough layouts of the new advertising material that incorporated photos of local suppliers. As usual, Louisa, who'd sat in on the meeting, hadn't said much but as the door closed behind Don and his assistant, she pushed back her chair and smiled at Jazz. 'You know, I really am pleased with how we're progressing. Don was a real find!'

Jazz had met Don almost by accident when she was checking out local markets nearly a year ago. He'd been running his own small business selling herbal products and, after a chat, he'd seemed to her to be a perfect fit for Edge of the World Essentials. When Louisa had met him, she'd liked him too, and, instead of advertising the place that needed filling, had gone with her gut instinct and employed him. Having been used to running a one-man band, the job had been a step up for Don in terms of scale and admin, but he'd risen to the challenge.

Jazz shuffled the layouts together. 'These are good too, don't you think?'

'I think they're charming.'

'Well, they're not down to me. It was Saira's idea.'

'Don't worry, you made that clear at the meeting. And that's the point, isn't it? We're building a team of individuals. I'm glad you were open to her input.'

Jazz held up a photo of an elderly man beaming into the camera with his arms full of marigolds. 'Doesn't Johnny Hennessy look like a star?'

Johnny, who was Mary Casey's neighbour, spent most of his time growing herbs and vegetables in his garden, and in the three big polytunnels he'd built behind his house. Jazz could remember him from childhood holidays at the bungalow, when she and her granddad would amble round in the evenings for a chat by Johnny's back door. He had wide-set, brilliant blue eyes in a deeply seamed face, and a tweed cap worn at a rakish angle. Following instructions, the photographer had posed him in the garden and, judging by Johnny's huge, gap-toothed smile, had known just how to relax him in front of a camera.

Louisa picked up a stack of shots of a little girl with a snub nose and cheeky smile. 'I think this "meet our growers" idea is splendid.'

'Those shots are really just there to indicate possibilities. Like I said at the meeting, her parents will be selling us camomile so, once this year's crop is established, we could go for an image of the kid surrounded by flowers.'

'Perfect.' Louisa stood up and reached for her handbag. 'I'd say let's have lunch but I promised I'd drive Mary into Carrick.'

'Give her my love.'

'Of course.'

There was a pause before Louisa spoke again. 'Have you heard from your dad lately?'

'Dad? No. But I haven't been expecting to. Why? Is he okay?'

'I haven't heard from him myself since I got back from London.'

Jazz frowned. 'Well, were *you* expecting to?'

'No.' Louisa straightened her shoulders briskly. 'I wasn't. Or, at least, I'm rather hoping I won't.' Seeing Jazz's troubled look, she laughed. 'We haven't fallen out! Nothing like that. I'm just a little concerned he may be at a loss for occupation. And you know what your father's like when he gets bored.'

Jazz knew only too well. That was why Mum had found the weekend retreat in Norfolk, where there was sailing and fishing and room for house parties. The Norfolk place had been sold when the divorce went through, and since then, Jazz had assumed, Dad's weekends had been taken up with whatever his latest girlfriend had demanded. Dining in Biarritz, possibly, or speeding round Paris in his male-menopause car. But, by the sound of things, he was without someone to keep him entertained. 'He's not planning to come on a visit, is he?'

'No.' Louisa sounded worryingly uncertain. 'No, I shouldn't think so.'

Jazz swung her bag onto her shoulder. 'Because I haven't got time to entertain him if he does.'

'Well, neither have I. And nor has your mother.'

'Oh, damn! He *is* planning to come, Louisa, isn't he?'

'Truly, dear, he didn't say so. But I do have misgivings.'

'Well, I hope you'll ring and tell him we're all up to our ears. Where would he stay, anyway? Not with you and Mary?'

Louisa laughed. 'There's no room at the bungalow. And even if there were I think he knows that he wouldn't be welcome. Mary's been remarkably careful in my presence, but I've no illusions about her opinion of Malcolm.'

'Where, then?'

'Carrick, I suppose. I shouldn't think he'd settle for anything less than The Royal Vic.'

'You're not just having misgivings, are you? You're pretty sure he's coming.'

'Well, if he does, dear, he'll have to fend for himself.'

As she crossed the garden on her way to the café, Jazz decided that she simply couldn't be bothered to think about Dad. The meeting had run late and she now had only half an hour for lunch.

It was a warm, windy day and one of the tables outside the café was standing in a suntrap so, leaving her jacket on the back of a chair to claim it, she whisked inside to get a sandwich. Then, as she sat down to eat, she realised she was the only person who seemed to be lunching alone. Briefly, she was stabbed by a dreadful longing for Sam. Everyone around her was either part of a group, one of a couple, or obviously waiting for a friend. The groups were chatting and laughing loudly, each person waiting seemed cheerful and expectant, and all the couples appeared to be holding hands.

For a moment or two Jazz tried to feel like a confident businesswoman, languidly sipping coffee with no need to do anything else. Leaning back in the rattan chair, she extended her legs sideways with her ankles crossed, like a film star, and rested her elbow casually on the table. Then, unable to find a convincing expression, she gave up on nonchalance and groped in her bag for *Brooklyn*. She was well into it by now, anyway, and fascinated by the differences between the book and the film.

After another few minutes, during which she was distracted by the need to keep avocado off the book's pristine pages, she finished her sandwich, wiped her fingers, and lost herself in the story, not raising her head again until someone approached the table with a tray. 'D'you mind if I join you?'

Slightly irritated, Jazz looked up and saw that all the tables around her were occupied. Then she recognised the guy who'd fallen over her feet when she'd been reading on the cliff. 'Oh, hi. Yes, no, of course ... sit down. It's nice to see you again.'

'But you're reading.'

'Yes, but it doesn't matter. I mean, it's only because one sometimes feels a fool eating alone.'

'Do you? I don't.' He balanced the tray on his knee, then moved his mug and plate onto the round table. His question, which might have sounded arrogant, appeared to be a genuine enquiry so Jazz grinned.

'Don't you? God, that's depressing, maybe it's a woman thing.'

'Or it could just be that I've got a brass neck.'

Johnny Hennessy, Jazz remembered, always called it 'a neck like a jockey's arse'.

Mike didn't seem to have a brass neck, though. More a steady air of containment, which Jazz continued to find vaguely familiar.

Deftly removing the cellophane from his sandwich, he asked if she was still enjoying *Brooklyn*.

'Massively. I keep wanting to talk to the guys who made the film, though. Like, last night I read the bit where Eilis is helping at the Christmas party in New York. You know, the community hall scene, with down-and-outs and knackered builders? Irish-American emigrants with nowhere else to spend Christmas Day?'

'Yeah. All smoky browns and greys, and guys getting drunk and falling asleep on their plates.'

'That's the bit. And in the film you get Iarla Ó Lionáird being a bloke in a cap who stands up and sings 'Casadh an tSúgáin'.'

'Is that what it's called? I remember something in Gaelic. Very powerful.'

'You call the language "Irish", not "Gaelic", but that's not the point. In the book Eilis finds herself drawn to the man. She nearly goes up and touches him because he reminds her so vividly of her dead father. And then when he sings he holds her hand.'

'Doesn't that happen in the film?'

'Yeah, you can see she's really moved but, if you hadn't read the book, you wouldn't know she's thinking of her father. Well, I dunno, I didn't. It was just sort of intense, distilled emotion.'

'Brilliant scene, though.'

'God, yeah. And you can hear the actual song, which is what produces the effect. But I wonder why they didn't focus on the link with her father. It seems to me that underpins what the book's all about.'

'I guess what happens when you're making a film is you shoot a lot of footage, and in your head you've got a narrative. But when you see what you've captured, you sometimes find that it's saying something else. Offering a different story.'

'You don't think they stick to a given script?'

'Well, there's masses of different ways to read a line or shoot a scene.'

'That's true.' Jazz put *Brooklyn* back in her bag. 'How's your own filming going?'

'My pathetic two-minute clips? Good. Really good, actually. Not pathetic at all. I met your mother this morning.'

'My mother? Why?'

'I went to the library to ask if I could do something on the Carrick Psalter. A bit in the exhibition, maybe vox pops with people in the queue. Your mum says there are illustrations in the psalter showing features in the landscape that can still be seen today.'

Jazz nodded. 'I know. It's cool. You can see the shape of Knockinver, and some of the coastline. And there's a huge rock that's still there in the forest. Some medieval monk working on the psalter must have known it, because he used it on the page that illustrates the Twenty-third Psalm.'

'Well, I'm thinking of demonstrating that you can visit the exhibition, and then travel round afterwards to places you've already seen in the book.'

'You'd need longer than two minutes to get that across, though?'

'I could probably do it in seven. Maybe five. It'd be harder to sell than a shorter piece, perhaps. But maybe not. Tourism websites are full of clips of lush-looking scenery. Travel porn, really – well, Bali Ha'i maxed up to the nth degree.'

'That bit about people longing for another island?' It was an echo from the song 'Bali Ha'i' which had come back to her from nowhere.

'Exactly. No place in particular. Just somewhere other than where they are now. Some place offering bigger dreams and more potential.' He turned to her and his eyes were very bright. 'I might do this, you know. It could sell. It'd be something specific and unique.'

'I think it sounds super.'

'Really?' Finishing his coffee, Mike stretched his arms above his head. 'It'd mean I'd have to stay round here a bit longer.'

'Would that be a problem?'

'Not at all. My time's my own, and I guess you could say that I came to Ireland looking for something.'

'And now you think you've found it?'

'Just in the last couple of days it's looking like I have.'

Chapter Twenty-Four

Rasher walked down the covered passage, turned left, and realised he'd been there before. There was a row of wheelie bins at the far side of the yard beside a long stretch of grating. Back in January, he remembered, when the weather had been awful, he'd slept behind those bins, warmed by a constant stream of air from below. He'd had two nights of relative comfort and safety before a bloke came out one morning and drenched him in freezing water by hosing down the bins.

He wasn't certain if the bloke had seen him lying there in his sleeping bag or if it had been an accident. Anyway, he'd known better than to get up and ask. Wide awake and shivering, he'd kept his head covered, hoping your man hadn't noticed him and, as soon as he'd got a chance, he'd scuttled away. There'd been no point in taking the sodden sleeping bag so he'd spent the day scavenging for another, and managed to find one, wadded in a dark doorway, just before it got really cold that night. His clothes had dried as he'd walked the streets, but by nightfall he was still shivering all over. It was the following morning that he'd woken up with flu.

There was a big double door saying 'STAFF ENTRANCE' not far from the bins. Rasher pressed the bell by the notice, like he'd been told to, and waited for a voice on the intercom to tell him to come in.

He hadn't known what you'd wear to be interviewed at a place called The Royal Victoria, but the Khan one had said a kitchen porter just needed to be clean and neat. Rasher had decided off his own bat that a hoodie would give the wrong impression so he'd worn a shirt with his jeans. The whiter-than-white trainers looked like a couple of searchlights after he'd gone at them with a nailbrush, and he was wearing a brand new pair of socks, the second in the pack of two he'd got from Martin. The jeans were still far too big but he'd hitched them up with a belt.

Mindful of the need to look super-scrubbed, he'd gone a bit mad at the shaving and ended up giving himself a cut. Still, there was a bottle of aftershave called 'Edge For Men' in the washbag he'd got from Martin, so he smelled good. Fergal had used some foul goo with a name like 'Wolf' or something, and, no matter what bathroom stuff Mum had bought for him, Dad always smelt of the pharmacy. Edge For Men was good, though. Kind of spicy and discreet. According to the Khan woman, it was made by Edge of the World Essentials, the crowd she worked for. They'd given a box of samples to Martin who, by the sound of things, was the best blagger on God's green earth.

The intercom buzzed and a foreign-sounding voice told Rasher to come in. He was met inside by a guy about his age, and taken upstairs and along a corridor to a room where the guy gave the door a knock. It opened and Rasher went into a room that seemed awfully bright. The corridors had had dim strip lighting, but here there was a desk in front of a big window, with a woman sitting behind it on a chair. She was wearing a black uniform suit, and a shirt with what his mum had always called a pussycat bow.

When Rasher came in the woman walked round the desk to shake his hand. This would have been unexpected except that the Khan woman had warned him it might happen, and told him what was needed was a firm, assured grip. He had a feeling his hand was a bit too sweaty for assurance but Pussycat Bow looked him up and down and indicated a chair. They sat down opposite each other, and Rasher attempted to look bright without seeming too eager.

The next chunk of time was a blur. She asked questions and he must have answered them but, afterwards, he couldn't remember a thing he'd said. It must have been okay, though, because she stood up eventually and said she was sure he'd fit in with The Royal Vic's team ethos. Rasher said he hoped so, and wondered if it meant he'd got the job.

'Right. Well, I'll take you down to the kitchen to meet our chef, Anton. And I suppose you'd like to see the accommodation.'

He followed her down a bunch of other corridors and waited while she opened a door and stood back to let him go in.

'As I said, our kitchen requires two porters and in the off-season there's normally only full-time work for one. But, obviously, we're going into our high season now, and I understand that live-in is your preference?'

Rasher said it was.

'Good. You'll probably have as many hours as you choose to work. I mean, overtime and night work if you want it. And this would be your room.'

It was much the same size as the one in the halfway house. Everything was a bit older, though, and more solid. The window, which was really big, overlooked the yard and the wheelie bins, and the grating where he'd once slept. Literally a case of coming up in the world. There was a bed with built-in shelves and drawers beside it, a wardrobe against the other wall, a table and chair under the window. Out of the corner of his eye he could see that the door had a lock.

'It's grand. Very nice.'

'So, let's take you down to meet Anton.'

They went down in a lift that was a bit scruffy, with marks on the walls where things had been banged in and out. As they emerged, Pussycat Bow showed him the staff lounge. It had sofas and armchairs and a big telly, all slightly knackered-looking. Peering through the doorway, Rasher thought about his mum's front room with its two-seater couch and footstool, and matching lounge chair. Last time he'd seen it, the couch had had a huge stain on the cushions, where he'd chucked Fergal's curry the day he'd gone berserk.

He'd never spoken to anyone about what had happened that day. He didn't plan to, either. Just thinking about it made him cringe — worrying about Mum and half wishing the bastard Fergal had left her, then panicking that, if he had, she'd be left all alone. In his first few months on the streets he'd kept having nightmares about her sitting on the stained couch with no one there to mind her. That was another reason he'd gone hitching down the country. Just to get away. He'd soon found that you couldn't run from nightmares. All the same, he knew he couldn't go home while he was a minor. Because the chances were that, if he did, he'd end up in care.

He still couldn't fathom the Khan woman. Sometimes she came across like a social worker, and Rasher would sit there waiting for her to start asking personal questions. She hadn't done yet, though. Instead she'd talked about daft things like herbs. She'd told him that, when she'd volunteered in the Lissbeg garden, she'd read a book in the local library, written by some nun. 'It's a history of the garden. Not old, because the convent is only Victorian and the book seems not to have been written until the garden was well established. It shows all the beds and the layout, though, and what used to be planted there before it got overgrown. With drawings and diagrams and notes. We used it as a manual when we restored the garden. The woman who got the project going was a lay sister in the convent.'

Rasher had got half interested. 'What's a lay sister?'

'She'd worked in the garden and the kitchens.'

'Like a chef?'

'More like a servant, I think. Nuns needed a dowry to be accepted into the order. If you had no money you entered the convent and worked.'

'Did she cook, though?'

'Yes. And she grew food. She was very knowledgeable.'

'And she read it all up in a library?'

'I doubt if Sister Michael ever spent much time in a library. She was given the book when they put her to work.'

'So how come the garden got all overgrown?'

'Well, the school and the convent closed. Sister Michael and another elderly nun were the only two still in residence. They were given a retirement flat there when it still belonged to the Church.'

Rasher reckoned it was just as well that the place had shut down. He'd heard plenty about care homes run by nuns, and what went on in them. Priests and brothers too, all beating the shite out of kids. It was part of the reason he'd stayed as far away as he could from Social Services. You'd never know what might happen to you if you found yourself in the hands of the Church or the state.

It seemed like Mrs Khan had got on with Sister Michael, though, so he didn't comment. And maybe the poor old nun was a decent skin. Actually, by the sound of it, she'd been shoved around a fair bit herself. Maybe not actually beaten but, chances were, treated like shite.

All the chat about convents had got him nervous, so he'd doubled back to talking about the book. 'Is it still in the library?'

'Yes. You should come and see it some time.'

Rasher had shrugged. All he knew about public libraries was that, generally speaking, you weren't thrown out if you sheltered in one from the rain. They were warm too and, at the end of a day, they threw out loads of newspapers, so they were good places to find something to put between you and the street.

Pussycat Bow had a confident walk, like she'd left school as a head girl and was on her way to becoming Head of Everything. You could tell they were approaching the kitchen by the great smell and the deafening clatter. There was a sanitiser on the wall by the door, reminding Rasher vividly of the hospital.

'They're clearing up after lunch service, so I'm sure Anton will have a moment to meet you.'

She clicked into the kitchen on her neat little heels and Rasher followed, his new trainers making sucking sounds on the flooring.

Clearly, Saira Khan had been right when she'd said that a kitchen porter was very low in the kitchen pecking order, so low that Anton hardly seemed to see Rasher was there. He nodded and shook hands okay, but he looked right through him, and it was left to Pussycat Bow to announce that she knew Rasher was going to become a valued member of the team.

Anton turned and let a roar at a guy who was scrubbing pots in some way that didn't come up to standard. Then he looked through Rasher again and asked if at last they'd managed to pull in someone who didn't balk at a night shift. 'You are going to be live-in, aren't you?'

Assuming that at this stage he'd got the job, Rasher said, yes, he was.

'Good. At least I can kick you out of bed if you start rolling in late on Monday mornings.'

Having roared at the pot-scrubbing guy again, Anton suddenly clapped Rasher on the shoulder. 'Don't panic, man, you'll be fine. Things just get a bit loud round here if people don't step up to the mark when they're needed.'

'Right. Well, that won't happen with me.'

'Good. Then I'll see you when I see you. When do you start?' He went charging off across the kitchen without waiting for an answer, which was just as well because Rasher hadn't a clue. Pussycat Bow smiled wanly and said that was all right, then. And a few minutes later, Rasher was back in the yard, with an envelope in his hand containing a roster, and the feeling that all that had just happened was part of some weird dream. He supposed he ought to get back to the house and tell Martin about it but, as he made his way back along the passage, he decided he'd cross the street first and take a proper look at the front of The Royal Victoria. You'd never know, there might come a time when he'd have his own celebrity chef television show, and be interviewed about where he'd begun his career.

Grinning at the thought, he stuck the roster into his pocket, and glanced round to check the traffic. But, just as he stepped off the pavement, a hand grabbed him by the shoulder. Even before he saw the uniform, Rasher knew it was Nugent. The big, bland face with its pale, piggy eyes glowered down at him and his stomach creased in fear.

For a minute he thought he was going to be hustled back down the passageway, accused of trespass or trying to burgle the hotel. But it seemed that the sergeant already knew that Martin had fixed him an interview because, instead, Nugent shoved him against the railings and hissed in his face, 'Respectable now, are we? Clean as a whistle and off the streets with Father feckin' Martin watching your back? Well, just remember this. If there's one thing I hate more than a lousy, stinking beggar, it's a dirty whinging scrounger getting a leg up from a priest. There's decent people up and down the length and breadth of this country that never got a handout in their life. Never asked for it and wouldn't get it if they did ask. Because of the likes of you.'

He stepped away from Rasher, brushing his hands together as

if to wipe off contamination. Then he leaned in again, and the weight of him made Rasher's legs shake.

'So you think you've fallen on your feet now but, trust me, I'll be watching you. All I need is a reason to move and you'll wish you'd never been born.'

Chapter Twenty-Five

Brian sat on his living-room floor, thinking he wouldn't miss this impersonal flat he'd chosen to live in simply because it was close to the council offices. Moving out was going to be easy, physically as well as emotionally. He'd come to Carrick with few possessions, and accumulated hardly any since he'd been here.

Looking round the bare room, with its desk, television and large, expensive armchair, he realised that the bulk of what he owned amounted to marks on paper and canvas – stacked portfolios of drawings, photos and sketches, and ridiculous numbers of books, which were also piled up on the floor.

In the first few years in his boring council job he'd walked endlessly, photographing Finfarran's beauty from every possible angle, until the walls of his rented rooms were lost under shots of majestic mountains and glorious sunsets. Eventually, when the last square of magnolia paint had disappeared under yet another study in scarlet and gold, he'd taken the photos down and lived surrounded by hundreds of pinholes, like constellations of tiny black stars. The shots of the mountains had appeared sterile, and it seemed to him that the scents and sounds central to the experience of a sunset had been lost in his efforts to stop it slipping away. So, telling himself that the exercise had been pointless, he'd thrust most of the photos into the bin.

Later he'd realised that what he'd really lost was shared experience. Life with Sandra, his wife, had been all about togetherness, so nothing had made sense without her presence, and no other human relationship could compensate for her absence when she'd died.

Confused, grieving and resentful, he'd ignored offers of friendship from colleagues in the planning office, where he was over-qualified for his job and most of the people he'd worked with had been younger than himself. Ironically, the age gap had added to his problem in ways that hadn't occurred to him when he'd chosen to take the post. The last thing he'd wanted was to be reminded of what he'd lost, but in seeking to escape from painful memories, he'd surrounded himself with colleagues whose main focus was finding love, getting married and having kids.

None of this had been clear to him until he'd met Hanna. Prickly, difficult and resentful of what life had thrown at her, she'd somehow jerked him out of his own self-absorption. To begin with, he'd been moved by nothing more than empathy, but before long, to his amazement, he'd found himself deeply in love.

In one of his portfolios there was a charcoal drawing he'd made more than a year ago. Getting up, he fetched it and took it out onto the balcony. He'd sketched it from a photo he'd taken of Hanna on their first ramble on the mountain. Softening the little wrinkles round her wide-set eyes with his thumb, he'd drawn her straight, uncompromising eyebrows, unconsciously adding the crease that appeared between them whenever she was troubled. This wasn't the open, laughing Hanna he now loved to spend time with. It was the reserved, thoughtful Hanna whom he'd first learned to love.

Shared experience had returned to his life since they'd found each other. But this time it was different, informed by what Hanna called his reticence, something which, until now, he'd felt no pressing need to examine. Why should he? He hadn't needed to. In the twenty years or so since Sandra's death, if he'd thought about his reserve at all, he'd dismissed it as a habit arising from circumstance, and one that, if it was damaging, could hurt no one but himself. But that was before Hanna.

Whenever he was alone in the flat he was conscious of her distant presence. Now, only a few miles away, she was probably working in her garden or sitting on her bench above the ocean, drinking a glass of wine. That jealously guarded space of her own meant so much to her that sometimes he wondered if she thought of him at all when they were apart. Though that, he told himself wryly, wasn't the worst of his troubles. Not now, when she might be thinking about her ex-husband.

And why should she not? Like Sandra and himself, Hanna and Malcolm had shared a life that belonged to them alone. Brian knew how deeply she'd loved Malcolm and how, even though she'd moved on, the bond between them endured because of their shared love for Jazz. Was Hanna's intense sense of privacy linked to that past life and those painful memories? If so, he, of all people, had no right to complain.

His finger moved across the paper, smoothing the crease he had drawn between her eyebrows. Her eyes were nothing like Sandra's. Her grave expression had nothing of his wife's brilliance, and the silver threads in Hanna's dark hair made Sandra, as she existed in memory, seem unnaturally young. Sandra had been young, though – younger than he was – and fragile as a fledgling bird by the time she died. Nothing of her was real now, and nothing they'd made or done together had ever seemed real without her. This was why he had cut all ties with the past. Or nearly all. Some ties came with responsibility.

Leaning on the balcony rail, holding the drawing, Brian remembered the day he and Hanna had gone for that walk on the mountain. In his first shot he'd captured a moment of stillness, her face composed and her grey eyes closed. The click of the camera's shutter had jerked them open and, in that moment, he'd taken the photo from which the sketch had been made. Somewhere in the field above them a lark had been tossing and singing, and far below on the beaches the waves were like turquoise silk. He'd known then that he didn't want to lose her, and the perfect trust in her eyes when she'd looked up into the camera lens had pierced him with a hidden stab of guilt.

Now he couldn't imagine his life without her. But did she feel the same?

Moving back into the living room, he returned the sketch to the portfolio and stacked it again with the others lining his bare walls. The house in the Hag's Glen had a custom-made desk for him to work on, and deep shelving designed to hold papers and plans. Right now, Fury O'Shea would be up there, probably trying to sneak in a splash of colour that wasn't wanted. But soon, Brian told himself, it would be finished: the final touches added, his possessions, such as they were, moved in, and the last tradesman gone. Living there, he'd be able to work out what he should do about Hanna. They couldn't go on the way they were, with so much unsaid.

The battered red van was parked outside as Brian drove up to the house. When he approached the door there was a deep growl and a burst of shrill barking, which made him smile. During the months of construction he'd been known to arrive with a bone, or the remains of a steak, and been lured into a secret pact devised by The Divil himself. Whenever Brian arrived accompanied by the smell of last night's dinner, the small, furry figure would appear without barking, take the offering silently, and vanish till it was consumed. But on foodless occasions he'd be met with snarls and aggression, as The Divil postured as the fierce guardian of the site.

Brian had imagined that Fury hadn't noticed. But one day, Fury, who'd been on his knees installing wiring, had looked up at him and winked. 'What was it this time, beef or mutton?'

It had been a ham bone, and The Divil had carried it off into the furze.

'How did you know?'

'Ah, I've known for months. It wasn't hard to work out.'

'Go on, then.'

Fury stretched his arms above his head. 'God, a man could be crippled trying to fit bloody sockets in the daft places you want them. I've had a crick in me neck all week.'

'I've told you before, get one of the lads to do it.'

'And I've told you that if anyone's recessing sockets in a timber floor of mine, it's going to be me.'

'Fine. Okay. So how did you know about the scraps?'

'Don't get me wrong, he's a sharp man, The Divil. But he doesn't always think outside the box. I got suspicious when he started to change his habits.'

'How?'

'Well, he has a great pair of ears on him, and he'd hear your car when you'd turn to drive up the glen. So, when he'd clock that, he'd dodge in to me and give me the nod in case I'd be having a fag. Then, when you'd pull up outside the house, he'd run out barking, as if he'd just realised you'd arrived.'

Fury stretched again and shrugged. 'So when you started turning up the odd time without him giving me notice, well, I knew he had to be working to some agenda of his own.'

'But if that's the case he can smell food half a mile away.'

'Looks like it, doesn't it? Unless he's got hidden cameras in your flat.'

Brian had felt rather like a guilty schoolboy. 'Would you prefer me not to feed him?'

'Not at all, he's welcome to what he can get. But don't go telling him I've rumbled him, or he won't know where to put himself. I wouldn't want us working this close to a river if the poor fella started to brood.'

'Oh. Right. Well, I won't say a word.'

He'd been rather proud of contriving to keep his face straight, but Fury had looked at him scornfully. 'Ah, would you have sense, man. He's a dog. They don't understand talking. Just don't you go behaving differently when you slip him the bit of food.'

Surprisingly, that hadn't been easy, but today, since Brian was empty-handed, the problem didn't arise.

He found Fury indoors, giving instructions to a workman who was about to go up on the roof. The airy rooms were now painted, their smooth white surfaces reflecting light exactly as Brian had intended. The kitchen appliances, which were brushed steel, produced the same luminous effect, and the open-plan layout ensured that his workspace would blend seamlessly with his living space.

Fury stood back, looking smug, and, pivoting on his heels to admire his creation, Brian's eyes came to rest on a large paint tin that was standing on a spotless dust sheet in the centre of the room. There was a decorative swirl on the lid to indicate the colour and the label on the side said 'COBALT'.

Brian stiffened. 'What's that?'

'It fell off the back of a lorry.'

'I don't give a damn where it came from, what's it doing here?'

'Well, that's a bit reprehensible, isn't it, not caring that it's nicked? Anyway, it didn't really fall off the back of a lorry. I got it off a mate.' Fury removed a roll-up from behind his ear. 'Mind you, it wasn't actually free, because I know yer man and he'll be back looking for a favour. But I'll absorb that, no bother.' He struck a match and squinted at Brian over the cigarette. 'So you've got a grand blue wall there at no cost to yourself.'

'I don't *want* a grand blue wall!'

'That's not the point, though, is it? Herself will be looking for a splash of colour.'

Brian gritted his teeth. 'You are building this house for me.'

'Well, you *say* that ...'

'I do. Repeatedly. And you'd better start listening.'

'Oh, fair enough.' Fury sauntered over and picked up the tin of paint. 'Forty-five euro that'd cost if you laid out cash.' He tilted the tin displaying the colour on the lid. 'You're a fool to yourself, do you know that? What woman could resist the hint of a sun-drenched Greek island?'

Brian gave him a basilisk glare and left the house.

Once outside, he strode down to the river, feeling he'd made a fool of himself and knowing he ought to calm down before getting behind the wheel of his car. It was a misty day and here, where the river was widest, shallow water chattered over stones and larger rocks were visible above the surface. Through the deep amber-coloured water Brian could see green weed shining on the river bed. Hunkering down, he watched foam-flecked ripples swirling round the obstacles in their path.

The water ran through his fingers like silk. Then he heard splashing and The Divil leapt out from behind a foam-fringed rock. There were droplets on his whiskers and, as he loped out of the shallow water, his wiry coat was wet and his lips drawn back. Brian reached out a hand, offering to scratch him, and The Divil opened his jaws and let something fall on the stones.

Picking it up, Brian felt a smooth surface polished by river water. For a moment he thought it was a pebble he was being asked to throw for The Divil. But it wasn't. It was a gold wedding ring.

Chapter Twenty-Six

From the moment Joe had suggested it, Conor had felt iffy about this meeting at the farmhouse. He was willing to bet that it hadn't been Joe's own idea at all. This was down to Eileen, and Joe should have had the sense to head her off. Instead he'd agreed to the six of them sitting down together – Conor and himself, the girls and the two chief bridesmaids. To make matters worse, old Dawson and his wife were due to turn up as well.

Conor had seen his mam's face when Joe broke the news that she and Paddy were expected to be there, too. If it turned out to be a bad day for Paddy, most likely the whole thing would go horribly wrong, but Una couldn't say so because Joe had made the announcement with Paddy there in the room. Not by chance either, Conor reckoned. By doing it that way he'd avoided any chance of Mam intervening. It was getting clearer day by day that when Eileen told Joe to jump he just asked how high.

Conor didn't really blame Eileen. Unless you actually lived with somebody suffering from depression, you wouldn't know how volatile things could get. There were days when Paddy's anxiety levels meant that he found it hard to cope with what the doctor called social contact. Joe knew that damn well and he shouldn't have let this happen – or at least he shouldn't have announced the plan as he had. But since the whole crowd was turning up at three, there was nothing to do now but hope for the best.

Their mam had pulled all the stops out. She'd made a cake and had it in the oven before they'd sat down to breakfast, and it was iced and on the table now, flanked by plates of biscuits and egg sandwiches. Poor old Marmite had been banished to the sheds, and the kitchen was clean as a whistle. Not that it wasn't always, but Una had gone round like a fiend this morning, polishing the range and washing the best tea set in the sink.

The sight of her doing that had set Paddy off. He wanted to know why she didn't just stick the damn ware in the dishwasher.

'Ah, I'm grand.'

'You are not. You're rushed off your feet.'

'Sure, it's nearly finished now, Paddy. It's nothing. And you can't put fine china in a dishwasher, not when it's as old as this.'

'Well, set out mugs, can't you? Or are the Dawson crowd too high-class for the likes of that?'

Most of the time Paddy was fine about the Dawsons, but every so often he decided they thought Eileen was marrying beneath her. Which was completely daft. Whatever you might say about old Dawson, he wasn't the least bit snooty. According to Joe, he never shut up about being just a small farmer's son who'd got lucky. Which was true enough, because his wife's people owned the machinery business he'd married into and built up. You couldn't find a decenter man, anywhere. And, according to gossip, you'd be hard put to meet with a nicer woman than his wife.

With the china on the table and the kettle filled, Una was

taking off her apron when the first knock came on the door. It was Aideen and Bríd with a box of pastries from the deli. They were followed ten minutes later by Jazz Turner carrying a bunch of flowers. Paddy and Joe were eyeing the food when there was barking in the yard and the Dawsons arrived in a snazzy-looking Land Rover.

As Joe went out to meet the car, Conor exchanged a quick glance with his mam. So far, things were okay. Paddy's eyes had lit up when he'd seen Aideen and, though he hadn't met Bríd before, she appeared to be going down well. He'd looked approving, too, when Jazz had praised the chocolate cake, which was topped with a crumbled Flake bar and little silver balls. Una had gone all shy and said it wasn't a patch on the pastries, and the chorus of denial had seemed to cheer Paddy no end.

The Dawsons came into the room in a flurry of chat from Eileen. She rushed into Jazz's arms and hugged her, and then pecked Una and Aideen on the cheek. Conor gave her a smile and kept his distance. He'd nothing against her but she wasn't really his style. The first time he'd met her he'd thought that maybe she was shy, and that all the bouncy stuff was just a cover-up. Since then he'd decided that what you saw was what you got. If you asked him, Bríd hadn't much time for her either, which probably wasn't ideal, but there it was.

Mrs Dawson, who said they must all call her Maura, seemed to be taking trouble to be polite. She was a lot quieter than Eileen but, all the same, with eight of them milling round the kitchen, Conor was already feeling he could do with a breather. Except for standing up to shake hands with Mrs Dawson, Paddy was staying put in his easy chair. The girls seemed to be everywhere, giving a hand to Una, while old Dawson and Joe were stood with their arses to the range.

Not quite knowing what to do with himself, Conor sidled across to the door and hooked his foot under one of the ginger kittens, sending it squeaking back into the yard. If Eileen saw it she'd probably go hyper about its cute fuzziness, and already the volume of noise looked to be stressing Paddy out.

'Come here to me, Joe, isn't this all gorgeous?' Eileen bustled over and took Joe by the arm. Then she linked her other arm through her dad's. 'D'you know what it is? I'm jealous of Aideen already! Her living in this lovely house and us going to be stuck down in Cork!'

Old Dawson winked across at Conor. 'How would you like this one for a wife, boy? Signs on it 'tis far from the farm she was reared!'

You could tell he'd only said that to tease Eileen, but Conor spotted Una shooting an anxious look at Paddy, who might well have taken it as a slight. Maura seemed to see it, too, because she intervened: 'Aren't they the lucky pair of brides to get two such handsome husbands? You must be very proud of your boys, Una, and I'd say they're great sons to you, Paddy, aren't they? We'll have a grand wedding altogether and, with any luck, a double christening as well!'

Conor saw the pair of lucky brides looking boot-faced. The thought of living their lives in perpetual tandem didn't appeal. Anyway, he and Aideen had already decided they'd wait a few years before trying for a baby; and, according to Joe, Eileen had said she wanted a bit of fun before she tied herself up to a buggy.

Things didn't get much better over the tea table. Eileen was in full flight almost before they sat down, producing her iPhone and scrolling madly through it. 'I'd no idea they did such fabulous apps for planning weddings! I mean look at these – *Bridal Joy* ... *Get Me to the Church* ... *My Dream Day* ...' She held the phone out to Una. 'See, literally everything you could want! We could set up a group log-in and get the whole thing organised with hardly another meeting.'

Jazz and Bríd both opened their mouths but Bríd got in first: 'Well, since we're all here now, let's take a step back and look at things in the round. To start with, you'll need a date.'

Eileen took an egg sandwich and looked round big-eyed. 'Well, we'll want June, won't we? I mean, who doesn't dream of being a June bride?'

Joe pulled a face. 'There's the farm workload to think about. June's a busy month.'

Eileen laughed at him. 'Ah, for God's sake, Joe, what month isn't busy on a farm? If we're putting another man in for you, can't we just hire someone else as well for the few days it'll take?'

Conor blinked. 'The few days?'

'Well, it's going to take three, at least, isn't it? Especially if we have it in Cork.' Eileen reached out helpfully and took the teapot from Una. 'Here, don't disturb yourself. I'll give us another drop.' She filled her mother's cup and got up to give more tea to Paddy. Conor saw Aideen turn and look at Bríd. It hadn't occurred to him that they might go off to Cork for the wedding and, clearly,

Aideen hadn't thought of it either. Before anyone else could speak, Eileen waved the teapot at Joe.

'Three days at *least*, Joe, I'm telling you.' Returning to her seat, she counted the days on her fingers. 'Driving down, settling in, dinner the night before. The day itself, with the ceremony and the gala dinner with speeches. Then breakfast or a buffet lunch next day, afternoon tea, some kind of do, and a barbecue in the evening. And that's without counting rehearsal days, so we could be talking more.'

No one said anything. Then Una asked what kind of do she had in mind.

'Well, there's dozens of options, aren't there? Depending on the venue. Paint ball for the lads, say, or a falconry class. Maybe spa treatments for the girls, or a foraged food trail – or some kind of installation.'

'What the hell is an installation?'

'Ah, God, Joe, have you never been to a wedding? I saw a thing in a magazine where everyone wrote a wish for the bride on a seashell, and then an artist created an image of a mermaid out on the hotel lawn. Afterwards all the guests got a personal video.'

'Of the ceremony?'

'No, eejit, of the mermaid emerging in slo-mo, with a soundtrack made up of all the wishes spoken by whispering voices. Now that's romantic.'

Eileen's mam looked doubtful. 'Whispering voices? Would you not say that's a bit creepy?'

'Well, it needn't be that exactly. Tell you what, it could be a dove release.' Eileen turned enthusiastically to Aideen. 'Wouldn't that be great? Say, one cage full of orange doves, and one of white. Or silver.'

This time Jazz got in before Bríd, while Aideen sat there gobsmacked. 'That would depend on the colour scheme for the whole wedding, wouldn't it? Which has yet to be agreed.'

Eileen nodded cheerfully. 'Orange is going to be next year's colour. Peach is already *passé*. Touches of white and silver never go out of fashion. But monochrome bouquets are going to be huge.'

There was a pause in which Conor was pretty certain Jazz gave Eileen a kick under the table. Then Jazz spoke again. 'Right, well, getting back to the big picture, I suppose the date is the important thing if you want to book a venue. And, broadly speaking, what kind of event you'd both like to plan.' She gave Eileen a gimlet look and turned to the rest of the table. 'In terms of size, say.'

Everyone looked at Aideen, who looked at Conor. Taking a gulp of tea, Conor cleared his throat. 'I reckon Joe and Paddy and me would want to get a grip on the implications. When to have it, like, and how taking the time off might play out in terms of the farm. And I guess me and Aideen need to talk about scale, like Jazz says.'

Aideen threw him a grateful look and Una turned to Eileen. 'A big wedding like that would cost an awful lot of money.'

'No, but you mustn't think about cost, that's down to us.'

Old Dawson nodded. 'It is, of course, pet, and you're not to worry, Una. I've always said I'll pick up the tab.'

You could see Una working out that a three-day wedding meant three different outfits.

Conor glared at Joe. 'I'd say we'll want to talk colour schemes too, won't we, Aideen?'

The flowers on the *Primavera* dress weren't orange, and Carol had already embroidered yards of stuff from which they'd planned she'd make it up.

Eileen scrolled through her phone again and found a photo. 'See? Donatella! I'm not going to ask Dad to fork out for Versace, obviously. We'll get something in Dublin. But that's the shape to be bang on trend next year.'

The model in the photo was wearing a strapless, skin-tight sheath of satin that exploded from the knees into a series of spangled net flounces.

Eileen, who'd handed the phone to Aideen, took it back and showed it to her mother. 'I'll have to lose a few pounds, of course, but haven't I time enough? Aideen's good to go, though. She was made for that dress.'

Bríd, Jazz, Una and Maura opened their mouths simultaneously, but before they could speak, Paddy stood up and walked out of the room.

'Oh dear.' Una half got up from her seat and sat back down, looking troubled. 'I ... he wasn't feeling great this morning. He might have gone to lie down.'

'Ah, poor Paddy, is it the flu, maybe? I saw he had no appetite for the tea.'

Una smiled at Maura and said that could be it. Then she sipped her own tea, clearly wanting to get up and follow Paddy but feeling it would be rude to desert her guests.

For the millionth time Conor wished that his dad wasn't so

touchy about his depression. There was no shame in it but, all the same, he hated people to know. Sometimes he'd be so lethargic that he hardly seemed to see or care what was happening around him. But other times he'd be super-sensitive and couldn't bear to see anyone looking anxious, so it wasn't surprising he hadn't been able to cope with the tension around the table.

He'd be back in the other room now, beating himself up for walking out on Una. On the other hand, Conor thought, you'd almost be grateful to him for the interruption. Seizing the opportunity, Jazz had got up and was talking fiercely in an undertone to Eileen, while Una put more water in the kettle and Bríd shoved the cake at Aideen and gave her a heartening wink.

When they sat down with a fresh pot of tea, Jazz and Bríd took over and, by the time the last pastry was eaten, some stuff was actually on the way to being settled. They'd even agreed to set up a closed group on Facebook, where they could be in touch and upload photos and info. And Jazz had announced firmly that by the end of the month they'd need to agree on a date and really begin looking for venues.

That was when the shit would really hit the fan, if you asked Conor. Still, they'd have to face it sooner or later and, given the way Eileen had the bit between her teeth, sooner might be best.

Chapter Twenty-Seven

Jazz rolled over and reached out for her phone. She'd been dozing for the past ten minutes or so, subconsciously waiting to hit snooze on the alarm, which she'd set for six thirty. But squinting at the screen, she could see that this was a call from Dad.

'Hello?'

'Dad. Are you okay?'

'Of course I am.'

Struggling into a sitting position, Jazz peered up at the clock on the wall. 'Because it's twenty past six.'

'I wanted to catch you before you went out to work.'

'Yes, well, you've done that. So what's happening?'

'Not a lot. I just thought I'd call and see how my daughter is.'

'Oh, come on, Dad, no, you didn't. What the story? Granny Lou said she'd got the impression you were planning to come over.'

She heard a second's hesitation before his bland response.

'Well, yes, I hope so, but I haven't firmed up my plans. Actually, I called to say I've had an offer on the house.'

'Cool. Or is it? Are you going to accept?'

'You knew I was selling?'

'Sure. Louisa told me that too.'

'Yes, I asked her to. When I got the offer it seemed important that you should be the first to know. After all, it is your home too.'

Jazz swung her legs out of bed, went through to the kitchen, and set about making coffee with the phone cradled between her shoulder and her jaw. If the house was her home too, she thought, it might have been good if he'd let her know before putting it on the market. But that was typical Dad. He'd have calculated that calling sooner might produce objections. Far better to leave it till an offer was on the table, when causing a fuss would make her look like a brat.

She sighed as she closed the fridge door with her hip. Seeing Dad in his true colours always made her feel bereft. The knowledge that, in his way, he truly loved her was never enough to make up for the loss of the father she'd thought she had. Not only that, but she hadn't found out the real truth for ages. When he and Mum had split up, Dad had told her no one was to blame. With no reason to doubt him, she'd believed him. So, of course, Mum had had to play along. It wasn't till she'd left school that she'd discovered what had really happened, and that was only because Mum had refused to keep on endorsing his lies. In the fallout, which had left her furious with both of them, each had claimed they'd been trying to protect her and, on a good day, Jazz could see what they meant. By now she'd mended her bridges, at least where Mum was concerned. But on a bad day it seemed as if nothing in her life could ever be relied on.

That wasn't something she wanted to dump on Mum, though – any more than she was prepared to admit that the news of an offer on the London house had caused her stomach to lurch. Given what Mum herself had been through, it didn't seem fair. Besides, when Louisa had first mentioned the sale Jazz really hadn't been bothered. But now, with Sam gone and her own world shaken, it felt like yet another blow to her sense of where she belonged.

Dad must have heard the sigh because his voice became concerned. 'You do know that my home will always be yours as well, sweetheart?'

'You've found a place to buy?'

'I think so. It's in a wonderful location. A very sexy block, right by Tate Modern. Not as big as the house, of course, but with two bedrooms. One of which will have your name on it.'

Hers, or Granny Lou's, or anyone else's who happened to be his house guest. Not a place where she could leave her clothes in the cupboards, or sleep under the quilt that Mum had made for her twelfth birthday, from patches of all their favourite colours, in velvet and brocade. Suddenly it seemed awfully important to know where that quilt was now.

'You haven't started to clear things out, have you? Because some of my stuff is still in my room in the house.'

'Of course I haven't. I've hardly had time to consider the offer.'

'But you'll take it?'

'Yes, I think I will. I'd like to close on the flat as soon as I can. These places get snapped up in an instant. Actually, it's not been listed yet, but I happen to know the agent. We handled a case for him once.'

Jazz pulled a face. Insider knowledge had always got Dad what he wanted. That and his weird ability to put people in the wrong.

It was a subtle form of bullying she'd lived with as a child and never even noticed, but now that she was alert to it, it always made her angry. 'Look, I'm glad you called, but I would have preferred to know about this sooner. You could have told me you were selling, instead of letting me find out from Gran.'

'But, darling, aren't you being a little selfish? I had to tell your grandmother first – after all it's her London pied-à-terre too.'

'Yes, but it's not *my* pied-à-terre, is it? You said it yourself, it's my home.'

'I thought Mum would tell you.'

'Oh, no! Stop right there! You're not going to blame Mum for this. Actually, she was gutted because *I* had to tell *her*.'

'Look, something tells me I've woken you too early. Let's talk another time.'

Jazz could feel a lump rising in her throat. 'And don't try blaming me either. I've every right to be fed up, Dad. And I am.' The lump in her throat got bigger so she decided to stop this now. 'I need to go, if I'm to have any breakfast. Leave it, Dad, it doesn't matter. You're selling and that's fine. Just keep me in the loop, please, from now on, will you? Gotta go. 'Bye.'

Louisa wasn't due in the office that day and Jazz was glad. Having her grandmother as her partner-cum-boss was complicated, not least in terms of how she was seen by the rest of the team, so she'd sworn from the start that she wouldn't let family stuff intrude at work. Dad's phone call had thrown her, though, and if his name or the sale was mentioned today, she had a feeling she might behave unprofessionally. Swear loudly, say, or burst into tears. It had been bad enough when Louisa-as-boss had delivered the swingeing pep talk about Sam. Having her turn into Granny Lou with sweeties and a paper hankie would be worse.

★

It was a gorgeous evening when Jazz left work after a successful day. Sauntering across the nuns' garden, where Saira Khan was chatting to a group of volunteers by the polytunnel, she saw Mike talking to her mum near the gate to the library courtyard. He waved and came along the path towards her, calling out cheerfully as soon as she was in earshot.

'That psalter is amazing. There's a page with pipers and fiddlers dancing down the margin. Little grotesque animals and fat, boozy monks. I'm going to intercut shots of them with snippets of trad music sessions in pubs.' Arriving at her side, he frowned and assumed a cod Yorkshire accent. 'You're looking a bit down. Trouble at t' mill?'

Jazz laughed. 'No, work's fine. I just started the day with a phone call from my dad.'

'And that's bad because?'

'Oh, because he's had an offer on the house where we lived in London. And he's planning to come to Finfarran on a visit.'

'And *that*'s bad because?'

She laughed again. 'You wouldn't understand. Anyway, it's a long story and I'd hate to bore you to death.'

'Okay, here's a thought. Do me a favour.'

'What?'

'Come and have dinner with me in Ballyfin.'

She stepped back and he shrugged. 'Look, it doesn't matter,

you've probably already got something planned with your boyfriend.'

'Nope. No boyfriend. Not since a couple of weeks ago. Actually, I was on my way to get fish and chips.'

'Well, come and have them in Ballyfin instead.'

As she hesitated he gave her a broad smile. 'How about I cut the crap and just say this? You're lovely but I'm not looking for a holiday romance, and if I were I wouldn't be targeting someone who's just broken up with her boyfriend. I am looking for company, though. What d'you say?'

'I thought you had family over here to hang out with.'

'I haven't got round to making that call.' Mike looked at her quizzically. 'Is this you politely giving me the brush-off?'

Jazz grinned. 'Why Ballyfin?'

'Because I haven't been there and I need to go. It's the tourist hub of Finfarran.'

'Where they charge a king's ransom for a bag of fish and chips.'

'In that case, let's push the boat out and go to a swanky hotel.'

'Yeah, right. Who's paying?'

'The swanky hotel. I called the manager of the Marina and said I was shooting these videos, and he said to come and interview a few guests and have a meal on the house. As well he might, since he'll be getting free publicity. But I don't fancy eating alone, so you really would be doing me a favour.'

'Blimey, is this how you journalists feed yourselves?'

'All the time. Us freelance types have to take things as they come.'

*

The Marina Hotel was a modern building set above the curved golden beach, with a glass winter garden where sofas and easy chairs faced the sparkling Atlantic. On the opposite side of the reception area was the entrance to a banqueting suite where a noisy post-wedding party was in full swing. While Mike arranged his next day's schedule, Jazz retreated to the winter garden with a glass of wine. Twenty minutes later she joined him in the first-floor restaurant, where they were ushered to a window table with a stunning view of the ocean.

As they sat down Mike asked Jazz how her bridesmaid's job was going.

'Oh, don't start me! I should have researched the role more carefully before taking it on.'

'Can't be easy when you've just had a bust-up of your own.'

Mentally, Jazz told herself that it wasn't. There'd never been any question of Sam and herself getting married but, now that he'd gone, Eileen's endless harping on about doves and flowers was sort of wearing.

Still, though Mike was nice he was a stranger and Jazz had no intention of turning him into a confidant. She shrugged. 'It's no big deal. I got dumped, that's all. First-world problem.'

'Okay, I get it, this time you *are* giving me the brush-off. Let's eat chips and talk about books and films. But, just for the record, I don't believe in the concept of first-world problems. Well, obviously I do if we're talking famine or no clean water. Or being stuck in a war zone. Getting dumped doesn't compare to that. But having food and water doesn't deny you the right to sorrow.'

'So what are you now? A psychiatrist?'

'No. I'm stating the obvious. Everyone everywhere feels the same human emotions. Okay, I guess feeling crap is worse when you're also being shot at or starving. But it's not a matter of one person's problems trumping someone else's. That's just daft.'

Later, when the sun had gone down, and lights on yachts and fishing boats were reflected in the dusky water, they strolled out into the warm night. Jazz paused where the wall of the marina seemed made for strollers to lean on, resting her elbows on stone and her chin on her linked hands. Together she and Mike watched as the last of the daylight faded and stars began to appear in the ink-dark sky. 'Weird to think of the rest of the world out there in darkness.'

'Well, half of it's just getting up to a new day.'

'Yes, but I think that's what I mean. All those lives being led in other places, and we don't see them. It's the Bali Ha'i thing. A sense of something out there in the distance that you can't reach.'

'Easy enough to reach them. You just have to jump on a plane.' Mike put his own elbows on the wall. 'Or take a slow boat to China. I've always fancied the idea of doing that. Or, better still, a slow boat to nowhere in particular. It's the journey, not the destination, that counts.'

'Yup. "A banging of the door behind you, a blithesome step forward, and you're out of the old life and into the new"!'

'Is that a quotation?'

'Probably not accurate, but it's a thing I remember from *The Wind in the Willows*. Did you read it when you were a kid?'

'Isn't there an animated movie?'

Jazz chuckled. 'You are so not a book person!' Turning round, she leaned back with her shoulders against the wall. 'I've no time for dreams about taking a slow boat to China.'

The look he gave her in response produced a spurt of irritation in her. 'I'm building a life, okay? It's hard work.'

'But life isn't something you build. It's what happens.'

'Not when the choices you make impact on other people.'

'Okay. Who?'

Once again, he didn't seem to be prying, just showing an interest. 'Well, I've taken on this bridesmaid's job. So Eileen, for one. And my grandmother. I'm a key person in a start-up business in which she's the prime investor.'

'But nobody's indispensable. Surely they wouldn't want you to stay if you felt like moving on?'

'Well, possibly, but Eileen's my best friend. And while I'm not saying I'm indispensable, if I left my job it would destabilise the team we've been building at work. People who've given up other jobs to join Edge of the World Essentials, and people like Saira Khan and our growers whose lives it's changed. Saira had never worked outside her home before she joined us. Some of our growers have taken out loans and expanded because we've offered them a new market for their produce.'

He didn't appear convinced, so she tried again. 'And, look, it's not just about work, it's about family too. My gran lives with my nan, and it's great that Nan has company. If Edge of the World Essentials went pear-shaped, that arrangement might have to change.'

'But your nan's domestic arrangements aren't your responsibility. Or are they? Am I missing the point?'

'Well, no, they're not. But, yes, in a way they are. Because if they did change, and I wasn't here, my mum would end up having to deal with the fallout on her own.'

'Why would there be fallout?'

'Because my nan's getting old and she's a difficult woman.'

'Okay, you've lost me now.'

Jazz groaned. 'I get lost myself sometimes. Don't get me wrong, I adore Nan, and she's sweet underneath, really. Families are just – complicated. Don't you think?'

Mike shook his head. 'Not if you don't allow them to be. At least, that's what I've found.'

Pushing herself away from the wall, Jazz grinned. 'Well, that's either wholly admirable or unutterably selfish. And now I reckon it's time I went home.'

They'd driven to Ballyfin in his car and he dropped her back at the flat, thanking her for her company and turning back for a moment before he went away. 'Look, I know it's none of my business, but it seems to me that you're longing to jump that slow boat to China.'

'You're right, it's none of your business. Thanks for dinner.'

'Okay. See you around.'

Upstairs, Jazz shed her clothes and shrugged herself into a dressing gown, then, remembering a memo she needed to send next day, looked round for something to write with. There was a notebook by her bed on which she often scribbled reminders but the pen she kept beside it had disappeared. Crossing to a pot on the console table in which she kept writing implements, she selected one at random and found it was a biro printed with the name of Sam's firm. Absurdly, the tacky logo brought tears to her eyes. Telling herself not to be a fool, she made her note, and took her copy of *Brooklyn* off the shelf beside the bed. She'd read until she felt sleepy, then turn off the light. Heaven knew, after Dad's early call and the late evening with Mike, that shouldn't take long.

But tonight, like every other night since Sam had left her, darkness brought a sense of the bed being huge and empty without him and, as she lay awake for hours, the walls of her flat seemed to close in like a trap.

Chapter Twenty-Eight

Rasher was still blown away by the thought of a big fry-up and several cups of tea in the mornings. In the past he used to hoard the price of a takeaway tea sometimes, but sleeping rough with money on you wasn't a good idea. If you got known for it, you could wake up robbed. Sitting round asking for the price of your morning tea was pretty awful, though, so sometimes he'd taken the risk and got away with it. Then you had to find a place that'd take your money, which wasn't easy. Half of them would smell you coming and throw you out.

At The Royal Vic, breakfast service began at seven thirty, to accommodate guests who were checking out early. Breakfast for staff on the first shift was at six, and you'd have a half-hour's work done before you'd sit down. You'd get tea or coffee in your hand first thing, though. And you'd have slept in a warm room and gone down to a hot kitchen, so you wouldn't need to wrap your hands around the heat of the mug.

The other thing Rasher had had to get used to was his bedroom. It wasn't much bigger than the one in the halfway house but it felt different. He liked the tall window overlooking the yard with the wheelie bins, and the fact that the sheets were washed in a laundry, and appeared in his room in plastic bags. One of the girls who cleaned the guestrooms had told him the staff duvet covers got changed every fortnight. She was friendly enough. When he'd first arrived, the bed had been stripped and looked a bit miserable, but she'd turned up with the bedlinen and, seeing him go at it cack-handed, offered to make it up. It took her about two minutes and the white sheets and pillowcase, and the red check duvet cover, almost made the place like home.

He hadn't seen that girl again. Chambermaids had their own room to eat in.

To begin with, the kitchen had seemed chaotic. Like Saira Khan had warned him, there was a hell of a lot of roaring and swearing, and a fair bit of passing Anton's aggression down the line. A few times Rasher had almost asked where the kitchen cat was so he could kick it. The other porters just kept going and said nothing, though. So he'd followed suit.

The two guys he saw most of were Romanian. Petru had a wife and kid here in Carrick, and Bogdan, who was Rasher's own age, was a student doing hotel work to pay for a holiday in Ireland. Rasher hadn't had much time to get to know them but they seemed decent enough. There'd been the usual surprise when he'd told them he was Irish. Then they turned it into a joke and started calling him Paddy. Most people in the kitchen were foreign – including Anton, who was Belgian – and you'd hear cursing in all kinds of lingo whenever things got stressed.

Scrubbing pots and spuds was pretty boring, and the huge, clattery space was hot and exhausting, but the buzz was fantastic. And the food Anton came up with was amazing. Back when Rasher's dad was alive, his mum had been mad for cookery programmes on telly, which was when he'd first got the notion that he might be a chef. The stuff he was dealing with now never got shown on the telly, but doing it made you feel you were part of the team. Bogdan and Petru didn't appear to see it that way, but Rasher – to his amazement – was having a brilliant time.

The only thing that got to him was the fierce long hours. Saira Khan kept telling him not to worry. 'You're not used to the physical exertion. I warned you when you said you were going to take every shift you could get. Good food and a warm bed will help you to build up stamina. Just take your time.'

'Yeah, but what if they reckon I'm not worth hanging on to?' If they did, it wouldn't just be a matter of losing a job he was loving. Without an address he'd be back to square one.

'They won't. You're doing the number of shifts required, aren't you? Plus a few extra. And they're lucky to get you. Think about it, Adam, you're hard-working, honest, committed, and you're ambitious. It's going to be worth their while to train and develop you. Martin has told them that, and they've agreed.'

'Really?'

'Really. So what you must do is work hard and prove that you're reliable.'

'Okay.'

'I promise you, demonstrating reliability is going to be the key to your future.'

It was decent of her to keep an eye on him. When he'd left the house he hadn't thought he'd ever see her again, but then he'd got a message suggesting they meet for another chat. He'd come away from that meeting feeling determined. He'd be super-reliable at

The Royal Vic and he'd go in to Carrick Library and get himself a card. The library thing had been Mrs Khan's suggestion. 'You have an address and a job now, and the application's been made for your PPS number. You need to start using the library as more than a place where you can go to keep out of the rain.'

Rasher hadn't ever asked himself what else he could use it for, but she'd told him he ought to apply for the card and find out. 'You don't need me to tell you. And you do need to build up your confidence, otherwise how are you going to build a career? So go into the library and ask about the facilities they offer.'

'Like what?'

'Like how to research what you'll need to know if you want to become a chef. Where to find courses and how much they'll cost you. How to get help to find yourself a flat.'

Seeing his worried look, she'd laughed, and smiled at him. 'This is about the future, Adam. Right now you're working at The Royal Victoria, which is fine. It's wonderful. But the future is going to offer you all sorts of choices, and to make choices you need information. So begin now. Discover how to find things out.'

Thinking about it afterwards, he'd known she was right. Before he'd taken the kitchen job, Martin had sat him down and said it wasn't his only option. He could always give his mum a call and consider going home to Dublin. But Rasher had stuck to his guns and told him that wasn't going to happen. No way. In which case, he reckoned, Mrs Khan was bang to rights. If he was on his own, it was down to him to work out what might come next.

The County Library was in a square, ugly building with rows

of blank windows and an automatic door. As Rasher approached, he saw Gracie's dog tied to a rail outside. Anyone who knew the streets of Carrick would recognise him instantly as Gracie's. He was a long-legged mutt, like a cross between an elephant and a sheepdog, with a matted ruff of rust-coloured hair and big yellow teeth. Gracie was an oul one who shuffled about loaded down with carrier bags, reminding Rasher of the rough sleepers he'd seen back home as a child. His mum called them bag ladies. There was one who used to sit on a broken bench outside the hospital and Mum would always slip her a few coins on her way in to work.

Rasher had no idea where Gracie came from. She seldom said much beyond announcing that she was eighty years old, and that no one was going to part her from Gussie, her dog. 'They've offered me nights in hostels, son, but there's no way I'll go in there. I'm not leaving poor Gussie out in the cold all on his own.'

Now Rasher hunkered down and scratched Gussie's muzzle before taking a deep breath and climbing the library steps. Immediately inside the door there was a hallway with a reception desk. Beyond that was the door to the reading room, which had rows of long tables and plastic chairs. When he'd been in before, Rasher had always stuck his head down, avoided the desk and made straight for the reading room. There was a stand of newspapers and magazines against the far wall and, as long as you looked like you were reading one, you could sit at a table for hours.

This time he approached the desk, smiled at the guy behind it, and said he'd like to register for a card. It was incredibly quick, but the effort of appearing nonchalant was knackering, so he decided he hadn't the strength to start asking questions and finding things out. He had to be back at The Royal Vic for a shift by four o'clock anyway, and it was one thirty now.

He took his temporary card and the pile of leaflets he'd been given, and went through to the reading room to find himself a seat. Gracie was there, sitting alone at a table by the window, apparently deep in a copy of *Ireland's Own*. She was wrapped in several layers of scarves and jackets, and had piled her plastic carrier bags at her feet. A few other people were reading at different tables. None of them close to hers, though, which wasn't a surprise. Gracie smelled strongly of Gussie, and Gussie smelled strongly of dog.

Flicking through his leaflets, Rasher reckoned it was just as well he hadn't started a conversation at Reception. If he read this lot carefully, he'd be better placed to ask questions, and it looked like there was masses here that he ought to know more about. There was a biro and a bit of paper left on one of the tables so he leaned over, whipped them and started taking notes.

Ten minutes later he was disturbed by the sound of high heels on the floorboards and, looking up, saw a tall lady marching out of the room. She returned almost immediately with a young girl in tow. The lady was making some kind of fuss and gesticulating, and the girl was looking flustered, when an older staff member came into the room. Rasher couldn't hear what the older woman said, but the lady raised her voice.

'Well, I must say, that's rather rich, to accuse me of making a disturbance! I'm the one who's trying to lodge a complaint!'

She waved her hand aggressively towards the window and the girl turned to her colleague, clearly distressed. 'It's Gracie but, honestly, Máiréad, she isn't being any bother. I've kept an eye on her since she came in, and she's grand.'

At this stage, their voices were getting louder and people around Rasher were looking up. Máiréad took the lady's arm and suggested they move outside. 'If you'll come with me, Mrs O'Brien, I'll find you a place to sit in the main library.'

'I want to sit here! And are you aware that that woman's dog is blocking the public entrance?'

Rasher saw Gracie raise her head from her magazine. Seeing the O'Brien one glaring at her, she pushed back her chair and began to grope for her bags. Furious, Rasher stood up, and went over to give her a hand. She was so intent on her carrier bags that he wasn't even sure she recognised him.

Everyone was looking up now and, seeing she was getting nowhere with Máiréad, Mrs O'Brien turned and addressed the room. 'The woman's a vagrant and the dog appears to be rabid!'

Some people looked away, embarrassed, but Rasher could tell that half of them agreed with her. The next thing he knew, the two staff members were beside him. Máiréad knelt down and smiled at Gracie. 'It's all right, Gracie. Let me help you with the bags.'

Gracie ignored her and waved her little fist at Mrs O'Brien. 'No, he bloody well isn't rabid, that's my Gussie!'

'This is disgraceful!' Still standing in the doorway, Mrs O'Brien brandished a phone. 'I've already called the guards and, evidently, it wasn't a moment too soon.'

Máiréad stood up briskly and took Gracie by the arm. 'Gussie's fine, Gracie, don't worry. Maybe it's time to go now, though, okay? We'll see you another day.'

If the guards were coming, Rasher reckoned she was right. The young girl was around on Gracie's other side, stuffing things back in a bag, which had split. At that moment a pint-sized female guard appeared in the doorway, with a second, taller figure looming behind her.

Gracie grabbed hold of Rasher. 'Jesus Christ, what have they done with Gussie?'

Mrs O'Brien went all dramatic and turned to the guard. 'Thank goodness you've come, the woman's getting obstreperous.'

Stepping forward, the guard extended her arms. 'Could everyone clear the room, please? Just for a minute? We'll deal with this.'

She moved towards Gracie, and Rasher lost his cool. 'You can't arrest Gracie! It was that oul bitch started it.'

'We're not arresting anyone, sir. Can you just leave the room?'

'No, I won't! I'm not leaving Gracie!'

Gracie suddenly started to wail. The guard reached out a hand to her and Rasher swiped at it angrily. 'Don't you touch her! Leave her alone!'

Though he didn't make contact with the guard's hand, she jerked away instinctively and, stumbling on the carrier bags, ended up on the floor.

Rasher's instinct was to bend down to see if she was okay but, as he stooped, a heavy weight struck him on the chest, driving him violently backwards against the metal stand by the wall. For a moment he had no idea what had happened. Then, blinking away tears of pain, he realised that the other guard had launched himself across the room from the doorway. There was a horrible smell of coffee-breath and, as Rasher's eyes refocused, he recognised the livid face inches from his own. It was Nugent's.

Chapter Twenty-Nine

TELL PAT FOUR O COCK GARDEN CAFÉ

Mary Casey glared at her phone and shot off a second text.

CLOCK NOT COCK tHIS yOKE LOUisa and me gOT iS
wORSE tHAN tHE ISAAST oNE

She stabbed at the screen again and found herself looking at her emails. There was a circulated reminder from Pat about the computer class in the library. Clicking her teeth, Mary tapped out, IVE JUST TOLD HANNA TO TELL YOU IM NOT GOING TO BE TYHER, and hit send. As she took off her glasses, there was another ping from the phone so, putting them on again, she discovered a reply saying that automatically generated emails didn't require a response.

Mary drew in her breath sharply. She had told Hanna several times that this phone was plain stupid, and here it was acting up again. Moving swiftly, so it couldn't catch her out, she shut it off and thrust it into her bag. Hanna would pass the message to Pat when she saw her and, anyway, it didn't matter a damn who turned up or didn't turn up to the class. After the last one Mary had decided she wasn't going back. They'd only start trying to teach her about her new phone.

It was two o'clock, so there was plenty of time to clean the kitchen before Johnny Hennessy gave her a lift to Lissbeg. Wrapping herself in an apron, and fetching a mop and bucket, Mary wondered if she might do the windows as well. Louisa had offered to pay for a man to come round with a ladder, but where was the sense in that when you could do them off a chair? That was the beauty of a bungalow. Anyway, cleaning round the place gave you something to do.

Turning the kitchen chairs onto the table, she ran the brush round the floor before setting to with the mop. Louisa was great company and she was glad to have her, but the fact remained that it wasn't Louisa's house. Not in any real sense – though of course they'd made an arrangement when they'd divided it into flats. Louisa had paid for doing up her own rooms, and for the new French doors that opened out from her bedroom into the garden, and they'd gone fair shares on the cost of the rest of the work. Their arrangement to share the kitchen had worked out grand too. It was nice to have someone to notice when you'd given the place a scrub. And, fair dos, Louisa was very appreciative. Whatever way her son had turned out, she was a lady herself.

With the floor done, Mary rinsed the mop and took it out to the garden to hang on the line. Casting a critical eye on the windows, she decided they'd do as they were for another week. She'd slip into her bedroom now, and get showered and changed. The world and his wife met in the Garden Café for afternoon coffee, and you wouldn't want to cut a shabby figure in front of the whole town.

She emerged from her front gate at exactly three forty. Johnny was reversing out of his drive and she sat in beside him, tucking her skirt away from the door. Jazz had told her that Johnny was going to have his photo on some billboard advertising face cream. You wouldn't know what the world was coming to these days, and that was a fact.

The sun was splitting the heavens when she got to the Garden Café. They did a lovely plate of shortbread with their afternoon cappuccino special, so she ordered that and took her tray out to a table by the fountain. You wouldn't find her drinking chai latte at four in the afternoon. Or eating churros either, for all they might be made by Bríd over in HabberDashery. You'd end up with hands like a couple of sugary oil slicks, and chai latte was only builders' tea with bits of twigs.

She'd only begun to drink her coffee, at a table beyond the fountain, when Pat came towards her, carrying a pot of tea and a scone on a tray. Before she could start blathering about computers, Mary hitched out a chair for her and asked if Hanna had passed on the message.

'She did, of course. Amn't I here?'

'I had a lot to do at home, so I couldn't make the class.'

'Ah, for God's sake, Mary, would you stop coming out with excuses? There's no pressure at all on you to come.'

'Well, I've never said I don't enjoy them, so don't you go putting words in my mouth.'

Pat poured herself a cup of tea and took a bite of her scone. 'I love the way they serve you these with the butter on them. It saves so much trouble.'

'Ah, would you have a bit of sense, girl? They do it to save the expense.' Mary leaned over and sniffed at the scone contemptuously. 'That's not a scone and butter at all, it's a scone with a scrape!'

Pat ignored her and asked if Bríd was planning to make the cake for Aideen's wedding.

Mary sniffed again. 'Not judging by what I've heard from Jazz. By the sound of things, Eileen Dawson won't settle for anyone less than Elton John!'

Pat looked puzzled. 'Singing?'

'Baking.'

'But ...'

Mary waved a hand dismissively. 'You know what I mean – someone famous. Bruce Forsyth, say, or Mary Berry.'

'Isn't poor Bruce Forsyth dead?'

'God, Pat Fitz, you're a fierce annoying woman!'

Pat poured milk into her tea. 'How is Jazz anyway?'

'Grand, I'd say. Fallen out with the boyfriend.'

'Sure, we all did that.'

Glancing over her shoulder, Mary leaned in conspiratorially. 'But d'you know how it is? I'm fierce worried about Hanna. Wait till I tell you what Louisa told me last night.' She pointed a teaspoon at Pat, who looked expectant. 'That pup Malcolm Turner's coming over.'

Pat's eyes rounded. 'Over here?'

'Now so! And a grand welcome for himself! Bold as you please, after the way he treated my Hanna. And there's worse.'

'No!'

'He's selling the house in London.'

'The marital home?'

'That's it. The house Hanna found for them when it was dripping damp and needed all sorts doing. Holy God, Pat, the months she spent getting it halfway decent! And the years of keeping it up and putting in all class of improvements! She had it like a palace by the end.'

'She did!'

'Don't you know she did!'

Shaking her head, Mary reprised the sorry story of Malcolm Turner's treachery. 'That floozy from his office he was cheating with was Hanna's friend. Did I tell you Hanna invited her to be poor Jazz's godmother?'

'She didn't!'

'With no notion of what was going on! I should've done a bit of digging meself when I heard the scamp turned it down.'

'I suppose she must have had some streak of shame in her.'

'Not at all, girl! Not one shred. No more than he had. Think of the way he behaved when Hanna found out. Going behind her back and telling the child a pack of lies!'

'What did he say?'

'That Mammy and Daddy just "fell out of love". And, of course, once he'd said it, Hanna had no choice but to go round backing him up.'

'God forgive him!'

'After bedding that trollop in the family home that Hanna was worn out caring for. And now he'll be living high on the hog off the back of all her work!'

'I'd say a place like that would be worth a fair bit now.'

'Ah, God help me, Pat, I looked it up last week on the internet—'

'Did you Google it?'

'I used Firefox. Sure, I had no choice. Wasn't that what you made me put on my bloody machine?'

'It wasn't.'

'Well, it's what came up when I hit the yoke anyway. And it's not the point. I found the price of the house, Pat, and d'you know how much he's asking? Two million!'

'Go to God!'

Mary took a gulp of her cappuccino. 'Two million sterling. Offers In Excess Of. That's the kind of money my Hanna added to that house over the years. And will she see a penny of it? Not one cent.' Exhausted by outrage, she sat back and glowered at the fountain, where birds were fluttering round the statue of St Francis.

Pat absent-mindedly reached for a piece of Mary's shortbread. 'Wasn't that what she said when they fixed up the divorce, though? That she wanted to go her own way and she wouldn't take a penny?'

'But she was out of her mind that time, Pat. I told her. I said she'd regret it. And if she hadn't married that pup in the first place, she could've been working herself all those years, building up savings and earning a decent pension.'

'Ah, sure, she's young yet.'

'We were all young once. She won't always be.'

'And is she wild upset?'

Mary slapped the flat of her hand on the table. 'Sure, how would I know, girl? I'm only her mother. She'll say she's not, anyway. I do know that.'

Pat wrinkled her nose. 'Isn't she settled down in Maggie's place, though, Mary? And hasn't she a grand new man?'

'What difference does that make?'

'Well, maybe she's not bothered about the money. I mean, she'll have enough to get by, and she's happy. And aren't you fierce lucky to have her and Jazz in Finfarran? God, I'd give a fortune to be that way myself, now poor Ger's gone.'

'Holy God Almighty, I'm surrounded by total eejits! What matter if she isn't bothered about the money? Who gives a toss what she said when they were divorced? This is about justice, Pat, and decency. I don't care what Hanna wants! I'm telling you what she's owed!'

Chapter Thirty

When the guard came in with a mug of tea Rasher was in despair. It was after five o'clock and it felt like the end of the world. For a while, when they'd frogmarched him out of the library, he'd thought that maybe things would turn out okay. The two librarians had followed them, and Rasher had heard Máiréad telling Nugent to calm down.

'We're perfectly capable of dealing with any problems on the premises, Sergeant. And it would have been courteous if you'd reported to the desk, instead of just marching in.'

Rasher had held his breath. His arms had been twisted behind his back and Nugent's hand was on his neck, pushing his head forward.

'We were responding to a call from a member of the public.'

'I know. But Mrs O'Brien herself was the problem, and you'd have found that out if you'd spoken to me first.'

Gussie had started making a racket then, because Gracie had appeared behind Máiréad on the steps. Nugent had ignored them and simply raised his voice. 'It's my job to act in the interests of public safety. I did what I saw fit.'

'What you actually did was make matters worse.'

Rasher had felt Nugent's hold slacken and, for a minute, he'd thought the bastard might back off. Then he'd caught sight of the female guard, who'd been clutching her own arm. He'd heard an awful crack when she'd hit the floor, and now she was leaning on the squad car, looking sick. That was when he'd known he was screwed.

Nugent had shoved him into the squad car, making a show of protecting his head and actually hurting him more. The last thing he'd seen through the car window was Gussie rearing up to put his paws on Gracie's shoulders, and the two of them standing there on the steps, like a couple of lovers, hugging.

At the garda station, Nugent had made a big fuss about getting someone to take the pint-sized guard to A & E. She had perked up a bit by that stage, and was saying she'd be fine. But Rasher guessed Nugent wanted her gone, so his own version of events would be the one down in black and white. From the look on her face, he'd had a feeling that she might have thought so too. Another guard took her away, though, saying he'd drive her to the hospital. So that had been that.

By then, all Rasher could think about was that he was due on a shift. There was a clock on the wall behind the desk sergeant, and he could see that, if they'd let him go, he might just make it back to The Royal Vic by four o'clock. Then Nugent had announced that he'd had to intervene to stop an assault on an officer, and that a member of the public had given in evidence that Rasher had threatened her and called her an oul bitch. The triumphant look on his ugly face, as the desk sergeant filled the form in, had told Rasher he hadn't a hope in hell.

When they'd shoved him into a cell he'd broken down. His

back and his shoulders were killing him, and his chest still felt like he'd been hit by a truck. But it didn't seem like his ribs were cracked so he'd probably just end up covered in bruises. Set against the possibility that the female guard's arm had been broken, that wouldn't count for much in front of a judge. Anyway, it didn't matter if they did bang him up. His job was banjaxed now, and without it he was homeless, so, with nowhere to go, he might as well be in jail. There was no way they'd take him back into the halfway house. Martin had warned him what would happen if he fell foul of the police.

Now the guard who'd come in with the tea asked him if he wanted a sandwich. 'I could bring you one from the canteen if you want.'

Rasher felt sick. He was also afraid that he might start bawling. So, he shook his head and said no. The effect on his muscles made him wince, and the guard frowned and asked if he was okay.

'Yeah. No. I'm grand.'

'You've a right to be seen by a doctor, you know, if you got hurt in the ruckus.'

'No, I'm fine. Thanks for the tea.'

'Right so.'

The guard went out and locked the door and, sitting with his hands tight round the mug, Rasher felt hot tears falling on his fingers. What he really wanted was for the door to open and his dad to come walking in. It felt like a million years since he'd died, of a stupid disease that Mum had said was just the luck of the draw. According to her, there was no point in asking, 'Why me?'

'Nature doesn't pick and choose, love. People get sick and they die, it just happens. Families are left grieving and there isn't a reason why. We just have to pick ourselves up and get on with things.'

She hadn't, though. She'd taken to the drink, let herself be used, and ended up useless, and Rasher hadn't realised till now how angry he felt about that.

In the beginning, he'd bought into the whole thing about being brave and keeping a stiff upper lip. It had seemed right because Dad had been a bit like that himself. If ever you asked him about the past, he'd tell you it didn't matter. Life was for living now, and looking back was a waste of time.

Mum had told him that was because Dad had been an immigrant. 'When you walk away from all you've known, you can't keep looking back. It's the kind of choice that takes courage and you have to hoard your strength.'

Rasher didn't even know why his dad had left Egypt. The fact that he didn't know his relations over there didn't bother him, though. He hardly knew his Irish grandparents either, and Mum's only brother had gone to Australia before Mum and Dad had got married. So there'd only been the three of them, facing the world together, and that had suited Rasher just fine.

Dad used to take him to matches in Croke Park, and out to Seapoint Baths. They'd go diving and splashing about like brown fishes while other kids and their freckly dads shivered and watched from the side. Well, not all of them, maybe. But plenty. Afterwards Dad would buy fish and chips and they'd eat them on the way home. That was about the only time he'd said a word about his childhood in Egypt. He'd told Rasher that his own dad used to take him fishing, out at sea in a timber boat with brown canvas sails. But he'd never said whether they'd gone on trips or if his dad had fished for a living. And, by the time it had occurred to Rasher to ask, he was dead.

It was weird that he hadn't inherited Dad's slim hands and long legs. Rasher was made kind of square, like Mum, with hands that she always said were like shovels. Maybe her ancestors had gone around shovelling spuds. Digging his heel into the floor, Rasher found himself sobbing – there'd be buckets of spuds by the sink now in The Royal Vic's kitchen, and people there cursing him for not turning up to his job.

The door opened and Nugent walked in, looking grim.

'According to Guard Sullivan, you'll be wanting to see a doctor.'

Scrubbing his sleeve across his face, Rasher got his back against the wall. Nugent moved closer.

'Apparently you hurt yourself when we were bringing you in.'

Rasher's eyes measured the distance between himself and the emergency button outside on the corridor wall. Deliberately, Nugent went back and quietly closed the door.

'I didn't say I needed a doctor.'

'That's good.' Nugent came back and stood in front of him. 'Because I wouldn't want you to have any reason to.'

Somewhere at the back of Rasher's mind he could hear his mum's voice telling him there was never any point in asking, 'Why me?' God alone knew why Nugent had taken a scunner to him. It didn't seem to be about his appearance. What had he said that time he'd cornered him outside The Royal Vic? 'There's decent people up and down the length and breadth of this country that never got a handout in their life.' But Rasher had never wanted to live on handouts. He'd never even thought he'd end up needing a hand up. None of this was his choice.

Instinct made him keep his head down but nothing happened for so long that he lifted it and looked Nugent in the face. The guy was plain mad. You could see a little tic pulsing in his cheek, and his eyes were like stones.

They stood there, like a couple of actors in a cop film, and Rasher got a weird feeling that Nugent couldn't think what to do next. It was like he was playing a role without having read the whole script. There'd been a film Rasher had seen at school, called *Schindler's List*, with a bit in it where the commandant of a World War Two concentration camp had been fed the notion that being really powerful meant being able to choose to let people off. For a mad moment, he wondered if Nugent was toying with the same idea.

Then the door opened a third time and Martin came into the room. Immediately Nugent seemed much smaller. Martin was wearing jeans and a grubby sweatshirt, and his hands looked as if he'd been clearing drains. Sullivan, the guard who'd brought Rasher his tea, had come in behind him, and the female guard was just outside the door. It struck Rasher that she was a lot younger than he'd thought.

Martin asked how he was.

'Fine. I'm grand ... Look, Martin, I never laid a hand on her. Honest. I didn't. I wouldn't. I did let a roar at the oul bitch, but I

... she was threatening Gracie. And they'll tell you at the library Gracie never did nothing wrong.'

Nugent had turned round and was staring at the two guards in the doorway. Rasher could see the young one looking nervous. Then Sullivan threw her a look and she kind of relaxed.

Martin looked from Nugent to Sullivan. 'Will we drop this now, or do we take it upstairs and do it by the book?'

Nugent's face went dead white, like a piece of blank paper. Then, to Rasher's amazement, Sullivan jerked his head at the girl and they walked away, leaving the door open. Nugent didn't move. Martin stepped in front of him and, taking Rasher by the shoulder, propelled him into the corridor and up a flight of stairs. There was a security door between the upstairs landing and Reception, and the desk sergeant released it without looking up from his screen. Feeling as if Martin's grasp had somehow made him invisible, Rasher found himself outside and walking down the street.

Martin took him to a café and ordered more tea. Before they sat down, he said Rasher had better go into the Gents and have a pee. 'I'd say you want one. You won't have managed to squeeze much out with your man Nugent glaring in through a bloody hole in the door.'

Actually, the thought of Nugent spying on him hadn't occurred to Rasher, but Martin was right, he was bursting. While he was in the Gents he scrubbed his blotchy face with cold water, telling himself he'd keep his cool, whatever happened next. Now that the fear of Nugent was behind him, he'd had time to be scared of what Martin might do to him. But, almost more than that, he wanted to hear how Martin had known where he was.

'That was Gracie.' Martin shoved the tea at him and told him to put sugar in it. 'She turned up at the house with Gussie and said you'd got yourself nicked.'

'Jesus, she must've put her skates on.'

It was a good couple of miles from the library to the halfway house, and Gracie moved at a snail's pace because of all the bags and her dodgy feet.

'Máiréad drove her over.'

'The *librarian* did?'

'Why not?'

'Well, I don't know her. She doesn't know me.'

'She's got eyes in her head, and she saw what happened.' Martin tipped sugar into his own tea and shrugged. 'Anyway, I know Nugent. Mad as a rat. So I thought I'd better come round and spring you before you ended up dead.'

'Are you serious?'

'Nah. I'd say today might not go unnoticed, though. He's getting a reputation for being violent.'

'You said if I got myself arrested, you'd find me and kill me yourself.'

'That was if you'd stuck your hand in a till, not if you'd met a psychopath.'

Rasher was about to laugh. Then his face fell. 'I've stuffed things up properly, though, haven't I? If I hadn't gone and got involved, I wouldn't be out of a job.'

'Ah, not at all, boy. We'll fix that as well.'

'How?'

'You stuck your neck out for Gracie. Leave this one to me. I'll find a way.'

And he did. Rasher could hardly believe it. There was a ghastly twenty minutes or so, when he stood out by the wheelie bins while Martin was inside talking to Pussycat Bow. And another five when he could hear Anton roaring. Then he was back up in his room with the white sheets and the check duvet cover, with instructions to get a few hours' sleep before starting a night shift.

Once he was alone, he found his hands shaking, and it took ages to get his things off and roll into bed. But, with the duvet pulled over his head, he realised that something had changed inside him. Back in the cell, he'd recognised how angry he'd been with Mum since Dad had died. Chucking that six-pack of beer at Fergal, and the laptop into the mirror, had sort of been ways of hitting out at Mum herself. And being angry with Mum was kind of a substitute for wanting to shout at Dad. It was like he'd felt that Dad had gone and left them alone on purpose, when the truth was that he hadn't had any choice.

Chapter Thirty-One

Botticelli obviously hadn't called carnations gillyflowers. The Italian word for them was *garofano*, though, and the old English name was gillyflowers, so that was how Aideen thought of them. When she'd explained the dress to her aunt Carol, she'd found it for her online.

'It looks like it's got three layers to it. There's an overskirt she's tucked up to hold the roses she's scattering. And one or two underskirts, see, and they're all embroidered. The hems and the sleeves are finished with lace, or something heavy like cotton crochet maybe? Would that be right?'

Carol had said she'd embroider enough fabric for a single overskirt, with some left over to add a few swags. 'It'd take miles and miles to make it just like the painting.'

'Oh, I know! The painting's only a starting point. I don't want a copy.'

'Well, that's good.' Carol had flashed a grin at her. 'Because, if you did, I'd still be embroidering by the time I was drawing my pension.' Yesterday she'd texted, asking if Aideen fancied dropping round to take a look. By offering to get up early and do the trip to the cash-and-carry, Aideen had got Bríd to agree to her taking the afternoon off. 'I won't leave till after the lunchtime rush.'

'I've said it's fine. Don't worry. Make sure you take photos.'

'We decided to go for lots of wine-red, and dark stems, not too much pink.'

'I know. You showed me the colour samples, remember? So did Mum, actually.'

'Yeah, sorry, it's just that I'm all excited. She says she's got a good few yards done.'

It would have been brilliant if the fabric could have been silk, but that would have cost a fortune so they'd chosen unbleached ultra-fine muslin and used silk thread for the flowers.

When Joe and Eileen had proposed the double wedding Bríd had told Aideen it was a shame that Carol had started work already. 'Eileen would have paid for whatever fabric you wanted.'

Aideen was secretly glad that hadn't happened. The dress was something special that belonged to her and Conor, and Carol had said that the muslin looked great. She'd been thinking of getting Pat Fitz to crochet some heavy lace to use round the hemline, or adding beads, to give it a bit of weight. 'It was the perfect choice though, I think, and the colour is almost exactly the same as the painting.'

Whizzing along on her Vespa towards Carol's cottage, Aideen wondered if all brides-to-be went a bit mad. Look at Eileen, buzzing around like a maniac, and herself, getting obsessed by embroidery and flowers. Suddenly she felt a sense of fellow-feeling for Eileen, which was weird because, up to now, she'd found her a pain. Look at how she never seemed to notice when Jazz, who'd just been dumped by her boyfriend, went awful quiet sometimes when they were all talking weddings.

Carol's sewing room, which was next to the kitchen, had a window overlooking the back garden. Outside, there was a lawn studded with daisies and, pinned to a board near Carol's desk, a piece of paper on which she'd sketched a daisy design for the dress.

'I thought I'd go for silver petals and pale gold centres. They won't jump out from a distance but they'll be lovely close to. Just a scattering of the flower heads, no stems or leaves. I'll do a few golden narcissi as well, like the ones on the dress in the painting.'

'They'll be gorgeous.'

The fabric was loosely folded in a dust sheet and, when Carol shook it out, the gillyflowers with their dark stems and wine-red petals seemed to flow across the creamy stuff and shimmer towards the floor. Aideen couldn't repress a squeak of excitement. 'It's stunning!'

'Now, I know you don't want a wreath of flowers round the neck.'

'Well, it's lovely in the painting but, like I said, it looks scratchy.'

'So I thought the dress could be Empire line. You know, with the skirt falling from under the bust. In the painting it falls from the big wreath, and there's more flowers lower down, like real roses twined across the fabric. If we give you a narrow embroidered belt below the bust line, you should get a similar effect. And the neckline can just be a plain scoop with a little edging of flowers.'

'Honestly, Carol, it's dreamy.'

'I don't know about bare feet, though.'

'Conor's all for that, but I think you're right. I might get sandals, like Venus has in the painting. Totally flat with thin gold straps.'

'And you're still going for no veil, just a wreath on your hair?'

'Yeah. Fresh flowers. That's about the one thing Eileen and I agree on. She wants a June wedding, and so do I. Because the right flowers would be out.'

Carol folded the fabric again and led the way into the kitchen. When they were both sitting at the table with coffee, she gave Aideen a look. 'Are you and Eileen having problems?'

'Not really. Well, she's a bit full-on.'

'All weddings are fraught with complications, so double weddings probably make things worse.'

'Joe says she just gets over-excited.'

'Well, if she's paying the piper she might think she's a right to go calling the tune.'

Aideen looked at her doubtfully. 'I don't think it's like that. Well, maybe a bit. The thing is, she's awfully generous. I won't let her push me around, though. I've told Conor that.'

'It could be that it's time you told Eileen.'

Aideen remembered feeling that unexpected flash of empathy. Maybe a chat with Eileen wouldn't be bad. Biting her lip, she looked across at Carol. 'We've set up this private Facebook group that everyone's pitching ideas at, but I suppose she and me could always sit down and talk.'

'That sounds like a good idea. You could go off somewhere and have a quiet drink.'

'Better not to phone her, you mean?'

'Phones are grand but nothing beats a proper sit-down chat.'

Aideen wasn't certain. There'd been that tense meeting around the farmhouse table, and the weird day at The Royal Vic when

Eileen had produced the wedding guy off the telly. But this would just be Eileen and herself.

Carol got up and went to make more coffee. 'Why not text her now and see if she's free today?'

As soon as Aideen did so, a text pinged back and, almost before she knew it, she'd fixed a meeting for five at the Garden Café.

Carol set the cafetière on the table and, sitting down again, said she was glad. 'Your mum would have been so excited about this wedding. I wish she could see how happy you are with Conor.'

'You think she'd like him?'

'I know she would.'

'Did she know before I was born that I was a girl?' Aideen wasn't sure why she'd never asked this before.

'She did. She rang me up the day they told her.'

'So she went in for scans and stuff on her own?'

Carol looked troubled. 'I would have gone with her myself if she'd only let me. But she didn't want anyone there. Your gran had got a bit upset when your mum told her she was pregnant.'

Aideen had gathered that already. Aunt Bridge and Gran had hardly ever mentioned her mum. 'Who decided that I'd be called Aideen?'

'That was Cathy. Your mum. She told me before she went into the hospital. They were concerned about her blood pressure, so maybe she was apprehensive. Anyway, that was what she said she wanted you called.'

'Do you know why?'

Carol shook her head. 'I don't, pet, I've no idea. Maybe she just liked it, or read it in a book.'

Aideen's face felt kind of stiff, so she held the warm cup against her cheek. 'It wasn't a name in my dad's family?'

'Not that I know of.'

You could see Carol looking bothered, which was the last thing Aideen wanted. Putting the cup down, she forced a laugh to clear the air. 'Well, that's good, because if it had been, I might have thought of changing it. Taken a new wedding name, like you do at Confirmation.'

Carol relaxed and laughed back. 'Like what?'

'Flora, after the *Primavera*?'

'Or the margarine?'

'Shut *up*! I was being romantic.'

'If I were you I'd stick with what I've got.'

Later on, weaving in and out of traffic on the Vespa, Aideen found herself smiling about her mother. Like people said, you couldn't miss what you'd never had, and Aunt Bridge and Carol had always made her feel loved. It was good to know, though, that Mum had chosen her name.

The tables round the fountain in the nuns' garden were crowded when she arrived, and Eileen was sitting on the edge of the stone fountain. Aideen crossed the garden and asked if they'd go and sit on a bench. 'I could nip inside and bring us out something to drink.'

'Actually, I've just had coffee.'

'Me too.'

'Will we go and sit down then, and not bother with drinks?'

They found a bench near the polytunnel and Eileen asked what the story was. Immediately, Aideen found herself starting to babble. 'You must be wondering what I wanted to say and it wasn't anything in particular. Just ... wedding stuff, really. You and me, we haven't sat down and talked it through on our own. I don't mean that I want to go micro-managing every bit of it. Though, obviously, that's not to say that I want to go dumping it all on you.'

Eileen looked baffled. 'You're not dumping anything on anyone. It's cool.'

'Well, that's great. But it's not actually. Not cool.'

'What's the matter?'

'Nothing. Well, that's not true. Take the wedding dress. Dresses. Our wedding dresses.'

'What about them?'

Aideen could feel her palms getting damp. 'It's just that the other day you were talking orange satin sheaths?'

'Yeah, but, you know, I'm not sure I'm going to manage the weight loss. So now what I'm thinking is we stick with the orange, but go for a more traditional kind of shape? Really tight corset bodices, huge veil and meringue skirt. We could do the veils in silver net with Swarovski crystals. You know what I'm saying? Bling but not over the top?'

Aideen suddenly realised why Carol had pushed her into arranging this meeting. If no one told Eileen to stop, she'd simply keep going, and probably change her mind right up to the wire. By which stage they'd end up with whatever they'd have to settle for, and the likelihood was that none of them would be pleased. It couldn't just be the bridesmaids trying to get a grip on things.

She needed to step in and do this herself. 'I've already made my mind up about my dress.'

Eileen looked blank. 'But you haven't put any ideas up on the Facebook page.'

'No. And I'm sorry. But my mind was made up long before this became a double wedding. And, let's face it, you've yet to make up yours.'

'Well, but we'll have to match.'

Having felt rather pleased with herself for her firm, definitive statement, Aideen now felt as if she'd been hit on the head with a brick. Of course they had to match somehow. And obviously they couldn't both turn up dressed as the goddess Flora. Anyway, that was *her* design and she didn't want it robbed. Staring at Eileen, she realised that she should have said all this sooner, but Eileen had bounced and talked so much that she hadn't had time to think.

Though that was a pretty lame excuse, now she came to consider it. Feeling horribly guilty, she pulled out her phone. 'Look, I'll show you the picture ... well, the sort of inspiration.'

The painting was her screensaver, so it came up at a touch. For once, Eileen seemed lost for words. Aideen tapped through to another image and pulled in on the dress, saying Carol was helping with the design. She could hear herself saying the fabric was unbleached muslin, and explaining the medieval language of flowers: carnations were emblems of love and fidelity, while narcissi stood for prosperity and good fortune. 'Daisies are for love too. They symbolise innocence. Carol's been at the embroidery for months. It's nearly done. I'm going to have a plain underskirt. Pat Fitz is crocheting the lace.'

She'd talked herself to a standstill and Eileen, who was holding the phone, was still sitting there staring.

Aideen twisted her fingers together in anguish. 'I know you won't want the same dress. And, anyway, it represents Conor's and my story, and you and Joe have a story of your own. But maybe we could use my colours as a basis for our theme?'

When Eileen spoke it was like the voice of doom. 'Pat Fitz is crocheting the lace?'

'Well, probably.' Aideen swallowed nervously. 'Or I might have pendant beads.'

Handing back the phone, Eileen took a deep breath. 'I don't quite know how to say this, but have you actually looked at that painting?'

'Well, of course I have.'

'And you haven't noticed that your one, Flora, is pregnant?'

'What?'

'Mind you, so's Venus. Ready to drop.'

'What? They're not!' Aideen looked at the picture again, her eyes out on stalks. Her voice faltered. 'Well, I know what you mean, but they're symbols of fertility.' Her lip trembled and she bit it painfully. 'My dress is going to be Empire line.'

'It's up to you, of course, how you want to present yourself. But I'm telling you, you're taking a big risk.'

There was a long moment in which Aideen looked at her aghast. Her face must have shown what she was thinking, because Eileen grabbed her hand. 'Ah, Jaysus, Aideen, I didn't mean anything about your mother! I was just saying the associations are dodgy. Like you said yourself, a wedding dress tells a story. You don't want to walk down the aisle looking as if you're already knocked up!'

Chapter Thirty-Two

No birds were singing as Brian got out of the car. Instead he could hear the repeated clack of a stone hammer and, walking round to the back of the house, he found the source of the sound. A week or so ago, he'd given instructions for one of the old dwellings to be rebuilt to make a garage. The original stonework stood to a height of several feet in places and now, while the rest of the lads had cleared up and gone home, the indefatigable Fury was working on a wall.

'For God's sake, Fury, what're you at?'

'What does it look like?'

The Divil, who had advanced on Brian, barking shrilly, now looked darkly at Fury and pattered off to the van.

Brian turned back to Fury. 'Even The Divil knows when it's time to down tools.'

Squinting at the string he'd rigged to provide a straight horizontal, Fury grunted dismissively and laid his next stone. 'You said you wanted this made up.'

'I didn't say I wanted a stonemason's job.'

'Well, a botch might be fine for you, but it won't do me. These walls were properly built the first time, and I'm not going to insult them now by making them up in blocks.' He jerked his thumb at the length of broken wall he hadn't yet got to. 'Look at that. Tidy work, the like of which you'd go far to find, these days. Why would I waste blocks, and go knocking up sand and cement, when I've stone to hand and masses of good subsoil? God, if you're not bankrupt by the time this job's finished, you damn well should be!'

Capitulating, Brian bent down, hefted a stone and passed it to him. Having given it a sharp glance to demonstrate that he wouldn't proceed until suited, Fury set the stone on the mortar. For the next ten minutes they worked together, shifting their weight to the weight of the stones, as rhythmically as dancers.

Though it was ages since Brian had built a wall, the mesmeric quality of the task returned to him at once. The swing of his body with his legs braced, the precise clack of Fury's hammer, and the wet thump as each chosen stone was bedded in the mortar. The old dwelling had been solidly built, parallel walls infilled with rubble to repel winter storms. Fury was right. The subsoil thrown up for the foundations of the new house was perfect for the mortar and infill needed to raise these old stones.

As each stone passed from his hands to Fury's, Brian knew it had already passed through many other hands. Whoever had first built this little structure had bent his back and reached out, choosing his stones by eye, and knowing each choice would affect the next. It wasn't enough to build straight, you had to have foresight.

The skill of the man doing Brian's job lay in the eye and the hand's choices, and the mind reaching ahead in the knowledge of what was yet to be done. The skill of the mason with the hammer lay in knowing how to strike a sharp edge or smooth an imperfection, and where to place a stone. Each must be set at the correct angle, to shed water, and each must lock with the next bedded beside it.

Reaching up with another stone, Brian glanced at the sky. Every man who had built walls in this valley had kept an eye on the clouds and tested the wind. Sudden rain or even a change in humidity during construction could affect the strength of a wall, and had to be allowed for. Bronze Age builders had used the same lime mortar that he and Fury were working with today. Its strength lay in its binding property when mixed with liquid and, traditionally, the secret of the perfect mix was passed from craftsman to apprentice across generations. From time immemorial, the tried and tested liquids added were organic. As late as the nineteenth century, horse or bull's blood or animal urine had been chosen, while builders of Fury's generation had still used their own piss.

When they came to the end of a lift, Fury stopped. Reaching for the pinched-out cigarette he kept behind his ear, he hunkered down and settled his back against a firm bit of wall. Brian joined him.

'You're not going to want to put thatch on my garage, are you?'

'If you think I'm going to spend weeks doing extras, forget it. You can roof it yerself and, if I was you, I'd shove up a sheet of corrugated. I might find you some Kingspan but it'll cost you.'

It wasn't a comment requiring response, so Brian ignored it. Rooting in the limy rubble beside him, he picked out a pebble and lobbed it towards the river. It fell short of the water and disappeared into a mass of silt and wind-blown grasses. High above, a swallow who'd been spooked by the sound of the hammer swooped past, catching evening insects.

Reaching into his pocket, Brian found the gold ring and held it out on the palm of his hand. 'The Divil gave me this. He took it from the river.'

'Well, that's a fair return for a few bones.'

'Not old, I think. Maybe nineteenth century? No mark, so you can't tell.'

Fury stretched his legs to dig in his own trouser pocket. 'You'll be into the house next month, I'd say.'

Brian, who hadn't smoked for years, accepted the offer of a roll-up. 'You know that kind of lethargy you get when something you've planned for months is suddenly imminent?'

'Would we be talking about the house or something else?'

'Part of me wants to walk away and pretend this place hasn't happened.'

Fury shrugged. 'I've known fellows build themselves houses and never move into them.'

'Seriously?'

'Why do you think property papers talk about dream homes? It's all fantasy, these days. No wonder people are scared to move in. The dream might turn out to be a nightmare.' He bent sideways and cupped his hands round a match to give Brian a light. 'That's not you, though, is it?'

'Nope, I don't do dreams. I know too much about sewage systems.'

'So we're not talking about the house.'

Inhaling deeply, Brian picked a shred of tobacco from his lip. They smoked in silence until he spoke again. 'When did you go over to England?'

'Nineteen forty-five. Just after the war. Plenty of work back then, building up fallen walls.'

'Were you over long?'

'Long enough.'

'I was at school there. Boarding school. It was a hellish building, freezing cold in winter.'

The Divil appeared down by the river and, seeing that they'd stopped working, bounded up. Fury scratched him between the ears and the little dog promptly curled up and closed his eyes. 'He's a divil for company.'

'That's pack instinct, isn't it? Generations of ancestors sleeping in a hairy heap at the back of a cave.'

'I'd say none of us was meant to live alone.' Fury cocked an eye at him. 'You ever been married?'

'Once.'

'Lucky man.'

'You weren't?'

'Nah. Well, I never settled. It's a hard life on the sites. You keep moving. And back then, I can tell you, you weren't welcome. They needed you for the dirty jobs but they treated you like shit. It's always the same story when you're an emigrant. So you're always making plans to be going home. Then you do come home and it's nothing like the place you had in your head.'

Brian took a pull on his cigarette. 'Did you ever read *Brooklyn*?'

'I'm illiterate, remember?'

'Oh, for Christ's sake, Fury, could you drop that for once?'

'No, I didn't read *Brooklyn*. What's it about?'

'There's a film too.'

'I don't go to cinemas. They won't let The Divil in.'

'It's about being caught between two countries and not knowing which to choose. No, that's wrong. It's about forgetting your life in the other place when you're not actually in it.'

'Yeah, well, that can happen.'

Brian flicked limy soil off his forefinger with his thumbnail. Then he tipped his head back and watched the swallow circling in the air. 'Hanna showed *Brooklyn* at her film club.'

'Did you see it?'

'God, no, I don't join things. I went and bought the book.'

Fury scratched the sleeping Divil, who curled himself into a tighter knot. 'I'll be letting the painters go at the end of the week.'

The tin of cobalt blue hung in the air. Determined to ignore it, Brian asked about Fury's next job.

'Ah, I pick and choose these days. Something will come up.'

'Hanna said you were round to do her roof tile.' He hadn't intended to mention Hanna again and, now he'd done so, found himself starting to gabble. 'You did a great job for her there on Maggie's place. I remember the panic she got herself into over the planning permission.'

Fury pinched his fag out. 'Why don't you just piss or get off the pot?' Uncoiling his long length, he got up and stood over Brian, his torn waxed jacket flapping in a gust of wind. 'You're dying to put that ring on her finger, so what's holding you back?'

'Oh, Jesus! Stuff. Complications. She had a whole life before she met me. So had I.'

'For Christ's sake, man, so has everyone. I was sixteen when I went to London, and I left a girl behind me. A lifetime later I left someone else to come back.'

'I need to talk to her.'

Fury bent down and picked up the hammer. 'Well, that's up to you, of course. I've never gone in for too much talking myself.'

'That's the point, isn't it? Nor have I. Mostly it just makes things more complicated.'

'You've built her a house, though.'

'All right, I admit it. Yes, I have.'

'So what's your problem?'

Brian stood up and stubbed his cigarette out on a stone. 'You can't ask a woman to marry you if there's stuff you haven't said.'

Chapter Thirty-Three

Hanna inspected her neck in a mirror. It was nearly two years since she'd seen Malcolm – at a fraught family gathering where they'd all been madly convivial – and she'd woken this morning with a sinking feeling that she wasn't wearing well.

This, of course, was idiotic. She looked a damn sight better now than she had in the stressful years immediately after she'd left him. Furthermore, Malcolm's opinion of her appearance was unimportant. Irrelevant. Totally beside the point. He hadn't come over to see her, he was visiting Jazz and Louisa. He'd be focused on his mum and daughter, not his ex-wife.

It was far too warm for a polo neck, but perhaps a jaunty scarf? Rooting through a drawer, she found a silk square and spent several minutes attempting to knot it securely. But each time she turned away and glanced back at her reflection the Audrey Hepburn effect had gone and she saw an anxious middle-aged cowboy wearing a badly tied neckerchief. Eventually she laughed at herself and tossed the scarf onto the bed. Her neck wasn't all that bad, and how could it matter what Malcolm thought, when Brian said that her beauty was in the bone?

Anyway, she had no reason to expect to see Malcolm today. Jazz had phoned the previous night with his schedule. He was flying into Cork this morning, and hiring a car to drive on to Finfarran. He'd booked himself into The Royal Vic in Carrick, but hadn't divulged how long he was planning to stay.

Pulling on her sweater and looking for her handbag, Hanna told herself grimly that, for someone who claimed to be so cool about Malcolm, Jazz needed a hell of a lot of attention when he was around. She'd announced again on the phone that he'd better not take her for granted. 'He always thinks I'll be free to entertain him. Well, I'm not, Mum. You know that.'

'I do. So does he, love. He knows you've got a job.'

'And I hope he's not going to start making demands on you.'

'He can try, but that doesn't mean I'll give in to them. I've got my own work, you know.'

'Yes, and so has Louisa.'

'Jazz, you've told me yourself, repeatedly, that Louisa's got the measure of him. Chill out.'

'Oh, God, Mum, what a ghastly expression!'

Hanna had laughed, but she'd ended the call with the thought that none of this was going to be easy. Louisa's suspicion that Malcolm was bored was probably spot-on, and no one knew better than Hanna herself what that meant. If they'd still been married she'd have strongly opposed his taking early retirement, given the effect it was likely to have on his ego. Malcolm needed a spotlight. He'd be lost without the excitement of the court room, where his charm and manipulative intelligence had made him such a star.

Pushing her packed lunch into her bag, and taking a last look at herself in the mirror, Hanna remembered Louisa's complaint after taking that trip to London. Malcolm had questioned his mother's ability to run Edge of the World Essentials, and wouldn't accept that her business was none of his concern. Hanna sighed. If he'd come to Finfarran intending to meddle, Louisa wouldn't be happy. And Jazz, in her present volatile state, was likely to go ballistic. She seemed to be coping well with the difficult job of being Eileen's bridesmaid, but Hanna knew it was adding to her stress.

Today was one of Conor's mobile days and, usually, there'd be nothing special happening in the library. Though the clubs and events were always well attended, significant feedback in the box on her desk had alerted Hanna to the need for balance. Several brisk notes had pointed out there was a distinction to be made between a public library and a jolly community centre, and that the writers would appreciate a chance to browse in silence, or avail themselves in peace of a trained librarian's knowledge and advice. So, aware of often being distracted by the demands of what else was going on, she tried to keep at least one morning purely for book borrowing, which appealed to a demographic that seldom came in on other days.

Today, however, she'd had to bend her rule. The County Arts Officer had declared it Children's Culture Day and a story session was scheduled for twelve noon. Volunteers had been working on crêpe-paper decorations, and a local children's author had been booked to give a reading. The author, a pleasant man whom Hanna had met socially, was important enough to warrant a page in the *Finfarran Inquirer*, so a reporter who doubled as a photographer was due to come along.

Even though there was nothing to do but set out the kids' chairs and hang the streamers, Hanna knew that at least one volunteer would be waiting for her to open up. Sure enough, as she entered the courtyard from Broad Street, Darina Kelly was standing on the doorstep, trying to control two unruly children. She was wearing ripped jeans and a tie-dye T-shirt, and her hennaed cornrows suggested Bo Derek on a bad day. 'Oh, there you are. Thank goodness! These two are being such twerps! I've told them they have to behave as it's a special day for kids – haven't I, monsters? But their dad fed them a ton of sugar at breakfast and now they're like a couple of bees in a bottle!'

Resigning herself to a difficult morning, Hanna unlocked the outer door and turned off the alarm. As she entered the lobby, the gift shop staff came clattering in behind her, and two of the psalter exhibition guides appeared at the foot of the steps. Darina bustled past her into the library. 'It's so *quiet* and *tranquil* here in the mornings! *Such* a joy after the hell at home! You must love your job, Hanna, don't you? I mean, what a *gift* to live one's life surrounded by all these books!' She dropped her drawstring bag on the floor, where her little girl pounced on it.

'Oh, hell! Gobnit, stop, leave Mummy's bag alone ...' The child pulled an iPhone from the depths of the bag and crawled under Hanna's desk. Wedging herself defiantly into a corner, she glared out through a fringe of blonde hair plaited with beads. Her little brother's face turned scarlet. Darina took him by the arm. 'Setanta! Stop it, d'you hear? I mean, don't start!' She bent forward and the heavy pendant she was wearing struck him on the head. The boy, who was only a toddler, dissolved into tears. Dropping his arm and casting her eyes to Heaven, Darina attempted to disentangle the pendant from her scarf, which, Hanna reckoned, must be at least four foot long. Definitely not the Hepburn look, more Dr Who.

Setanta was now screaming like a fire siren. Basely ignoring Darina's line about the sugar, Hanna took him by the hand and suggested a biscuit. Immediately Gobnit emerged from under the desk. 'Me too. He *can't* unless I do. Gimme one.'

Darina threw up her hands. 'Oh, fine, gorge yourselves, see if I care! Say "thank you" to Miss Casey, though. Be nice. D'you hear me, Gobnit? *Nice*.' She delved into the bag for her crêpe-paper streamers, leaving Hanna to pilot the kids to the kitchenette.

Once there, Hanna closed the door and looked down at them sternly. 'One each, and you're going to sit down to eat them. Is that clear?'

Both children smiled at her angelically, and Gobnit pointed to the row of hooks on the wall. 'Do you want us to put on coveralls?'

Hanna took down two children's plastic aprons, kept for the library's Kiddie Crafts group. 'Yes. And I also want you to be quiet. Can you do that?'

'Of course.' Gobnit held up the iPhone. 'We'll turn the volume right down and play *Dora the Explorer*.'

Back in the library, Hanna settled them in a secluded corner. There were sure to be ructions when Darina found them with the iPhone, but at least she'd bought herself breathing space to get set up for the day.

By eleven thirty Darina had been joined by the three other

mums who'd organised the event. In the interim Hanna had persuaded her to take the kids to play in the nuns' garden. Before they left, she'd managed to whip away the iPhone and return it to the bag unnoticed by Darina. Gobnit's justifiable outrage had been taken by her mother for characteristic naughtiness, and the reproach in little Setanta's eyes had left Hanna smitten by remorse. Still, she'd got them out of the way for a couple of hours, which had allowed her to help several elderly readers to find books.

She'd also dealt with a call from Mary Casey, who knew perfectly well that she shouldn't have phoned. 'Don't go putting this down on me now. I'm only ringing because you ignore my texts.'

'Mam, I ignore your texts for the same reason I don't take personal phone calls. I'm at work.'

'And when is your poor mother supposed to talk to you?'

'You can call me whenever you like, you know that. Just not when I'm working.'

'God above, do you know what it is, you're worse than our Jazz!'

'You haven't been ringing Jazz at work, have you?'

'How well you don't ask if I'm all right!'

'And are you?

'I am, of course. Never better.'

'So what do you want?'

'I want to know what you're going to say to your pup of an ex-husband!'

'Mam ...'

'Don't you Mam me, Hanna Mariah Casey. This is crunch time. I'm telling you now, I won't sit down in that man's company unless I know that you've thrashed this money thing out.'

'Well, in that case you're going to be doing an awful lot of standing. Because there's nothing to be discussed.'

'He owes you—'

'Mother! Stop. Right now. I'm going to put the phone down. Don't ring me back on this line. And I'm warning you, don't go winding Jazz up. I mean it. Back off.'

The call had upset her so much that she'd nearly rung Brian. But he, too, would be working, so that wouldn't be fair. Anyway, it really wasn't okay to be making personal phone calls so, to calm herself down, she'd raided the library biscuit tin instead.

Three KitKats later, she'd returned to her desk and motored through a huge list of emails. But now, as the author arrived, along with the reporter, she felt that, like Darina's kids, she'd overdosed on sugar and, having had the initial rush, was suffering from its effect. All around her, children were squealing and quarrelling over chairs. Irritated, Hanna cursed herself for having agreed to host the story session. This was supposed to be a calm, composed day in the library, when her time was spent simply dealing with books. No crêpe paper. No reporters. No affable female from the County Arts Office, turning up with her hair done, eager to be featured in a photo.

But that was churlish. The author was charming, the kids were excited, and this was a special day. Pulling herself together, Hanna went and shook hands with the arrivals. Darina appeared beside her with Setanta and Gobnit in tow. It was evident that she was longing to be introduced to the author and to tell him how much Gobnit adored all his books.

'She really is a remarkable little reader, aren't you, Pumpkin? And a critic too! She wasn't at all happy about what Brona Bear did in *Brona's Burp*! We thought she was very greedy and we tore that page out!'

Hanna's eyes met the author's registering apology, though she could see that he'd weathered worse mothers in his time. Gobnit crossed her eyes at him and announced that Brona Bear was Very Boring. 'I like *Dora the Explorer* because I can get her in hi-res.'

Darina retired discomfited and Hanna steered the author – who was shaking with repressed laughter – to his seat. Then she returned to her desk and watched the magic of a really talented storyteller addressing a group of kids. They sat in a circle around him, their eyes wide and, in many cases, their thumbs firmly in their mouths. Listening to the low voice, and observing the fluid movements of the author's supple hands, Hanna could see each child falling under his spell.

Setanta was lying on his stomach on the floor with his elbows planted on the author's feet. Even Gobnit, who'd hung around by the shelving, was edging towards the group. Observing the pointed face under the ridiculous beaded fringe, Hanna was stabbed by a memory of Jazz as a little girl.

As a stroppy teenager pained by the marriage break-up, Jazz had insisted that Malcolm in the midst of a case had always been distant and unavailable; and, fuelled by Mary Casey, that had become an accepted myth, which Hanna never challenged. But the whole truth had been far more nuanced than Mary or Jazz was prepared to admit.

Now, as Gobnit slid into the author's spellbound circle, Hanna recalled a May evening in London after a shopping trip to the West End. She'd let herself in at the front door and run down to the basement, where she'd piled her bags on the scrubbed kitchen table. The conservatory door was open and the pear trees in the brick-walled garden were in leaf.

Outside, Malcolm was sitting on the garden bench with Jazz. Their heads were bent in intense concentration, and Jazz's eyes beneath her dark fringe were alight. She'd been the same age as Gobnit then, seven or eight. Standing in the doorway, Hanna had watched the two beloved faces, and strained to hear Malcolm's murmuring voice. He was telling Jazz a story about a mouse who lived in a pear tree.

Every detail of that scene was still etched in Hanna's mind. The evening sun through the green leaves and the grey slabbed surface of the garden, where she'd planted big scarlet tubs of rosemary and mint. The Liberty print smock that Jazz had worn with a pair of Doc Martens, and the muscular curve of Malcolm's arm around their daughter's waist. He'd removed his jacket and rolled up the sleeves of the crisp, formal shirt he'd worn to work that morning. The jacket and a discreet silk tie were tossed on the garden bench and, as his quiet voice rose and fell, his handsome, hawk-like face was full of delight. Leaning together in perfect trust, he and Jazz were like two absorbed children and, rather than disturb them, Hanna had crept away, leaving them to finish the story together.

That sharp snapshot of the past was only one of many. You might say that Malcolm's betrayal negated all such moments, but Hanna knew she could never pretend that they hadn't happened at all.

Chapter Thirty-Four

When Conor got home from the day's mobile-library run he was worried. He'd texted Aideen several times and she still hadn't replied. Having left the van in Carrick and started back home on his Vespa, he'd been tempted to take a right turn off the motorway and nip into Lissbeg. He couldn't, though, because he'd promised Joe that he'd grease and oil the tractor, a job that needed doing before the following day.

Eileen was coming to tea at the farm and Joe didn't want her arriving while he was up to his elbows in muck. That's what he'd said, anyway, though Conor had noticed that, ever since Old Dawson had come up with the offer of a desk and a business card, Joe had taken to copping out of the dirtier jobs on the farm. He was all for swaggering round the mart, talking to fellows he'd soon be selling gear to, but you seldom saw him clearing a ditch with a shovel, or wrestling a bunch of sheep through a stinking bath of dip.

Conor remembered his mam saying long ago that Joe had never really been suited to farming, which was why he was prone to kicking over the traces once in a while. Not regularly, but sometimes, as if he'd suddenly had enough. The accident to Paddy's back had happened the day after Joe had been on a pub crawl in Lissbeg. He'd arrived home totally wrecked, and the next morning he hadn't been concentrating so, when a pregnant cow in a pen went for him, she'd nearly trampled him down. It was Paddy getting him out of there that saved him, but Paddy himself had rolled over the rail at the last minute, and he'd come down on his spine in the cobbled yard.

Paddy had never blamed Joe for his accident, nor he wouldn't neither. But if your man hadn't gone off on the tear, it mightn't have happened at all. Conor reckoned that Joe himself hadn't got over the shock of it. So it was a good thing for the lot of them to be facing a new beginning and, by next year, with a new man worked in, things might be better all round.

Steering the Vespa into the yard, he rode it round the hay shed and parked at the back. Then he took off his helmet and texted Aideen again. There was no response and, since it was closing time at the deli, he hit speed dial and tried giving her a call. But her phone seemed to be off.

Fed up, Conor went and changed into his overalls. Paddy was inside in the room going through dockets, while Joe was up having a bath and, according to their mam, using the very last drop of the hot water. She was standing at the kitchen table, slicing tea brack, and there was no sign of Marmite or the kittens. Conor nicked a piece of brack as he passed her, and went back to the sheds to deal with the tractor.

Once he got properly mucky there'd be no point in trying to use his phone so, before opening the tin of grease, he had another go at calling Aideen. Her phone was still off. Conor wondered if he might nip into Lissbeg later and find her. He had a dawn start next morning, though, because the vet was coming, and it might be late to go looking for her by the time they'd finished tea. It could be that she, too, would need an early night, anyway. She'd been kind of down the other night when he'd seen her — sniffly and red-nosed and saying she might be starting a summer cold.

His mam had made it crystal clear that she wanted him at the tea table. Conor didn't blame her. She liked Eileen well enough but, at the same time, she'd be glad of a bit of support. Beneath all the generosity and the over-the-top enthusiasms, there was a steely sort of assurance about Joe's fiancée. Maybe it came with the money. Or maybe, like Joe, she was just used to getting her own way.

Back when he and Joe were growing up, their mam used to say that Joe had what she called 'older-brother syndrome'. When he and Conor used to row over something, Mam would always try to laugh them out of it; and, while Joe usually threw a strop, Conor would join the laugh because he hated her to be worried. Anyway, when push came to shove, he was never all that bothered. If Joe wanted the ball or the biggest bit of cake, what matter? It was easiest just to give in to him and find something else to do.

It couldn't have been like that with Eileen, though, because she was the youngest in her family. Maybe she had 'only-child syndrome'. Her five brothers were well grown before she came along, as an afterclap. According to Joe, the house the brothers were reared in had opened onto a street, and the lads had slept in two rooms, stacked up in bunk beds. Eileen was the only one born into the big place in the country with the tennis court and the gardens, and the bedrooms all en-suite.

So, maybe you couldn't blame her for being a bit of a lady of the manor. And, actually, she and Joe were well matched. It was typical of the two of them to want to pay for the wedding. Slapping grease onto the tractor's bearings, Conor told himself Joe'd always had a mad generous streak. Once he'd claimed the football, he was happy for you to choose what position you played in, and he'd break the bit of cake in two and give you the bigger half. There was nothing complicated about his generosity either. It just had to be his way or the highway.

Reaching up to the shelf where it stood in a jumble of obsolete tools and ends of wire, Conor turned on the ancient transistor radio, which was so knackered it seemed to be impervious to muck. Then, as his body automatically kept working on the tractor, his mind floated off on a dream of bliss.

They seemed to be settling on a wedding date some time next June. So by high summer next year Aideen and he would be living here on the farm.

Conor whistled happily along with the song on the transistor. Aideen's house in Lissbeg was one of those modern council boxes where you could hear all that went on in one room from the next. The inside walls at the farm weren't like that because most of the building was more than a hundred years old. The upstairs rooms were small, though, so Joe's bedroom was going to be knocked through into Conor's to make a room for him and Aideen twice its current size. There'd be room for a built-in wardrobe and a king-sized bed. His window had a view over the garden, which in June would be full of the flowers Aideen loved. There was a bathroom across the landing that would be theirs.

To begin with, he'd wondered if Joe would mind them appropriating his bedroom but, from Joe's description, Eileen's room at the Dawsons' house was palatial, and her dad had fixed to get them a big place of their own in Cork. Anyway, when their mam had first thought of knocking through into Joe's room, she'd managed to get Joe thinking he'd had the idea himself.

And the little parlour at the front of the house was going to be done up as theirs. That had been his mam's idea too. She said he and Aideen would want a place to relax together. If Conor knew Aideen, she'd probably want to spend most of her free time down in the kitchen. But a room of their own with a sofa and a telly would be great. They could put their wedding photos on the mantelpiece, Aideen in her gorgeous dress and himself probably looking like a dog's dinner. And they'd find a print of the *Primavera* and frame it on the wall.

Everything was going to be hunky-dory. Paddy had even had wind of the word of a man who'd be willing to take on the farm job. The guy had a proper agri degree from uni but he'd been born and raised on a farm east of Carrick. His granddad was still farming, though, and his dad was only in his sixties, so for the next while he wanted to hire himself out.

Paddy had told Conor that the final decision was his. 'You're the one who'll be working with him and, ultimately, when you're out on the farm, it's you who'll be the boss. If you like him, we can take him on and, whatever happens, we won't end up stuck with him. He has his own place to go off to in a few years' time and, meanwhile, we can be taking a view of what comes next for us here.'

There had been times since the accident when Joe had treated Paddy almost like he was thick. Not unkindly, but sort of over-solicitous, as if the poor man had lost the power to think. But, as their mam always said, Paddy was a great man for the big picture. He'd stand back and say nothing and then you'd find he had it all taped.

Still whistling, Conor went back to dreaming about Aideen. Though she'd grown up on a council estate, she had no fear of any animal. The first day they'd gone up for the cows with her on the back of his Vespa, she'd hopped off and stood in a gap instinctively, and the cows had sensed her assurance and turned the way they should. She was daft about cats and went moony over Bid the sheepdog, but she understood that farming was a business, and she'd come up with more than a few suggestions that made sense.

Conor didn't want to jump the gun and start raising them with Paddy but, once they were married and settled in, there'd be plenty to discuss. Moving towards getting a few acres certified as organic, say, and looking at her notion of raising pigs. You couldn't just keep plodding on, doing what you'd always done. And the new man with the uni degree might contribute ideas as well.

It was twenty to six by the time he'd finished with the tractor and he'd just managed to get himself showered when he saw Eileen's car driving round to the kitchen door. Joe went out to meet her, fierce natty in a Hilfiger shirt and a pair of new chinos. Looking down from the open bathroom window, Conor could see he was getting a bit thin on top. Eileen's hair, which used to be short, now reached her shoulders. It was weird, though you'd have to admit it suited her. She seemed to have lost weight too.

As Conor came into the kitchen, she was telling his mam that she probably shouldn't eat brack. 'I'm on a really strict diet. I fancy myself as svelte now that I've got these extensions. Not the Atkins diet exactly – the same thing but with a modern herbal twist. I won't stick to it, though, will I, Joe? Honestly, Una, I'm dreadful! Show me a lovely brack like that and I'm slathering on the butter!'

Una laughed and invited her to sit down. 'Have something to eat anyway. The brack isn't mandatory.'

'But I daresay I'll succumb to it. Actually, I'm sure I will. Wouldn't you think I'd have a bit of self-control?'

Joe gave a laugh and smacked her on the bum. 'Sure, you've no bloody self-control whatever! Look what you said to Aideen the other day.'

There was crackling silence in which Conor looked at him sharply. This was typical. A couple of weeks back Joe had chosen a safe moment to break the news of the family meeting at the farmhouse, and now he was using the same trick again. A lifetime of living with him told Conor this had to be a set-up and, by the look of their mam's face, she thought so too.

But clearly it wasn't a set-up that Eileen was in on. Looking from Una to Conor, she shifted in her chair. Having said his piece, Joe was sitting back, waiting to see what would happen. Conor turned to Eileen and asked her what he'd meant. At the back of his mind he knew he was dancing to Joe's bloody fiddle but, right now, he needed to find out what on earth she'd said to Aideen.

'Honestly, Conor, I didn't mean to upset her. Hasn't she told you?' Turning to Joe, Eileen spread her hands. 'You see? It wasn't a big deal. Aideen hasn't even mentioned it.'

Her eyes were sending darts at Joe, asking why he hadn't kept his mouth shut.

'Mentioned *what*?' Feeling his mam's hand on his arm, Conor lowered his voice and controlled himself. 'Sorry, I didn't mean to shout. What did you say to Aideen?'

'We were just having a chat about what she'd planned to wear.'

'At the wedding?'

'Well, yes. And it does sound lovely, and perhaps we could even find a way around it ...'

Conor's eyes narrowed and, seeing his face, Eileen changed tack. '... I mean, *she* said maybe we could use her colours as a theme. She did. And I'd be fine with that, Conor, really. I just thought I ought to mention something about the design.'

'So what did you say?'

'Oh, dammit, I didn't mean it! She took it the wrong way!'

Conor turned to Joe, who shrugged his shoulders. 'Look, if Aideen hasn't said anything, the chances are that it's fine. And, let's face it, Conor, she couldn't waltz down the aisle looking pregnant. Eileen's right. What would people say?'

Conor felt the colour drain from his face. 'You told her people would say she looked *pregnant*?'

Eileen looked at him beseechingly. 'Well, that's the way the girl is in the painting, Conor, you've got to see that.' Turning round, she held out her hand to Una. 'Honest to God, I never intended to upset Aideen. I never even *thought* about her mum.'

'Jesus Christ Almighty!'

Without waiting for his mam's response, Conor blundered through the kitchen door out into the yard. Digging his phone out of his pocket, he frantically hit speed dial, praying incoherently that Aideen would pick up. But she didn't. Her phone was still turned off.

Chapter Thirty-Five

Hanna stood at the courtyard gate and considered the nuns' garden. It was what Pat Fitz always called 'a pet day'. An extraordinary amount of growth had occurred since the last film club meeting. At the beginning of May the predominant colour in the garden had been the grey of the gravelled paths that ran between the herb beds. The conifers edging the far perimeter wall had added an unrelieved note of dark green, and the beds, which were mulched with bark, had still shown wide expanses of dark brown chippings.

Back then, the eye had been caught by the flash of birds' feathers and sunlight on the fountain. Now, wherever you looked, there seemed to be hundreds of shades of green, and the clipped box hedges enclosed tracts of blue hyssop, white and yellow feverfew, and deep red bee balm, all flowering or breaking into blossom. It was too early for purple and pale blue lavender flowers, and for deep blue rosemary, but their grey-green leaves made a spreading background for lemon-yellow Moonshine yarrow, silver sage, and shimmering Firewitch dianthus.

At Hanna's elbow, the red-brick wall of the old school was warm under green creeper; and at the far side of the garden, at right angles to the school building, stained-glass saints in the old convent's windows glowed like tall flowers between their grey stone arches. As she stood there in the sunshine, movement by the polytunnel at the far side of the garden caught her attention. She stiffened. Beyond the fountain, Louisa was talking animatedly to some of the volunteers who tended the herb beds. Beside her, listening with his sleek head bent, was Malcolm. Instinctively, Hanna stepped into the shadow of the gateway. Even at this distance, viewed through the veil of shining water, his figure was unmistakable. And she could see he was charming the socks off the group gathered around him.

Though he'd arrived at The Royal Vic yesterday, Hanna had yet to encounter him. The previous night he'd given Jazz and Louisa dinner in Carrick and today, according to a text from Jazz, Louisa was taking him out to lunch and showing off Edge of the World Essentials. Presumably, having shown him the garden, she was about to take him into The Old Convent Centre. Hanna considered retreating into the library. But, as though he'd sensed her presence, Malcolm turned and waved.

It would be idiotic to pretend not to have seen him so, feeling absurdly like Alice in the looking-glass garden, she started down the gravelled walk, half wondering if, like Alice's, the path would give a sudden twist and shake itself and lead her back in the direction from which she'd come. Instead, Malcolm and Louisa moved steadily along the path at right angles to hers and, unlike Alice and the Red Queen, they met within moments on the old convent step.

Malcolm was wearing Armani. He usually did. Hanna, who'd slept through her alarm, was wearing whatever had come to hand when she'd scrambled out of bed. The Audrey Hepburn scarf was at home at the bottom of a drawer. Uncomfortably conscious of the contrast between her own jeans and T-shirt and Louisa's neat, calf-length dress worn with a string of pearls, she pushed back a stray strand of hair and pecked Malcolm on the cheek. 'Good to see you. Are you comfortable at The Royal Vic?'

Knowing Malcolm, it was a toss-up between whether he'd find the Vic delightful or complain that it was provincial and badly run. Apparently, he'd decided on the former. 'Extremely comfortable, and they keep a very good wine cellar. And a remarkable barman. We ate like lords there last night, so we're planning a sandwich lunch here today.'

There was nothing for it but to admit that she'd been on her way to pick up a sandwich in the café.

Louisa beamed. 'Well, join us, Hanna, won't you? We're popping up to show Malcolm round our offices. It shouldn't take long. If you'll find a table we'll meet you there.'

'Okay. Lovely. Will Jazz be with us?'

'No, I'd hoped she would, but she's off to a meeting.'

Hanna managed to keep her face in neutral. Leaving them to go upstairs, she walked briskly across to the Garden Café, telling herself that she couldn't go round dodging Malcolm for ever. Anyway, she'd already agreed to attend a family dinner tomorrow, when Malcolm was hosting the Turners and the Caseys at the Vic, with Brian thrown in. It was likely to be excruciating. Mary would take issue with Malcolm's house sale; Jazz would be feeling the lack of Sam; and she herself was already wishing that Brian hadn't been invited. So perhaps a sandwich with Malcolm and

Louisa would serve as a kind of rehearsal and make her feel less apprehensive.

Having found a table and sat down with a coffee, she gave Jazz a call. 'Where are you?'

'On my way to a meeting. Where are you?'

'Sitting in the nuns' garden about to have lunch with your dad.'

'And feeling that I've abandoned you?'

'No. But I wondered if all went well last night?'

'Of course it did. But, honestly, Mum, he's already driving me crazy. He's full of bright ideas about how we should grow the business. That's why I've bunked off to this meeting. I was buggered if I was going to sit up in the office watching him making mental notes of what we're doing wrong.'

'There is no meeting, is there?'

'Actually, I'm having a sneaky pub lunch with a book.'

Twenty minutes later, when Malcolm and Louisa joined her, Hanna could tell that he'd irritated his mother as well as his daughter. Louisa was being determinedly upbeat. She praised Hanna's choice of table and announced firmly that the café's food and ambience were better than anything comparable in London. 'Such delicious sandwiches and so much local produce!'

Malcolm laughed indulgently and said that, where Finfarran was concerned, all her geese would seem to be swans. 'It is a charming garden, though, I'll give you that.'

'Thank you, Malcolm. I was an avid gardener before you were born, so I suppose I may be allowed an uncontested opinion on that.'

Malcolm's dark eyes danced. 'Darling Ma, there's no need to be prickly! All I said was that you might find a better place to rent as your HQ.'

'And I've told you already that this place couldn't be bettered. The facilities are splendid, and one could hardly find an environment more suited to our brand.'

Determined not to be caught in the crossfire, Hanna was leaning back in her chair with her coffee. Malcolm's way of calling his parents 'Ma' and 'Pa' had always slightly annoyed her. It felt like a habit picked up at his expensive public school.

Louisa had told her some years ago that the manor in Kent had been bought by Malcolm's dad, who'd started out as a solicitor and become rich by investing in stocks and shares. 'We began married life in a rather dull country town.'

'I don't know why, but I'd always assumed that the family had lived in the manor house for ages.'

'Well, that was the impression George liked to give. He gave up work as soon as we could afford it. He was in his father's office, you know, and the job bored him stiff.' Louisa had assured her earnestly that her husband wouldn't have lied. It was simply that he was happy to have achieved a home that Malcolm could be proud of.

Hanna, who'd always been fond of her late father-in-law, had smiled. 'I can imagine that. George was a very sweet man.'

This information, which had emerged long after the divorce had gone through, had given her another reason to feel that Malcolm had deceived her. But, after all, why should he offer her chapter and verse on his background? She'd never asked for it.

Louisa's family must have been better connected than the Turners. Malcolm had been sent to Harrow, where her father had been, not to his own father's minor public school. When he and Hanna met he was very much the son of the manor, and it was the most hospitable home she'd ever been in: a relaxed, spacious house imbued with Louisa's good taste and George's genial charm. Theirs was a civilised, very English world in which the copies of the Mitford books that Jazz remembered had shared shelves with works by Iris Murdoch and Doris Lessing. Sipping her coffee, Hanna reflected wryly that Malcolm could easily have grown up calling his mother 'Louisa' and addressing his tall moustachioed father as 'Fa'.

And that was the world she'd recreated in their homes in London and Norfolk, the one in which she'd chosen to raise Jazz. Except that Jazz had also had those long summer breaks in Finfarran. She'd played on the seal beach with kids from Lissbeg, and known the joys of new-laid eggs, milk from the cow, and brown soda bread. Her first crush had been on a freckled boy who'd taken her out in a boat to haul lobster pots. Knockinver and the ocean, the green fields and the complex web of Irish small-town relationships were as much a part of her life as Malcolm's privileged world of professional contacts at the right level and suitable social connections.

Tuning in again to the others' conversation, Hanna found Malcolm was still raising Louisa's hackles.

'Tell me again how you're sourcing the herbs you'll use.'

'I've told you twice already. You can't have been listening.'

'Nonsense! I always listen. But I do wonder if you're taking the right tack.'

'We are. So you mustn't let it trouble you.'

'Darling, do stop it. I might have something useful to offer.'

Louisa put down her sandwich and folded her hands on the table. 'All right. Tell me what I'm doing wrong.'

'Well, those photographs you showed me of your suppliers ...'

'Yes?'

'Isn't it all a bit amateurish? I mean, a gap-toothed yokel and a curly-haired moppet?'

'Those shots are for a marketing drive. Rather a good one put together by your daughter and the team.'

'I grasped that. But I understood that these are your actual growers. Not models?'

'Well, the little girl is the daughter of a couple who'll be supplying us – we haven't yet sunk to child labour. And Johnny Hennessy has been growing herbs all his life.'

'On an industrial scale?'

'No. Which is fine. Because that's not the kind of supplier we employ.'

Malcolm sat back and joined the tips of his fingers, a gesture Hanna had always told him he'd stolen from Rumpole of the Bailey. 'And that, Ma dear, is precisely my point. If you start out on an artisan level you'll see no return for your investment. Not in the long run. You'll grow to a certain stage – assuming you're lucky – and simply stagnate.'

Hanna was about to intervene when Louisa laughed. 'For heaven's sake, Malcolm, stop being pompous. You may be able to browbeat a witness, but you're wasting your time with me. I married a canny businessman, remember? And together we managed our finances rather well.'

Malcolm threw up his hand in another stagey gesture, this time indicative of good-humoured acquiescence. It struck Hanna that his pomposity had grown with the passage of time. Or perhaps the increasingly juvenile girlfriends meant he could now indulge in it? He wouldn't have got away with that tone when he was married to her.

But, though she hadn't gone in for serial cradle-snatching, she too could be accused of moving on to a younger partner. And, in a looking-glass way, she and Malcolm had each succumbed to a form of menopausal vanity. While he'd embraced the role of an archetypal sugar daddy, she'd rejected Brian for months, afraid of being seen as a clichéd divorcée dating a younger man.

Sometimes she looked back now and gasped at the thought of all she would have lost had Brian given up on her. After what felt like a lifetime of betrayal, it was extraordinary to think she was now loved by a man she could wholly trust.

Chapter Thirty-Six

Slapping a 'Beef and Gherkin' sticker on a wrapper, Aideen put a freshly made sandwich on the rack.

Bríd came up behind her and whipped it out again. 'For feck's sake, Aideen, do you not know egg and cress when you see it?' She peeled the sticker off the cellophane and went to write another, while Aideen leaned on the counter looking contrite. They were alone in the deli in a mid-morning lull before the lunchtime rush.

There was a shrill ping from Aideen's bag, on the shelf behind her. Stalking back with the sandwich, Bríd gave her a thump. 'If you're going to ignore Conor, will you turn that damn thing off?'

'It mightn't be Conor.'

'Then answer that text.'

'No. I know it's from him.'

Bríd went to serve a couple of backpackers. When they left, she came and glared at Aideen. 'As soon as he gets a chance he's going to be round here to find you.'

'Well, it won't be today. He has the vet coming.'

'Tomorrow, then. Or the next day. He's going to want to know what the hell you're playing at, Aideen. So do I.'

Aideen stuck her chin out. 'Oh, shut up, will you? Mind your own business.'

'This *is* my business. I'm your bridesmaid and you're refusing to talk to your fiancé.'

'I wish you'd both just back off. I need some space.'

Bríd rolled her eyes and squared her shoulders. At that moment Pat Fitz and Mary Casey came in looking for fairy cakes and, seeing her chance, Aideen grabbed her bag.

'Hi, Pat. Hello, Mary. Isn't it grand weather altogether? Listen, Bríd, I'll do that thing now and see you in a couple of hours.'

'What?'

Aideen dodged past Mary and Pat, who were standing in front of the counter. 'Bríd made some gorgeous cupcakes this morning, ladies. You'll love them.'

For Mary Casey the word 'cupcake' was a red rag to a bull. As Aideen had known she would, she turned on Bríd. ''Tis far from cupcakes you were reared, Bríd Garvey! When did we lose our native language and start talking like Yanks?'

Under cover of the lecture, which was moving on to muffins, Aideen slipped out the door. It was a bit mean to have started a row on purpose but, if she didn't get off on her own somewhere, her head was going to explode.

At the rear of the deli she took her helmet out of the box on the back of her Vespa, locked her bag into it and set off with no idea of where she was going. Half an hour later, she found herself on a back road between ditches surmounted by foxgloves, and realised that the farm was only a mile or two away. Slowing down, she stared at a clump of tall spires covered in clustering purple flowers. Some caterpillar or grub had eaten away at the pointed foliage, leaving an intricate pattern of holes, which drooped from the stems like delicate green lace.

Aideen's eyes filled with tears. How *dare* Eileen sneer at the thought of Pat Fitz crocheting lace for her wedding dress? And how could anyone fail to see the beauty of Conor's idea? Her mum would have *loved* the thought of Aunt Carol doing the embroidery, and no one would think she was pregnant. No one. Or if they would she didn't care.

At the thought of her mum, the tears began to fall. Eileen would have a church full of ghastly, noisy relations, with Maura and Old Dawson up at the front, looking smug. Conor and Joe would have crowds of cousins and connections, as well as Una and Paddy. And they'd all be looking over at Aunt Carol and Uncle Justin, and Bríd's three little sisters, who'd be the only ones in the place to support her. She'd been so sure that it didn't matter, but it did. Well, it did if Eileen was right and the whole church would be sitting there saying she'd got herself into trouble.

Nobody used that awful expression 'got into trouble' these days. Though maybe the Dawsons did, with their swanky house and their money. Maybe the telly would be there, or some awful society magazine, and they'd think she was pregnant too. And then her dad's family would see the pictures and say she was no better than her mum.

Dragging off her helmet, Aideen put her head down on the handlebars and bawled. It wasn't *fair*. No one had asked her if she wanted this stupid double wedding. Why hadn't Conor seen the kind of eejit Eileen was? Why hadn't Bríd known that everything would go wrong?

There was a rustling noise above her and, looking up, she saw four cows peering down from the ditch. Their wide pink nostrils quivered with curiosity and their big heads were sticking through garlands of curling briars. Seeing the wide-eyed faces, Aideen choked on a laugh. They seemed so concerned that she stopped crying and gave them a daft thumbs-up. One cow stretched her neck and lowed deeply and the others swung their heavy heads, lipping the leaves and flowers on the briars. Three had white curly polls and black patches, and the other was russet red.

Having wiped her face with the back of her hand, Aideen began to gather up her own red curls. The four heads above her swung sideways simultaneously, and she realised that, from their vantage point, they'd seen a car approaching round a bend. Turning her back, Aideen concentrated on pulling her hair up into a scrunchie but, instead of going past, the car slowed down.

'How's it goin', pet?' Paddy leaned out of the window and waved. It must be one of his good days, and Aideen was ashamed to find herself wishing fervently that it wasn't. Normally you wouldn't see him out driving the roads, but now she'd have to talk to him, and he'd see that she'd been crying. Not only that, but she wouldn't know what to say.

Letting her hair down again, she shook it forward. Then she gave him a wave back, trying to look casual. His expression changed, so her face must look dreadful. He didn't say so, though.

'You're not at work.'

'No.' Aideen reached for her helmet. 'I had to go out for a thing.'

Paddy nodded, as if she'd made sense. Then he looked at her again and squinted at the cloudless sky. 'I'd say there could be a shower coming shortly. You wouldn't fancy a drink till the weather clears? Or a coffee, say? We'd get one below in Feeney's.' Without waiting for her to reply, he slipped the car into gear and moved off, shouting back that Feeney's wasn't far. Aideen jammed the helmet on and followed him. He was already well down the road, so she hadn't any choice.

When they got to Feeney's he climbed out of the car, using his stick. Aideen got off the Vespa and said she didn't really fancy going indoors. He didn't ask why, and together they crossed the road and leaned on a gate. There was something growing in the field so she asked what it was.

'Red clover. You sow it for forage or fertiliser.'

'Oh? Right.'

'They'd undersow it or put it in after a cereal crop. You want to watch out for stem eelworm, though.'

'Okay.'

Paddy glanced at her. 'I hear you've been off radar the last day or so.'

'Conor didn't send you out to find me?'

'Christ, no, I'm just driving round trying to get some head space.'

Aideen rested her elbows on the top bar of the gate. 'So am I.'

'Is it nerves? Una was a dreadful mess before our wedding.

You've a whole year yet, pet. You don't want to be panicking too soon.'

She gave him a reluctant smile. 'I'm not nervous. The actual being married bit is fine.'

'Not the actual wedding bit, though?'

'It's just ... we're not going to have the wedding we dreamed of. No way. It's not going to happen. Eileen has all these notions ...'

'I've noticed that.'

'And I'm not saying I'm not grateful, honest. She's awfully kind. So is Joe.'

'Yeah, but we're talking about your wedding, here, not theirs.'

'Well, that's just it. Me and Eileen are coming from different places. On every possible level. And I don't know what to do.' She turned her head to look at Paddy and found him still staring across the field. After a silent minute or two she asked him what he thought.

Paddy grimaced. 'I'm the wrong person to ask, love. I can hardly get my head around my own life at the moment. Mostly I'm living in a big black hole.'

'Is that what it feels like? Depression?'

'It's not really about feeling. More like just being there. The hole is my home.'

'That's horrible.'

'You can say that again.'

'Like someone came and blotted out all your hopes and dreams.'

'I wouldn't know, pet. I don't do hope any more. And I'm not sure I ever believed in dreams.'

Paddy turned round and put his back against the gate. Aideen kept looking at the clover. There were bees hovering over the field, which was bounded by posts and wire. Paddy spoke again, staring at the road. 'I sure as hell don't believe in them now.'

Aideen realised she'd entered unknown territory. One thing she did know was that she shouldn't get all positive and bracing. According to Conor, people with depression could get overcome by self-loathing and trying to argue them out of it only made things worse. Anyway, Paddy himself changed tack. 'Sure you're not having second thoughts about coming to live at the farm? I told Conor we didn't have to accept this notion of Joe's unless you're happy with it.'

'I know. And I am.'

'You don't think this double wedding is part of the deal with Dawson, and that he won't help with the farm unless you and Conor play ball with Eileen?'

'No, of course not! He's not like that. Nor is Eileen.'

Paddy shrugged. 'No, I don't think they are.' He turned and looked at her. 'But it beats me why you'd want to marry into our family. Not when it means moving onto the farm.'

'Because I love Conor. And because the farm is where I want to be. Truly.'

'Things can get pretty grim living round me.'

'Will you stop it? You and Una are great. I've even thought I might be marrying Conor because of his parents.'

'God, the inside of your head must be almost as weird as mine.' He pushed himself away from the gate and stood leaning on his stick. 'Well, at least you're not still crying your eyes out.'

Aideen frowned for a minute, trying to get things to make sense. Talking to Paddy had somehow brought them into sharper focus. 'Eileen's all about chasing dreams, isn't she? Mad, makey-uppy stuff that isn't even real. Conor and me want a dream wedding, but not one like that.'

Paddy shook his head. 'Now you've lost me.'

'Well, there's a difference, isn't there? Between real dreams and ones you've just borrowed. You know, from stuff on the telly and things in celebrity mags.'

'Or a Renaissance painting?'

Aideen blushed. 'Okay, I see what you're saying.' Then she frowned and shook her head. 'But the point is that the painting's an inspiration, not an aspiration. Conor and I don't want to buy into some package. We want to make our own dreams.'

'I suppose that makes sense.'

'And talking to you is what's made me think it through.' Aideen grabbed Paddy's arm and hugged it. 'Listen, do you mind if I go? I've got to see Conor. I'm sorry, I know that's awfully rude, but there's something I've got to do.'

Chapter Thirty-Seven

The family dinner at The Royal Vic was to be held in a private room booked by Malcolm. Having no desire to spend a perfectly good Saturday dreading the coming evening, Hanna had arranged to drive up to the Hag's Glen for a picnic lunch with Brian. Sitting in her kitchen in her dressing gown, she gave him a call to confirm. 'I'll bring a loaf of bread and a salad. Malcolm will probably regale us with steak tartare and foie gras.'

'Do you reckon he'd mind if I asked for a tin of spaghetti hoops instead?'

As she ended the call, Hanna told herself things would be just fine. It had been daft to wish Brian wasn't coming, when the chances were that he would make the whole thing work. Despite his solitary habits, he was never fazed by social occasions. He got on well with Jazz and, like Louisa, was always more amused than annoyed by Mary. And Mary herself frequently announced that, in finding him, Hanna had landed on her feet.

Having assembled a bowl and utensils, and fetched a bag of flour, Hanna reached for the tumbler in which she always measured her buttermilk. It occurred to her as she went to the fridge that she'd first known the weight of that glass in her hand when she was a child. It had still been standing on a shelf in

Maggie's dresser when she'd rediscovered the derelict house more than forty years later.

In her childhood home bread had come ready-sliced and shrouded in plastic bags. But here in this room, all those years ago, Maggie had taken a tin bowl from under the kitchen table and swirled in flour and soda with her hand, adding salt and a brimming glassful of sharp-scented buttermilk. The rim of the thick tumbler was uneven, and the glass had a green tinge. The milk was the residue of an elderly neighbour's butter-making, passed on for a few coins a pail. Maggie had baked bread every day, sometimes adding fistfuls of oats or currants, and she and Hanna would eat it hot from the oven, hunkered on the doorstep or sitting over the fire.

As she drove up to the Hag's Glen with the car window open, Hanna marvelled again at the beauty of Brian's chosen site. While Maggie's place was a fortress against the power of the Atlantic, this glen, several miles inland, seemed to hold all the mellow warmth of the sun. The soil might be no better than it was in the stony field Maggie had dressed with seaweed, but the surroundings suggested a tranquillity that the clifftop never knew.

Pulling up in front of the house, Hanna was conscious of the constant song of the river, very different from the sound of the waves at the foot of her own cliff. At the head of the glen the waterfall fell between clumps of golden furze that clung to the rock face. And, now that the scaffolding had been removed, Brian's house seemed no more than another outcrop of rock and green growth on the valley floor.

He came out to meet her, kissing her and swinging the picnic basket out of the back seat of the car. 'Shall we go for a climb or eat down by the river?'

'The river, I think. But let me see the house first.'

'I haven't moved anything in yet. Fury's fitted the kitchen, though. And I've managed to stop him painting everything blue.'

'Why blue?'

'Don't start me! He has a tin of paint.'

Hanna laughed. 'Can we go up on the roof?'

'Sure. It hasn't reached anything like its promised glory. That'll take years.'

'You can show me the view.'

'It's pretty knockout.'

She had to agree. You could see the forest from the green roof, and the effect of the wind in the distant treetops echoed the moving light on the river here in the quiet glen. Hanna raised her hand and pointed south. Out beyond the forest was a glimpse of the blue ocean.

Brian laughed. 'I told you you'd still see it.'

'It seems so remote.'

'No, it's not. Just part of a wider picture.' He turned, as if about to say something.

Hanna looked up at him. 'What?'

He hesitated, then shook his head. 'Nothing.'

'No, what?'

'Nothing at all, sweetheart. Just that it's lovely to see you here.'

Down by the river she unpacked the picnic, tearing the cake of bread into pieces and opening a bottle of wine. Brian took the lid off a pot of olives. 'These are perfect, where did you get them?'

'HabberDashery. They're doing amazing business. Aideen must have been in the back making sandwiches because Bríd was behind the counter, rushed off her feet.'

'Fair play to them. It takes a lot of guts at that age to set up a business partnership.'

Hanna supposed he was thinking about his own architectural practice, which had hardly been up on its feet when Sandra, his wife, had got cancer. No one could have anticipated her illness, or that the shock of her death would have such an impact on his work. Hanna had often wondered if Brian had ever been back in touch with his business partner. Wouldn't the amends he'd tried to make have compensated for the loss of that all-important contract? After all, he'd sold his own home and stuffed the proceeds into his partner's letterbox. She knew they'd been friends before they'd set up in practice and, in such circumstances, it seemed unlikely that a friend would hold a grudge.

But even if his partner had put it behind him, she knew Brian hadn't. His memories of what had happened back then were still as raw as ever. Having once told her his story he'd never talked about it, and the thought of raising it herself felt aggressive, like ripping a piece of Elastoplast off someone else's wound. Perhaps it might promote the process of healing, but whether and when to inflict that pain should surely be his choice, not hers.

She poured a glass of wine and held it out to him. 'This won't be up to what Malcolm gives us tonight.'

Brian took it without answering and gazed out across the river. Then he spoke without taking his eyes off the water. 'The other day Fury and I were building a wall, and it got me thinking. You lift those stones and you remember all the men who were here before you. Generations of them, passing down stories and secrets from father to son. Yet, despite all that masculine presence, it's called after the hag.'

'Famine memories are powerful.'

'Yes, but it could be the name is older than that. You get it in other parts of the country too. That's what struck me. In folklore a hag can be a witch, but she can also be a goddess. Maybe this place has always had a female presence. Maybe it's what it needs.'

Hanna realised that, once again, most of her attention had drifted to the potential disasters of the coming evening. Giving herself a mental shake, she tried to focus on Brian's train of thought. 'So, you're saying Fury's famine story is nonsense.'

When he turned to her she wondered if he was feeling tense about the evening as well. But the impression passed when he smiled.

'I'm saying that seeking a definitive version of any story is pointless. Look at you and your film club. Which is the real story? The one in the book or the one in the film?'

'Well, according to Mr Maguire, the one that comes first.'

'But the function of art is to observe life from different angles, and no one angle is more valid than another.' Brian took a sip of wine. 'Anyway, everything that happens emerges from things that have happened already. That's the nature of life.'

Hanna grinned. 'Saira Khan told Mr Maguire that it's good to challenge one's assumptions by looking at things from new angles.'

'Good God! And she's still standing?'

'She's not troubled by the rural Irish tendency to fawn on retired teachers. Actually, I think she said "in different lights". But the principle's the same.'

'Precisely.' Brian turned his head and smiled at her. 'You, for example, are looking particularly beautiful in this light.'

'Well, that's good to know. May I stay at the flat this evening?'

'I was hoping you would.'

★

When they met again, six hours later, it was in a candlelit room in The Royal Vic. Malcolm had booked what the management called 'a salon'. The table, set for six, stood in an anteroom, beyond swagged velvet curtains. Armchairs and sofas were scattered about between the open window of the salon and a large fireplace, where a small fire was burning for purely cosmetic purposes. There was a high marble mantelpiece, low polished tables, and a vast arrangement of hothouse flowers.

Mary and Louisa, who'd arrived before Hanna, were sitting by the window sipping champagne. Malcolm was being charming, and Hanna was wondering what had become of Jazz.

Having shaken hands with the others, Brian crossed the room with a glass in his hand. 'You're looking troubled.'

'It's just that Jazz is late.'

'She'll turn up.'

'Well, I hope so, because my mother's getting bolshie.'

'Inferior champagne?'

Hanna stifled a snort. 'She's got it into her head that Malcolm's doing me out of a fortune. I told you he's selling the London house? Well, Mam's convinced that I'm owed a cut of the proceeds.'

'Right. Well, tonight should be entertaining.'

'I just hope Jazz gets here soon, and we move on to dinner. Maybe a plate of food will distract Mam.'

'She's responding well to PJ the barman.'

Knowing that Brian was trying to relax her, Hanna threw him a smile. Then, looking across at the group by the window, she saw he was right. PJ, resplendent in his tartan bow tie and short white jacket, was bowing as he topped up Mary's glass. With her ankles crossed in imitation of Louisa, Mary was perched on the edge of her chair attired in what Hanna recognised as a brand new dress. Inclining her head majestically, she dismissed PJ with all the condescension of a queen. Watching her, Hanna felt an unlooked-for spasm of affection. Infuriating though her mother was, the decision to share her home with Louisa had been brave. The bungalow had been Mary's palace, built to her exact demands by an adoring husband. Choosing to remodel it and move on hadn't been an easy call.

The phone in Hanna's hand buzzed and she saw it was a text from Jazz. 'Oh, damn!'

Malcolm, who'd seen her look at the phone, strolled across the room. 'Something wrong?'

'No. Just Jazz's car. The exhaust's misbehaving.'

'Tell her to take a taxi.'

'She won't find one in Lissbeg on a Saturday evening.' Hanna looked at the phone, which had just buzzed again. 'She's called a friend and he's giving her a lift.'

'No problem, we can wait. Do ask him to come and join us for dinner.'

Strolling away again, Malcolm summoned PJ with a finger. Hanna obediently sent the text and pulled a face at Brian. 'They're well on their way, so it shouldn't be too long now.'

At that moment, over at the window, Mary raised her voice. 'Do you know what it is, Malcolm, you must be doing fine for the money!'

To Hanna's annoyance, Malcolm's look of amusement was reflected on Brian's face.

'Take this champagne. Now, that cost a pretty penny! Still, I suppose we should all be glad you invited Hanna along to share it. God knows, it's the least that she deserves.'

The door to the salon opened to reveal a waiter with a trolley, and PJ shimmered over to escort him through to the alcove. Hanna recognised the boy as the teenage son of one of the greatest gossips in Lissbeg. Abandoning an attempt to remain detached, she hastened towards the window, as Mary tapped Louisa smartly on the arm. 'Not that I'd insult your son, Louisa, and I eating his dinner. Or I will be if our Jazz ever gets here at all.'

Arriving at Malcolm's side, Hanna beamed at Mary fiercely. 'She's going to be here any minute, Mam. She's getting a lift from Mike.'

Louisa smiled peaceably and remarked that Mike must be a nice lad.

Mary tossed her head. 'Ay, well, that may be but God knows where he came from! I don't know what it is with Hanna and Jazz that they want to go picking up with all these foreigners.'

'Mam …'

'No offence in the world now, and I've never been a racist, but when it comes to finding a man, a girl does best to stick with her own. Signs on it when things go wrong and she's left without a penny. And now there's Jazz and this Mike. I hope to God we're not going to have the same story over again.'

Hanna could see the waiter's ears flapping. She glanced across to where Brian was leaning against the door jamb. Because, of course, there was no point in his getting involved. There was no point in her intervening either but, to her own dismay, she found herself turning to Malcolm. 'It's only a few weeks since Jazz broke up with her boyfriend. Mike's a friend, that's all. We mustn't embarrass them by suggesting they're a couple.'

She glowered at Mary and, idiotically, turned back to Louisa. 'He does seem a nice lad, doesn't he? Apparently he comes from the end of the District Line.'

At that moment, her phone buzzed and, looking at it, she felt a rush of relief. 'That's them! They're here. They're downstairs now!'

Brian crossed the room and placed his glass on a table. Putting his arm around Hanna, he gave her shoulders a squeeze. 'Well, that's good news, I'm looking forward to dinner in that really magnificent room. You've chosen a lovely setting, Malcolm. It's good of you to ask me along.'

With Brian's arm around her, Hanna relaxed. Hopefully Mary would shut her gob as soon as they got her to the table, and a genuine outsider would leaven the Turner–Casey family mix. She could feel the warmth of Brian's grip and the reassuring solidity of his long body pressed against her side.

The door swung open, and Jazz, looking pretty and dishevelled, rushed in followed by Mike. In the flurry of introductions, Hanna felt Brian's hand tighten painfully on her bare shoulder. Glancing up in protest, she saw an indefinable expression cross his face. Then Jazz was beside them, laughing and presenting Mike.

'I'm so sorry for the hold-up, Mum, but I'm here at last and Mike's going to join us! You guys have already met, of course – and, Mike, this is Mum's partner, Brian.'

Hanna expected Brian to release her shoulder to acknowledge the introduction. But instead of offering to shake Mike's hand, his whole body tensed.

Mike beamed. 'Well, talk about happenstance! I had no idea you'd be here.' To Hanna's amazement, he leaned in and punched Brian lightly on the chest. 'This is so great! I was planning to call you tomorrow. How's tricks, Dad?'

Chapter Thirty-Eight

Life on the streets hadn't involved much talking. Mostly it had been about keeping warm and finding the next meal. Rasher had often spent days, and even weeks, when all he'd said to anyone was 'Spare a bit of change, please?', 'Thanks, missus', or 'Cheers for that, mate.'

Bogdan and Petru, the other kitchen porters, had turned out to be nice enough. Work in the kitchen didn't involve much chat, though. There wasn't time, for one thing, and the noise level didn't give you a chance of it. Between shifts, everyone seemed to go their separate ways. So, when Rasher wasn't peeling veg and scrubbing surfaces, he spent a lot of free time sleeping or just sitting in his room. Which was fine by him. It was brilliant to be able to close a door and know you were safe.

At his last session with Saira she'd asked if he'd done any more research in the library.

'Nah. I will. I'll get round to it.' Actually, he didn't fancy going there again. If Gracie was round she might get noisy, and if the O'Brien one appeared she'd probably tell them to kick him out. But he couldn't say that to Saira in case he seemed wimpy or ungrateful.

'You saw that having a library card gives you access to all

sorts of online services and courses? You just need a PIN to log
on.'

'Yeah.'

'Well, you don't have to access them from the library in
Carrick. There's another branch in Lissbeg.'

'Is there? Well, I don't know about courses.'

'You could choose just to watch video tutorials. No homework
or assessments. It's up to you how you use what's there on offer.'

He'd stuck his head down and said nothing and she'd smiled.

'Maybe it would be best to leave the library for the moment.
Making friends and spending time out of doors might be better.'

Rasher had been tempted to say he'd spent quite enough time
out of doors already. He wasn't sure he'd liked the idea of being
told to make friends either. It felt like being chivvied about when
you were a kid. Yet here he was, on a Sunday morning, sitting in a
bus to Lissbeg. Saira had suggested they meet in the nuns' garden,
and he hadn't been able to think of a way to say no without
sounding rude.

Lissbeg was much smaller than Carrick. The bus stopped in
a wide street with benches and a trough full of flowers on a
traffic island in the middle. There were shops on one side, and
across the road was what must be The Old Convent Centre.
You could see where the wall had been levelled to make an
entrance to the garden, which had a café and a fountain, and
there was a pedestrian gateway to a courtyard with a sign saying
'LIBRARY'.

Obeying Saira's instructions, Rasher crossed the road. She'd
said she'd be working on the herb beds or in the polytunnel, so

he walked across the garden, hoping he wouldn't have to ask someone where to find her. He was always forgetting that people didn't turn away now when he spoke to them.

As soon as he'd walked round the fountain, he spotted Saira fairly quickly. She was sitting on a bench chatting to an oul one. When she saw him, she stood up and waved. 'Adam! Come and join us.'

Feeling like an eejit, he went and sat down and shook hands with the oul one, who told him her name was Pat Fitz.

'Well, it's Fitzgerald really, of course, but my late husband was always known as Weazy Fitz.'

Rasher hunched his shoulders. 'Was he? Right.'

Pat turned to Saira. 'Though, having said that, I'm not sure how many people remembered it by the time poor Ger died. It was a nickname he had at school. Not a very kind one at the time, you know, but people forgot that after. It was one of the Brothers calling him a weasel that started it. Then for years he was just Weazy Fitz, and no one remembered why. And by the end, sure, the name itself was half forgotten. Time heals all wounds, as they say.'

Rasher wondered if Saira had decided he needed a garrulous oul one for a friend. Maybe Martin had told her he'd seemed to get on well with Gracie? Then he saw an amused look in her eye. 'Pat was just passing, Adam. She lives across the road.'

'That's right. I'm in the flat above the butcher's. My son has the shop below now poor Ger's gone. Mind you, Frankie has a manager in – he wouldn't go cutting up carcasses himself. But it's still the family shop.' She smiled at Rasher, her watery blue eyes looking earnest. 'Isn't Adam a lovely name. Is it in your family?'

'I dunno. I think my mum just liked it. Most people call me Rasher.'

'Would you look at that! A nickname. Just like Weazy Fitz.'

Saira pulled off the pair of gardening gloves she was wearing. 'I've told Adam about the garden. How it's manned by volunteers.'

'Well, isn't that great altogether? Are you coming to join them, Rasher? It's great work they do here, you know. Some of the herbs get sold to Edge of the World Essentials and the money's put back into the garden.'

'And the volunteers get nothing?'

'Well, no, love. Like I said, they're volunteers.'

Saira explained to Rasher that the place had been in rag order when they'd started on it.

'If it hadn't been for volunteers, nothing would have got done. The council's bought the site now, and they put money into the garden fund too, but it costs an awful lot to maintain a place like this. Pat gives a hand sometimes. Lots of people do. It's a very relaxing way to pass the time.'

'And doesn't it get people out of the house and talking to each other?' Pat tapped Rasher on the knee. 'It never does anyone any good to go shutting themselves away. That's the rock you perish on if you get too wedded to a screen. I'm always saying that to the crowd I teach computers to. "Cyberspace is enticing," I say, "but you don't want to make it your home."'

'Oh? Right.'

Rasher wasn't paying her much attention because he had a

feeling Saira was planning to put him to work. The garden was nice enough, with the birds flying round the fountain, and the herb beds looking pretty good in the sun. He didn't fancy the notion of getting his hands dirty for no pay, though. Or hanging out with a crowd of oul ones like Pat.

As if she'd read his mind, Saira smiled again. 'We get volunteers here of all ages. Pensioners. Middle-aged mums like me. My daughter Ameena comes along when she's home from college, and lots of people from her class at school are working in town now. They give a hand sometimes. Some of them belong to the film club in the library too. You should think about coming to that, Adam.'

Still feeling chivvied, Rasher shrugged. 'I haven't a clue about growing things.'

'No? But you should have.' Saira turned to Pat. 'Adam plans to become a chef.'

'Do you, love? Well, fair play to you, that's a grand job! Oh, you'll want to know all about growing things for that. And rearing meat. Ah, I wish Ger was alive now, and he'd give you a bit of a low-down on the meat trade. Poultry too – we did great business with turkeys round the Christmas.'

It was an aspect of things that hadn't occurred to Rasher. He looked at the herb beds shimmering in the sun. 'I suppose I could come for an hour or two if I wasn't on a shift.'

Saira stood up and laid the gloves on the bench. 'There are plenty of people here who'd help you learn.'

Looking at it that way, he was the one who'd be getting something for nothing. Though, on the other hand, once he picked it up, he supposed he'd be of use. As he sat there getting his head round it, Saira said she'd go and fetch some tea. She walked off in the direction of the café, leaving Rasher there on the bench with Pat. Stuck for something to say to her, Rasher asked if her son wasn't interested in butchering.

'Ah, no, love, he'd be more of a businessman.'

'And is he the only one? I mean you've no one else that'd take on the shop?'

Pat ducked her head and, to his horror, when she looked up her eyes were glistening. 'Well, no. My other two sons are off in Canada. They have their own lives now, over there. I have a granddaughter that's just about your age. She'd come back and forth. Not the lads, though. Well, they left a long time ago, and for years they didn't come back. They never got on great with Ger, you see.'

Wishing he hadn't started this, Rasher nodded.

Pat ran a forefinger under her eye. 'I'd say they kind of blamed me for not making things better. I'd say half the time I did the wrong thing but, sure, you do the best you can. They were here in the end when he died, though. Both of them. Sonny and Jim. But too much time had passed, I think, by that stage.'

'How d'you mean?'

'Ah, I don't know, love. It's not that I want to drag them back to live here. A phone call every week, say, that'd be good. Just knowing they haven't put me out of their minds entirely.'

She looked up and asked him if he'd ever read a book called *Brooklyn*.

'No.'

'It's a good book, that, you know, Rasher. We're reading it here for the film club in the library. They'd show you a film, and you'd read the book it was based on afterwards. Anyway, *Brooklyn*'s about this woman, and her man's dead and one daughter dies, too, and the other decides to go off and live in America. The end of the film was all about the new life this lassie would have. Sunshine and marriage and plenty of money. And that poor woman left at home in a town that was grey and cold. But, sure, the young are like that, Rasher. They have to be. They don't think.'

'But maybe your kids are always thinking about you.'

'Maybe so. I don't know that, love, though, do I? And it's not them thinking of me that matters, I just want to know they're all right. They'll be back again, I'd say, when I'm in my coffin. And what good will that be to me then?' She dabbed at both her eyes with a paper tissue and gave him a sweet smile. 'You're not from round here. I can tell that by the look of you. Where were you born?'

'Dublin.'

'Do you tell me that? And are your parents still there?'

'My dad's dead. I'd say my mum's still there, yeah.'

'But you're not sure?' He opened his mouth but, before he could speak, she put her hand on his knee. 'God, you must think I'm a nosy old biddy! Never mind me, Rasher, you keep your business to yourself.'

'No, it's okay ...'

'Look, if you're not in touch, there must be a good reason. But would you do this for me, love? Would you give the poor woman a ring and tell her you're safe.'

Ten minutes later, having drunk a cup of tea, Rasher was on his knees beside a herb bed. It was tarragon, with its deep flavour of aniseed and vanilla, and Saira was showing him how to prune back the plants. The scent of the clipped leaves was much stronger here in the sunshine than in the kitchen and, according to Saira, the basil growing in the bed beyond the tarragon was stronger and improved in flavour because it was planted beside them.

'Companion planting is a big thing for us here. We work on it a lot.'

'Yeah? That's cool. I've got a shift this afternoon but I could come and give a hand next weekend, maybe.'

'Why not? And you could come to the film club this Tuesday. We have it once a month. It's free.'

'I might do.'

On the way back to Carrick, he told himself he and Bogdan might fix their shifts and go to the film club together. Petru, the other porter, had a wife and a kid to go home to, but Bogdan, like himself, seemed to spend most of his free time in his room. They could come on the bus to Lissbeg and go for a pizza after the movie.

Maybe he'd ask Bogdan when they were taking a break tomorrow. Sitting back in his seat, Rasher watched the patchwork of green and gold fields flash by the window. It was pretty crap to think of Pat sitting there blaming herself for what had gone wrong in her family. And worrying about being dead and gone before her kids got back in touch. Like his own mum had said, things happen in life and there wasn't much point in asking why or going round handing out blame.

As the bus reached the outskirts of Carrick, Rasher made a decision. The chances were that the bastard Fergal had moved on or was banged up in prison and, if not, he'd find a way to cope. One way or the other, when he was back in the Vic he'd pick up the phone and ring Mum.

Chapter Thirty-Nine

I KNOW WHEN MY ADVIE CISNT WANTED

Pause. Buzz.

YOUD DO RIGHT 2 HAV A WORD WITH HIM WHEN UVE
GOT HIM THERE ON UR OWN

Buzz.

THINK OF UR OLD AGE IF U DON'T NO ONE ELSEWILL

Hanna groaned and buried her head in her hands. With a fleeting vision of Harriet Beecher Stowe's Uncle Tom, she decided to think of her mercies: at least while Mary remained focused on the price of the house in London she wasn't demanding to know why she hadn't been told about Brian and Mike.

As she lifted her head, a figure passed outside the window and, slamming her phone onto the table, she went to open the door. Malcolm, in a polo shirt, khaki chinos and loafers, was standing on the step with a bottle of wine. Having driven home the previous night in a state of turmoil, Hanna had woken wishing she could cancel the Sunday brunch she'd offered to cook for him. Given last night's dinner, and the fact that Louisa had already taken him to lunch, an invitation to Maggie's place had seemed only fair. But that had been last week. Now, having hardly slept till the small hours, kedgeree and conversation with Malcolm were the last things she felt up to.

Everything that had happened last night after Jazz and Mike's arrival had felt like a blur. The party had chatted, drunk excellent wines and eaten a delicious dinner. After a flurry of surprise, the revelation that Jazz's friend had turned out to be Brian's son had hardly been discussed. Jazz, Malcolm and Mike himself had seemed delighted by what Mike had called the happenstance. And all the time a voice in her head had reminded Hanna loudly of the day she'd told Brian how much she admired his reticence.

Whether or not she'd seen Hanna's confusion, Louisa had stepped in discreetly and monopolised Mary. After his initial rigid reaction – and the moment when Hanna had felt him remove his painful grasp on her arm – Brian had clapped Mike on the back and, for the rest of the evening, kept up a flow of inconsequential conversation.

Astonishingly, Hanna had contrived to do the same. She'd been aware, however, of both Malcolm and Mary shooting her curious glances. And now here was Malcolm on her doorstep, wanting brunch.

Crossing the threshold, he looked round in approval. 'How nice to be here. And what a lovely room you've made of this!'

Taking the proffered bottle, Hanna indicated a chair. Like the management of The Royal Vic last night, she'd lit a cosmetic fire. It was a beautiful day, and all her windows were open, but, given that the fireplace was the room's focal point, a cold hearth would have felt like a hostile gesture on Malcolm's first visit to her house.

He took the seat and, as she opened the wine, continued to admire the room. 'No one but you could have created exactly this ambience.'

Hanna snorted. 'Most of it's still dominated by Maggie, and much of the rest was imposed on me by my builder.'

'I find that hard to believe.'

'You don't know Fury O'Shea.' The thought of Fury suddenly reminded her forcefully of Brian.

Malcolm's eyes narrowed. 'You're looking a bit seedy. Is everything okay?'

'Perfectly.' Hanna sat down on the other side of the fire. 'I'm just not used to fine dining and late nights.'

'A pleasant evening, though.'

'Lovely. It was good of you to host it.'

'Oh, for heaven's sake, don't be po-faced! It was a family meal, not a banquet.'

'Yes. Sorry. And I know Jazz is glad you've come.'

'As glad as she ever is.'

With an effort, Hanna refrained from asking him whose fault he thought that was.

Malcolm frowned. 'I'm never quite sure if there's something up or if she's just edgy around me.'

'She's pretty upset about the boyfriend, I think. It seems she just came home and found him gone.'

'Well, no one knows better than I how difficult that can be.'

Hanna stiffened. 'If you're trying to suggest ...'

'I'm not suggesting anything.'

'Yes, you are! You're drawing a pathetic comparison between my decision to get out of the farce that was our marriage and a boy in his twenties moving on from a love affair of six months!' Taking a deep breath, Hanna controlled herself. 'Look, can we stop this? I am feeling a bit seedy, actually, so I'd rather hoped for a quiet, civil brunch.'

'Tell you what.' Malcolm stood up and removed the glass from her hand. 'You never could drink wine when your tummy was rough. Stay where you are and I'll make us both some tea.'

She was about to protest when she realised that a cup of tea was precisely what she was craving. 'Okay. You'll find the things on the counter. But my tummy's fine. I've made kedgeree and I'm looking forward to it.'

As soon as she'd spoken, she wished she hadn't. At least the fiction of an upset stomach would have accounted for her appearance. As it was, Malcolm would keep digging, like a dog scenting a bone.

Having made the tea and come back to the fire, he sat back and looked at her. 'Brian seems a nice chap.'

'He is.'

'Nice boy too. I gathered you hadn't met him before.'

Suddenly something inside Hanna snapped. 'Mind your own business, Malcolm! My relationship with Brian has nothing to do with you.'

'I merely mentioned Mike.'

'I know you did. Don't.' She glared at him, daring him to continue. Then he raised his hand in an acquiescent gesture that was nothing like the stagey one he'd used at the Garden Café.

They drank tea in silence until Malcolm spoke again. 'I suppose it would be idiotic to say that I hate to see you upset.'

'Idiotic? I'd have said offensive.'

He lowered his eyes and, looking at him, she realised how much he'd aged. The arrogance he'd had since she'd first known him had changed from something fiery into a brittle shell. Hanna was swept by a profound sense of weariness. All the troubles of their past seemed nothing compared to the confusion of her present.

Last night, as he'd helped her into her coat, Brian had spoken urgently: 'Hanna, come back to the flat like we planned. Please. Don't just disappear.'

Biting her lip, she'd shaken her head and driven herself home, seeing the lights on the motorway through a haze of unshed tears. He'd tried to ring her three times since then, but she hadn't taken the calls.

Now she realised Malcolm was looking at her again. To her surprise, his jaw was clenched and, when he spoke, his voice sounded strained. 'You know what I couldn't stop thinking of last night? William would have been older now than Mike is. I can't imagine having a son in his thirties. God, what would it be like?'

William was the name they had chosen for the baby she'd miscarried. Hearing it, Hanna pressed her hand against her mouth. It always seemed mad that the pain of that loss could still leap up and choke her. Yet it did, and on the strangest of occasions. Sometimes in the street, out of the blue, her heart would jerk at the sight of a mother with a baby. Or she'd wake at night from a dream that seemed to come from nowhere, in which she'd felt the ominous stream of blood between her legs.

Malcolm was the only person on earth who could understand and feel that loss as she did.

When she'd found out she was pregnant they'd been living together. But they'd had no plans to marry. The happy-ever-after ending had been his dream, not hers. 'Please, Hanna. Let's do this, let's get married. I love you. I want to look after you. I want us to raise our child together and be happy.'

'But none of this was planned.'

'Speak for yourself. I heard wedding bells the first moment I saw you.'

'And what? Sabotaged a condom to make it happen?'

'No, but I should have thought of that. You'd never have found out.'

She had laughed down at him as he knelt beside her, his arms around her waist and his eyes full of excitement. Later, in the bitter years after their divorce, she'd realised they'd been joking about a central part of his nature. He'd always assumed he'd a God-given right to anything he wanted, and that whatever he did to achieve it was just fine.

But the tears in his eyes now were real, Hanna was sure of that. Gulping her tea, she fought to remain composed. Here was Malcolm, more than thirty years on, weeping for the son he'd never had. How could Brian, whom she'd thought she knew, have a son about whom he'd never said a word?

There was a buzzing noise from the table. Quicker to recover than she was, Malcolm nodded at the phone. 'Sounds like a text.'

'Oh, damn and blast my mother! Yes, it is.'

Before the phone could buzz again, she shut it off smartly. Malcolm grinned. 'One thing I don't miss is Mary's intense need to communicate.'

'Well, I can't say I blame you.'

'I take it she's still unhappy about the house sale.'

'Yes, but that's nonsense. You owe me nothing, Malcolm. And I apologise for Mam.'

Malcolm stood up and went to put more water in the kettle. 'I'm not sure that, in this case, she hasn't got a point.'

'Well, I am. Absolutely. So don't even think about it.'

Coming back, he hunkered down to place the teapot on the hearth. Then he turned his head and looked at her. 'You know why I'm selling it? Because Mary's right and you're wrong. Okay, maybe not about the money, if that's how you feel, but it was always your house, Hanna. Always has been. I can't sit there growing old in it without you.'

Then why the hell did you bring Tessa Carmichael into my bed?

As soon as the thought screamed in her mind, she saw Malcolm acknowledge it.

'Look, I've said this already but I swear to you, Hanna, it's true. Tessa and I only made love in the house that one time. And, as God's my witness, I never intended to live a lie all those years. She was kind to me after the miscarriage and I was a fool and one thing led to another. I fell in love with her. Yes, I did. And I would have told you then. But you were in bits after we lost

William. And I loved you too. I couldn't just walk away and leave you. Not then.'

'Well, leave it now, will you? Please. I'm not up to this today.'

'No, but I have to say it. Because I buggered everything up and I know that now. And the worst of it was that I kept going, thinking I could square the circle. I thought I could make us all happy.' He held out his hand. Then, seeing her expression, withdrew it. 'Truly. I thought I could. And then there was Jazz.'

Hanna's face felt like stone. 'Yes. The baby you let me conceive while you were cheating on me. The daughter who was going to grow up to find her dad was a scumbag. And *don't* say that you were the one who tried to keep it from her! Have you any idea how much worse that made things, Malcolm? You lying to her, saying the split was amicable, and me having no choice but to play along?'

'Hanna ...'

'Christ, though it pains me to say it, my mother was right! She said I should have told Jazz the truth when I left you. And I would have, if you hadn't got in first with your weasel words and your lies!'

'Look ...'

'And then you had the gall to accuse *me* of destabilising our daughter! I was the villain for packing my bags and taking her out of that house!'

'Hanna, please. You're right, I know you are. I've said it already. I buggered it up all round.'

'Yes, you did. You absolutely did, Malcolm. So don't try to justify your actions to me now.'

'I'm not. I can't, I know that.' Malcolm stood up and leaned against the chimneypiece. Groping for the shawl on the back of her chair, Hanna pulled it round her. The familiar oily smell of the wool reminded her of Maggie.

There was silence, broken by the hiss of the fire and the sudden violent cawing of crows from the trees outside the house. Then Malcolm shoved his hands into his pockets and swung round to face her. 'I'm going to say this because I have to, even though I know how you'll react. I don't want to sell the house, Hanna. I want you to come back to it. I haven't exchanged contracts yet. I could pull out of the sale.'

'What?'

'Look, I don't know what's going on with you and Brian. And, you're right, it's none of my business. But the house was always yours, Hanna. Yours and mine. It could be that again.'

'For Christ's sake, Malcolm!'

'It could. I don't mean you and I would get back together. Not at once. Of course not. But maybe ...' He kept going before she could speak again. 'Look, the house could be your base over in London. It's lovely here, but it must be bleak in winter. Isolated too. And I'm not stupid. I know you needed a place in which you could find yourself again after you left me. I do. But you've done that now, and isn't it time to move on? Think about it – you could go to galleries, see old friends. Ma could still use it as her London pied-à-terre. It's a family house, Hanna. Remember our Christmases there when Jazz was small? And I know you have a job and, of course, you won't want to leave it. But what about when you retire?'

Hanna had a disturbing memory of Mary's text on her phone:

THINK OF UR OLD AGE IF U DON'T NO ONE ELSEWILL.

'This is crazy.'

'Okay. But the offer's there for the taking. I want you to know that.'

Chapter Forty

Eileen almost fell into the room. 'OMG! You are NOT going to believe this! SERIOUSLY, TOTALLY NOT going to believe it!' Suddenly she stopped shouting and looked sharply at Jazz. 'You're still in your pyjamas.'

'It's Sunday.'

'And it's practically lunchtime. For God's sake, girl, you'd want to get a grip.' Eileen wrinkled her nose. 'This is a seriously Bridget Jones vibe you've got going on.'

Jazz removed a yoghurt pot from the unmade bed. 'No, it's not. The place is so small that it looks untidy if I leave a thing out of place.'

'There's untidy and there's grot, Jazz Turner. You've been sitting there wrapped in a duvet watching telly.'

'Look, are you here for a reason?'

'I most certainly am!' Kicking off her shoes, Eileen bounced onto the bed. 'Check out what Aideen and Conor have done!' She held out her phone to Jazz. 'Only flown to Italy and got married!'

'No!' Jazz scrambled onto the bed beside her. 'When? How?'

'They flew over on Friday evening and they're coming back tonight.'

'But – got married? Over a weekend?'

'Well, that's the thing …'

Eileen swiped through the photos on her phone and revealed a shot of Aideen's radiant face. Her head was thrown back, caught in a shout of laughter, and there was a wreath of carnations and daisies in her hair. 'Look at her! Can you believe it? No, but the thing is that she texted me and she's right, Jazz, a priest doesn't marry you. Nor does a registrar. They're only witnesses. People marry each other. That's the point.'

'No, they don't. Not legally.'

'Yeah, but the legal stuff is something else again. They're going to go to a registry office after they get home.'

Jazz looked at another photo of Aideen, sitting on the back of a Vespa with her arms around Conor's waist. Her legs and feet were bare and she was wearing what looked like a white satin mini dress, with yards of flower-strewn embroidered fabric falling from her shoulders to the ground. 'Is that white thing the dress you made all the fuss about?'

'No. It's a slip she bought in a lingerie shop at the airport! Isn't it stunning? She packed all that fabric her aunt Carol embroidered, and came up with different looks when she and Conor got over there.'

The series of pics looked like a magazine photo shoot. Conor sitting on the Vespa, holding a glass of wine and wearing a crown of vine leaves. Aideen with the embroidered muslin worn like a toga, and a huge bunch of wildflowers in her arms. There was a close-up of her feet, poised like a dancer's on emerald green grass starred with creamy, brown-tipped clover; and another of a kiss, with the fabric in the background, thrown over the branch of a tree.

Eileen sighed. 'Don't they look stunning? When she texted she was all apologetic, but how could she think I'd mind?'

'You don't?'

'Of course not. Look at their faces! And look at this.' Turning to her phone, she touched the screen to run a piece of video. It had been taken at sunset on a gorgeous evening in what she explained was 'a trattoria up the hill from the Piazzale Michelangiolo'. You could see that it stood on a hillside with a stunning view over the city below. The front of the restaurant was smothered with vines growing over beams that formed a battered loggia, with three sides open to the air and a kitchen at the back.

'Conor took this on his mobile. They made their vows up the hill in a grove of cypress, and Aideen says they just stumbled on this little place as they came back down.'

There was a long table with benches round it on the loggia, where a crowd of locals and a few backpackers were sitting drinking wine. As the camera panned along the smiling faces, a woman bustled into shot and began clattering bowls of food onto the wooden table.

Eileen squeaked. 'Look! *Ribollita* and *crostini di fegato*! And tripe!'

'What?'

'*Trippa alla fiorentina*! It's really authentic, Jazz. Proper regional food.'

Evidently, Eileen had spent the morning Googling Florence and its culture.

A little boy joined the woman, carrying a basket of bread. As he placed a series of round loaves at intervals along the table, people raised their glasses and gave a cheer.

'Oh, my God!' Jazz's eyes widened in amazement as the camera pulled in on Aideen's foot stamping on the wooden table top. Her toes were grubby and there was a chain of blue cornflowers round her ankle.

Conor must have stepped back at that point to take in the full view because, amid cheerful whistles and noisy pounding glasses, Aideen could be seen dancing along the table. She was stepping deftly between plates of *crostini* and painted bowls of pasta, and the flying toga was now kilted up above her knees. Whirling round, she scattered daisies from a fold in the flower-strewn fabric and, as a man produced an accordion, people began to sing.

The video ended and, instinctively, both Eileen and Jazz punched the air.

'Go, Aideen!'

'I know! Isn't it magic?' Eileen turned round, her eyes narrowed in excitement. 'God, Jazz, Joe and I are *so* going to do that!'

'Dance on tables?'

'No, eejit! Fly off on a whim to somewhere wildly romantic. Bali ... No, the Eiffel Tower ... No, I tell you what, the Maldives!'

'I don't think it counts as a whim if you're going to sit here and plan it.'

'Stop being so literal.'

'And I'm not sure I'm equipped to organise a romantic overseas do.'

'Ah, well, yes ... That's the other thing.' Eileen gave her a guilty glance and bit her lip. 'It wouldn't feel spontaneous if I had a gaggle of bridesmaids.'

'I see. Or even one?'

'You wouldn't get all upset if I stood you down?'

Jazz responded with a deadpan look, just to teach her a lesson. Then she burst out laughing and rolled off the bed. 'Of course I wouldn't, you dork. It's your wedding! And, if you want the truth ...'

'You're actually over the moon?'

'Well, you *have* been a bit like the Bride from Hell.'

'That is so not true!'

'Look, really, if that's what you want, then I'm delighted. And I haven't seen Aideen looking so happy for weeks.'

'She does look like a million dollars, bless her.' Eileen swiped through the photos again and enlarged one, looking thoughtful. 'I wonder if I could get that effect with designer silk flowers?'

Half an hour later Jazz sauntered down Broad Street. It was weird how much better she felt without Eileen's daft wedding looming ahead. Now, showered and dressed, and with a pristine flat to come home to, she swung her handbag cheerfully on the way to find coffee and a Sunday paper. She'd finished reading *Brooklyn* in time for the film club on Tuesday, and now it was time to get back in touch with the real-life world.

HabberDashery was still open for the morning-coffee trade. Jazz went inside and grinned at Bríd. 'I take it you've heard?'

'Aideen sent me a text. They're stone mad!'

'She does look happy, though.'

'They both do. And they're dead right, really. I mean, you and I know what kind of disaster lay ahead.'

'You're not kidding!'

Bríd expertly feathered the top of a takeaway cappuccino. 'It wouldn't be my choice for a wedding, mind. I wouldn't be as mad as Eileen, but I would want a proper do.'

'Orange blossom and a veil?'

'Nothing wrong with that. Or a church and a nice traditional reception. But, listen, good luck to them. I was afraid my mum might be bothered but she thinks it's the best thing out.'

'I think I'll have an almond Danish with that coffee.'

'No problem.' Bríd furled the pastry in a napkin and slipped it deftly into a paper bag. 'I suppose you're still on the hook with Eileen's wedding, though, aren't you?'

'Nope. I've been stood down. Her latest dream wedding doesn't require the presence of a bridesmaid.'

'God, if I were you I'd flee the country before she changes her mind!'

As Jazz carried her coffee out of the deli, Broad Street was wearing its usual weekend air of relaxed bustle. The sun was shining on the council's scarlet geraniums in the horse trough, and the benches on either side of it looked inviting. Crossing the road between idling Sunday traffic, she sat down and took the pastry out of its bag.

As she bit through its buttery flakes to the almond paste at the centre, it occurred to her that for months she'd been in thrall to Eileen's endless demands on her time. And now, at onc stroke, she'd been proved to be dispensable. So why should she think that her being here was so important to her family and her work? Maybe Granny Lou and the rest of the team would be fine without her as well. Nan would be grand, and Mum would be happy to lose the burden of a daughter who'd never managed to find the right man.

Suddenly Jazz felt energised and empowered. Bríd's remark had just been a joke, but perhaps it contained the answer. Why not give in to that secret urge to escape from here and be done with it, to get on a plane to somewhere else and find new roots and new love?

Chapter Forty-One

Hanna had hardly slept the night before. Between Malcolm's unexpected offer and the discovery that Brian was Mike's father, she felt as if her life had been turned upside down. When she opened the library on Monday morning, it was all she could do to smile and exclaim on hearing Conor's news.

He was glowing with excitement and eager to show her all his Italian photos. 'Because the whole Italy thing was down to you.'

Startled, Hanna looked up from his phone. 'Was it?'

'I don't mean getting married there – that was Aideen's idea. But we'd never have found Italy in the first place if you hadn't shown me that art book. Remember?'

Hanna considered this in amazement. He was right. When she'd ended up back in Lissbeg running a local library, she'd thought she'd followed her dream of being an art librarian for nothing, and that her training in London had been a waste of time. Yet, without it, she'd probably never have had the urge to share her pleasure in that antiquated art book. And Conor's life had fundamentally changed as a result.

Mine too, she thought wryly. Had she never gone to London, she'd never have met Malcolm and dumped her dream to become a stay-at-home wife.

Conor revealed yet another photo. 'You wouldn't believe how amazing people were when they saw Aideen's dress. Like, we just stopped in that trattoria for a drink and they laid on a huge feast. And more people kept turning up with instruments and, in the end, we were all dancing under the vines.'

Hanna laughed. 'It looks like you had a wonderful weekend.'

'It was the best wedding you can imagine, Miss Casey. Like Aideen said, you don't need all the official stuff. It's about two people making a choice, that's all.'

They'd get round to the registry office too, he assured her earnestly, and to having a party for the family, but that, and getting the work done at the farm so that he and Aideen could move in there, would have to wait until after the harvest was done.

'Jazz tells me Eileen and Joe are still thinking of a June wedding next year. But I hear you've made Eileen reconsider how big it's going to be.'

Conor rolled his eyes. 'I'd say she'll have her mind changed twenty times before then. Wouldn't you think people would know what they wanted, Miss Casey? I mean, honestly, how can they not?' Whistling under his breath, he trundled a trolley of weekend returns towards the shelving.

Hanna sat down, wishing devoutly that she knew what she wanted herself. Throughout the night her mind had leapt from one conclusion to another, always coming back to the thought that she couldn't face Brian. Not now. Maybe not ever. What could she possibly say to him, given that he hadn't told her the truth?

At least, though, she could rely on his sensitivity. Having seen that she was ignoring his calls, he wouldn't just turn up and demand to be heard.

At that moment the door opened and Brian strode into the library. Grabbing the sides of her desk, Hanna looked at him in dismay. 'You can't come in here. Please, not now when I'm working.' She glanced covertly at Conor who was only a few feet away. 'Brian, really. Please.'

Instead of moving, he waved at Conor. 'I'm going to steal her for a minute, Conor. We'll be through in the exhibition.'

Conor gave him a thumbs-up and moved on, replacing books on the shelves.

Glaring at him, Hanna got up and preceded Brian through the lobby and into the exhibition space. No visitors had arrived yet and the guide on duty was out of earshot, chatting to the girl in the gift shop.

Pausing by the glass case that housed the psalter, she spoke in a fierce undertone: 'Why the hell are you here?'

'You know why I'm here. I have to talk to you.'

'This is ridiculous.'

'No more so than you refusing to pick up your phone.'

'Go away.'

'Hanna, I know you're upset but you're making far too much of this.'

Hanna felt herself swept by a wave of fury. Gritting her teeth, she took a step forward, forcing him to step back. 'Don't you *dare* tell me how I should think or what I should feel! I trusted you and you lied to me.'

'I didn't! I never lied.'

'Oh, stop quibbling like a schoolboy! You didn't tell me the truth!'

'Hanna, you've got to be reasonable.'

'I don't have to be anything. Go away.'

He took another step back, and the anguished look on his face nearly made her cry out. Beyond his shoulder, she could see a tourist peering round the lobby door.

'Is the exhibition open?'

Just as Hanna was about to go and deal with this, the guide came through from the gift shop. With her impulse to move inhibited, she dithered. Brian grasped her by the elbow. 'I'm sorry. You're right. I can't tell you how to feel. But you mustn't call me a liar.'

'All right. I apologise. But that's not the point, is it? I thought I knew you and now I find I don't.'

'That's not true either. You do know me. What you didn't know was that I had a son.'

'For Christ's sake, Brian, don't you see? I spent twenty years married to a man who thought it was fine not to mention the fact that he had a mistress. And when I found them together he gave me every excuse in the book. He hadn't wanted to hurt me. He'd intended to tell me. Their relationship had nothing to do with us.'

'But there's no comparison.'

'There is! There is because I feel there is. There is because God alone knows what else you've kept from me. Why didn't you tell me about Mike?'

'Look, I didn't know he was here in Finfarran.'

'That's not the point – that's not the *point*! Why didn't you tell me he existed?'

'Oh, Hanna …'

At the other side of the room the guide was reciting dates and facts about the psalter. Turning away to avoid Brian's eyes, Hanna found herself looking down at the book. No bigger than a large paperback novel, it stood open on a carved, gilded stand in its state-of-the-art case. The text appeared as a narrow block on each of two facing pages, and the broad illustrated margins were lavishly embellished, so that the vellum glowed beneath the glass.

It was a book of psalms dating from the eighth century, when Finfarran had been home to a powerful monastic settlement. The principal house of the order had been in Carrick, close to the Anglo-Norman Castle Lancy, which now overlooked the bypass. In the background, Hanna could hear the guide telling the tourist that the de Lancys, who were once lords of Finfarran, had acquired the psalter at the dissolution of the monasteries. 'Under Henry the Eighth, religious foundations in the British Isles were closed down. All the artefacts were sold off, and the buildings were granted to noblemen who supported Henry's divorce and his right to marry Anne Boleyn.'

Beyond the glass wall, Conor was cheerfully shelving books in the library. It occurred to Hanna that Henry VIII must have been like Malcolm, a man so determined to have his own way that the destruction of other people's lives would be seen as collateral damage. She wondered how the abbot had felt when the house he'd ruled was sold off, and the book was taken away. How had he survived the sense that he ought to have done more to protect it? How had he borne the knowledge that he'd never see it again? She herself knew the joy and responsibility that went with being the psalter's current custodian, and the thrilling sense of being in touch with the hands that had made it, and those that had kept it safe for a thousand years.

Across the top of this double-page spread was a painted frieze of doves with golden feathers, outlined in cobalt blue and set against a curling lattice. Green leaves and purple grapes trailed down the margins, interspersed with other birds feeding on the fruit. Among them, precisely observed and painted, were goldfinches, robins and blue tits, sparrowhawks and wrens. Across the lower margins, men and women strolled in a golden landscape dotted with sheep and tiny jewel-coloured flowers. Behind the figures, black and edged with purple, was an immediately recognisable mountain range. The monk who had painted the scene had set it in the foothills of Knockinver, hardly a mile from where Brian had built his house.

The poster outside the exhibition told visitors that one page of the psalter was turned each month. Tomorrow, before she opened the library, Hanna would unlock the case and reveal the next psalm. Though she'd studied the psalter, and been part of its digitisation process, the moments when she turned the pages always felt like discovery.

It was nonsense to think that they changed between each viewing, but perhaps she herself had changed in the passage of time since she'd last seen them. One way or the other, they always offered a different angle to her view. Some previously unseen bird or grotesque face would look out through fantastic foliage, a line of text would wander down a page, like the steps of a celestial staircase, or a city on a hill would appear within the curves of a gorgeous illuminated letter.

Mike had been filming the current double-page spread the other day. He'd interviewed Hanna standing beside the psalter, and she'd said that, while the mountain could still be seen as the monk saw it, the scene was probably meant as an image of Heaven. She'd explained to the camera that the lore of place names was a whole branch of medieval learning. Then, repeating what Brian had told her, she'd laughed and mentioned 'the meadow of desire'. 'It's an old name for a valley in those foothills, and a perfect example of how Irish place names can be confusing for tourists. Because it could equally well mean "the rough grassland of yearning". Or "the poor place of need".'

She'd been rather proud of remembering that, and of giving Mike such a neat snippet of colour for his film. He'd been delighted and thanked her, saying if he sold it he'd come back and stand her a massive celebratory drink. Jazz had recently told her that Mike was great company. He reminded her of Brian, she'd said, because he was unlike Malcolm.

'You know what I mean, Mum? Brian's so straightforward. What you see is what you get.'

Now the irony of that earnest statement tore at Hanna's throat.

The guide was ushering the tourist to the far end of the room. Now was the time to move away in the hope that Brian wouldn't make a fuss in front of strangers. But he began to speak in a monotone, so quietly that even Hanna could hardly hear his voice.

'Sandra was breastfeeding when we found out she had cancer. Mike had to be weaned when they started the chemo. My sister Kate took him because, pretty soon, Sandra and I couldn't cope. We couldn't cope with anything. It was exactly like a nightmare. A chasm opening at our feet. Kate didn't even bring Mike to visit. It distressed Sandra too much. Me too. I'd wanted a son desperately, and we'd been so happy. It didn't seem strange to me when he wasn't there, though. It just felt like part of the same nightmare. And when she died it somehow seemed right that he was gone as well.'

The dove's golden feathers shimmered through the tears that filled Hanna's eyes.

'I didn't see Mike again till he was three. Kate and her husband made brilliant parents. You could tell he was happy, and they were happy to keep him. They didn't have kids of their own and we decided they'd adopt him formally. It made sense, and what would have been the point of my uprooting him? They lived in London, where he had cousins of his own age, and he'd just settled down in a kindergarten. I had a stupid bachelor flat over here.'

'Didn't you visit?'

'Sometimes. I doubt if he remembers. Back then I was just a relation passing through. I stopped after a while. Kate wanted to wait till he'd left school before she explained things to him. That was her choice and she had the right to make it. And everything was pretty straightforward when I eventually saw him again. Effectively, I'm still just a relation on the periphery of his life.'

'So why keep it a secret?'

Brian raised his clenched hand in a gesture of hopeless frustration. 'Oh, God, Hanna, how can you not understand? It was never a secret. Never. Why should it be? It all just belonged to a different time and place.'

Chapter Forty-Two

The group that gathered to discuss *Brooklyn* at the film club was big. As well as the core members who always turned up for discussions, there were newcomers Hanna didn't even know by sight. As soon as the doors were opened and people had congregated by the tea urn, Saira approached with two awkward-looking lads.

'This is Adam Rashid, Hanna, and his friend Bogdan Vidraru. I invited them along.'

The boy called Adam had a broad Dublin accent while the other lad, who seemed a little older, had good, though slightly eccentric, English, and rather formal manners. Saira explained that they both worked in Carrick at The Royal Vic.

'Bogdan is doing kitchen work to subsidise his visit to Ireland, and Adam is planning a future as a chef. They've both offered to volunteer in the garden over the summer. Bogdan's only here for the next month or two. And at the end of the season Adam's going back to Dublin, aren't you, Adam?'

'Yeah. For a while. I'll probably spend some time there with my mum. I looked up some stuff online too. I might enrol on a course.'

Bogdan thanked Hanna gravely for allowing them to attend the film.

'Not at all. You're both very welcome. Have you read *Brooklyn*?'

The lads shuffled and Saira intervened: 'I'm afraid I raised the subject too late for them to get hold of *Brooklyn*. I've explained that we'll be discussing that first and then watching *The Revenant*.'

Hanna smiled and said that if they wanted to borrow either book, they'd only to drop to the library and ask. It was something she'd said dozens of times on former film nights, but now she was aware of mouthing it without her usual warmth. Irritated to find she was thinking of Brian when she should be doing her job, she tried again. 'It really is great that you came along. Enjoy the evening!'

Having done her best, she moved on to greet another arrival, shaking hands and ushering people to seats. One group was gathered around an elderly lady from Ballyfin, who'd arrived with two tiny kittens asleep in a covered basket. She hoped Hanna wouldn't mind, she explained, but she'd thought the club was the perfect place to find someone who might like to adopt them.

'It's that ginger tom across the way, Miss Casey. He's back and forth all the time bothering my girls up in the cowshed. Last time it was poor Fluffy and now, lookut, Fang's after having a litter of six. I have four placed already and these two are the last of them.'

Tactfully suggesting that the kitchen might be a better place for the kittens to nap in peace and quiet, Hanna removed the basket and found its owner a chair. Mr Maguire was already ensconced in the front row, with a cup of tea and a fistful of Bourbon biscuits. With a handkerchief placed over his knees as a napkin, he was lecturing the beady-eyed lady with the claw-like clutch. He was flanked by Aideen's aunt Carol, looking sceptical, and Darina Kelly, in a crushed velvet top and Lycra leggings.

At the other side of the room, Ann Flood was edging towards the KitKats, and Conor, who should have been serving teas, was swiping through photos on his phone for a group of friends. Aideen was laughing with Bríd over the teacups, and showing off the twist of red gold she now wore next to her engagement ring. Conor had explained to Hanna that they'd bought it in a shop in Florence.

'I think your man just made them up out of fuse wire, Miss Casey. Still, Aideen loves it, and we managed to haggle the price down to something sane.'

Looking at Aideen's radiant face, Hanna reached into her own pocket. Her fingers touched the heavy gold band that Brian had thrust at her before he'd turned on his heel and walked away. It had been a ridiculous moment, freighted with echoes of Louisa May Alcott's *Little Women*, with Brian and herself as improbable middle-aged casting for Laurie and Jo.

Having told her the story of why Mike had been raised in London, he'd opened his clenched hand. 'The Divil found this in the river. I've been carrying it round like a fool for the last few weeks.'

'What do you mean, The Divil found it in the river?'

'Like magic gold. Like treasure carried down from the mountain and caught in a golden fleece.'

'But surely not. Is it old?'

'It's yours.' Taking her hand, he'd placed the ring on her palm and closed her fingers around it. 'I was going to talk to you, Hanna. About Mike. About everything. I tried to lots of times but I couldn't find words. I know I left it too long but I had to find the perfect time. Because I want you to marry me.' Releasing her hand, he'd stepped back, looking defeated. 'Fury said I was an eejit not to have spoken out sooner.'

'Fury knew about Mike?'

'No, of course not! I said there was stuff I needed to say before I could mention marriage, and he told me I should piss or get off the pot.'

That sounded authentic. Though the thought of Fury as an agony aunt seemed unlikely. But later, when Hanna had come to examine it, the assumption that men didn't talk about weddings had seemed shamefully trite. At the time, she'd simply stared at the ring on her palm. 'If this is a proposal, your timing is really bad.'

'I know. But nothing's changed. I want us to marry. I want you to live with me and be my love.' Then he'd turned and walked away, leaving The Divil's ring in her hand.

Now, shoving it deeper into her pocket, Hanna went to the front of the room and began the discussion of *Brooklyn*, though most of what was happening was just a blur. She was aware of being a painfully ineffective facilitator, but Saira Khan was sketching the plot for the benefit of the newcomers, with various contradictory interpolations from the group. Soon Jazz and Mr Maguire had formed an aggressive alliance on the subject of revisionist screenplays, and Bríd was declaring that she hated indecisive people in books.

Pat Fitz, who was crocheting, remarked that a mother in mourning for her child now seldom wore black. 'And that's a bit of a shame, you know, because people aren't mind-readers. Though the funny thing is that, when people did wear mourning, we knew each other's stories already because, back then, we lived in each other's laps. So you might say there was no need for a black coat or a cardigan. It was a nice custom, though. I don't know why we gave it up.'

One of the lads from the council offices asked if the Korean War hadn't been on in the 1950s. 'Wouldn't the American guy she went back to have had to cope with the draft?'

Mr Maguire had begun to pronounce on artistic licence when Ann Flood interrupted to say that reading the end of the book had made her cry. 'It didn't end happily, not the way the film did. I don't think people make choices in life, anyway. All kinds of things happen to us that we can't control at all.'

'Yeah, but you can't just do nothing for fear of what might happen.'

'I know, but the thing is you can't control what's going to happen next.'

When Conor dimmed the lights to show *The Revenant*, Hanna's mind was miles and years away. A bouquet of expensive flowers had arrived at her door that morning, wrapped in crackling cellophane and accompanied by a note: *Thank you for brunch by the Atlantic. I enjoyed it. Here's to many more beside the Thames.*

With no vase in the house that was large enough to hold them, she had dumped the flowers in a half-full sink of water, aware that their musky scent would fill the kitchen when she came home.

It was typical of Malcolm to choose a gesture that asserted his presence even when he wasn't there. Still, his arrogance had always been balanced by a keen sense of humour, and Hanna knew he'd be the first to laugh if she pointed out what he'd done.

Even when the lie that lay at the heart of their marriage had been exposed, the intimate knowledge of each other's quirks and foibles had remained true. Malcolm was the devil she knew, with all the charm and power to open doors and make life easy. Perhaps at this stage of their lives she could find comfort and companionship rooted in what was true and real in their past. Love of their daughter. Memories of triumphs and failures in a career that they'd built together. And that continued awareness of William, which she shared with no one else.

As Leonardo DiCaprio struggled through the snow, Hanna suddenly realised that she'd never told Brian about William. She, too, had kept silent about a son. Biting her lip, she told herself that, of course, there was no comparison. None at all. But was that true? To her, William wasn't a miscarried baby, a potential child that had never really existed because he had never lived outside her womb. He was her son, just as Mike was Brian's. And there hadn't been a day since she and Malcolm had lost him when William hadn't lived on in her mind.

Yet the thought of talking to Brian about him had never entered her head. As Brian himself had said, when he'd spoken of Mike and Sandra, some things just belonged to a different time and place.

Chapter Forty-Three

Jazz stood in front of the sink and looked out at the garden. The sky was still faintly gilded by the sunset, and feathery grass between the potato ridges moved in a salt-laden breeze. Once again, she and Mum had left the film club together and driven to the house in convoy for a meal. It was a glorious evening of pearly skies after soft rain, and the catkins on the oak trees by the road were heavy with golden pollen.

On the way they'd passed the ditch where, this time last month, she'd seen the two badgers cross the road at midnight. Jazz sighed, remembered how she'd gone home that night to a flat full of Sam's presence: his papers piled on the bed and the floor, and his washing-up in the sink. When she'd slid under the duvet, she'd found his foot and tickled it, and afterwards they'd made love half the night. She still missed him dreadfully.

Not having to think about Eileen's wedding had been a big relief, but now she had far too much time to spend alone. Her flat was so small that it took no time to clean; the furniture only fitted if laid out exactly as she'd found it; and the lease stipulated that she couldn't paint the walls or even hang a picture. The only thing there that belonged to her was the narrow console table on which she kept her laptop, and to fit that in she'd had to move out another, provided by the landlord, and pay him to keep it in store.

Getting to the office early and working there until late wasn't an option. Not under Louisa's watchful eye. And hanging out in clubs and pubs to get away from her own four walls would be horrid. Everyone out on the town was either one of a couple or on the pull. Wearily, Jazz wondered how long it would be before she was back having tedious one-night stands. Or even falling for someone inappropriate. Last year there'd been a dangerous few months when she'd almost begun an affair with a married man.

Now she leaned over Mum's kitchen sink and threw open the window. 'God, this scent is intense!' She looked round as Mum came through from the bedroom. 'Who sent the flowers?'

'How do you know I didn't buy them myself?'

'I bet you didn't. That's about fifty euros' worth. Was it Dad?'

'Yep. And now I'm going to have to find somewhere to put them.'

'If I were you I'd stick them out on the step.' Jazz went and sat in a fireside chair. 'You know, I arrived home with exactly those lilies the night that Sam left. I didn't rise to the musk roses, though. Trust Dad to go over the top.'

Mum poured two glasses of wine and came to sit by the fire. She'd lit a twist of dry grass and a pine cone under a couple of sods of turf when they'd come in. Normally the scent of the rising turf smoke would have filled the room by now, but Dad's lilies and roses were winning the battle.

Restlessly, Jazz got up and went to look down the garden, where midges drifting in swarms were being feasted on by swifts.

The salty air outside was delicious, and the smell of the wet earth after the recent shower of rain made her smile. 'So what's Dad after?'

'Don't be cynical, love. He was thanking me for brunch.'

'Hmm. At least you've got space here, and a garden. My lilies ended up on the communal staircase outside the flat, and the neighbours knocked them over and complained.'

Mum sipped her wine and said nothing, possibly feeling that, while the subject of Sam was no longer off limits, it wouldn't be wise to start asking too many questions. Jazz was never sure how she felt about Mum's tact. It certainly beat getting endless advice in a stream of texts from Nan. On the other hand, there were times when she wished that Mum wouldn't always treat her with kid gloves.

Still, having mentioned Sam, she realised that she didn't actually want to discuss him at all. Coming back to the fire, she picked up her glass. 'D'you remember that summer in London when you read me *The Wind in the Willows*? I must have been six.'

'I remember you loved Badger.'

'In fairness, you did do a brilliant Badger voice.'

'I think I ran out of voices pretty soon. Toad ended up just sounding like your dad.'

'Did he? I never noticed. Mole was my favourite character. Well, not Mole himself. I just loved his house, and the way he called it Mole End. And that bit about the "small inquiring something" animals carry inside them, saying unmistakably, "This leads home!"'

Jazz stared into the flames. 'But then I loved that "Wayfarers

All" chapter too. When Ratty gets overcome by the urge to travel after he meets the seafaring rat by the road.'

'You didn't love it when I first read it. You got scared when Mole looked at Rat and saw that his eyes had changed.'

'Did I?'

'Well, it's powerful stuff. They were "glazed and set and turned a streaked and shifting grey", don't you remember? "Not his friend's eyes, but the eyes of some other animal".'

'Yes. I'd forgotten that.'

Mum smiled. 'I remember the description of the forecourt of Mole End. The skittle alley with the tables marked with rings that hinted at beer mugs. And the busts of Garibaldi, Queen Victoria and the infant Samuel.'

'"And other heroes of modern Italy".' Jazz laughed. 'Mole had a garden seat in the forecourt, remember? And a pond with a glass ball in the middle that "reflected everything all wrong with a very pleasing effect". I loved the language.'

The breeze from the open door was beginning to cause the sods to spurt flames. Mum picked up another scrap of turf to feed the little fire.

Jazz looked around the room. 'You've kind of recreated that here.'

'Plaster statuary, sardines on toast and a bourgeois Victorian lifestyle?'

'I didn't mean that and you know it. I meant the bit about "familiar, friendly things which had long been unconsciously a part of him".'

'Which makes me Mole?'

'I guess so.'

'He moved on, though, didn't he? Ratty recovers from the spell laid on him by the seafarer. When he comes to his senses, he sees he has all that he needs right there. But Mole's story is more subtle. At the end of the chapter he realises that he doesn't want to creep into his safe burrow and stay there. The call of the upper world is too strong and – what's the phrase? – "he knew he must return to the larger stage".'

Something in her voice made Jazz look at her sharply. Mum looked away and asked her what she'd thought of the film.

'Tonight's? I dunno. A bit blokey. All that stuff about fighting the forces of nature. I mean, it looked amazing, didn't it? And Leo was really powerful. But it's a film about a guy who's going through hell on earth to avenge his lost son, and it doesn't even touch on how he felt about being a dad.' Suddenly Jazz giggled. 'Oh, lor', I announced back there that *Brooklyn* ought to have made more of the stuff about the dead father. Do you think I'm obsessed?'

'No, but I think you might be in need of some proper space and a garden.' Mum added another scrap of turf to the glowing fire. 'Did you know that Maggie wanted this place to be a haven? A fortress for the women who'd come after her. She left it to me because she thought I might need it when I grew up.'

'Did she say so?'

'Maggie wasn't a talker. She wrote it in her diary. "Maybe one day she'll need a place where she can feel safe and be happy."'

'Cool. She must have been nice.'

'I'm not sure "nice" is the word I'd use. Your nan always called her "a bad besom". No, there was absolutely nothing cosy or nice about Maggie. She'd had plenty of hard knocks in her life, and learned the value of standing on one's own two feet.'

'And in the end it was she who got you out of Nan's back bedroom.'

'Yes, but that's not the point. I didn't need a place to escape to. What I needed was to discover how to be happy where I was.'

'I bet if you'd stayed at Nan's we'd have ended up with a murder inquiry.'

Mum laughed. 'Fair point. But you do see what I'm saying? It was a bloody hard lesson to learn, so I might as well pass it on to you.'

'You're saying I don't know how to be alone.'

Mum was looking tentative, concerned she'd said too much. Jazz leaned forward, feeling herself on the brink of something important. 'Mum, forget being tactful, this isn't the time.'

'Okay, yes, that *is* what I'm saying. Look, your dad let you down badly, first by cheating on me and then by lying about it to you. And I didn't help by trying to protect you from the truth. You lost your home and your friends and ended up living in a new country. Then, when you thought you'd got some stability back, you lost your first real boyfriend. After that there were all those guys abroad that I don't want to think about. Then there was Sam, and now he's gone as well. It isn't surprising that you keep trying to fill what feels like a gaping hole. You have this dream in which the perfect life requires the perfect man. And you keep thinking he's out there beyond some unreal horizon.'

Mum stopped abruptly and clasped her hands on her knee. 'Maybe you borrowed that dream from me and, if you did, I'm sorry. It's a dumb dream, Jazz, because there's no such thing as perfection. And you don't need someone to love you. What you need is ...'

'... to Learn to Love Myself.'

'I know it sounds like a Hallmark card but, yes, exactly that. It's sure as hell what I needed when I moved out of your nan's. I'd spent so long focused on you and your dad that I hadn't a clue who I was myself, or even what I wanted.'

For a long moment Jazz said nothing, digesting what, for the first time, she realised was the truth. Then she took a gulp of wine and said something she'd wanted to say for years. 'You do know I'm grateful, Mum, don't you? For everything. All the stories in the conservatory, and the walks to the library in London. The way you tried to protect me from Dad's asinine behaviour. And how you never blamed me for being a hellish teen.'

'You weren't hellish.'

'I took up a hell of a lot of your time. I still do. I don't know what I'd do without you, truly. Even if mostly I'm too bloody-minded to admit it.'

Mum knocked back her own wine, looking kind of wobbly. Afraid that they'd both end up in tears, Jazz gave her a grin.

'So you're focused on yourself now, and you know what you want, do you?'

There was a pause in which Mum looked into the fire, turning the stem of her wine glass. Then she nodded. 'Heaven knows how your nan will react but, yes, I know what I want. Your dad said it, Jazz. It's time for me to move on.'

Chapter Forty-Four

The Hag's Glen at sunrise was full of drifting mist, and the back road that approached it was wet. A herd of sheep blocked the way as Hanna approached the turning, so she kept her distance and slowed the car to a crawl. The farmer up ahead of her was riding a quad bike, with a dog running in front controlling the herd.

Hanna watched the dog's eager body weave to and fro. His dark flanks and waving tail hardly showed against the sheep's skinny black legs but when he turned his head his russet face showed like a whiskered fox's.

The car crested a rise in the road and Hanna looked down at a river of woolly backs. Crammed between the ditches, the herd skittered, like water running over stones, their hooves clicking on the wet tarmacadam. The rhythmic sound became the rhythm of an old folk song that, for the last few days, had been playing in her head.

I wish I was on yonder hill
'Tis there I'd sit and cry my fill
And every tear would turn a mill ...

As the leaders increased their pace, and the dog urged the others on from the rear, the sound of the hooves deepened and became like urgent drumming.

I'll dye my petticoats, I'll dye them red
And round the world I'll beg my bread ...

When the herd passed the turning, the farmer raised his hand in salute without looking back. Hanna accelerated and swung the wheel, taking Brian's newly built road up to the river valley. The mist ahead began to lift with the heat of the rising sun.

After Jazz had left the previous night, Hanna had walked down Maggie's field to the cliff edge. Gulls had been soaring above the ocean and the night was so still she could hear the sound of shingle dragged by the waves. Standing there on the cool grass, she'd remembered the click of her own heels in the West End of London. Those stylish shoes worn on shopping trips with friends, and outings with Malcolm, hadn't been among the things she'd thrown into her suitcase when she'd left him. Tasting the salt on the wind, she'd wondered what had become of the designer outfits that had once crammed her wardrobe. Not that any of them would still be in fashion now.

In a ghastly row years ago, just after she'd left him, Malcolm had told her that bolting with Jazz had been selfish, and that a conscientious mother would never have acted as she did. The other day, over brunch, he'd apologised. Of course, Jazz's reaction when she'd seen the flowers had been right: she'd recognised her dad in manipulation mode. Hanna herself had been aware of that too. But it was also true that Malcolm was genuinely lonely and –

as Louisa had said – failing to cope on his own. Now Hanna told herself that for Jazz to come out and say thank you, and Malcolm to say he was sorry, had been amazing. It almost felt as if her fractured family might yet be restored.

The mist was still drifting over the river and the pale sky became streaked with gold. At the head of the valley there was a flash of light from where the waterfall fell between high rocks.

Hanna knew that from up there, and from the green roof of the house, you could look across distant treetops to the patch of blue ocean where waves dragged the rolling shingle forward and back again. Beyond the waves was a shimmering horizon, and beyond that, if the stories were true, was the Land of Heart's Desire, where the streets were paved with gold.

This was the first time she had seen the house with no sign of building work or human habitation. When she stopped her car she wondered if Brian was gone.

Then he opened the door. Behind him the room was empty, except for a camera on a tripod standing against a cobalt blue wall.

Hanna blinked and Brian pulled a wry face. 'Fury doesn't believe in tins of paint going to waste.'

'So I see. Are you going to keep it blue?'

'If I don't he'll probably break in and do it again.'

Standing with his back to the startling wall, he looked older. He put his hand on the doorframe and glanced up at the sky. 'Isn't it kind of early?'

'I'm sorry. I needed to talk.'

I'll sell my rod, I'll sell my reel
I'll sell my only spinning wheel
To buy my love a coat of steel …

Brian stood back and held the door open, but Hanna shook her head. 'No, I just want to tell you something.'

But, now that they were face to face, she couldn't, so she told him Jazz was thinking of going away with Mike.

'What, for good?'

'No, of course not. For a holiday. To run a marathon.'

'Okay.'

'Not for a couple of years yet, though. Because she'll have to get in shape first. And, the thing is, Brian, I'm going to give Jazz Maggie's house.'

'In a couple of years?'

'No. Immediately. Well, as soon as I get things sorted. It's what she needs and it's time for me to move on.' Hanna clasped her hands, eager to finish what she'd started. 'I've always thought Jazz was the one who suffered when we came here from London. But I lost so much too. Not just Malcolm, or security, or the home we'd built together, but the person I was when I lived over there. That's who I'd been for most of my adult life.'

Brian nodded, as if he was thinking about it deeply. Hanna reached into her pocket and took out the ring. 'You said The Divil found this in the river.'

'I said it was yours. You should take it with you.'

Hanna looked at the amber-coloured water chattering over the stones. The mist was almost gone now. Raising her hand, she drew back her arm and threw the ring away. It rose in a high arc, spinning over the rough grassland, the sun striking light from the polished gold. In the quiet glen, they both heard the sound as it hit the water. Then Hanna stepped back and gritted her teeth.

'I won't marry you. I can't do that again. I know you didn't lie to me. And I know Malcolm did. But life is complicated. Making choices takes courage, Brian. I think that the older you are the harder it gets.'

They looked at each other in silence. Hanna took a deep breath. 'Malcolm's reconsidered the sale of the London house. He's recognised that it doesn't belong to him. Not really. It was ours as a family.'

'And you've made your choice.'

'Yes. I'll never have all of you, Brian. I know that now. And the truth is that you'll never have all of me. Too much has happened in both of our lives for that. So I've made up my mind. I don't want to marry you.'

Brian's face was bleak. He nodded again and stepped backwards. Then Hanna held out her hand and grasped his, and crossed the threshold.

'I don't want to be married. I want to be happy. I want to be your love and live with you here in the Hag's Glen.'

Acknowledgements

Heartfelt thanks to my editor Ciara Doorley, copy editor Hazel Orme, Breda Purdue and everyone at Hachette Books Ireland.

Also to my husband, Wilf Judd, and, as ever, to my agent, Gaia Banks, at Sheil Land Associates UK.

And special gratitude to the readers worldwide who've got in touch by email, letter and on social media to tell me what they enjoy about Finfarran – in particular, the medievalist librarian who tweeted to say how much he likes the Carrick Psalter. Every message, whoever and wherever it comes from, is hugely appreciated, and adds to the great pleasure of creating the lives of Hanna Casey and her neighbours.

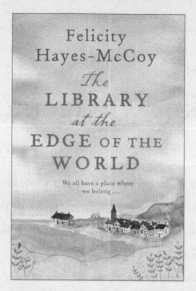

The Library at the Edge of the World

Local librarian Hanna Casey is wondering where it all went wrong ...

Driving her mobile library van through Finfarran's farms and villages, she tries not to think of the sophisticated London life she abandoned when she left her cheating husband. Or that she's now stuck in her crotchety mum's spare bedroom.

With her daughter Jazz travelling the world and her relationship with her mother growing increasingly fraught, Hanna decides to reclaim her independence.

Then, when the threatened closure of her library puts her plans in jeopardy, she finds herself leading a battle to restore the heart and soul of the fragmented community.

Will she also find the new life she's been searching for?

Also available as an ebook

Summer at the Garden Café

A place where plans are formed and secrets are shared, the Garden Café is nestled at the heart of the town of Lissbeg, on Ireland's west coast.

But Jazz – still reeling from the truth about her parents' marriage – has more on her mind than the gossip at the café. Increasingly isolated from her friends and family, she finds herself developing feelings for a man who is strictly off limits …

Meanwhile Hanna, Lissbeg's librarian, is unaware of the turmoil in her daughter Jazz's life – until her ex-husband Malcolm makes an appearance. And she begins to wonder if the secrets she's carried for him might have done more harm than good.

Then Hanna discovers a long-lost book buried in her garden. Could this help to turn Jazz's summer around, or is she too late?

Also available as an ebook

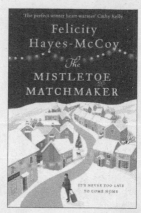

The Mistletoe Matchmaker

It's winter on the Finfarran peninsula and, as Cassie Fitzgerald, fresh from Toronto, is about to discover, there's more to Christmas on the west coast of Ireland than mistletoe and mince pies.

Enchanted by the small town where her dad was born, Cassie gets involved in a competition for the best local Winter Fest, and joins local librarian Hanna Casey's writing group in Lissbeg Library.

But the more she's drawn into the town's run-up to Christmas, the more questions Cassie encounters. Why does her sweet-tempered grandmother Pat find it so hard to express her feelings? What's going on between Pat and her miserly husband Ger? What happened in the past between the Fitzgeralds and Hanna's redoubtable mother Mary Casey? And what about Shay: handsome, funny, smart and intent on making Cassie's stay as exciting as he can. Is he the one for her?

As Christmas Eve approaches, Cassie discovers that love, family and friendship bring the real magic to the festive season – even if the locals of Lissbeg need an outsider to help them see it.

Also available as an ebook